The silencwaited
for him
posed. Bu
ing at th
zinging betw
him up.

Finally she looked up at him. "I never get involved
with employees." The need blazing in her eyes
protested the statement.

"Technically, I'm not an employee." His voice was
husky. He wanted to touch her but didn't dare. He,
too, had a rule against getting involved with a
client…but technically she wasn't his client.

"Guess not," she agreed. She licked those lush lips
again. "Truth is, I haven't been kissed in more than
three years. I may have forgotten how it's done."

He reached out and removed the clip that held her
hair. He wanted her to feel what a kiss from the
right man felt like.

First published in Great Britain 2012
by Mills & Boon, an imprint of Harlequin (UK) Limited,
Eton House, 18-24 Paradise Road, Richmond, Surrey TW9 1SR

© Debra Webb 2012

ISBN: 978 0 263 89573 5
ebook ISBN: 978 1 408 97254 0

46-1112

Harlequin (UK) policy is to use papers that are natural, renewable and recyclable products and made from wood grown in sustainable forests. The logging and manufacturing processes conform to the legal environmental regulations of the country of origin.

Printed and bound in Spain
by Blackprint CPI, Barcelona

HIGH NOON

BY
DEBRA WEBB

Debra Webb wrote her first story at age nine and her first romance at thirteen. It wasn't until she spent three years working for the military behind the Iron Curtain and within the confining political walls of Berlin, Germany, that she realized her true calling. A five-year stint with NASA on the space shuttle program reinforced her love of the endless possibilities within her grasp as a storyteller. A collision course between suspense and romance was set. Debra has been writing romance, suspense and action-packed romance thrillers since. Visit her at www.debrawebb.com or write to her at PO Box 4889, Huntsville, AL 35815, USA.

To my family, for always being there for me.

Chapter One

Beaumont, Texas, Sunday, May 26th, 9:50 p.m.

Joel Hayden had lingered in a dark corner of the High Noon Saloon for the past two hours. Finally a patron vacated a stool at the bar and Joel settled there before anyone else in the happy crowd could commandeer the prized position.

Whatever Laney Seagers was doing, she was doing it right. The century-old tavern she'd resurrected with her own two hands was hopping even on a Sunday night. The music flowing from the jukebox was country all the way and the atmosphere pure Texas from the murals on the walls depicting one-horse towns from the West's heyday when duels were carried out in the street at high noon to the restored original wood floor that had seen its share of two-stepping boots and bloody brawls. The patrons carried the mood with their cowboy boots and Stetsons.

He'd watched Laney Seagers for the past three days. Wasn't a hardship. The lady made his job easy, a vacation almost. Each time she laughed, the sound, sultry and sexy, left every single male customer within hearing range slack-jawed. Her honey-blond hair swung around her shoulders, making his fingers itch to see if it felt as silky as it looked.

Joel had handled a generous list of personal protection gigs for businessmen, celebrities and politicians alike, but he had to admit, this one was different. His new employer, the Colby Agency, wanted those with the most experience in the field on this case. This was Joel's first assignment for the Colby Agency and not one to be taken lightly, despite the spirited setting and the sexy blonde in the tight jeans and formfitting T-shirt sporting the saloon's logo.

Laney Seagers was in danger. And that was the easy part. That she didn't realize the threat nipping at her heels was the element that made the situation less than optimal. Though Joel would rather watch the lady scurry around behind the bar than eat at chow time, there was only so much even the most highly trained bodyguard could do under the circumstances.

Throw in the mix a five-year-old kid who was scared to death of his own shadow and things were a little complicated. Since the boy wouldn't start kindergarten until the fall, he spent most of his time attached to his pretty mother's hip. Even now, as she worked the Sunday-night crowd, Buddy slept on a cot in the office. Whenever he was awake, he played video games in the kitchen where the cook, Tatum, a landlocked former sailor he called Uncle Tater, kept him company. Every other moment he clung to his mom. Thing was, the kid didn't play just any old kind of games; they were the learning kind, reading, math and the like. As seemingly introverted as he was, little Buddy Seagers was as smart as a whip.

Joel had three brothers and they had all grown up hard. Their mother had developed multiple sclerosis when Joel was about Buddy's age. By the time he was ten, she was helpless. Their father had been busy trying to keep a roof over their heads and food on the table. Later, when Joel was older, he also understood that it was easier for his dad to work all the time than to come home to an ever-unfolding tragedy.

Basically, the Hayden boys pretty much learned to take care of themselves out of necessity. Made Joel wonder if shy little Buddy had a chance against the bullies he would face in school. Without a proper father figure or even an older brother, preparing him to take care of himself fell on the mother's shoulders. He didn't know many mothers who taught their boys how to land a nice uppercut.

It wasn't really his business whether or not Laney Seagers was up to that particular challenge, but being a kid from a primarily one-parent household, he wondered. She sure seemed to take by the horns the other challenges life tossed her way. Her background reflected a tough lady who preferred being a survivor to being a victim. A guy had to respect that. Rather than rely on entitlements, she got out and made things happen.

Laney sashayed over to where he sat at the center of the long counter. She smiled that big, bright smile that made her brown eyes twinkle and left a man a little dazed, and then she glanced at his half-empty glass.

"Somehow you just don't look like a soda pop kinda guy to me, handsome. Can I get you something else?"

"I have a one-drink limit when I'm doing the driving home." He gifted her with a wink and a smile of his own. "Unless you're planning on taking me home, I guess it'll be soda for me the rest of the night."

She belted out another of those sultry laughs. "I have

to give you credit, that's the first time I've heard that one." She picked up his glass. "You having regular or diet?"

There went that dazzling twinkle in her eyes again.

Beyond the fact that she was a knockout with a killer smile and inspiring eyes, he genuinely liked the lack of pretention in her manner and her looks. No fussy makeup or hairdos. She seemed completely comfortable in her own skin. He liked that a lot. She had spirit in spite of the hard luck she'd survived.

"Regular."

She filled his glass and placed it on a fresh napkin in front of him. "We've still got wings and ribs in the kitchen," she suggested.

He held up a hand. "I'm good."

"You don't know what you're missing."

Watching her walk away wasn't in his job description, at least not the part where he zeroed in on those tight-fitting jeans. But then he was only human. Any woman who looked that good in plain old denim deserved a long, lustful stare from any man breathing.

Since this was work, there was very little chance he would have the opportunity to see what he was missing beyond watching her swing those hips. That alone was worth hanging around twenty-four/seven for however long it took.

Tonight, if all went as planned, he'd get his opportunity to get a little closer. He'd overheard the one remaining member of her security make the statement that he wasn't getting paid enough to deal with the boss's ex. The frustrated guy intended to give Laney the bad news tonight. He'd already accepted another position with the competition downtown and he wasn't feeling inclined to give even a one-week notice.

A lot of that had been happening this week.

A raw deal for Laney but a much-needed opportunity for Joel to gain a better surveillance position. He'd laid the necessary groundwork with subtle comments to some of Laney's employees.

He swiveled on the stool, his back against the counter, and surveyed the crowd. At a table near the jukebox, a belligerent and clearly inebriated jerk annoyed the waitress attempting to take his order. From a distance he appeared your average had-a-little-too-much reveler. But that was far from the case.

He was the rub. The no-good baby daddy himself. Terrence "Terry" Kingston. Poster boy for thirty-something men with failure-to-launch syndrome. And missing in action ninety percent of the time for the past five years under the guise of finishing his law degree so he could follow in his rich daddy's footsteps. Though he and Laney had never married, he was the father of her son.

A self-absorbed, egotistical leech who just wanted to play from time to time with the one girl smart enough to walk away. His serial stints in rehab had prevented him from taking legal action to obtain partial custody of his son. Not that he'd actually wanted the responsibility but the threat worked well when he wanted something else from Laney. Knowing the kind of money his father had put Laney at a serious disadvantage. Fear had likely prevented her from taking legal steps to get the guy out of her life once and for all.

But now Kingston had a new motive. Rich daddy had cut off his trust fund after the last round of detox following his son's surrender to his never-quite-relinquished relationship with cocaine. So slacker Kingston junior needed a way back into rich daddy's good graces. A brief background check and a few questions asked of the right folks and Joel had the whole sordid story.

There was nothing like a grandson, an heir, from an only son—an opportunity for a do-over—to get rich daddy's attention. The desire to do it right this time, with a grandson when he obviously failed with his only son, was a powerful persuader for a man marching toward sixty. The senior Kingston had built his empire with no time for anything else and the guilt had caught up with him.

Kingston junior, on the other hand, was banking on his five-year-old investment to get his fingers back in the money jar.

And Joel was counting on human nature.

The cocky man swaggered up to the bar, his right tilt giving away his increasing level of intoxication. He elbowed aside a couple of patrons and bellied up to the counter. The unhappy folks grumbled but walked away rather than risk trouble.

The exchange between the ex and the saloon owner was muted by the lively music roaring from the jukebox, but Joel didn't need to hear the words to get the gist of the conversation. The body language of both participants telegraphed the story loud and clear to anyone who bothered to look.

He wanted something and she wasn't having any part of it.

Dekker, the security detail for the night—and every night since Joel's arrival—cut through the crowd and stationed himself next to the troublemaker. Dekker was a big guy. Six-three or four. Two-forty or two-fifty. Looked like a linebacker for a pro football team.

Joel finished off his soda and stood. Things were about to get interesting and he didn't want to miss the show.

Kingston turned on the big guy wearing the High Noon Saloon T-shirt and whatever he said didn't sit well. Dekker turned to Laney, shook his head and walked out.

Based on the gossip Joel had heard from the waitresses, Dekker was sick of throwing Kingston out night after night and getting nowhere. The local cops wouldn't give the guy what he deserved for fear of reprisals from his rich daddy. Adding to the pressure, Kingston had started threatening Dekker's wife's position at one of the elementary schools. Old man Kingston had friends in high places, the smart-mouthed jerk liked to brag.

Well, Joel didn't care who his daddy was or where his friends fell on the food chain. He just wanted to kick the crap out of him on principle.

By the time Joel made his way down to that end of the bar, the patrons had scattered and Laney and Kingston were going at it loud enough to drown out the music.

A few more minutes and they would successfully clear the house. Bad for business. And Joel happened to know Laney couldn't afford any dips in revenue.

"You can't keep me from seeing my son," Kingston slurred. "I'm petitioning the court for full custody. My daddy says this time I'll win. And you can't do a damned thing but cooperate or forfeit."

"Do what you think you're big enough to do," she dared. "Until then, you can see Buddy when you're sober and only when you're sober. Right now, I want you out of here. This is my property and I have the right to kick your drunken butt out if you can't behave."

The arrogant fool laughed. "The way I hear it, that may be changing very soon. Money makes the world go round, in case you haven't learned that yet."

Laney was fighting mad. But beneath all that bravado she was terrified. Didn't take a degree in psychology to see that. She wore her emotions on her sleeve. It worked for her because they were honest, no-drama emotions. Something else Joel liked about her.

"I thought I might go for bourbon after all. Straight up," Joel said as he cozied up to the bar next to the sleazebag harassing the lady.

Laney took a breath, shifted her attention to him. "Sure." She pivoted and stalked over to the rows of liquor bottles lining the mirrored shelves behind the bar.

"Who the hell are you?" Kingston glared at Joel, his bleary eyes reporting his alcohol-consumption level better than any breathalyzer could.

Joel leaned closer to the man and said for his ears only, "I'm the guy who's going to ruin those new veneers your daddy's money bought if you don't leave the lady alone and get the hell out of here."

Kingston reared back, swayed. He patted his pocket. "Old switch might have something to say about that."

Joel grabbed him by the collar, lifted him just high enough to prevent his boots from settling square on the floor, and hauled him across the room and out the swinging doors.

The drunken SOB cursed and swung repeatedly at Joel, missing every time. Joel snagged the key ring from the weasel's belt and shoved him away. "If you have any friends, call someone to pick you up. Otherwise, call a cab."

The guy charged at him. Joel stepped aside. Kingston went down face-first on the wooden walkway created as authentically as the ones straight out of an old Western movie. In fact, the whole scene could have been out of a classic John Wayne movie. Except Laney wore those body-hugging jeans instead of an ankle-length dress and petticoats.

"Show your face in here again," Joel warned, "and I won't be so nice next time."

Joel waited at the door until Kingston staggered away, cell at his ear, hopefully calling for a ride.

Joel turned around and came face-to-face with the boss.

"Is he gone?"

"For now." Joel glanced over his shoulder. "He'll be back eventually for his ride." He passed the keys to her.

"I wish that was the only reason for him to come back." She stared across the parking lot, probably hoping the bastard would fade into the darkness never to be seen again.

"You okay?" The question wasn't necessary. He could see that she was far from okay, but she had no way of knowing he understood far too keenly the unappealing facts of her financial and personal situations.

She shrugged, threw the bar towel over her shoulder. "I'd be a lot better if my security hadn't bailed on me. That really blows."

Joel made a show of considering the idea for a moment. "Maybe it is my lucky night."

Her eyebrows shot up in skepticism. "Look, mister, your pickup lines will have to get a lot better than what

I've heard so far for you to get lucky." She looked him up and down. "Packaging isn't everything."

Joel laughed. "I wasn't referring to that kind of luck, ma'am."

Her cheeks flushed. She hitched a thumb toward the swinging doors. "I have to get back in there. Without someone keeping an eye on the crowd, anything could happen."

She had no idea. The Kingston men were just the beginning of her troubles. As frustrating as things were for her at the moment, he hated to eventually be the one to let her know that it was going to get a lot worse before it got better.

He gave her a nod. "If you decide to hire a new bouncer, let me know. I'm in the market for a new job."

Joel tipped his hat to her and stepped down from the walkway. He'd taken another two strides when she called out to him.

"How can I get in touch with you?"

He turned to face her, backed up another step. "I'm right here." He shrugged. "I'll probably be back tomorrow night."

"You'd have to fill out an application."

He paused.

For a lady who wanted to play it tough, she looked damned vulnerable at the moment. But then he knew why. Couldn't blame her for feeling that and more.

"I'd need references," she tacked on.

"I can handle that."

She hitched her head toward the door then disappeared inside. Joel followed, enjoying the view. Wasn't often that the backside was every bit as gorgeous as the front, but this lady was definitely all-around gorgeous.

His job was to protect all of her and he finally had his in. Being employed at the High Noon would make his work a whole lot easier.

She skirted the end of the bar and poured that bourbon he'd had to walk away from. When she set the drink on the counter, she grabbed a pen and a napkin and placed them in front of him.

He glanced from the napkin and pen to her.

"The application. Just jot down the usual stuff. Name, address, phone number and references. I need their numbers, too. Use both sides if necessary."

"Yes, ma'am." Joel scrawled the requested info on the napkin. He flipped it over and provided a couple of names with numbers he retrieved from his cell. When he'd added the final digit, he passed it to her.

"Anything else?"

She studied the information. "When can you start?"

He grinned. "I thought I already had."

She tried to look serious but one of those breath-stealing smiles peeked past her cautionary business persona. "All right. The pay is a percentage of the night's take. It's nothing to brag about some nights, but others make up for it."

"Works for me."

"I will call your references," she reminded him.

"Then you'll really be impressed."

She held his gaze a moment. "We'll see."

Chapter Two

Monday, May 27th, 1:00 a.m.

Laney perched on the edge of her son's bed and watched him sleep all snuggled up with his bear. He'd had that ragged old thing since he was born. It was the first toy she'd bought her child. She'd walked into the gift shop and immediately been drawn to the cute brown bear with its red bow tie. Made her feel safe and it seemed to do the same thing for Buddy. As silly as that sounded.

Regret settled heavily onto her shoulders. These late nights were hard on him. She had hoped to have a good solid staff on board before school started in late August so she could get her boy home at a decent hour, but with Dekker's abrupt departure that was looking less and less likely.

Last week it had been two waitresses.

What was she going to do?

Getting home after midnight on Sunday night—a school night come this fall—was not going to work. She had to get a good team in place soon.

Terry was running off all her best help. The police

would do nothing for fear of a backlash from his father. How did you fight that kind of trouble?

After all these years, why in hell did he have to hunt her down now? She hadn't seen the bastard but twice in five years. Both times he'd been looking for a place to crash when things got too hot for him in Houston. Which generally meant his father had gotten fed up and decided to actually act like a father. Too little too late, unfortunately for both Terry and her.

She'd let him fool her the first time, but not the second. He'd been furious when she wouldn't let him into the little apartment she'd had at the time or into her bed. The Kingston men weren't used to hearing no for an answer.

They weren't kids anymore. The time for playing games was over. She had a home and a business, as well as a son about to start school. She had responsibilities that needed her full attention and her best efforts. Terry needed to grow up.

Laney might have gotten a rough start with her life, but she was a quick learner. She was a bit of a sap but she was no dummy. The idea of allowing her mistakes to damage her son's future hurt too much to even think about.

She tucked the covers around her baby, gave him a kiss and checked the window by his bed. Locked, shade drawn. Relieved the day was mostly done, she made her way to the kitchen. There hadn't been time for even a five-minute break tonight, which was a good thing for her bank account. Now, however, her stomach was demanding attention.

As she took sandwich fixings from the fridge and deposited them on the worn wooden counter of her make-

shift island, she considered that tomorrow she had to
hire at least one of the new waitresses she needed. And
she'd have to check the references on her new security guy.

Her fingers slowed in their work. Joel Hayden had
been hanging around most of the week. One of the waitresses had told her he'd recently gotten laid off from his
work as a bodyguard at some swanky security company
that had closed its doors. Jobs were tough to come by
these days and he'd opted to take a break from Houston's big-city noise and mayhem. Beaumont, he insisted
to the waitress who was clearly enamored with him,
fit the bill.

Part of her couldn't help thinking that it was not a
coincidence that he hailed from Houston. Terry and his
family were Houstonians. But, after the way Hayden
had rousted her ex out of the saloon, she figured that
wasn't very likely. Unless the whole scene had been
staged.

Damn. She hadn't thought of that until now. Great.
Something else to worry about. Maybe she'd do some
checking beyond his references. Google him or something.

After stuffing two slices of bread with ham, cheese,
mayo and tomato, she grabbed a beer and found her favorite spot in the living room. Her little corner on the
sofa. Most of the living room served as a play area for
Buddy. He had his Legos in one corner. His game station in another. And miscellaneous toys in yet another.
At five, the kid was already more organized than most
adults. He kept Laney on the straight and narrow when
it came to clutter.

He was so smart that he scared her sometimes. Not in

Debra Webb 21

a bad way, though. Her biggest fear was that she would never be able to provide him with the opportunities he deserved. College tuition was outrageous. She had already started saving for that but it wasn't much to speak of. She had thirteen years and so far her math was way off reaching the necessary sum.

"That plan's really holding together," she muttered. Between the walk-in cooler in the High Noon's kitchen going out and that fancy automatic toaster oven Tatum had insisted he needed to make sandwiches folks would love, the almighty dollar was tough to hang on to.

Laney sighed as she settled into her corner. She clicked the remote and set the station to a movie channel that featured classic love stories. What could she say? She had to get her happily-ever-afters from somewhere. And there was nothing like getting lost in a sappy movie after a long, hard night at the High Noon.

Truthfully, she couldn't complain. Her life had sucked for a while after her parents died. The accident had devastated her entire life. Just a ten-year-old kid with no relatives to take her in. Foster care hadn't been so bad, but Laney had. She'd been a pain in the butt until she was eighteen and then she'd been an idiot.

As stupid as she was and as many mistakes as she had made, she had a beautiful son because of at least one of those errors in judgment. She couldn't regret Buddy.

Man, she hadn't realized how starved she was. Something as simple as a ham and cheese sandwich shouldn't have a girl moaning but Laney had learned enjoying the simple things in life came with the single-mom territory.

As a single mom and a business owner, there was

rarely any time left for a social life. Hayden's image tried to nudge its way into her thoughts.

Hayden was business. She had to keep that fact firmly in front of her. He had trouble written all over that sexy frame.

She gave herself another fifteen minutes of me time before reluctantly moving on to the other chores that would not be put off. Laundry, dishes. Forget about picking up around the house. She was way too exhausted.

Her hodgepodge kitchen wasn't exactly state-of-the-art. Far from it actually. She'd spent the past two years scrounging for castoffs from folks remodeling their kitchens. Few of the cabinets matched; none of the appliances were the same color or from the same decade, but they all had one thing in common—they worked! Even Tatum saw the beauty in her vision when it came to getting that toaster oven secondhand.

The vinyl floor tiles were of a mixed variety as well, all leftovers from those same remodeling ventures. But her prized find was the old butcher's chopping-block stand that she used as a center island to ground the assorted eras she'd converged in the room. The island didn't sit level and the surface was beat all to hell and back, but still she cherished it.

She'd managed to replace all the broken windows in the house, again with castoffs from those moving to more energy-efficient choices. She'd painted the eighty-year-old wood siding herself. She'd painted the whole house as a matter of fact. Looking at it now made her proud even if she wasn't likely to be featured in *House Beautiful*.

The saloon was a similar project. The building and

five acres she'd gotten for a song at a tax sell-off. Some-one had abandoned the place and Laney had grabbed it, using her measly savings to purchase it flat-out and do the necessary renovations. She'd talked the president of a small local independent bank into taking a risk and lending her the money on her newly remodeled house so she could buy and renovate the saloon.

That had worked great at first. Problem was, she hadn't seen the nice older gentleman's bad side until it was too late. The loan had been on a balloon note which wasn't a problem at the time. Time flew and now that note came due in a mere ninety days. He had just in-formed her that he wouldn't be renewing the loan so the full amount was due in three months.

If she didn't pay, she would lose her business and her home. Worry crushed down on her shoulders.

Last month's receipts had looked stellar, and she had felt confident she had proof of steady-enough income to get a new loan elsewhere. But now the trouble with Terry and good workers walking had started a trend in falling revenue.

Many of her regulars were complaining that the guy made them uncomfortable. With all the wackos shoot-ing up restaurants and the like, she could understand. But the last thing she needed was a drop in cash flow as the drop-dead date on getting a new loan approached.

She needed the books to look good. Laney choked back the anxiety and reminded herself that there was still time.

With the washing machine churning and the dishes done, she walked through the house to ensure the windows and doors were locked. Before Terry reap-peared, she left her windows open at night during good weather. That was a risk she couldn't take with him lurking around. She couldn't trust him as far as she could throw him.

Keeping her .32 handy once Buddy was asleep was another new addition to her nightly routine. She hated that feeling of being afraid. She'd lived it too many times. Seemed just when life was looking up something else came along and rained on her parade.

She hesitated at the front window, one hand on the paper shade ready to drag it down. Her house sat a good fifty yards off the road and there were no streetlights on these old county roads, but the moon was big and bright tonight, giving her a clear view of the road that ran in front of her house.

A Jeep had parked on the shoulder directly in front of her house. With the convertible top removed, she could see that someone was behind the wheel but she couldn't begin to determine whether the driver was male or female. Definitely wasn't Terry's fancy import. Since his keys were at the High Noon, she could safely assume it wasn't him.

Unless he'd hitched or borrowed a ride from some jerk friend of his.

There was no logical reason for the driver to be stopped in front of her house unless he'd run out of gas. Since the closest convenience store was nearly all the way in town, a long ways from these twisting, winding roads, it wasn't smart to joyride out here without at least half a tank.

Evidently the guy didn't mind being seen since a few yards to the right or left of his position and her view would have been blocked by the trees in her yard. Not scary but definitely unsettling.

She didn't have any binoculars but she could get closer to have a better look and assess the situation. Knowing old man Kingston, he had a P.I. or member of his personal staff watching her, hoping she would make some sort of unfit-mother mistake. She had decided that making his old man happy was the only possible reason Terry was interested in Buddy after all this time. There had to be an agenda.

"Not happening, old man." He wasn't getting her son and she wasn't about to screw up. The thought that Kingston might be behind her banker's change of heart had crossed her mind. Failing to keep a roof over her son's head and food on the table might push her firmly into the unfit category.

"Don't borrow trouble, Laney."

She slid her cell into her back pocket and tucked the .32 in her waistband. She eased out the back door and made her way to the front of the house using the grapevine trellis and the old well house as cover. The trees and an abandoned tractor that was nearly as old as the house gave her a few points of cover from there. She'd considered having the old tractor hauled off when she first bought the place but she'd decided it gave the yard character. Her five acres had once been part of a huge family farm. It came with all sorts of funky character, like a leaky roof and unlevel floors.

The final tree available to shield her was only about ten yards from the road. She should be able to have a decent view of the interloper from there.

She rushed through the ankle-deep grass until she made her destination. Cutting the grass was something else she needed to find the time and energy to get done. Laney added the chore to her growing mental list.

Crouching behind the tree, she studied the vehicle and its driver. Male. The cowboy hat prevented her from making out his profile or his face.

As if he'd picked up on the thought, he removed his hat and placed it on the passenger seat. He leaned the seat back and appeared to be settling in for the night.

Strange.

He checked the screen of his cell phone and the glow highlighted his face.

Joel Hayden.

What the heck was he doing here?

Before her brain assimilated the best course of action, she pushed to her feet and strode toward him.

When he glanced her way, she demanded an answer. "What're you doing out here?"

He hopped out of the Jeep. The doors had been removed, leaving nothing between him and making that cocky move.

Her right hand rested on the butt of her Smith and Wesson. She kind of liked this guy, but the truth was he was a stranger and she had to be smart.

"I guess I should've knocked on the door and let you know I was here."

"I guess you should've." A frown nagged at her. "What're you doing?" How was it that her eyes couldn't stop surveying him from head to toe? The guy looked even better in the moonlight, but that was no excuse to go stupid.

He shrugged, set those big hands on his lean hips. "I was worried that guy might show up at your house after I kicked him out of the saloon."

Laney beat back the smile that tickled her lips. She did not know this man or his motives. As much as she wanted to be flattered by his chivalry, she couldn't ever be a fool again, especially when her son's safety was at stake. Still, she was flattered.

"That's very noble of you, Hayden, but your pay ends when you walk out the door of the High Noon."

"This isn't about getting paid overtime," he assured her.

"What's it about, then?" Her hand still rested on the weapon he could plainly see. "I warned you about those pickup lines. Persistence doesn't add any points."

"I have no patience for men like the one who gave you a hard time tonight," he explained in a firm tone that still reeked of charm. "Maybe I was a little rougher on him than I should have been. I don't want him taking out his frustration with me on you."

Wow, that really was sweet. "Nice of you to care, but honestly, you being out here now is kind of strange unless there's a hidden agenda. I don't know very many men—actually I don't know any—who would go so far out of their way just to be nice. So, what's the hitch?" Her cynicism was showing. That was never attractive.

He took a couple of steps toward her.

Her pulse reacted, but not in fear. She was attracted to this guy and that was dangerous.

You don't know him, Laney!

"I like you." He didn't stop until he was standing right in front of her in the grass that marked her property from the gravel road the state owned. "I don't have anything else to do and this felt like the right thing."

Before she could respond with something intelligent, he added, "I can leave if that's what you want."

"That'd probably be best."

She gave him her back and marched toward the

house. In those few minutes in the moonlight she understood one very important thing about Hayden. He was trouble.

"Are you certain he won't come back?"

She hesitated. She shouldn't have. But he had a legitimate question.

Laney turned to face him. "He might but I doubt it."

He'd been damned drunk. Terry was probably sleeping it off at some dive motel with a honky-tonk honey who didn't have any better sense.

"Are you prepared to use that weapon if he does?"

That was none of his business. "If I have to."

"Do you know how to use it?"

No. "Of course. Why would I carry a weapon I can't use?"

"Because it makes you feel safe even when you have no idea how to use it."

Heat scorched her cheeks. "I said I know how to use it."

"You don't need to be afraid of me, Laney. I'm only here to help. No hidden agenda."

Okay, so maybe the guy was bored. As much as she felt sure providing him with entertainment would be equally entertaining to her as well, that wasn't happening.

The last time she'd been in bed with a man was three years ago when she'd been stupid enough to believe more of Terry's lies. As much as she recognized her own needs—needs that she had ignored for far too long—she had a son to protect.

"Good night, Hayden."

"I'll be out of your way at sunup."

"Suit yourself."

To her amazement, she made it all the way to the house without looking back. A repeat of her nightly rounds in the house proved the doors and window were secure.

In her room, curtains and shades drawn, door closed, she stripped off her clothes. A shower would just have to wait until morning. She was way too tired. Besides, the washing machine was still running and that meant the water pressure in the shower would suck.

No, thanks.

She dragged on her favorite T-shirt, the one with that silly sponge character her son loved. Tucking her .32 on the shelf above her bed—way out of Buddy's reach even if he climbed up on the iron headboard—she realized she was sore from unloading that supply truck this afternoon.

She crawled into bed and her whole body sighed.

Her bed was the most awesome piece of furniture she owned besides the lumpy sofa.

Lying on her back, she stared at the slow turn of the ceiling fan blades in hopes that sleep would come quickly.

Didn't happen.

How could she hope to sleep with him out there watching?

Instead, her brain started throwing out scenarios that had nothing to do with a good working relationship with the cowboy.

Not smart, Laney.

The folks who liked her called her hardworking, nice, friendly…but not a one had ever accused her of being savvy when it came to spotting the devil behind a nice smile and good manners.

She had a feeling it was going to take her savviest maneuvers to head off this collision course.

Joel Hayden was going to be way, way more than she could handle.

Chapter Three

6:30 a.m.

The sun was up and the promise of an early summer scorcher was in the air.

Joel walked back toward his Jeep. The need to stretch his legs had awoken him before sunup. All remained quiet. The last of the lights had gone out in Laney's house around two. He doubted she and the boy would be up any time soon.

The past five nights had been spent like last night, only without Laney's knowledge. Parked out of her line of sight, Joel had slept in his Jeep—what sleep he'd gotten—in order to keep watch on her.

It wasn't the most comfortable assignment he'd had as far as getting any shut-eye but there was no way around it. For now, he couldn't ensure her safety via any other means.

Clare Barker was still unaccounted for. Her whereabouts unknown since her great escape from the apartment in Copperas Cove. Rafe, her husband, remained on death row. His execution was barely more than three weeks away.

He'd been the one to contact the Colby Agency yet

he'd shut down completely since learning of Clare's disappearance. In part, possibly, because he had learned the one person he had trusted and communicated with in recent years had double-crossed him by helping Clare elude the agency's surveillance.

Not a whole lot about this case made sense.

The necessity to keep the principals in the dark was primarily to ensure their safety. Until the Colby Agency discovered what Clare Barker was up to, these women's safety had to be top priority. If word got out, the media circus would hinder the agency's investigation. Disrupting the lives of the three women who had been confirmed as the long-missing Barker daughters was going to be problematic enough, mostly for them. Sadie Gilmore, the youngest, had accepted this new reality well enough, but there was no way to guess the reaction from the remaining two women. For now, keeping the investigation quiet and finding the truth as quickly as possible was essential.

Bottom line, it didn't have to make sense to Joel or anyone else. His single mission was to protect Laney and her son.

He settled his Stetson in place and leaned against the front fender. A few more minutes and he would relocate to ensure Laney didn't grow any more suspicious than she already was.

Laney Seagers had no idea that she had been born Lisa Barker, middle daughter of Clare and Rafe Barker. Prints from her one arrest for assaulting the same jerk who was giving her a hard time at present had confirmed her identity. She had no idea and Joel wasn't looking forward to sharing that information. And he wouldn't until one of two things happened—the danger had passed or he was forced to do so in order to keep watch.

The lady seemed reasonably happy considering the less-than-kind hand fate had dealt her. Like most these days it was a rough go on the financial front, but she was managing or she had been until her banker decided to turn testy. To Laney, getting that loan taken care of was her biggest worry at the moment. She had no idea that far larger problems were brewing like dark clouds over her head.

Rafe and Clare Barker were two of Texas's most heinous criminals, the Princess Killers. The two had allegedly kidnapped and murdered more than a dozen young girls. That number didn't include their own daughters, who had disappeared under suspicious circumstances the morning of their arrests. The Barkers were sentenced to death. Though Clare's conviction had recently been overturned, according to her husband she was the one who had actually committed those gruesome murders more than twenty years ago.

Both had been arrested and charged, after so many young girls had gone missing in and around the community of Granger. Several bodies had been recovered from the Barker property. But the bodies of some of the missing as well as those of their three little daughters had not been found.

Now Joel and the other folks at the Colby Agency knew the reason why. Rafe Barker claimed he had turned the girls over to a trusted friend to ensure their safety from their crazy mother. To that end, he'd staged the family car and their room to make it look as if he'd killed them. But now that Clare's conviction had been overturned, he feared for their lives.

The Colby Agency had no idea as of yet if there was any validity to Rafe's claim of innocence, but he had been right about his daughters. The woman, Janet Tolliver, he had alleged was his accomplice in that eleventh-hour move to protect his girls had, in fact, arranged for their private, off-the-record adoptions.

Regrettably, she had been murdered within twenty-four hours of Clare's release. So far there was no proof Clare had anything to do with the murder, but they now knew that Clare had an accomplice. A one-armed man by the name of Tony Weeden.

As an infirmary nurse, Weeden had befriended Rafe Barker. Weeden was the one person to whom Rafe had told his story—until Rafe contacted the Colby Agency. His letter to Victoria Colby-Camp had been smuggled from Polunsky Prison by Weeden.

Whatever scheme was in motion and whoever was telling the truth, there was damned good reason to believe the Barker girls were in danger. The only question was from whom.

Sadie Gilmore, born Sarah Barker and the youngest of the three, was already in the capable hands of Colby investigator Lyle McCaleb.

Russ St. James had his eye on the unpredictable Olivia Westfield, born Olivia Barker, the oldest of the three. When reviewing the background files on the Barker girls, Joel had expected that his assignment would prove the most troublesome. Laney Seagers had a record of violence, though not exactly a rap sheet as long as her arm. She'd been in and out of one kind of trouble or another during her teenage years. She was also the only one of the three sisters with a kid in tow.

So far the biggest issue was with her ex-boyfriend

and the father of her child. Still, Joel hadn't attempted to move in close to his mark until last night. He supposed the next couple of days would reveal a clearer picture of what lay ahead as far as his ability to gain her trust.

As if his thoughts had summoned her, Laney stepped out onto her front porch, settled her attention directly on him and headed his way.

He'd promised to be gone by sunup. Maybe he'd lingered too long. Laney seemed to appreciate his charm to a point, but she was far too wise of the ways of men to be fooled for long. She had no intention of falling into a trap of any sort. The lady was definitely jaded when it came to all things male. But she was attracted to him.

Jeans skintight, T-shirt just as formfitting, she strode purposefully toward him. Her hair bounced around her shoulders, the gold catching the early morning sun and shining like silk.

Now that would be a hell of a vision to wake up to every morning for the rest of a guy's life. Even a hardcore bachelor like him could appreciate that prospect.

"You're up early." He smiled, gave her a nod.

"Saw you walking around out here at the crack of dawn yourself." She set her hands on her hips and looked him up and down. "I imagine you could use a cup of coffee before you go back to town." She shrugged. "It's the least I can do after you stood guard all night."

He cast a speculative glance at the waist of her jeans. "Decided you didn't need your weapon this morning?"

She smiled. Not one of those full-blown make-his-heart-thump kind but sexy as hell nonetheless. "I'm a little paranoid at night. Afraid of the dark as a kid. You know how it goes. Some of us just don't grow out of it."

"Never had any trouble in the dark." He matched her smile. "But I have my moments with paranoia."

"So, you interested in coffee? I grind the beans every morning."

"Hard to refuse an offer like that."

"Is that a yes, Mr. Hayden?"

"Hop in." He grinned. "Considering the miles you walk most nights from one end of that bar to the other, taking a load off won't hurt." Not that he minded watching her walk.

"That's a nice Jeep." She climbed into the passenger seat. "Looks new."

"It's a couple years old." He cranked the engine. "Bought it for my thirty-second birthday. I guess it's my midlife-crisis car."

"At least you didn't get a massive truck." She shook her head as he rolled along her dirt driveway. "Some guys think they either have to buy the biggest truck or the fastest car. For some crazy reason they think it's a chick magnet."

He glanced at her as he parked in front of her house. "You mean it's not?"

"Definitely not." She admired the interior of his Jeep. "A vehicle should suit the man and his purpose in life."

"Never really thought about it that way."

Her gaze settled on his. "What's your purpose, Hayden? You got a house? A wife? Kids?"

He laughed. "No. No. And, no. Did I pass the test?"

She swung her legs to her right and hopped to the ground. "I haven't decided yet."

He wondered what her old beat-up Chevy said about her purpose. Just getting by? Or laid-back and happy to go with the flow?

"I know what you're thinking." She strode up onto the porch.

If she was a mind reader they were in serious trouble. "Is that right?"

She nodded. "You're wondering why I drive that old truck."

He pushed up his hat and studied her a moment. "The thought has crossed my mind." He wouldn't mention how recently.

"It was my father's." She turned toward the old blue vehicle. "It was the only thing left after the fire. A buddy of my dad's saved it for me. Took him a while to find me with the bouncing around from one foster home to the other. It's a damn good vehicle. Since I was sixteen it's been the one reliable thing in my life. Got me where I needed to go. Even served as a home sometimes."

"That beats the hell out of a high-tech sound system and power windows any day of the week."

"Damn straight."

The screen door whined as she swung it open. The old house had a comfortable feel about it. Swing on the front porch. Pot of colorful flowers near the door. Old-fashioned screen door fronting an even older slab door with glass so old it had that wavy look. Inside, the place was well-kept and smelled of fresh-brewed coffee.

Likely every part of the decorating and furnishings were secondhand but she'd done a nice job making the place feel like a home for her and the boy.

"Buddy still asleep?" Joel didn't have a doubt that if the kid was conscious he would be either following his mom around or designing the next rocket for space ex-

ploration. As smart as he was, he didn't appear to have
any playmates his age. The kid didn't seem to mind.

"He'll be up soon and then he won't slow down until
he crashes for the night."

Joel laughed. "Kids that age never slow down unless they're sick."

"Thought you didn't have any kids."

The remark was tossed offhandedly enough but Joel
suspected it was one of those self-protective measures.
"Lots of nieces and nephews."

In the kitchen, there was more of Laney's eclectic
decorating. Again, lots of repurposed items. He was
impressed with her ingenuity. A lot of things about the
lady impressed him. She grabbed a mug from the rack
and poured the coffee.

"Smells good." He accepted the cup and savored a
long swallow. "Hmm. You have a special blend?"

She patted a glass container. "I mix a few different
beans to get the perfect combination of light and dark,
French and Colombian. It's the best mix I've come up
with so far." She wrinkled her nose. "Sounds kind of
tragic but it's a hobby of mine."

Judging by the large pot rack hanging over her island
and the broad selection of cooking implements, the lady
liked to cook. "Did you do the decorating yourself?"

She cradled a mug of her special brew in both hands.
"I did. The remodeling and the decorating. I spent a lot
of time in salvage stores and hustling to remodeling
sales. It got to be a kind of competition with myself to
see how much money I could save."

"Looks like you have a knack."

"That's what my grandmother said." She smiled, remembering. "I was just a kid when I helped her remodel

her old farmhouse. She was all by herself and my parents were on the road with business all the time. One day we just tore into the place and started fixing things up. It was a learning experience, let me tell you."

"Your folks live around here?"

She shook her head. "They're all long gone. Died when I was a kid. Had foster parents through my crazy teenage years and, believe it or not, I just got a little crazier after that. I didn't get my act together until I had Buddy."

He knew her history but asking the logical questions was necessary for his cover. "Well, you turned out pretty damned good, Ms. Seagers."

Those brown eyes searched his. "What's a guy like you doing hanging around the High Noon and tossing out compliments to lonely women?" She heaved one shoulder then let it fall. "Or here, for that matter? You're clearly educated, polished. Not the usual cowboy who hangs out in saloons."

"The company I worked for went south. I have some savings. I decided taking a little time off to just chill would be a good thing."

"You seem a little young to retire."

He laughed. "True. But there's a high burnout rate in security services. A lot of pressure and a lot of long days and even longer weeks."

"You're on break," she suggested, her expression a bit wary and openly disappointed.

He nodded. "I guess I am."

"Why bother with working for me? I mean, it's still security work. Last night can't be your idea of chilling."

"Definitely not the same." He finished off his coffee. "Most of my work involved high-risk principals.

Politicians, celebrities. Lot of pressure. Last night was a cakewalk."

She poured him another cup. "You meet anybody really famous?"

"You mean like a rock star or movie star?" he teased.

She scooted up onto the counter. "Yeah, that's exactly what I mean."

"A few. A former president and vice president impressed me the most."

"Wow." She pursed her lips. "I may have to get you a special T-shirt for work."

"Does that mean I have the job?"

She held his gaze for a bit. He didn't miss the hesitation in her eyes. "I don't usually trust people right off the bat. I take a while, most of the time. But for some reason I do trust you, Hayden."

That should have made him relax. It sure would make his assignment a hell of a lot easier. But it also meant that she would eventually learn that he wasn't telling her the whole truth. Knowing that she had decided to trust him made that part a whole lot harder.

"I'm flattered," he confessed. A woman like her didn't trust easily.

"Just make sure you don't make me regret it. And when you're ready to go back to your real life, I expect a two-week notice."

The tension held a moment. "You have my word."

Another second or two of that thick silence elapsed.

"I guess you have the job, then. Barring any unflattering information from your references."

"Fair enough." He narrowed his gaze at her. "Now I have a question for you."

Her expression turned skeptical. "Be aware, I reserve the right not to answer."

"Agreed."

"So ask."

"Why're you lonely?"

She looked confused.

Before she could put two and two together, he went on with the question that had nothing to do with his assignment. "A woman as young, smart and hot as you should never be lonely."

Surprise flashed in her eyes but quickly reverted to wariness. "I was trying to be funny, Hayden. I don't have time to be lonely."

He'd hit a nerve there. He glanced at the array of hanging pots and pans. "You must be a heck of a chef."

"I can hold my own." She set her cup aside, visibly relaxed. "The only time I've ever known a man to be interested in kitchen utensils was if he was a chef himself or if he was hungry."

Joel grinned. "I'm afraid my culinary skills leave something to be desired."

Laney folded her arms across her chest. "I'll make a deal with you, Hayden. You cut the grass and I'll make you a breakfast you'll tell your grandkids about."

"Deal."

Joel was only too glad to help.

One step closer to where he needed to be.

Chapter Four

Victoria Colby-Camp reviewed the records they had amassed on the Barker case. What was she missing?

Each step taken by the investigating detectives after the arrest of the Barkers was spot-on. There was every reason to believe that the Barker girls had died that final morning before their parents' arrests. The blood at the house and in the family car had suggested foul play. The blood type was consistent with that of the little girls. The bodies were not recovered and no trace of the girls had been discovered in all these years.

Until now.

If Janet Tolliver, Rafe Barker's friend who had helped with whisking away the children, had lived, perhaps she would have been willing to cooperate with the agency's investigation and solved at least part of this mystery.

But she had been murdered and the killer was still out there. Had she been killed by another of Rafe's confidants? That wasn't logical and no other resource he might have used had been discovered.

And why would he kill the woman who had kept his secret all these years? To cover his tracks? Had Janet

Tolliver known incriminating information beyond the location of the three Barker daughters?

If Rafe hadn't orchestrated her murder, had Clare? Not likely. Lucas, Victoria's husband, had been keeping watch on Clare until she vanished with Tony Weeden, the one-armed man. There simply had been no real opportunity for Clare to have gotten to Janet. Unless Weeden had committed the act for her or for Rafe.

Weeden was the only variable. It had to be him. For one thing, he was left-handed, out of necessity, but a leftie nonetheless. The police in Copperas Cove had determined that the blow that ultimately killed Janet Tolliver had likely been wielded by a person who was left-handed. The murder weapon was thought to have been a heavy marble angel statue from Janet's home. The killer had obviously taken the time to clean it thoroughly as well as anything else he or she may have touched in the home. But trace amounts of Janet's blood had been found on the statue. Since the statue hadn't been lying near her body, the blood hadn't simply splattered there.

But if Rafe hadn't ordered Janet's murder, which his doing so would have made no sense, why had Weeden turned on Rafe and murdered the woman who had ensured the safety of Rafe's daughters? That scenario made no sense, either. But someone had murdered her and that murderer had a motive. Had Weeden been waiting for just the right opportunity to take vengeance on Rafe or Janet?

For what reason?

Was Weeden somehow connected to Clare beyond the role of accomplice? If so, why had they not found a connection in his history? Weeden was raised by foster parents but his birth record was ambiguous to say the least. Simon Ruhl, the head of the Colby West offices, was convinced the record was a forgery.

So many questions and hardly any answers.

Victoria heaved a weary sigh. The day had scarcely begun and already she felt emotionally drained.

Time was short and all at the Houston Colby office were working overtime to solve this complex puzzle, including Victoria and Lucas.

The idea of an innocent man being put to death twisted her insides. But was there time enough to prove who was innocent and who was guilty?

Victoria thought of the way Rafe had looked at her when she revealed that Weeden had deceived him. The devastation had been clear in his eyes but it was the other emotion—something like rage—that disturbed her immensely. Forced her to rethink his motives and his story.

Was she working with the devil himself?

A rap at the door drew Victoria from the troubling thoughts. Simon and Lucas entered the small conference room where, together with Victoria, they had created a timeline of events along a whiteboard that extended across the better part of one wall. Photos, newspaper clippings, it was all there.

"We have a new development that may prove our first real break in the case," Simon announced as he and Lucas joined Victoria at the conference table.

"We could certainly use one." Though they had uncovered small details over the course of the past few days, not one had propelled the investigation forward.

"As you know," Lucas began, his expression cautiously optimistic, "I've spent the past forty-eight hours attempting to track down anyone who knew either Clare or Rafe in college, before their marriage."

Anticipation trickled in Victoria's veins. Lucas had that look in his eyes. He'd found something. "And?"

"A Francine Parks was a close friend of Clare's for the first year they attended the same university. She claims Clare was raped by one of their professors but she refused to report the incident for fear that the scandal would somehow cause the loss of her scholarship. This woman believes a pregnancy resulted from the rape."

"This would have been thirty-one or thirty-two years ago?" Clare was about the same age as Victoria.

"Thirty-two," Lucas confirmed.

Simon picked up where Lucas had left off. "Ms. Parks is certain Clare gave birth to a child conceived in the assault. But she has no proof. She is basing her assumption on excessive weight gain and repeated bouts of something like morning sickness those final few weeks of the spring semester. The following fall, Clare returned looking and behaving as if nothing had happened. According to Parks she refused to discuss the incident at any time."

"But this Francine Parks can't be sure," Victoria guessed.

"She cannot," Simon confirmed.

It was definitely a possible lead, though not a particularly reliable one. Hearsay was just that, hearsay.

"According to Parks," Lucas noted, "the incident occurred in late November which would suggest a July or August delivery date. The timing could imply that perhaps Tony Weeden is Clare's son and, frankly, I'm inclined to believe the Parks woman. She has no horse in this race."

"The age would be right." Victoria resisted jumping to the immediate conclusion. "Did Ms. Parks have any other reason to believe that a child resulted from the attack? An overheard conversation? Rumors around the campus?"

"None," Simon answered. "Clare requested a different roommate that fall and apparently kept to herself since we haven't been able to find anyone she was close to until she met Rafe." Simon sat back in his chair and seemed to consider the possibilities. "Clare was young, only twenty-one. Her parents, the Sneads, were murdered when she was a kid. At eighteen, she left her foster parents without looking back. But," he countered, "she did have a sister, Janet Tolliver. Might she have turned to her? That would provide the connection between the three."

"You're assuming," Victoria suggested, "that Clare knew where her biological sister ended up."

"We've learned the Tollivers, the people who raised Janet, and the Sneads, Clare's parents, were friends," Simon reminded her. "Our thinking when we first discovered that Janet and Clare were biological sisters was that the Sneads gave Janet up due to financial reasons but that may not have been the case. The one source we found who knew the Tolliver family at the time Janet came to live with them suggested the Sneads had been afraid of Janet. There was talk that she tried repeatedly to harm her younger sister, Clare, and that was the reason for the Sneads sending Janet away."

"Is this source that reliable?" Victoria was sure both Lucas and Simon understood that accuracy was key not only for finding the truth but also for moving forward in the proper direction. "We have little time, gentlemen, for running theories that prove groundless. We need something solid. And we need it now."

Lucas joined the conversation. "The woman who lived next door to the Tolliver family is old, and her memory is sketchy on some aspects of how Janet came to be a part of the Tolliver family, but she was absolutely certain of that point. The Tollivers had no other children at home. They were all grown, so they never saw any trouble out of Janet. She gave the appearance of a nice young girl but the neighbor was not comfortable around her."

"We're checking with old schoolmates and any living teachers," Simon explained, "to determine if Janet had any problems at school."

"We learned nothing else from Janet's neighbor in Copperas Cove who held the photo albums of Rafe's daughters for her?"

Simon shook his head. "The neighbor knew the aunt who left the house to Janet. She and Janet saw each other occasionally as children but their friendship was more recent and, I suspect, relatively superficial."

Were they wasting their time digging up information on a dead woman? Maybe, but they simply had no other leads. There was nowhere else to go in light of Rafe Barker's abrupt silence.

"Would Clare turn to a sister who had tried to harm her as a child?" Seemed a more than reasonable question to Victoria. Victoria had a younger sister of her own who had proven that blood was not always thicker than water.

What exactly had happened to tear apart Clare's

family and to set her on a course to connect with Rafe Barker? Had he turned her evil or had she changed him?

"Clare may not have known about the incident or perhaps didn't comprehend the magnitude of what actually happened." Simon had children of his own and would certainly understand the capacity of young ones for forgiveness. "She was three when Janet was sent away. Her parents may have chosen not to tell her or she may have simply blocked the incidents from her memory."

"Then again, Janet may have sought out Clare." Victoria understood the need to find long-lost loved ones. "She was certainly old enough to remember a sister even if she chose not to remember certain events." Then again, the prison logs listed no visitor named Janet Tolliver for Clare or for Rafe.

"Janet may have done more than that," Lucas interjected. "After Clare's parents were murdered, a couple of neighbors stated they saw a teenage girl outside the home. The lead proved a dead end. But what if it was Janet? What if she came back—she would have been fourteen at the time—and killed the parents who deserted her? Perhaps she even hoped it would be blamed on Clare as punishment for being the daughter they kept."

"Then why would Clare see Janet again? Even after being raped and feeling utterly alone?" That part didn't feel right to Victoria. The police reports from the time Clare's parents were murdered indicated that she had come home and found the tragedy. Yet she had been covered in blood. From her attempts to save them, she had claimed.

So much death and devastation. Would this tragic cycle end with the surviving Barker daughters? Victoria intended to ensure the nightmare ended with this investigation.

"Clare may have blocked the horror of that evening from her mind, as well," Lucas offered. "It's far easier to fall back into a pattern that worked once than to stand up and face such a terrible truth."

Her husband had a very good point. Victoria had long thought that the tragedy of her own son's abduction and the twenty years they had lost was the worst a woman and mother could suffer. This frightening family saga had her rethinking the definition of "worst-case scenario."

"If the two were in contact again," Simon proposed, "Janet may have taken care of the child born to Clare just as she did her three daughters years later."

But Janet Tolliver had taken the three girls for Rafe, not for Clare.

"That possibility, however, gives Clare less of a motive for murdering Janet," Victoria suggested. "Why kill the person who helped her with such a tremendous burden at a critical time in her life?"

"Because she discovered that Janet had hidden her daughters from her…and then refused to tell her once she was released where they are," Simon offered.

"Janet had even gone so far as to hide the photo albums she had saved," Lucas pointed out. "With the woman next door. Seems to me she wanted to make sure Clare didn't get her hands on them."

The photo albums. All three were well-documented biographies of the girls' lives, from their original birth certificates to current photos. All apparently recorded by Janet Tolliver.

"Assuming Weeden is, in fact, Clare's son, he may

have killed Janet in an effort to help his mother," Simon summed up. "The flip side of that is that possibly Weeden is only pretending to help his mother. He may have an entirely different motive and agenda."

"Revenge," Lucas agreed. "He was the child his mother abandoned. Subsequently marrying and having three little girls."

More theories and scenarios and no answers, Victoria thought. She banished the mounting worries. "Where are we on Laney and Olivia?"

"Hayden called in this morning," Simon reported. "He's making good progress. St. James is still watching Olivia from a distance."

"Both are very good at what they do," Lucas tacked on. "Laney and Olivia are in good hands, even from a distance."

Victoria prayed they could keep these women safe.

And she hoped solving this puzzle would not be too late to stop an innocent man from being executed.

If he was indeed innocent.

Chapter Five

Beaumont, 9:16 a.m.

Laney leaned in the open doorway to watch what she typically considered a boring task. But with Hayden pushing that lawn mower, his shirt long ago tossed aside, she had to confess there was absolutely nothing boring about the view. Broad shoulders, lean waist with those ripped abs… Very nice.

That little voice that always reminded her of how often she'd been an idiot tried to intrude but she ignored it. Hayden had no idea she was watching and she deserved a little stolen pleasure here and there.

Lonely. Yes, she was lonely. No use lying to herself. But she had no time to quench that particular thirst.

Couldn't hurt to look. It was the touching that led to trouble.

In the living room behind her, Buddy watched his one hour of television. The restriction wasn't one she had enforced; it was his own. He had two thirty-minute programs he considered his must-watch TV then he was done. On to one of his games or to his Lego corner to design and build something new. Having such a bright kid was intimidating at times. No matter the cost to her personally, she wanted him to have every opportunity in life.

As for Laney, she could be happy just to daydream. Her attention wandered back to the man finishing up the nice job in her yard. She couldn't remember the last time anyone had done a menial chore for her. In part because she was so independent she rarely allowed anyone to know she needed help. But mostly because she'd always picked the wrong kind of guys. The ones not at all interested in helping with anything other than separating her from her panties.

At twenty-six it was darned well past time she'd recognized her destructive pattern and changed course. Her gaze tracked Hayden a moment longer. Falling back into bad habits was a bad idea. The next man she allowed herself to get involved with would earn the right to be with her.

A good-looking cowboy on break from his life wasn't the right starting place.

The smell of biscuits browning in the oven tickled her nose and reminded her that the only promise she'd made to her new sexy security guy was breakfast.

After a quick check on Buddy, she headed back to the kitchen. Eggs and bacon were staying warm in the covered cast-iron skillet. She grabbed an oven mitt and peeked in on the biscuits.

"Perfect." And homemade. That was another thing her grandmother had taught her. How to make super-fluffy biscuits. One of these days she intended to start opening the saloon for breakfast. Experimenting with coffee was a fun hobby that had her hankering to take it to the next level. The interstate passed right by the saloon. She was far enough out of Beaumont proper to make going for breakfast from that end of the city limits a pain. Why not capitalize on the convenient location?

The roar of the mower stopped. Laney glanced out the window just in time to see Hayden drag his T-shirt back over his head. If her stomach weren't rioting with hunger pangs from the smell of the biscuits she'd swear it was gawking at him that was tightening her insides.

She grabbed a strip of crisp bacon and tore off a bite. "You're just hungry, girl. And not for him."

With her mismatched stoneware on the kitchen table and a fresh pot of coffee filling the room with its robust aroma, she smiled as he strolled in through the back door.

"My yard looks more like a lawn now than the makings of a hay field. Thanks." Fact was, she couldn't remember when the lawn had looked so well manicured.

"I'm the one who should be thanking you." He rubbed his flat belly. "Breakfast smells fantastic."

Oh, yeah. The man was a bachelor all right. Otherwise plain old morning staples wouldn't have him tossing around words like *fantastic*.

"Nothing you couldn't get at any old breakfast hut."

He raised his eyebrows at the platter of biscuits. "I'm reasonably confident you're wrong about that."

"Bathroom's down the hall. Wash up and I'll serve."

"Whatever you say, boss lady." He winked and strode off to follow her order.

Laney shook her head. No one should fit that well into a pair of jeans. Or look that good all sweaty and smelling like fresh-cut grass.

Buddy wandered over and leaned against her leg. "Does he live here now, Mommy?"

"Of course not. This is our house. We live here. Just

you and me." Laney lifted her munchkin into her arms and gave him a hug. "Wow, you're getting almost too big for me to pick up, young man."

He pressed his nose to hers. "Biscuits. I need more energy for the town I'm buildin'."

She grinned. "Biscuits will do it." Laney settled him on the floor. "Pick your seat." He never chose the same chair twice in a row.

"Purple feet!" He slid into the one on the far end of the table.

"That's the best one." Same thing she told him every time no matter which chair he selected.

Like the rest of her furniture, her table and chairs were mismatched. She'd decided to throw a little excitement into mealtime so she'd given each chair a personality by painting each a different color with faces and painted-on hair. She'd even attached small wooden shapes to the legs and painted each as a foot or a shoe. She might have gone a little overboard with the beads and bow ties on the backs of the chairs but Buddy loved them.

The air changed in the room when Hayden returned. Maybe it was the breeze from the window. The chill bumps on her skin certainly weren't the result of him simply entering the room.

"Good morning, Buddy."

"You have to sit down there." Buddy pointed to the other end of the table. "That's for company."

"Sounds like the best seat in the house. Definitely the chair with the best feet."

Laney threw off her apron and joined them at the table. "Actually it's the one with an uneven leg." She arrowed a look at her son. "I'll take that one."

Hayden pulled out the chair. "Love the feet."

Laney settled in the chair, and it immediately tilted a smidge to one side. "I got the idea from a magazine."

He took the seat to her left. "You have a very artistic flare and a vivid imagination."

"I'll take that as a compliment."

"That was the point." Hayden sent her another of those unabashed winks.

Laney focused on the food. Buddy had already filled his plate with far more than he could possibly eat. Laney loaded Hayden's and then her own. She was starving.

At the same time, he poured the coffee, their movements choreographed as smoothly as if they shared breakfast every day.

She speared a clump of scrambled eggs. What the heck was wrong with her? Evidently the financial worries and frustration with Terry were messing with her brain.

"You looking forward to school this fall?" Hayden asked her son.

Buddy looked up, a biscuit halfway to his mouth. "I'm not sure yet."

That was her boy. "You liked it when we went for that orientation visit a couple weeks ago."

He chewed off a big bite of biscuit and shrugged.

"He's a little worried that he won't fit in," Laney explained. "He doesn't know any of the other kids who'll be starting with him."

"Sounds like you need to join one of the ball teams," Hayden said to Buddy. "I've seen flyers all over town about sign-ups."

Buddy turned up his glass of milk then pursed his lips while he considered the suggestion. "I'm not really T-ball material. I prob'ly couldn't hit the ball and then I'd get bored."

Hayden nodded. "Yeah, that would be kind of boring."

Laney focused on her plate and hoped the men wouldn't notice the laughter she was barely restraining.

"'Course," Hayden went on, "a man puts a little practice into it, he could probably hit that ball every single time."

"I don't have a ball or a bat," Buddy explained. "That makes practicing a problem."

"I'm sure we can do something about that." Hayden glanced at Laney before he turned back to the boy. "I made all-star every year in high school. I could give you a few pointers."

Buddy's face furrowed in concentration. "That was a long time ago. You might be rusty."

Laney couldn't help herself; she laughed. She tried to cover her mouth but there was no holding it back.

Hayden nodded, managed to keep a straight face somehow. "How about I get the gear we need and we practice together?"

Another fierce moment of concentration puckered her little boy's face. "We'll see."

"Good deal." Hayden glanced at her again, amusement shining in his eyes.

Laney wanted to smile at the idea but would Hayden really stick around long enough to keep that promise?

The screen door whined, announcing someone was at the front door before the firm knock echoed.

"Excuse me, gentlemen." She flashed a smile at Hayden. Maybe he wouldn't break her boy's heart... or hers.

As much as her son's vocabulary and intelligence thrilled Laney she did worry about him fitting in at school. She sighed. That was one worry she couldn't do anything about right now.

Laney opened the door expecting to have to kick Terry off her porch or to see the mailman dropping off a package. But the man waiting on her porch was a stranger. He wore a suit and tie, glasses and sported a slicked-down comb-over. He carried a black leather briefcase, the thin kind that was useless for anything other than a few papers.

"Ms. Seagers?"

Apprehension needled its way under her skin. "That's me."

"I'm Howard Samson from Samson and Lott Appraisers. Mr. Teague from Beaumont Independent Bank commissioned me to execute an appraisal of your property."

What the...? "I'm afraid you have me at a disadvantage, Mr. Samson. I wasn't aware an appraisal had been ordered." The apprehension swelled into downright fear.

"I assure you, Ms. Seagers, it's standard procedure when a loan nears maturity and the refinancing is questionable."

Standard procedure. Old man Teague just couldn't wait to assess the value of her property. Damn him and damn Kingston if he had anything to do with it.

"We're in the middle of having breakfast." She was angry now. How dare that old goat do this? "Maybe you could call for an appointment next time."

"I understand," he offered in that monotone that matched his neutral expression. "I'll be taking mea-

surements and photos outside first. When you're ready
for me to come inside you can let me know."

"The lady said you needed an appointment."

Laney's breath caught at the warning in Hayden's
voice. He'd moved in right behind her and she hadn't
even noticed.

Samson's eyebrows reared up his forehead. "I see."

"Good," Hayden offered. "You have a good day
now." He closed the door in the guy's face.

Laney stared at him. She wasn't sure whether to kick
him or to hug him.

"Sorry," he muttered irreverently. "I have no patience
for jerks and that guy was a jerk."

Heat singed her cheeks. She walked past him to
check on Buddy. He'd finished and was busy piling
his dishes into the sudsy water now filling the old por-
celain sink, egg and biscuit remains going for a swim.

She turned back to Hayden. "I guess you've heard
the rumors about my impending loan crisis." Her staff
had a bad habit of eavesdropping.

"I did," he admitted.

She blew out a breath of frustration. "It's not pretty
but I'm not giving up."

"Giving up is for wimps." He gave her a reassuring smile that felt more reassuring than it should have.

This man was almost as much a stranger as the one
who'd just showed up at her door.

"Thanks for the breakfast. I'll stow the mower." He
ran a hand through his hair. She shivered. "I noticed
the barn needs a few repairs to the roof. Unless my boss
tells me different, I'm free all day to work on that."

Laney ignored the floor shifting beneath her feet.
This was too much. It wasn't that she didn't appreciate

the help and he'd been really nice to her son…but this was a risk she wasn't prepared to take.

"You're a really nice guy and all," she said, searching for a kind way to say what needed to be said.

He held up both hands. "I get it. You don't trust me."

Wow. Hearing him say it sounded a lot worse than she'd been aiming for. "I guess that's what I'm trying to say."

"I get it. Really." He set his hands on his hips. "Call my references. You'll feel better then."

"You're right. Sure." She slid her fingers into her front pockets. "I'm sorry but my son is my top priority and as much…"

Stop, Laney. That was enough. She didn't have to explain herself. This was the right thing to do. He would either understand or he wouldn't.

"I'll see you tonight at the High Noon."

She nodded. "Thank you for…helping out."

He patted that amazing six-pack. "Thanks for the home-cooked meal. It's been a while."

"Mom!"

Laney pushed aside the mixed feelings she couldn't seem to shake. "What you got, sweetie?"

He held up one of his latest art endeavors she'd had hanging on the fridge. "This one is extra good."

Laney crouched down to his eye level. "It sure is." He'd drawn a picture of the two of them flying a kite. This was his first year to be able to hang on to the kite string all by himself.

"Can I give it to the lady?"

Laney frowned. "What lady?"

Buddy looked at her as if she should know exactly

who he meant. "The grandma lady who played with me in the kitchen last night."

Fear ignited deep in Laney's gut. "What grandma lady?"

Buddy huffed. "The one who washed dishes for Uncle Tater."

Laney relaxed. "A friend of Tater's?"

Buddy shrugged. "I don't know. She was nice. I wanna give her this."

Hayden crouched down next to Laney. "Is this lady your uncle Tater's grandmother?" he asked Buddy.

Laney frowned. "He doesn't have any relatives in Texas."

Buddy eased closer to his mother and shrugged again.

"I guess it'd be okay to give her the drawing." Laney hugged her son. "That's very sweet of you."

Buddy wiggled out of her arms and smiled. "She'll like it."

"How do you know the lady was a grandmother?" Hayden asked.

What was with all the questions? she wondered. Before she could ask that very question, Buddy answered. "She had grandma hair."

"Gray hair?" he prompted.

Buddy nodded. "That means she's old."

"Was her hair long like your mother's?" He tugged on a lock of Laney's hair.

With a big shake of his head, Buddy touched her chin. "Short like there."

"Did she ask you any questions, little man?"

Buddy frowned. "I'm not a man. I'm a little boy." He turned to Laney. "Tell him, Mom. He's confused."

Laney searched Hayden's eyes. "You heard him. You need to see his driver's license to confirm his age?"

"Mommy." Buddy made a face. "That's silly."

"Did this nice grandmother ask you any questions about you and your mom?" Hayden rephrased his question.

"Nope. She asked me about Mr. Bear."

Hayden swung his attention to Laney. "Mr. Bear?"

"Why don't you introduce Mr. Bear to Mr. Hayden?"

"Okay." Buddy hustled off to his bedroom.

Laney pushed to her feet. "Why all the questions? I'm sure the lady was a friend of Tatum's. He has friends stop by and hang out with him in the kitchen occasionally."

Hayden stood. "I saw something on the news before I left Houston about an older woman involved with a human-trafficking ring that deals in young children."

The very idea made Laney's chest hurt. She rubbed at the tightness there. "Are you serious?"

"Afraid so."

"Jesus. I'll have to talk to Tatum."

"You should ask him to keep the kitchen door locked."

That barb of fear twisted a little tighter inside her. "Absolutely."

Buddy shuffled back into the room, Mr. Bear hugged to his chest. He glanced shyly at Hayden.

He crouched down and pretended to shake the bear's hand. "Nice to meet you, Mr. Bear."

Buddy smiled, something he rarely did with strangers. "The grandma lady said her daughter had a teddy bear just like him."

The notion that this woman could be the one in the

news report Hayden mentioned seemed like a long shot. She was probably just one of Tater's friends. A silly coincidence.

But the sudden grim expression on Hayden's face sent a chill straight through her.

As protective as she was of her son, surely she hadn't been totally oblivious to that kind of danger walking right into her own saloon.

But then she'd been overwhelmed lately.

Had Buddy's safety suffered because of her inability to handle the stress load right now?

Laney chased away the worries. It wouldn't happen again. She would see to that.

Chapter Six

Noon

When Tatum Motley, aka Uncle Tater, arrived half an hour ago, Joel had given him and Laney some space. Though she hadn't said as much out loud, she had clearly wanted to talk to her employee and friend privately.

Joel understood her situation. As much as she would prefer to have her son at her side at all times, she had to run the bar—which meant Buddy had to be in the kitchen or the office away from the dispensing and selling of liquor. Laney trusted the retired sailor but she would need to get it through his head that extreme caution was necessary from this point forward.

Laney had suggested maybe Kingston had sent the old lady to freak her out or to prove Buddy wasn't safe at the High Noon.

She just didn't know.

Joel offered to keep an eye on Buddy while he played in the backyard. It gave Joel a chance to call the agency with this latest development. Simon Ruhl agreed that despite the lack of proof that the grandmotherly woman, as Buddy had described, was in fact Clare Barker, there was every reason to suspect she was here and, at the very least, watching.

Lucas Camp, Victoria's husband, and a former CIA agent, was en route. Clare Barker had given him the slip in Copperas Cove a few days ago. Lucas had been attempting to pick up her trail again since. He would be nearby and available if Joel needed backup.

Hopefully it wouldn't come to that but better to be safe than sorry. This was a highly sensitive situation with charged emotions for all involved.

At this point Joel would have no choice but to add the next layer to his cover profile. As much as he disliked lying to the lady, it was, unfortunately, necessary to ensure she didn't grow suspicious of his interest in this mysterious visitor.

Leaning against the post nearest the steps on the back porch, he watched Buddy climb the ladder to the slide, then squeal as he slid down. The kid was cute and so damned smart. But he was still just a kid and had no concept of the danger associated with talking to a stranger. The kid needed playtime with others his own age.

Joel had no real experience with kids but that requirement seemed logical to him. If he bothered to say as much, Laney would likely put him in his place. The woman was seriously protective of her son and defensive of her mothering skills. He supposed dealing with a sleaze like Terry Kingston had generated that touchy situation.

Buddy hopped into a swing seat and struggled to get the thing going. The seat needed to be lowered a bit. Joel could handle that.

He strolled over and propped against the slide ladder. Like his mother, the boy had a strong sense of independence. Approaching the suggestion from the wrong perspective would offend the little fellow.

"When I was your age," Joel commented, "I liked to be able to push off with my feet."

Buddy started grunting and wrestling with the momentum and stared at the ground a good six inches below his boots. "I'll have to grow some more before I can do that."

"Guess so." Joel pushed his hat up a notch. "Unless you lower the seat. It's pretty easy. Just climb up there and bring it down a couple of links."

The kid stared up at the hook where the chains holding the seat connected to the frame of the swing set. "I'd need a ladder to do that." He turned to Joel and visually measured him. "You could reach it."

Joel considered the cross bar of the frame. "I can try it."

Buddy hopped off the swing seat and braced his hands on his jean-clad hips. "Try it." He made a hopeful face. "Please."

Thirty or so seconds later the seat was lowered by three links of chain on either side. "Try that out."

He settled in the seat, no hopping in required this time, and shuffled his cowboy boots over the grass. He grinned at Joel as he launched into a wide swing.

The new squeals were thanks enough.

When Buddy had slowed to a relaxed back and forth motion, Joel broached a few questions. Better to ask the stickier ones without his mom around. "The grandmother lady was nice, huh? Did she give you a present?"

"Yep she was nice. And funny, too. She promised to bring me a present next time."

"Did she tell you her name?"

"Nope." He kicked at the grass. "She said it was okay to call her grandma."

Uneasiness settled heavy in Joel's gut. "Did she talk to your uncle Tater?"

"Nope. Just me. She was busy washing dishes."

Took some nerve to waltz in through the back door of an establishment and just pretend to work there.

"Your mom ever talk to you about not talking to strangers?"

"She wasn't a stranger. She was nice."

That was what he figured. "Maybe next time you see her you can introduce her to your mom or to me first."

"She's shy. She doesn't like to talk to people she doesn't know. Just me and Mr. Bear."

Joel had seen the crime-scene photos from when the Barkers were arrested. The middle daughter Lisa—Laney—had had a teddy bear exactly like the one Buddy lugged around.

He doubted that was coincidence. Laney had most likely been drawn to the bear when she saw it. The mind worked that way sometimes. Even if a memory didn't surface, sensations could be triggered by one or more of the senses.

"Is she coming to see you again?" he asked Buddy.

"Hope so. I want to give her that picture."

Something else he'd have to pass along to Lucas when he arrived in Beaumont.

"I'm ready for juice!" He hopped out of the swing and ran for the back door.

Joel followed. He smiled as the boy shouted for his mom. Reminded him of when his mother was still well enough to be a mom. Many, many years before she died a withered and drawn ghost of the person she had once been. He and his brothers were young. Stair steps, folks called them. Church every Sunday, grace at dinner every night.

In the kitchen, Tatum looked as if he'd lost his best friend. Laney was pouring juice for Buddy, who sat on a stool at the island, boots dangling back and forth. She placed a couple cheese sticks on a napkin, glanced at Joel then Tatum and jerked her head toward the living room.

Joel locked the back door—just in case—before following the two. Maybe the cook had some additional details Laney wanted Joel to know.

If it helped track down Clare Barker, he would be grateful for the info.

Once in the living room, Laney told Tatum, "Tell him what she told you." She nodded toward Joel.

Tatum "Tater" Motley heaved a woeful breath. "She said Laney hired her to come in and help weekends. Wash a few dishes and then go." Tatum glanced at Laney. "Wouldn't be the first time somebody new showed up that I didn't know was coming."

Evidently she had dressed the guy down pretty good.

"From now on whenever I hire anyone new," Laney promised, "I'll make the introductions."

Tatum nodded. "And I'll keep the door locked."

"Sounds like a good plan," Joel noted. He sympathized with the older man. The High Noon hadn't exactly exercised any real security measures. Now probably wasn't a good time to point that out to the boss.

"I'm sorry as I can be that this happened, Laney. You know I love Buddy." The older man shrugged. "But she looked like a nice lady. Harmless."

Might as well take the first step in adopting the deeper cover. Joel fished his cell phone from his front pocket. He pulled up the photo of Clare Barker taken just before her release. He passed it to Tatum.

"Is this the woman who talked to you and Buddy last night?" He hadn't wanted to confuse the kid by showing it to him. A kid that age would think any picture Joel carried around in his pocket had to be of a friend.

Tatum nodded. "Her hair was shorter. But that's her."

Shooting a glare at Joel, Laney reached for the phone. "Let me see that."

Her shoulders seemed to sag as she studied the photo. She might not notice the resemblance at first, but when she'd had time to absorb the details and to think about it, the questions would begin.

Laney thrust the phone at Joel. "Thank you for coming over to discuss this, Tater. I apologize if I overreacted a bit. The whole idea terrifies me."

"Yes, ma'am, I understand. Like I said, I never left Buddy alone with her for a second. But you have my word it won't happen again."

"I know." Laney gave him a hug. "I'll see you tonight."

When the old guy had gone, Joel braced for her interrogation.

She closed the door and turned to him. On him, actually.

Before she could make her first demand, Buddy sauntered into the room and collapsed in the corner with his mound of Legos.

"Coffee?" she asked, her frustration seething under the surface of her cordial tone.

"Sounds good."

He hung his hat on the coatrack near the front door, made a point to lock it, then wandered into the kitchen. The sound of coffee beans grinding once again delayed the launch of her questioning.

"Why do you have a picture of that woman in your phone?"

He braced his hands on the old butcher counter to prevent crossing his arms over his chest. Any defensive or withdrawn body language would make her all the more suspicious. "The woman's name is Clare Barker. She was released from prison recently and apparently has decided that her best career opportunities can be found working with lowlifes who steal kids and young women for trade. Drugs, money, guns. It's a nasty business."

"So you're not a laid-off security guy, you're a cop." She crossed her arms over her chest, her shoulders back. This was going to be an uphill battle.

"I'm not a cop. I work for a private-investigations agency and I, as well as others, have been hired to keep an eye on potential victims."

Her eyes widened with fear. "Potential victims?"

God, he hated this part. "When it comes to young kids, they're usually looking for certain ages, eye and hair color. Boy versus girl or vice versa."

"I'm absolutely certain that Buddy is not the only five-year-old boy in Beaumont with brown hair and eyes. What made you decide he was in danger?"

Her expression was openly wary now. The cover he'd intended to use was not going to work. That was way too clear to ignore. And the truth was, he didn't want to lie to her.

"All right." He drew in a breath. He was taking a risk

here. "I'm not here because of Buddy or any human-trafficking ring." He steeled himself for the disbelief, the anger and then the pain. "He's your son so that makes him my responsibility, too."

"What the hell are you talking about?"

The fight-or-flight response flashed across her face. Keeping her calm was essential. He had to tread carefully here.

"We need to sit down and talk about this." Buddy was in his own little world in the living room but his mother's raised voice would draw him into the room in a heartbeat.

"So talk." There came the anger.

He hadn't given her anything yet to prompt the shock but that was coming. "There are some things I need to get from my Jeep, then we can sit down and go over the facts you don't know about your past."

She stormed out of the kitchen. Joel followed her into the living room where she snatched up the cord-less handset.

"I'm calling the sheriff."

Buddy looked up.

Joel glanced from him to Laney. "Bring the phone with you. We'll sit on the porch. Hear me out, and then you can call the police if you feel the need."

Several seconds passed before she reacted, most of which she spent eyeing him with something akin to contempt.

"Five minutes," she warned. "Then I'm calling the sheriff and getting some real answers."

He couldn't blame the lady. He'd shown up in her life just days ago and suddenly he was here, in her home, with secrets to reveal. She had every right to be suspicious and angry.

But she had no idea that what he was about to tell her would change her life forever. However complicated her finances and the situation with Kingston were, that was nothing compared to what she was about to learn.

And he couldn't stop it.

"We'll be right outside on the porch if you need anything, Buddy," she said to her son.

He nodded. "I know. Grown-up talk."

Joel smiled. Damn, that kid was smart.

JOEL STRODE OUT to his Jeep. Laney wilted down onto the top step of the porch, the phone clutched in her hand. Part of her wanted to make that call right now. This man—this stranger—had been too good to be true and she had known it.

"Damn you, Laney," she muttered.

She thought she'd learned her lesson when it came to trusting the wrong guys and here she was about to be scammed for God only knew what reason.

Her fingers tightened around the handset. But he'd taken care of Terry… He'd watched her house all night. And then he'd gotten rid of that damned bank appraiser. Was all of that nothing more than an act?

Instinct warned that if Hayden was up to no good it was motivated by the Kingstons. To her knowledge she had no other enemies. Her banker was likely getting his palm greased with Kingston money, too.

Every single problem she had could be traced back to that crazy short-lived relationship with Terry. What an idiot she had been!

No. No. That doomed relationship had given her

Buddy. She hadn't been a total idiot. Or maybe God had known she needed an angel to help her rise above the troubles in her life.

Hayden joined her on the porch, settling next to her. After the way she'd watched him play with Buddy she'd started to feel more comfortable with letting her guard down a little more.

He carried a case, like a portfolio. Black leather. Much larger than the one the appraiser had carried. His body language told her that whatever he had to say he wasn't looking forward to doing so. What could this stranger possibly know about her past?

Wait. He'd said he worked for a private-investigations agency.

"Before you start," she said, cutting him off when he would have spoken, "I'd like to see some kind of credentials."

He dug out his wallet and showed her his Texas driver's license which identified him as Joel Grant Hayden of Houston, Texas. Then he pulled out another picture ID which showed he was an investigator for the Colby Agency.

"I can give you the number if you feel inclined to call."

She hadn't checked his references. Too much had happened. "What's in the case?"

He opened the leather case and removed a photo album. "Did your parents tell you or leave a will informing you that you had been adopted?"

An old but familiar terror trickled into her veins. "No. Of course not. Why would they?" She banished those old feelings that hadn't haunted her in years.

"When you were almost four you and your two sisters were taken—"

"Sisters?" She stood, moved down the two steps and glared at him. She couldn't sit and listen to this. "I don't have any sisters."

"You do. Two. One younger, one older. Both right here in Texas."

"You must have me mixed up with someone else." She shook her head but there was a distinct storm of uncertainty brewing in her head. "My parents had baby pictures of me from birth." She hugged herself, felt suddenly cold despite the warm midday sun.

"The attorney who handled the private adoptions was in Austin. When the woman came to him with the three girls to be adopted, she provided baby photos for all three of you."

"That doesn't make any sense. Why would anyone do that?" She shook her head. This was nonsense. Crazy. "And why split us up?"

"There are a lot of questions I can't answer." He tapped the album in his lap. "This will help but there are some things you may never know."

"What about the woman who—" she shook her head "—had the photos and supposedly did all this?"

"She was murdered six days ago."

Fear sparked anew. "What? Murdered?" She held up her hands, the phone still clutched in one. "This is like something from a bad movie."

"Why don't I start from the beginning?"

"Start wherever you like but I think there's been a mistake." Denial and fear and other emotions she couldn't even label twisted wildly inside her.

"Twenty-six years ago you were born Lisa Barker. Parents Clare and Rafe Barker of Granger, Texas."

She stood still as stone, his words echoing in her soul. This was impossible and yet some part of her couldn't refute the words. Sounds and sensations continued to echo.

"Your father was a veterinarian. Your mother his assistant. The five of you lived in an old sprawling farmhouse. The barn had been remodeled into the office and clinic for your father."

Images too vague and dark tumbled one over the other through her head. She blinked them back. This whole thing was like mass hysteria or something. She was only feeling this way because he sounded so convincing. He was wrong. He had to be wrong.

"When you were almost four, your parents were about to be arrested. Your father claims he wanted to protect the three of you so he whisked you away in the middle of the night and left the three of you in the hands of a family friend with instructions to see that you were taken care of. He alleges that he wanted you to have happy lives free of the Barker name and legacy."

"What legacy?" Claims? Alleges? Why was he talking like that? "You talk as if this man is still alive."

"They both are. Rafe is in Polunsky Prison awaiting execution. His wife, Clare, was on death row in another prison but her conviction was recently overturned so she's free."

Goose bumps started to crawl along her skin. "What were they convicted of?"

"Multiple homicides. Rafe and Clare are the 'Princess Killers.'"

Laney felt the color drain from her face. In the middle of the night once when she couldn't sleep she had watched some true-crime special about criminals of Texas. That couple had been the stars of the show. "They killed all those little girls?"

Hayden nodded.

Wait! Laney remembered something else from the show. "They killed their own daughters, too." Ha! She had known there had to be a mistake. "How could I be one of their daughters when I'm obviously alive?"

"As I said, Rafe claims he had the three of you taken to safety and he made it look as if you were murdered. He insists Clare was the murderer and that he was protecting the three of you."

He'd said that. Yes. But he had to be wrong. "If that's true, why is Clare free and he still awaiting execution?"

"He never said a word in his own defense during trial. His goal was to keep his daughters safe even if it meant execution. Clare insisted the entire time she was innocent. She finally won an appeal."

"Okay." Laney started to pace. "Why is your agency involved in this? Why track me down now after all these years—if you can even prove what you say?"

"Rafe claims his wife wanted the three of you dead. He broke his silence after more than twenty years to contact our agency after Clare was released. He begged us to find the three of you and protect you from her."

"Sounds like he just wants a ticket off death row," she argued. No way this could be about her. She had no sisters. Maybe she was adopted. She'd had freaky dreams when she was kid. Sometimes even now. But this was way off the charts unbelievable.

"He says he has no interest in clearing his name. He only wants his daughters protected."

"Show me your proof." She sat down next to him and reached for the photo album.

The first page opened to a newborn photo and a birth certificate for Lisa Barker. She pointed to it. "That doesn't prove a thing."

He said nothing, just let her keep looking.

As she turned the pages, Laney felt the bottom drop from her stomach. The pictures were all of her. Duplicates of what her parents had had in their family albums. Maybe not duplicates but photos taken from the same time frame.

The photos of her as a toddler with a man and a woman took her breath. She pointed to the couple. "That's them...the Barkers."

She remembered vividly the photos of the couple on the television show. It had been one of those investigative shows. The woman—Clare—had even granted an interview. But not the man. The woman...

Laney turned to Hayden. "That was her." The words were scarcely a whisper. "She came into the High Noon and talked to my son."

"I'm afraid so."

Her hands shaking, Laney flipped through the pages that showed snapshots in time of her life up until now— the good, the bad and the ugly. How was it that someone had gotten close enough to take these pictures and her not have known it?

When she reached the final page, packed with photos from her renovations on the house and the saloon, she quickly closed it and handed it back to him as if it were poison.

And it was.

She stared forward, at nothing at all. He was telling

the truth. Dear God. All she had thought she knew…
The entire foundation of her life was a deception.

"What does she want?" The voice that came out of
her sounded nothing like hers.

"According to her estranged husband, Clare wants
to find each of you and do what was supposed to have
been done twenty-two years ago."

Ice closed around her heart. She turned to him, stared
straight into his eyes. "She wants us dead."

"We can't confirm that's her goal, and until we do
it's imperative that you're protected twenty-four/seven."

"And that's why you're here. To provide protection."

His face grim, he nodded.

"For how long?" There was no way to even guess
how long it would be before this woman was stopped.

Was she really buying into this? She blinked back the
images she had seen in the album. How could she not?

"As long as it takes."

Chapter Seven

Laney went back inside her house.

Joel stood. He hadn't wanted to tell her right away. Too much risk that she would go to the authorities or make some other move that would get the media's attention.

The less Clare Barker knew about her daughters, the better. Keeping the situation contained until a resolution was reached was absolutely essential. Warden Prentice at Polunsky Prison and the Texas State D.A.'s office wanted this investigation off the record until the puzzle was solved.

He climbed the steps wishing there was something he could say to make this easier but there was not.

Laney would have to come to terms with this nightmare in her own time. At the moment he felt confident that her priority was protecting her son. If Clare was desperate to get at Laney, she might not think twice about using her son.

If the woman was innocent, which seemed highly doubtful after her escape from surveillance and the steps she had taken since, last night was the first time she'd seen her grandson. She may not have known until she tracked Laney down that she had a grandchild.

But there were two looming questions. Why had she evaded Lucas's surveillance? And how had she found Laney? There was no positive proof as of yet that she had tracked down Sadie, her youngest. But there was no doubt this time.

Clare Barker was here and she was growing bolder.

Since Laney left the door ajar, Joel figured it was safe to go inside without knocking. Laney sat on the sofa. Buddy was still occupied with his building project.

Joel placed the photo album on the steamer-trunk-turned-coffee-table and took a seat in a chair across from her. He doubted she wanted him too close, and from the blank expression on her face, talking wasn't on her mind, either.

Buddy wandered over to the sofa. "I'm ready for lunch," he announced. "Breakfast was a long time ago."

"Come on, big guy." Joel stood and rubbed the kid's head. "Since your mom made breakfast, why don't we whip up lunch?"

Buddy looked from his mom to Joel. "Why do we have to whip it? Whippings are bad."

Joel laughed. "You got me on that one, Buddy."

Laney didn't say a word as they left the room. Damn, this had to be hard.

Buddy went straight to the fridge. He opened the door, then dragged one of the chairs over so he could stand on it and survey the offerings.

"No baloney. No cheese. No ham."

He continued naming off the unacceptable options lining the shelves. Joel had a feeling this was going to turn into an ordeal.

The kid turned to Joel. "Can you make sk'hetti?" He leaned closer and whispered, "Not the stuff in the cans."

"Possibly." Unless there was bottled sauce on hand, that might be a no-go.

Joel checked the cabinets. To his relief he discovered a jar of warm-and-serve sauce. And pasta. They were in business.

Buddy had already climbed on the island and retrieved the necessary pot and pan.

Joel watched as he carefully climbed back onto the chair and down to the floor. Instead of dragging the chair back to the table, he scooted it over to the pantry.

"We gotta have something green. Lunch and dinner has to have green."

By green Joel presumed he meant a vegetable. "Got any green beans in there?"

Buddy went from door to door perusing the supplies. "No green beans but we got spargut." He made a face. "Takes like yuck but it's green."

Asparagus. The kid was right. It did taste like yuck from a can. Roasted or grilled, fresh was best.

Joel had the water on to boil and the sauce and asparagus in pans when Laney appeared. She looked emotionally drained and her arms were still wrapped around her waist. Drained and shaken. The entire structure of her life had just been jerked from beneath her feet.

"Buddy, why don't you go finish your project and start figuring out what you'll take to the High Noon this evening?"

Buddy frowned. "But I'm cooking." He had dragged his chair over next to Joel and stood in the seat to watch his every move.

"I think Mr. Hayden has it under control."

Buddy huffed a big breath. "More grown-up talk."

He hopped down and dragged his chair back to the table. "I want to help drain the noodles, please."

"I'll let you know when they're ready," Joel promised.

Satisfied, Buddy shuffled off to do as he was told.

"What are the police doing about this?" she asked without preamble.

He leaned against the counter near the stove so he could see when the water started to boil. "They aren't involved yet."

"Why not?"

Time for the anger. "We have no evidence. All we have is the allegations of a man on death row who may be jealous that his wife got off and he didn't."

"But she came into my saloon and talked to my son," Laney argued. "That's trespassing or something."

"And she's gone. We can't prove it was her. It was a woman who looked like her is all we can claim. We have no idea where she is. We can't connect her to having broken the law. She can do as she pleases until she crosses that line."

"The bottom line," Laney said as she squared her shoulders, "is that you have no idea what her intent is."

"We can only speculate based on her husband's allegations and her actions since being released. But we're not willing to take the risk that she is an innocent woman who only wants to be reunited with her children. If the only thing she wanted to do was talk to you, she had the opportunity. But she didn't."

She rubbed at her forehead. "So no one can stop her?"

"Until she breaks the law, all we can do is watch her."

"Why wasn't someone watching her last night?"

"A few nights ago she gave the man watching her the slip and until now we couldn't be sure where she was. But, trust me, every effort is being made to get her back on the radar."

Laney moved closer to him, leaned against the counter on the opposite side of the stove. "If it's true that she killed those girls, she could be capable of anything."

"That's why we can't take any chances."

"So you're asking me to allow you to stay with us every minute until this situation is resolved?"

"Call the Colby Agency and those references I gave you. I'm here to help, Laney. I know it's difficult to trust someone you've known only for a few days. I wish I could make you see that there simply is no other way to do this."

"Give me those numbers again."

"I'll do you one better." He handed her his cell phone. "Call anyone in my contact list. Ask anything you want to ask. Then make your decision."

She stared at him for a good long while, then she accepted his phone and walked away. He heard the front door close as he dumped the pasta into the boiling water and then added a dash of olive oil. He'd learned that trick from his older brother. Kept the noodles from sticking together.

He set the flame under the sauce and the asparagus. He'd noticed lemonade in the fridge. It wasn't wine but then his assignment had just elevated to a new hazard level. Extra precaution was needed.

Clare Barker was here.

"Hey, Buddy! You want to give me a hand in here?" It wasn't time to drain the pasta but there were a few things they could get ready.

The kid set the table while Joel monitored the stove.

Once the pasta was drained and the meal was transferred to serving dishes, they were ready.

Laney was still outside.

Joel helped Buddy get his plate ready and ensured he was settled at the table before going in search of her.

He crossed the porch and sat down on the swing next to her.

She handed him his phone. "I should not only trust you, I should marry you."

He frowned. "I'm afraid to ask who gave you that advice."

"One of your brothers. The oldest I think."

"Yeah, he bugs me about being single all the time. Especially now that they're all married except me."

"Why aren't you married?" She pushed against the floor with the toe of her boot and set the swing in motion.

"Never ran into a lady who made me want to divert from the status quo. I like my life."

"You mean you're afraid of change."

He laughed. "I'm not afraid of change."

"That's what they all say." She stopped the swing and got to her feet. At the steps she leaned against the porch post and stared out over her yard.

He studied her a moment. "Does this mean you will accept my offer of protection?"

"I don't really have a choice, do I?"

"I wish I could give you a different answer but I can't. The situation is escalating and I need to ensure you and Buddy stay safe."

She stared at her hands a moment. "From the moment Buddy was born the only thing I wanted was to make sure he was safe and happy. And now everything's going to hell because of my mistakes."

"This isn't your mistake, Laney." He came to her, took one of her hands in his and gave it a squeeze to get her to look at him. "You can't help who your parents are or what they do."

She nodded, didn't try to tug her hand from his. "But I sure screwed everything else up. I'm probably going to lose our home and my business." She glanced out at the old truck in the driveway. "I never thought I'd have to resort to making Old Blue home again."

"Never surrender, Laney. The battle isn't over until you win or you give up."

"Easy for you to say."

He hitched his head toward the door. "Come on. Sk'hetti and spargut will do you good."

She laughed but the emotion shining in her eyes told him she felt more like crying than laughing.

They made it just inside the door when the house phone rang.

With a weary sigh, Laney answered.

Joel checked on Buddy, who had spaghetti sauce all over his face. He smiled. "I guess we make a pretty good team."

The kid nodded. "'cept for the spargut."

Laney appeared at the kitchen door. "That was the

Beaumont police. Vandals hit the High Noon last night. The officer said it's pretty bad."

Damn. Couldn't the lady get a break?

3:05 p.m.

A COUPLE OF WINDOWS were broken. Ugly words were scrawled in white paint across the antique front door that opened into the lobby-style entry. Big splats of paint stained the wood walkway that ran across the front of the saloon.

That was the good part.

Inside, several chairs were broken—eight if she counted right. Two tables were damaged.

Dozens of liquor bottles were shattered, their contents soaking into the old hardwood floor.

The kitchen and office had been spared. The latter was the strangest part of all. Why didn't they tear the office apart looking for money?

Fury tightened Laney's jaw. Because it wasn't about money. This was Terry's kind of tactic. She doubted he would have the guts to do it himself, but one of his scumbag friends would be only too happy to wreak such damage.

Hayden had already started sweeping up the broken glass from the liquor bottles. Buddy was seated at one of the untouched tables playing an electronic learning game.

Laney needed paint remover to scrub the slurs from the door. The rest of the cleanup would be more about manual labor.

She'd have to make do with fewer tables and chairs until she had the cash to buy some replacements. But the liquor supply would have to be taken care of immediately.

Outside, Terry's car still sat in the lot. That was the only part that mystified her. If he'd put someone up to this, why leave his car? Maybe to make it look as if he hadn't been back. But then why hadn't the vandals touched his fancy car?

The police had made the report, but doubted their efforts would be anything but futile considering the crowd in and out of here every night. Thousands of fingerprints and loads of trace evidence but nothing that would likely help find the lowlife who had done this. Her money was on Terry, but Hayden had a different theory.

Laney's insurance would cover the damages but the darned deductible was so high that she would be better off not even filing a claim.

"I need to get some paint remover." She opened at six. There was no time to stand around here pretending the cleanup would get done on its own. Even if the doors had to be sanded and restained, they were opened and pushed against the walls during operating hours, except in the winter. The Old West style swinging doors that separated the lobby from the saloon hadn't been touched. Thank God.

"I already called the nearest hardware store. They're delivering the paint remover and some shop towels," Hayden told her. "I also called the supply store and someone is pulling together a liquor supply run based on what you typically order."

He called and asked for a delivery? No, two deliveries. Laney had no idea something as simple as paint remover was a deliverable item. Maybe he'd promised a big tip which would greatly impact her pocketbook.

But she wasn't about to complain. She needed his help.

"Thanks."

Tater would be here within the hour to help.

Grabbing a bucket, gloves and cleaning clothes, she started with the liquor shelves and counter. Whoever had done this hadn't exactly been methodical which was to her benefit. Just random damage as if the person or persons who'd done it had been angry.

Had to be Terry. Jerk.

She checked for her Louisville Slugger behind the bar. A friend had given the bat to her when she first opened the saloon. *If you ever have any trouble, this'll do the trick.* Laney smiled. So far she'd never had to use it. Buddy had asked her a dozen times why he couldn't play with it.

Hayden was right. She needed to introduce her son to sports.

Her son. At least Buddy knew who his parents were.

She had been adopted.

The emotional wallop came out of nowhere and made her quake inside. Why hadn't her parents told her? Maybe they would have if they hadn't died so suddenly.

She tugged the gloves onto her hands, stared at them a moment. How could she be the biological result of two killers? Was that why she'd gotten into so much trouble in her teen years? Was she bad deep down inside?

Laney shook off the horrible thoughts and focused on the work. Her parents had died when she was ten. These other people—Rafe and Clare—were not her parents. Just the reproductive donors.

Something else to protect her son from.

The sound of tires spinning in the gravel outside drew her attention to the door just in time to see Terry swagger in. Judging by his walk he was already well on his way to intoxication at this early hour.

"I need my keys," he shouted. "Hey, Buddy boy."

Buddy glanced up, then lowered his face closer to the screen of his game.

Laney stripped off her gloves and snagged his keys from under the bar. Joel set his broom aside but Laney stopped him with a look. "I've got this.

"You see this mess?" she demanded.

Terry glared at her as if she were a lesser life-form.

"Did you do this, Terry?"

He looked around as if for the first time. "You know when I left last night." Terry shot her another of those condescending looks. "I haven't been back until now. Now give me my keys."

Later, Laney would look back on this moment and still the reason she lost it so completely would elude her.

She tossed the keys to him. He missed the catch, of course. She waited until he'd swaggered out and then she did what she had wanted to do for years.

Louisville Slugger in hand, she strode out the door with Hayden calling her name.

With Terry fumbling with his keys, she walked right up and swung. The impact left a fair-size dent in the hood of his prized car. She moved on to the windshield.

"What the hell are you doing?" he screamed.

Laney made her way around the car, bashing windows, denting metal.

Terry rushed around to her and started wrestling for

control of the bat. The desire to use it on his head was nearly more than she could resist.

Suddenly Hayden was there. She had a feeling he could have stepped in earlier but decided not to spoil her fun.

Hayden gained control of the bat and held it aside. With the other hand he manacled Terry by the collar. "It would be in your best interest not to come here again."

"You touch me and my father will make sure you regret it."

Hayden shoved him aside. "Tell him not to waste the effort. I already regret it. Now go and do not come back without making arrangements with Laney."

"Finally got you another guy," Terry accused. "I see how it is." He sent an accusing look at Laney. "I don't care what you do but you will not keep my son from me."

Laney got right in his face. "I don't have to. You're doing a stellar job yourself. No judge with half a brain is going to entertain your petition of custody with your record."

"You mean like he's going to entertain the idea of a kid hanging around a bar all night every night?"

Before Laney could do something even more stupid, Hayden pressed the bat to Terry's chest. "I'm certain you want to keep breathing. Now go."

"This is nothing compared to what you've got coming," Terry threatened. "Watch your back, Laney!"

He climbed into his car and revved the engine. Despite the cracked glass and dents, he spun out of the lot.

Good riddance.

Hayden turned on her, fury flashing in those bronze eyes. If he'd been gripping the bat any tighter it might have splintered. "This isn't a .32," Hayden warned. "When you attack a guy's vehicle, you attack him. No more of this, Laney. It could have gone way wrong."

Now she was mad all over again. He had no right to tell her how to conduct her personal life. They weren't in a relationship. As much as she appreciated him being here considering what he'd revealed to her this morning, she didn't need him deciding what was best for her.

"I need you because of this other crap, but I don't need you to tell me how to protect my kid or my property."

With the truth in his words stinging her cheeks despite her proclamation, she wheeled around and stalked back into the saloon. She had plenty to do that didn't involve discussing the subject of her ex or her son with him or anyone else. She yanked the gloves back on and set to the work of cleaning up the mess behind the bar.

Hayden walked into the saloon a few minutes later, wagging the paint remover and plenty of cleaning rags. Like her, he had gotten worked up over this whole mess. He'd probably been out there cooling off.

"I can work on the paint if you can finish up here."

That was exactly her point. The man thought he was the boss and they'd hardly done more than hold hands. She could only imagine how territorial he would be if they'd so much as kissed. Why was it guys always thought they knew best?

"Whatever." This whole day had just been too much.

The plunk of items on the counter made her jump but she didn't turn around. When he invaded her space behind the counter she had no choice but to meet his fierce gaze.

"You've done a fine job raising your son," he said,

the words tight with restrained tension. "I just don't want you getting hurt any more than you already have by that deadbeat guy."

His expression relaxed just a little. He looked away before she could analyze the change further.

"I appreciate your concern." She surrendered. "It made me angry that you were right. I lost control and that was a mistake. I just didn't want to admit it."

He touched her arm. It was nothing really. Just a simple slide of his fingers down the length of her upper arm from shoulder to elbow, but the heat that blazed inside her was not simple at all. She was attracted to this man. Had been since he walked through those swinging doors that first night.

She couldn't go there. The move would have been dumb enough before but it was downright foolish now. His revelation this morning had stolen something from her. The certainty of who she was and where she'd come from. She couldn't handle anything else.

"You've had a lot dumped on you when you were already carrying more than your share. I wish I hadn't been the one to do the dumping. But this is not going away until we learn the truth. I need you to use caution in all you do."

She nodded. "I understand. It'll take some time for me to get my head on straight." She wished he wasn't so nice. Maybe then she wouldn't feel like a complete idiot for going stupid in the parking lot.

"We'll get this place back in shape and you do what you do." He smiled and her knees went a little weak. "I'll have your back and I'll help Tatum keep an eye on Buddy."

Laney closed her eyes and fought the urge to cry.

That was the part that terrified her the most. She needed to know her baby was safe. As torn up as she was at learning her life was one big fabrication, his safety was all that really mattered.

Hayden's fingers tightened around her arm. "Trust me, Laney. That's all I'm asking."

He had no idea what a monumental request that was for her. Trusting him to do his job was easy. Actions spoke louder than words and she had seen in him action. But that personal trust she sensed he wanted as well was a whole different arena, one where she'd made the wrong decision too many times already.

"I'll give it my best shot."

Chapter Eight

5:00 p.m.

The house was pretty.

It reminded Clare of the one where she had raised her children…until *that day*.

The sickening ingredients of fear and hatred stirred into the pot of misery simmering inside her. *He* had taken all of that from her.

She could not change the past but the future was hers. Clare was free and in twenty-four days *he* would be dead. Her soul would rejoice.

If there was any justice in the universe he would burn in hell for all eternity. It would almost be worth joining him there just to watch him fry. She wished she could watch him gasp for his last desperate breath, but that was impossible.

Her mission had only just started. She had those same twenty-four days to see her goal accomplished. Rage kindled deep in her belly when she considered that *he* had so many on his side. The Colby Agency in particular. They were strong and smart. But they would not stop Clare.

She had almost been stuck in that rat hole of an apartment in Copperas Cove. But a blessing in the form of rescue had come at just the right moment.

Clare turned to Tony. What a good man he had become. No thanks to her.

"You're not safe here." He studied the house and its nice plot of property. "They could come back."

Clare smiled. "I think they'll be too busy to come back. You did a good job." Maybe too good but she wouldn't scold him for showing ambition.

Tony ducked his head. "I promised I would. I was careful this time."

"Let's hide the car and have a look inside."

He scowled. "That might be dangerous."

"Hmm. I don't think so. There's no security system. The house is old. Getting in should be very easy." She gifted her firstborn with a reassuring smile. "And I have you. What could go wrong?"

Reluctantly he obeyed. Farther up the road was a turnoff that led to nowhere. Just one of those places added for turning around or for hunters perhaps since it only led a few yards into the woods. These old country roads were full of little niches like that.

From there she and Tony marched through the field. The sun felt good on Clare's face. She had lived in that ugly gray cell for so many years. Her youth had vanished in the darkness of that awful place. Nearly half her life. But that was behind her now. She was free. And nothing was going to stop her from making them pay.

One already had.

Clare wrapped her arm around Tony's. He had made sure no one could harm her. He was a far better son than she deserved. If he only knew what she had suffered before his birth he would understand. But she dared not tell him for fear that the ugly truth would only add to his own suffering.

They had both suffered far too much.

It was time for the rest to suffer.

She had ensured Gus Gilmore could no longer keep his secret. Sadie was not his daughter. He had pretended all these years that she belonged to him. He'd given her a new name—Sadie, of all things—and kept the truth from her all those years. In a moment of heated emotions she had called him and warned that she was coming for her baby girl, but that had been wrong of her. Still, now Clare's baby girl knew the truth. And one day soon they would be together.

She squeezed Tony's arm. They would all be together.

"We'll try the back door."

"Whatever you think."

Tony was smart, too. He'd gone to school to be a nurse. He'd used that skill to get to that devil waiting on death row for his time to come. Tony had promised to take care of Clare now that she was free and they were reunited. With him and her three girls, the rest of her days would be filled with happiness.

A mother should be happy. Memories of locked doors and darkness…of her girls crying out for her tore at her heart. Never again… Never again.

With just a minute of manipulating Tony had the back door open. Clare entered the kitchen of her middle daughter and felt right at home. Her kitchen smelled of frequent use. Spices and the aroma of something recently baked. A plate of leftover biscuits sat on the counter.

Clare tasted one. "Mmm." Made from scratch. "Have a biscuit, Tony. Your sister made them."

He shook his head, too bashful to be so bold as Clare. She understood. He had spent his life cowering in fear. That was her fault. She intended to make that up to him.

Clare wandered to the fridge and admired her grandson's artwork. "He's like you, Tony." She turned to him. "Gifted."

One of those rare smiles lifted his lips. "He's a fine-looking boy."

"He is."

Clare made her way through each room. She studied the framed photographs and touched the things that held a place in her daughter's and grandson's lives. A good, comfortable home.

Tony hovered near the front windows, nervous about being caught. Lisa and this man from the Colby Agency were too busy to worry about anything else just now.

In Buddy's room, Clare sat down at his little desk and drew him a picture with the crayons and craft paper. When she was finished, she put everything back exactly as it had been. Then she placed the picture on her grandson's pillow.

"Just for you," she said softly. There were so many things they would soon be able to do together.

In Laney's room she found a photo album with oodles of pictures of her and Buddy. Clare took one and slipped it into her pocket. She hated to steal from her own daughter but she wanted desperately to have something to remember her by. She had one of Sarah already.

Tony had handled the situation there a bit poorly. He had left that ugly message to frighten the girl. Clare had chastised him for doing such a thing. He'd sworn that he hadn't set fire to her house but Clare worried that he might have accidently caused the fire and then feared telling her.

Since no one was harmed, she decided not to torture him about it. He had suffered enough.

With a deep sigh of contentment, Clare joined her son in the living room and took his hand.

"Let's be on our way. We have much to do."

No one would stop Clare from reuniting with her daughters. Rafe was going to pay anyway…far more than he knew. And that Victoria woman and her agency had better stay out of Clare's way or she would pay, too.

Chapter Nine

5:51 p.m.

Lucas had been in Beaumont less than three hours and already he had canvassed most of the hotels, motels and any other dives advertising rooms for rent.

He'd prioritized his list by the ones with the least visibility.

Victoria was worried. She would have preferred that he stay at the office and that one of the agency's new recruits have taken this task.

But this job belonged to Lucas. It was his responsibility that Clare Barker had jumped off the radar. He had fallen down on the job and now others were at risk. Lyle McCaleb had Sadie Gilmore under close watch; no problem there. But Olivia Westfield was not fully covered at this time. St. James was still watching her from a distance. Joel Hayden had shown Laney the photo album and explained the risks but it was yet to be seen whether Laney would go for around-the-clock, up-close-and-personal protection.

She had no idea how badly she needed that kind of security.

At least one person was dead. Whether Clare Barker,

which was highly unlikely since Lucas had been watching her apartment at the time, or Tony Weeden committed the murder—and Lucas suspected it was the latter—dead was dead.

Lucas pulled into the parking lot of the next motel from his Yellow Pages list. Another dive, but those types presented the lowest profile and required the least in the way of identification for anyone looking to stay under the radar.

The air was cooling down, a nice contrast to the unusually warm day. He'd already made his own arrangements to bunk in the office at the High Noon. Clare's appearance at the saloon as well as the vandalism had ensured Laney's cooperation. Hayden said Laney kept a cot in the office for her son. That would work. He wanted as close as possible. Particularly since vandals had hit the saloon at some point this morning.

Both he and Hayden understood that this was most likely the work of Clare Barker's sidekick but convincing the police, or Laney for that matter, without evidence wasn't likely to happen in time to reap any benefit.

Also because of the vandalism at the saloon, the police had offered to make extra drive-bys the next few days but that was the best they could do until they had a lead on a suspect.

Lucas entered the motel office. The manager looked up from the book he was reading. A small fan sat on the counter stirring the stale air.

"I'll need a driver's license and cash up front," the man informed him. "No credit cards."

Lucas moved to the counter, his limp a little more

pronounced than usual. He'd spent too much time behind the wheel today. "I'm not looking for a room."

The guy set his book aside. "You a cop?"

"No need to get into the technicalities." Lucas passed
him the photos of Clare Barker and Tony Weeden.
"Have you seen either of those two? Maybe they rented
a room."

The manager nodded. "I saw him all right." He shook
his head and handed the photos back to Lucas. "Felt
sorry for him because of the missing arm. Even gave
him a discount. Sorry sack of—"

"Is he still registered here?" Anticipation sharpened.

"Nah. They cleared out this morning, but they left a
hell of a mess for me to deal with."

"Have you cleaned the room already?"

"No use cleaning it. It's gonna need a new paint job."

"Can I see the room?"

The other man's eyebrows reared up. "I figured you
was a cop." He grabbed a key, the old-fashioned kind
attached to a plastic placard sporting the room number.

Outside, the twelve rooms were divided in half by the
office. A row of six fanned out on either side. The motel
was a one-story place with little recognizable landscap-
ing and even less visible upkeep. Shabby.

Room ten sat near the end to the left of the office.
Lucas followed the manager to the door, his aching leg
forgotten.

"Yeah, the cleaning lady came into the office raising cane this morning. I figured it was the usual kind
of mess. Drugs, alcohol or some freaky sex-party leftovers." He hesitated before opening the door. "Didn't
expect this."

He pushed the door inward and motioned for Lucas to have a look.

Dozens of stick-figure drawings littered the walls. Some were what appeared to be three little girls in a row. Others featured the three girls along with a mother and a larger male stick figure. Some had a sixth stick figure, this one much smaller. Clare, her three grown daughters, Weeden and the grandchild.

Dread settled in Lucas's gut.

"The freak used a felt-tip marker that won't scrub off. It'll take some work to cover that up."

Lucas surveyed each drawing. All were meticulously drawn. Then, as if the artist had decided the work wasn't right, he'd come along and hastily slashed each one with a large X.

Whether it was Clare or Weeden, Lucas couldn't be sure. Whichever it was, they were dealing with one very sick individual. Or maybe they were both over the edge.

Either way, in Lucas's opinion, the desperation of the situation was intensifying. The urgency or hatred one or both of the suspects felt was obvious.

It was only a matter of time before the urgency evolved into sheer desperation.... And then anything could happen.

Chapter Ten

High Noon Saloon, 11:15 p.m.

Joel joined Lucas at the table farthest from the rowdy crowd gathered around the jukebox. Considering it was a Monday night it was hard to believe any one of these folks had to go to work in the morning.

The beer was flowing and the music was loud. Most were either dancing or huddled in throngs talking and laughing. So far nothing but good clean fun. And no sign of Kingston, which Joel appreciated. As much as the guy deserved to have some good sense beat into him, he was still Buddy's father and Joel had no desire to be the one to get the job done.

But he would, if the need arose. The guy wasn't getting another chance to make Laney miserable.

Between the woman getting so close to Buddy and the news Joel delivered today, the dead-last thing she had needed was more hassling from Kingston. The destruction they'd found here was nearly the straw that broke the camel's back. Laney hadn't been herself all night.

She'd rushed to the kitchen, and later the office, so many times to check on Buddy that customer service had suffered. Most had been patient but a few had given her a hard time. Joel had wanted to step in but she'd given him that look that said *back off.* He'd checked on Buddy repeatedly, but no matter how often Joel made his rounds, she had needed to see the boy for herself.

"No word yet on Janet Tolliver's murder?" he asked Lucas. There hadn't been much time to talk. Lucas and Laney had hit it off immediately. He'd even thrown in with her behind the bar as if he'd tended bar his whole life. Joel had no idea the man could draw the draft with such skill.

"Nothing new. Marble angel statue from her own home was the murder weapon, it seems. No prints or other trace evidence discovered so far. The coroner suspects the killer was left-handed. Simon has contacted the great-niece to see if she has any background on the angel." Lucas sipped the same beer he'd been nursing since he took a seat. "Its use as a weapon may or may not be significant."

"Based on what you found in that motel room," Joel suggested, "we may be dealing with a bigger problem than Clare Barker. This Weeden character sounds like he may be a little over the edge."

"There's nothing in his background that suggests a mental disorder. Prentice, the warden at Polunsky Prison, insists Weeden was a stellar employee who never missed a day of work until he disappeared last week. And his background is clean."

"Maybe reading the letter Rafe wrote to Victoria tripped some sort of trigger that sent him over the edge." It happened. A shocking and debilitating illness could lie dormant for the better part of a person's life, only to surface when an intense physical or emotional trauma occurred.

"That's certainly possible," Lucas agreed. "I just hope we can contain it before the onset of more violence."

"The motel manager reported the vandalism?"

"He wasn't going to but I pushed the issue." Lucas checked his cell phone. "I also gave the Copperas Cove police a heads-up on the connection. If the slightest piece of evidence between the motel room and Tolliver's house could be found, we might be about to turn some aspect of this investigation over to the police."

That would take a big load off the Colby Agency. Both Lucas and Victoria were bearing a significant burden with this case. For a retired couple, they worked damned hard. One death during the course of a Colby investigation was one too many.

"Hayden." Mike Kelso, a waiter, paused at their table. "You might want to check what's going on outside. That guy from last night is messing with your Jeep."

"Thanks, Mike. I'm on it. Don't mention this to Laney."

"No prob." The waiter hustled to the next table, the tray loaded with beers balanced in one hand.

"Go ahead," Lucas assured Joel. He pushed to his feet. "I'll check on Buddy and stick close to the bar."

"Appreciate it."

Joel made sure Laney was preoccupied before crossing the room and heading out the door. He didn't want her following.

The parking lot was well lit. A small crowd of onlookers was gathered a safe distance away to watch Terry Kingston wave what appeared to be a tire iron.

A blonde female dressed in a super-short skirt, a halter-style top and thigh-high boots was trying to talk him into leaving before trouble started. Evidently her powers of persuasion were proving futile.

Joel cut around behind the arguing couple and approached from the rear.

"Really, baby, let's go," the woman urged. "I can't be caught in no trouble. I still got three months of probation."

Joel came up behind Kingston and snagged the tire iron before he could swing it. "I'd listen to your friend if I were you."

Kingston spun around, stumbled. He stared at his hand and then at Joel's grip on the wrench as if he couldn't understand how the transfer happened.

He looked up at Joel, squared his shoulders and cocked his head. "I don't know who you think you are, but you're messing with the wrong guy, hotshot."

Joel figured Kingston was too drunk then and maybe now to remember anything from the previous night. "Actually, I know exactly who you are and that's my Jeep. So I think you're the one who doesn't understand who you're messing with."

Realization dawned on the man's face. "You may think just because you and Laney have hooked up that you got some say over my son, but you're wrong. I will find a way to get you."

Joel tossed the tire iron aside and grabbed Kingston by the shirt. "We need a word." Holding Kingston far enough away that he couldn't get a swing in, Joel said to his female companion, "Get his keys and drive him to wherever he's staying. If you don't and something happens, I'll make sure the police know you were with him."

Her eyes widened. "I got the keys."

"Good. Where're you parked?"

The woman led the way to another snazzy sports car, this one as nice as the one that was no doubt in the shop after Laney took that Louisville Slugger to it. Kingston tripped and stumbled all the way to the car, mostly in an attempt to connect one of his fists with Joel's face.

Joel slammed the guy against the car, rattled him for a moment. "You listen to me, Kingston. I don't want to have to say this again."

Kingston swore at him. Joel had him pinned to the vehicle so he wasn't moving.

"As long as I'm with Laney," Joel warned, "you'd better stay clear." Before Kingston could interrupt he went on, "I'm not trying to keep you from your son. This—" Joel looked him up and down "—is keeping you from Buddy. Get smart. Find some help and this time stick with it."

Kingston told him where he could shove his advice.

"This is your mistake to make, pal," Joel cautioned, "but next time I won't be so nice." He released the fool and stepped back. Beating up on a guy too drunk to defend himself would be wrong, even if he deserved it.

Kingston smoothed his hands over his shirt. "I'll be back. You can bank on that." His threat fell short of the mark when he staggered sideways.

"And I'll be here," Joel promised. "Now go before I call your friends in uniform."

Joel waited until Kingston had loaded into the car and his girlfriend had driven away. Despite having won this round, he understood that the fool would be back.

When the taillights had faded in the distance, he turned and headed back inside. A round of applause from the crowd of bystanders followed him.

Laney's gaze collided with his and he knew she'd heard about the trouble outside.

LANEY COMPOSED HERSELF and moved on to fill her next order. Hayden looked no worse for the wear. Whatever had happened outside, obviously he'd handled it without violence.

Her hands stilled on the lever as the suds overflowed the glass. Why couldn't Terry get his act together? Her son would need his father at some point and the man lacked the skills to provide that necessary element.

She wiped the foam from her hand and delivered the beer, producing a smile for the customer. Between the bank, Terry and this…other…thing, she was a mess.

With two more beers delivered, she stepped from the bar and hurried to her office to check on Buddy again. He slept like an angel. He had no idea of the storm brewing in their lives.

Careful not to let the latch click too loud, she eased the door shut and joined Mr. Camp. She didn't have the exact chain of command but she got the impression that Camp was Hayden's boss. The man was really something.

When she'd first met him earlier in the evening he'd fooled her. Given his limp and the dark hair peppered thickly with gray, she'd expected the typical old man. Boy, had she been wrong. Lucas was not old by any definition. He was charming and intelligent and a gentleman all the way.

Laney strolled up to him. "We caught up for the moment?"

"We are." He flashed a killer smile, his gray eyes shimmering with kindness. "I think the boss needs a break."

"Oh, I'm sorry. Of course. I can handle this." It was almost midnight. He'd been all over town looking for leads on that woman...Clare Barker. Her mother. Unfamiliar emotions clogged her throat. "I didn't think, Mr. Camp. I'm sure you're exhausted."

The man laughed. "Call me Lucas. And I've got plenty of kick left in me. I meant *you* needed a break."

Laney's hand went to her throat. "Well..." She hadn't sat down all night. Five minutes off her feet would be a blessed relief. "I shouldn't impose."

"Go," he ordered in a tone she doubted few dared to ignore. He nodded toward the far side of the room. "Hayden's holding a seat for you."

"Okay. Five minutes." She started to back away. "If you need me before then—"

Lucas gave her a look and she turned tail and headed through the crowd. Though she had never heard of the Colby Agency, she was definitely impressed. If these two were any indication of the caliber of folks who worked there, they were the best. Her feet slowed as she neared Hayden's table.

He was watching her move toward him and something about the intensity on his face took her breath away. When his gaze made the slow, thorough journey up her body and connected with hers, she stopped. Only a few steps away but she just couldn't make those last three or four strides.

He stood, the movement slow and fluid, and closed

the small gap between them. When he was toe-to-toe with her he smiled, stealing her breath all over again.

"You okay?"

She nodded. *I will be as soon as I catch my breath.* "What happened outside?" Truly she didn't want to know. It wouldn't be good. But it was her responsibility to be aware.

One of those sluggish, syrupy country love songs floated from the jukebox and he reached for her. At first she was so startled she couldn't respond. But when he pulled her into his arms her whole body responded.

His arms were strong around her and she felt weak with need. He left the smallest margin of space between them but she closed it. She needed to lean on him. She needed to close her eyes for just a moment and let the rest of the world slip away.

He moved with the rhythm of the music, slow enough they could have been floating on air. His body felt warm and inviting and so powerful. She hadn't been held like this in so long. Maybe she'd never known this sensation of pleasure accompanied by a feeling of safety. She'd been on her own for too long.

She rested her forehead against his jaw. The late-night stubble made her shiver, made her want to reach up with both hands and explore the lean and intriguing contours of his face. She longed to get lost in all these wondrous sensations.... To forget the world.

He stopped moving. Her whole being protested. A couple of seconds were necessary for her to realize why he'd broken the trance.... The music had stopped.

Time and place flooded her senses, washing away the pleasant escape. Humiliation singed her already-flushed face. What had she been thinking? Thankfully no one had stopped to stare. They were just another couple in a packed house.

"I should get back to the bar."

"Take a break in the office with Buddy." Hayden glanced around. "The crowd is thinning. Lucas and I can finish out the night."

Laney started to argue, but he was right. She needed a few minutes away from the demands of the crowd.... Away from how he made her feel.

Tuesday, May 28th, 1:00 a.m.

"LANEY."

Her eyes opened to Hayden leaning over her.

Laney sat up. "Sorry. I guess I dozed off." She'd curled up on the narrow cot with Buddy for just a second.... Or so she'd thought.

"Come on. I'll get Buddy."

"What about cleanup?" Good grief. What had she been thinking? Her staff must be frustrated with her for abandoning them at closing.

"It's all done." He took her hand and pulled her to her feet.

By the time they were loaded in his Jeep, her brain was working again. Everyone had gone for the night. Lucas stood in the doorway watching them go. He would be staying the night.

With her son buckled into his car seat in the backseat and still sound asleep, Laney relaxed and considered that she hadn't allowed herself to collapse like that in ages.

Everything around her felt out of control.

Not that her life had ever been sedate or organized,

but usually there was some amount of structure to her chaos. Certainly not now.

"You got the receipts and the cash?" For God's sake, she hadn't even taken care of the books for the night.

"It's all taken care of. You had a particularly good night judging by the previous two or three Mondays' takes."

At least there was some good news. "Thank you."

Funny, she mused. This man had brought a whole new layer of uncertainty and disruption to her life, through no fault of his own, yet he'd also somehow injected a bit of new hope. Not so funny was the idea that she desperately needed him.

Strong, independent, ambitious Laney never needed anyone.

How had that happened in the space of a few short days? However it happened, he was a godsend. She glanced at her hero. Problem was he was only temporary. He was here for his job. So was his boss. She couldn't dare allow herself to get too attached. Laney felt reasonably sure that surviving any more loss and heartache was not in her.

She'd had enough for several lifetimes.

"What's it like…" The words were out of her mouth before she could stop them. She cleared her throat. No point stopping now. "What's it like growing up in a normal family? I mean, past early childhood?"

He glanced at her. "Some days it's a pain but most it's reassuring. You always know you have each other. Even if you have a knockdown drag-out with a sibling, you know if the chips were down, he would be there for you. I can count on my brothers anytime, anyplace."

Since she was ten, Laney hadn't known that kind of

support. Since she'd had no siblings—none that she'd known about—she'd missed that special bonding.

"What're they like?"

He glanced at her. "My brothers or your sisters?"

Wow. Sisters. "My sisters."

"Sadie, the youngest, lives in Copperas Cove. She has a small ranch and she rescues horses. Olivia, the oldest, lives in San Antonio. She's a paralegal. She spends a lot of time working for those who can't afford legal aid."

Impressive. "Do we look anything alike?" There had been a couple of photos with her and the others, but only when they were really young.

"Hair color is the same. Sadie's is a little lighter. You and Olivia have the same brown eyes. Sadie's eyes are green like Clare's." He seemed to consider the question a bit. "You're obviously sisters but you're each also unique. You're the tallest. Sadie is kind of petite. Olivia falls somewhere in the middle."

"It's funny. We all rescue something just like our parents did." The Barkers had rescued cats and dogs. Sadie rescued horses and Olivia those in need of help with legal troubles. Laney rescued things. Old houses. Furniture. All sorts of things. She'd tried to rescue Terry but he'd almost drowned her in the same cesspool he couldn't seem to drag himself out of.

He made the turn into her driveway. "That's because you're all three good people."

For the spawn of cold-blooded killers. But she didn't bother pointing that out.

He shut off the lights and the engine, leaving nothing but the moonlight to illuminate the house. She felt suddenly afraid to go inside for fear of finding some awful message from her recently released-from-death-row mother or her crazy ex.

Not once had she ever thought twice about arriving home at this hour and being afraid.

Hayden was already at her side of the Jeep before she snapped out of the disturbing thoughts. She unbuckled Buddy from his car seat and lifted him into her arms. She walked beside Hayden to the front door. He unlocked it and went inside ahead of her. Once the lights were on, she followed. Those old fears of the dark were back with a vengeance.

He locked the door and checked the kitchen as well as the back door for signs of forced entry before leading her deeper into her own home. A place where she had never felt anything less than safe.

"All clear," he assured her.

Frustrated with herself, she moved ahead of him to Buddy's room. There were only two bedrooms in this old house and the first one as she entered the hall was his. She flipped on the light with her elbow and her little boy's magical realm enveloped her. His things were here. His scent. It was home. Maybe she'd never had siblings or a real family life after the age of ten but she had it now.

She moved to the bed, threw the covers back and snuggled her little boy against his pillow. He burrowed into the soft sheets and never roused. She covered him and kissed his sweet forehead. Yes, this was their home and she would not lose it.

Then and there she decided that she wasn't going to play the victim here. Yes, she had to do as Hayden said until the issues with her biological parents were resolved. But she intended to take charge of this financial crisis. No one was taking hers and Buddy's home.

She moved to the other side of the bed and switched on the night-light. Something crinkled beneath her foot. She looked down and made a face.

Some of Buddy's artwork had fallen on the floor and she'd stepped on it. Dang it!

She picked it up and stared at the drawing. It was different from his usual highly imaginative drawings. Just a row of stick people. The first was obviously a woman. Next to her were two more slightly smaller girl stick figures. Then a little one, a boy since he didn't have the triangle shaped dress. Then another girl stick, the same size as the second and third figures.

How strange.

"What's this?"

Hayden moved to her side and studied the drawing.

"Something Buddy drew…I guess."

Hayden rushed from the room. What the…?

Laney wandered into the hall just as he burst from her bedroom. "What's wrong?"

"Stay right here."

She studied the drawing. Had something about it set him off?

By the time he returned she was more than a little freaked out.

"Someone tampered with the lock on the back door." His face was grim.

"You think someone came in my house?"

He nodded. "Whoever did it was good. He knew what he was doing and left very little evidence of his handiwork. And he locked it when he left."

Laney didn't understand. "Why did this drawing make you feel the need to check the doors again?"

He pulled his cell from his pocket and opened the photo library. "Lucas sent this to me after he found the place where Clare Barker and Tony Weeden stayed last night."

Laney stared at the image in disbelief. Hundreds of stick figures, exactly like the ones in the drawing she'd found in her son's room, marred the walls of the motel room. Only the ones from the motel had been crossed out.

What did this mean?

She stared up at Hayden. "They were here."

He nodded. "They were here."

Chapter Eleven

Beaumont Independent Bank, 10:00 a.m.

The small waiting area outside the bank president's office was nothing more than a hallway, a narrow one at that. On the other side of the glass wall in front of her was the bank's VP guiding a client through a mountain of paperwork. Laney wondered if that client, too, would be sitting here a few years from now wondering what would happen next.

Behind Laney was the president's office. She noted a client in his office when she'd taken her seat. Obviously that appointment was running long. The delay gave her a few minutes more to bolster her courage.

She understood that times were hard, but why make it even more difficult for a working woman to keep her head above water? Whatever happened to teamwork?

Speaking of which, Joel Hayden had happily agreed to take Buddy across the street for ice cream at the Dairy Dip. How had she gotten so lucky to have a man like him show up in her life at this pivotal moment?

No, luck had nothing to do with it. Evidently it was fate. And fate had taken its sweet time pulling this particular rug from under her feet.

How could she be twenty-six years old and not know who she was in the literal sense? Maybe her adopted parents had intended to tell her when she was older. Or maybe they'd never intended to tell her at all.

The idea that she was the daughter of convicted murderers lowered her already-sinking self-esteem down into the vicinity of her boots. The only saving grace that she could see was that she had two sisters. Buddy had aunts.

It was all a little overwhelming. Who was she kidding? It was a lot overwhelming. Not only could she and Buddy possibly be in danger, but once the media got wind of what was going on there would be fallout, too. Buddy started school this fall. Would the other kids make fun of him for being the grandson of Texas's most notorious killers?

Would business at the High Noon dwindle away? Or maybe it would pick up. Patrons might hurry in to see the freak show. Kind of like passing an accident and stopping to stare.

Most troubling of all was her concern for Buddy's safety.

Either Clare Barker or Tony Weeden, maybe both, had come into their home last night. Laney shivered at the memory of that stick-figure drawing. Had the same person drawn the one left in Buddy's room and the ones on the motel wall? What kind of sick person did that? And what the hell was the idea behind marking them out?

She wasn't sure she could deal with the answer to that question right now.

As soon as the hardware store opened this morning, Hayden had changed the locks on the doors at the house.

He'd ensured the locks on all the windows worked and he'd called a reputable security-monitoring company. Unfortunately they couldn't get her on their schedule until next week.

Meanwhile, Hayden was the protection. Warmth spread through her at the thought of having him near. She didn't usually let anyone this close but she hadn't had much of a choice and, if she were honest with herself, she would have to admit that it had been easier than she'd expected.

He was nice and seemed to genuinely care about her and Buddy. And her son loved him. Buddy had never taken to anyone the way he'd latched on to Hayden.

Then again, that swiftly developing relationship was worrisome, as well. How would Buddy take it when Hayden went away? He was only here for work.

For that matter, how would *she* take it?

Apparently, having just met the guy wasn't going to deter that long-neglected romantic side of her that still existed. She'd thought that foolish part of every young woman's fantasy had died years ago. Had to be some renegade gene she'd inherited from her crazy biological parents.

She'd had those old nightmares last night. The ones she hadn't experienced since right after her parents— the only ones she'd ever known—had died in that awful car accident. The screaming... God, she hated the screaming. Children sobbing, a woman screaming and the darkness. That nightmare had haunted her for years. But it had gone away after Buddy was born. All she'd had to do was cuddle up with Buddy and Mr. Bear and she slept like a baby.

Didn't take a self-help talk-show host to tell her that the mental stress was re-creating those same feelings of fear and insecurity she'd suffered after her parents had died.

Laney shoved her hair behind her ears and tried to relax. She couldn't get worked up about any of that and expect to be coherent in this meeting. She'd dressed in her best jeans and most conservative and businesslike blouse. Her grandmother always said that there were two times in a person's life when they needed to look their best. When asking for a loan and when going to the doctor. As a kid, Laney had giggled and asked her grandmother why it mattered if you looked good for a doctor's appointment. Most folks only went to the doctor when they were sick anyway. Her grandmother had lifted an eyebrow and given her a nod before saying, "You want 'em to think you're worth saving, dear heart."

Good advice in Laney's opinion.

The gentleman with the appointment ahead of her exited the president's office.

Finally.

"Ms. Seagers."

Laney stood and rearranged the worry on her face into something she hoped was optimistic. "Mr. Teague."

"Let's have a seat in my office."

Laney followed, took the seat in front of his desk. Because he hadn't smiled or made more than fleeting eye contact with her, fear twisted in her belly.

"I understand you ordered our appraiser off your property." Still no eye contact. He focused on the file she presumed to be hers.

"I did." She steeled herself. "Since I didn't receive

advance notice from your office, I wasn't sure if the gentleman was legit." He looked up then. "Allowing a stranger into my home is not a common policy of mine." She didn't need to remind him that she was a single woman with a small child. That was all in the file.

Mr. Teague heaved a big breath and leveled his gaze on her then. "Your profit and loss statements for the first quarter look very good, Laney. Last year's net profits gave you a strong year."

She nodded. "That's exactly why I don't see the problem with refinancing."

He sighed. "I'm going to be completely honest with you."

Fear kicked her heart against her sternum. "I appreciate that, sir."

"I don't have an issue with renewing your loan. You have gone above and beyond to show your credit worthiness. The collateral assets are in place. As an independent bank we're not as constrained as the larger banks when it comes to making loans. I do, however, have to answer to my board. Therein lies the problem."

"I always pay on time, Mr. Teague, and as you just said, I'm showing the necessary profit margin."

"All true." He closed the file and leaned back in his chair. "The board is made up of powerful businessmen who have stock in this bank. I am only one voice on that board. There are others who are considering the proposed loan renewal from a *different* view."

What the heck did that mean? "I don't understand."

If her credit and her income were solid, what was the problem?

He looked away a moment, then seemed to come to a decision. "I'm taking a great risk in telling you this, but I feel you should know."

Laney braced for the worst.

"There is outside interference from a very influential man in Houston."

Terry's father. The bastard. Fury blasted her. "How can anything he say make a difference?"

"It shouldn't," Teague admitted, "but this is not a perfect world and, unfortunately, there are those who love nothing better than wielding their power."

"What am I supposed to do?" She squeezed the chair arms to keep herself seated. "My profit and loss statement for the year before last was a little in the red. You know the other bigger banks are going to need two solid years of strong profit for me to qualify."

"I have a friend at another independent bank," Teague offered. "I'm hoping he can help you. You have my word that I'm doing all I can."

Laney understood that he was unmistakably under tremendous pressure. She couldn't fault him and she sincerely appreciated him being honest with her.

"Thank you, sir." She stood, offered her hand across his desk.

"Don't give up on me."

Laney promised not to and left the bank feeling somewhat better about Teague and outright livid about Kingston. No wonder Teague had given her such a hard time last month. He'd been under major pressure himself.

Somehow she had to stop the Kingston family from trying to ruin all that she'd worked for.

Buddy deserved better.

5:15 p.m.

JOEL HESITATED IN THE HALL outside Laney's room. He hadn't meant to stumble into the part of voyeur but here he was and there she was.

She'd bent forward to brush all that honey-colored silk into a manageable bundle before securing it into a French twist that turned out all tousled and sexy instead of neat and serviceable. His gaze remained riveted to that cute bottom encased in worn denim. It wasn't until she straightened and reached for the hem of her blouse that he made a sound of warning. He cleared his throat.

Laney whipped around, jerked her T-shirt back down over that slim waist.

"Just wanted you to know the security system is up and running." And that his body was hard as a rock from merely looking at her.

"That was fast." She hugged her arms around her waist. "Thank you for pulling some strings or whatever you did to get them out here today."

He acknowledged her appreciation with a nod. He told himself to walk away but his need to stand right here and look at her and smell that subtle, sweet scent she wore held him prisoner. Hell, it was just lotion but, on her, it smelled soft and womanly and made him want to get closer.

She glanced around the room, visibly nervous or at a loss as to what to say next. Her attention locked on the window. "So those things on the windows will make the alarm go off if the glass is broken?"

When her gaze found his once more her eyes were wide. She licked her lips, waiting for him to answer or to make a move. Too hard to tell—in more ways than one.

He crossed the room, drew back the curtain and pointed to the sensors. "These are for letting you know if anyone raises a window. If you forget to lock it for some reason or if the glass break fails and someone reaches inside and unlocks the window and attempts to raise it. There's a sensor on the ceiling at the other end of the hall that triggers the alarm if the distinct pitch of glass breaking is detected."

Laney nodded. "Oh. Well, good." She took a breath. "You'll show me how to arm and disarm the system?"

"It's simple." He moved back to the electronic keypad by her door. "You have two keypads. One here and one at the front door since that's the one you use most often."

He might have made it through this teaching session just fine if she hadn't moved in so close to watch. Forcing his attention on the keypad, he took her through the steps of arming and disarming, delayed and instant status.

"If you press these two buttons simultaneously, that's the panic mode. The police will be notified immediately. If the fire detectors have picked up any smoke or excessive heat, the fire department will be notified, as well."

"Man. I need something like that at the High Noon."

She definitely did. "I can see what kind of package deal they can offer for the two."

"Remember," she cautioned, "my budget's limited."

The silence thickened for several seconds. She waited for him to say something, he supposed. But his mind wasn't on talking at the moment. The electricity zinging between them was burning him up. Moving away from that hypnotizing pull was out of the question. If they were lucky she would break the spell with a word or gesture…anything.

Finally she looked up at him. "I never get involved with employees." The need blazing in her eyes protested the statement.

"Technically, I'm not an employee." His voice was husky and there wasn't a damned thing he could do about that. He wanted to touch her but didn't dare. He, too, had a rule against getting involved with a client… but technically she wasn't his client.

"Guess not," she agreed. She licked those lush lips again. "Truth is, I haven't been kissed in more than three years. I may have forgotten how it's done."

He reached out and removed the clip that held her hair. Joel had been dying to touch that silky mane since the first time he laid eyes on her. He threaded his fingers into the mass and massaged the back of her neck.

She trembled. "I'm usually a lot more cautious than this."

He lifted his other hand and traced the soft contour of her cheek. She was a beautiful woman but she didn't seem to have a clue. Wide brown eyes. Lush lips set in a creamy complexion. Even her nose was cute.

"Caution is good," he murmured. "You're a beautiful woman, Laney. You work hard. You deserve a man who'll treat you right."

"I know you'll be leaving when this is over." She leaned into his hand. "But," she said as she searched his eyes, "I have this feeling that if I hold back with you, I'll regret it for the rest of my life. I already have enough regrets."

He leaned down, brushed his lips against hers and she trembled again. He kissed her slowly, tenderly, the way a man should kiss this kind of woman. She'd been treated badly, neglected and thrown away. He wanted her to know that it wasn't always like that. He wanted her to feel what a kiss from the right man felt like.

Her arms went around his neck and he slid his hands down her back and pulled her close. She made the sweetest sound as her quivering body formed to his as if they were made to fit together. She tasted like the peach she'd eaten a few minutes ago, soft and ripe with need.

He wanted to strip those clothes off her and make love to her right now but they had to be at the saloon in an hour and though Buddy was occupied for the moment with his new building set, he was awake and that made the option unacceptable.

She drew her lips from his and pressed her forehead to his chin. "That was really nice." She toyed with the collar of his shirt. "I hope I didn't scare you off with my neediness."

He lifted her face to his and looked directly into her eyes. "That was very nice. And I don't think you needed that any more than I did."

She backed up, managed a smile. "I have to get ready to go." She gestured to the High Noon T-shirt lying on the bed.

Joel gave her a smile and decided a walk was in order.

Maybe a long walk.

Chapter Twelve

Wednesday, May 29th, 7:45 a.m.

Heat glided along her body…made her sweat. Laney curled deeper into the warmth. She didn't want to wake up…. She wanted this to last. To feel his body tangled with hers for just a little while longer.

Stranger. She ignored the voice. Yes, he was a stranger but she needed to trust him. She could trust him. Her mind grew dark and darker still…. Where was he? She felt cold, alone. The screaming wouldn't stop.

Mommy!

She held her bear tighter and squeezed her eyes shut tight. *Please make it stop!*

Mommy!

I'm here, sweet girl…. Mommy's here.

"Mommy!"

Laney's body quaked. She tried to open her eyes, but the darkness wouldn't let go.

"Mommy, wake up!"

The shaking started again. Her eyelids lifted, fluttered. The light was bright. Too bright.

"Come on, sleepyhead."

Laney came fully awake and found her boy perched

on the edge of her bed shaking her again. "Morning, Buddy."

"You have to get up!" He jumped off the bed and rushed over to the window. "Mr. Joel is on the barn roof but he won't let me play up there with him."

Laney threw the covers back and climbed out of the bed. She stared at the clock in disbelief. Almost eight o'clock. Good Lord, she never slept that late.

She slid her feet into her house slippers. "I'm sorry, baby, you must be starving."

"We ate already." Buddy rushed over and grabbed her hand to tug her to the window. "I need to help Mr. Joel."

Laney stood at the window and stared across her backyard. Hayden was on the roof of the old barn nailing down the loose tin. The sun glistened on his bare back. The feel of his lips moving over hers had her body growing warm. They'd barely skirted a repeat performance after she'd put Buddy to bed last night.

She'd wanted more. Oh, how she had wanted more. But she had known that she would never be able to stop with a kiss. No way. His body felt so strong when he'd held her against him. Strong and powerful and somehow humble and gentle.

The way his jeans fit his body made her want to explore every part of him over and over until she knew him by heart. She turned back to her bed where she'd curled into the covers leaving them a tangled mess. She'd dreamed of lying with him that way, their bodies connected completely.

But then that old, too-familiar nightmare had intruded. The screaming and the sobbing...and the bear. That was the first time she'd remembered the bear from the dream. She'd always sensed she'd been holding on to something in the dream.

Maybe it was symbolic.

"Mom-mee!"

"Okay, okay. Let me get dressed and make the bed."

"I make mine, too!"

Buddy dashed from the room. Moving slower than usual, Laney changed into jeans and a cami. She roamed a brush through her hair and watched Hayden. It was guilty pleasure but who would know?

He finished nailing down one section, scrubbed the sweat from his brow with his forearm and moved on to the next. Her gaze followed that bare torso down to his low-riding jeans. Even from across the yard the delineated, sinewy lines were enough to make her throat go dry.

"Snap out of it, Laney." *If you want him that badly, take him,* a wicked voice taunted.

But would that really be fair? Extreme stress wasn't a good reason to have sex. That was something two people should do in a relationship…a mutually beneficial relationship. Not this one-sided neediness.

What was wrong with her? She had worked hard to be an independent, self-reliant woman. Now this insanity from the past blows into town and suddenly she's all squishy and wishy-washy. Enough with the fantasy world.

Buddy was still fiddling with his bedcovers when she paused at this door. "Need some help?"

He dropped the corner of his quilt and sighed. "I think so. It won't cop'erate."

Laney smiled. What big words her boy used. "Okay. Let's see what we can do to get some cooperation."

As she tidied the linens and then the quilt, Buddy frowned. "What's wrong? You don't like the way I'm doing it?" This wouldn't be the first time her son had decided a task could be done better or a different way. His little mind worked a mile a minute.

"She wouldn't come inside," he said with another sigh. "I told her to but she didn't listen."

A chill slithered over Laney. "Who wouldn't come inside?"

He scrunched his face and looked up at his mom. "You know, the grandma lady."

The chill turned to fear. "Where did you see her?"

He pointed to his window. "Right there."

"When?" The word was brittle with the ice freezing her blood.

He shrugged. "Dark time."

Stay calm, Laney. If she scared him he might not get all the facts straight. "You woke up and saw her there? In the dark?" Maybe it was just a dream. He couldn't have seen her in the dark…maybe the moonlight. She couldn't remember if the moon had been particularly bright last night.

"The light woke me up." He picked up Mr. Bear and propped him on his pillow. "It shined in my face."

"What kind of light?" Laney sank to the bed, her knees too weak to keep her standing.

He puckered out his bottom lip and shrugged again. "I dunno. It was in my face and I woke up. Then it was on her face. I could see her there." He pointed to the window again. "I tried to open the window. It was too hard."

"Come here." Laney tried to control the way her body

trembled so he wouldn't notice. She patted the bed. "Let's talk about the grandma lady a minute."

Buddy bounced up on the bed. "She's old."

Laney tried to smile. "Old to you."

Buddy smiled and gazed up at her. "Old to you, too."

She ruffled his hair. "I'll take that as a compliment." *Deep breath. Keep it low-key.* "This grandma lady is a stranger, Buddy. It's not safe to talk to strangers or to let them in our house. We've talked about strangers before."

He nodded emphatically. "But she's a grandma. Old people are nice."

Laney hugged her sweet son. "Sometimes they can be bad, too. We can't be fooled by how nice someone seems." God knew she had half a lifetime of experience with that one. Her gaze drifted beyond the window to where Hayden worked on the barn. Maybe she hadn't learned her lesson yet.

"You don't want me to be nice to her?"

Laney turned his face up to her and looked him in the eyes. He knew this was the listen-good signal. "You be nice to everyone, William Seagers. But you never, ever let yourself be alone with strangers. No matter how nice they look. You don't go anywhere with them and you don't let them get too close to you."

He nodded, his head moving up and down in her hands.

"If anyone, even the grandma lady, comes to your window or to the door again, you come and get me. Promise?"

"Promise. But she didn't say anything. She was just smiling at me."

More of that fear crowded into her throat. "And you're sure this wasn't a dream?"

He nodded. "After a while she turned off the light and then she was gone." He moved his shoulders up and down. "Least I couldn't see her no more."

"Just remember to come get me next time."

"I promise."

"Now." Laney gave him a hug. "Let's go see what's left of breakfast." She had to talk to Hayden but she didn't want to upset Buddy.

The woman had come back.

"Bacon," Buddy called out as they raced to the kitchen. "Biscuits." He skidded to a stop at the island. "But not your biscuits."

Laney laughed out loud when she saw the little mound of small, knotty biscuits. The scrambled eggs looked fine and the bacon nice and crisp. But the poor biscuits. She laughed some more. Buddy jumped up and down and laughed with her. Tears streamed from her eyes. Maybe the hysteria was more related to what Buddy had told her than the pitiful biscuits.

"What's so funny?"

Laney jumped. She'd been laughing so hard she hadn't heard the screen door. With her lips compressed to stifle the mirth, she attempted to compose herself.

"Mom was laughing at your biscuits!"

"Buddy!" Laney couldn't help it. She burst into laughter again. This time it sounded more like sobs.

Hayden searched her face as she once again struggled to compose herself.

When she could speak without the words jerking, she said, "Buddy, I'd like you to tidy the living room for me this morning. You know how."

"Okay." He lumbered off as if she'd just grounded him for a whole week.

When he was out of earshot, Hayden frowned. "What's wrong?"

Was the front door locked?

"Just a minute." Laney rushed to the front door and checked to ensure the screen was latched and the door was locked, dead bolt included.

By the time she returned to the kitchen she had swiped her eyes and caught her breath. Hayden waited, his expression serious. He'd pulled his T-shirt back on and had his hands planted on his hips.

"A light woke Buddy last night." The idea that she had been asleep in her room just a few feet away and Hayden had been on the sofa stunned her. Did this woman have no fear? "Someone was at his window shining—" She shrugged. "I guess, shining a flashlight in his face to awaken him."

"Was it her?" Fury simmered in his tone.

Laney nodded, tears welling once more. "She shined the light on her face so he could see that it was her."

"Did she talk to him?"

"No. He said she just stared at him for a while and then left." Laney hugged herself. "What does she want?"

Hayden closed in, pulled her into his arms. "I wish I knew. Until we find her, we can't take any chances. I'll add motion sensors to the exterior lights. That way she won't have the cover of darkness."

Laney closed her eyes and tried to block all the worries with the feel of his strong body and that scent of clean, sun-kissed sweat. As much as she wanted to be strong and take care of Buddy and herself on her own, she knew she could not do this alone.

He drew back, then ushered her to a stool. "Sit. Eat.

When you've had a minute to relax, we'll look around outside and I'll give Lucas an update."

She poured herself a cup of coffee while he readied her plate. Prepared for the worst, she nibbled on one of the biscuits that looked more like a stubby dinosaur egg. To her surprise it was good.

"Not as bad as you thought, huh?"

She rolled her eyes. "Not as bad as I thought. Actually they're pretty good." She concentrated to pinpoint the flavors. "Garlic and cheese. Really nice."

He slid onto a stool and smiled at her from across the old wooden countertop. "When you've been a bachelor as long as me, you have to learn to whip up a few things."

She realized there was a lot more she didn't know about him. "How old are you?"

"My thirty-fifth birthday is in December."

"Wow." She made a face. "You're like an old maid except you're a guy."

He scowled. "Funny."

"You always lived in Houston?"

"Grew up in Galveston. Most of my family still lives there." He plucked a biscuit from the bowl and tore off a bite.

Laney got distracted for a moment by his mouth. She blinked. "I find it hard to believe you've never even gotten close to marriage." A guy this good-looking, nice, great job... He was a catch.

"Let's just say I went through a long *me* stage," he confessed. "I wasn't interested in complications. I was focused on my career and having a good time."

"Aha." She sipped her coffee. Not quite as good as her own, but close. "You were a player. A heartbreaker."

He grinned. "I guess I was."

"What changed?" Obviously something had. Since it wasn't first love or a wedding or a child, it had to be a significant event. Her pulse rate slowly returned to normal. As normal as possible considering just being in the room with him seemed to have some impact on her ability to breathe.

Under normal circumstances she would chastise herself for going off into romantic fantasyland, but right now she desperately needed an escape. Tension started to knot in her belly. *Don't think about it. Not yet.* It was all still too painful and overwhelming.

All that mattered was that Buddy was safe. As his mother, whatever was required to keep him that way was her job. But she was only human. Finding a little relief—even if only in a moment of romantic fantasy— was not such a bad thing.

Hayden seemed lost in thought for a moment, as if trying to decide if he wanted to remember whatever had made him take a step back and assess his life.

"My older brother—they're all married." He laughed softly. "But he married the one woman for him. High-school sweethearts. Bought the house with the picket fence, two kids and a dog. Life was perfect. Exactly what marriage and family should be. The kids came home from school one day and she was gone."

Laney felt her eyes widen in dismay. "She left?"

Hayden shook his head. "She had an undiagnosed heart defect. She finished the laundry that day, sat down to fold the towels and she was gone."

"That's just awful."

"Really awful." He turned to the fridge and helped himself to a bottle of water. One twist of the cap and he chugged down about half of it. "I watched him go through the stages of grief. The kids were devastated. His whole life fell apart for a little while. Then he sucked it up and did what he had to do."

"Did he eventually find someone else?" Laney decided this was about the saddest story she'd ever heard.

"There's someone now but it's a slow go." He deposited the bottle of water on the counter. "The point is I realized that the relationship between men and women—that kind of relationship—was too precious to treat with such insignificance. Hearts aren't meant to be broken. And I broke more than my share."

Now Laney was confused. "So, you avoid relationships altogether?" Exactly why she felt so intensely disappointed at the prospect escaped her at the moment.

"I'm cautious. I don't lead anyone on and I don't play games."

"That's a good thing," she offered, hoping that was the right thing to say. "People shouldn't play games with other people's lives." The way Terry was playing with hers and Buddy's.

Laney couldn't avoid the subject any longer. The fear was gnawing at her again. "What does this woman want from us?" Surely she didn't expect herself or the others to see her as their mother. Dear God, the thought was unbearable.

"That's the problem." He braced his hands wide apart on the counter and showed with his eyes that he was dead serious. "If Rafe Barker is right, Clare is a killer. If he's straight-up lying, she falls somewhere between accomplice and victim. Either away, she has an agenda. And until we know what that agenda is, none of you are safe."

"What about this man who's with her? The one-armed man?" As much as she hated to prejudge, this whole thing felt like something from a horror flick.

"We haven't confirmed the suspicion, but we believe Tony Weeden is Clare's son from her college days. She may have been raped by a professor. We don't know how the two reunited. Maybe Weeden learned the identities of his biological parents and sought them out. We can't be sure."

Laney thought of the two people who had raised her until their untimely deaths. William and Lana Seagers were her parents. Her grandma Seagers had been her most beloved companion. She took care of Laney whenever her parents were away on business. It was her grandma's heart attack that had her parents rushing home. Her grandmother had died in the hospital that night. Before dawn, her parents had been killed in the crash.

And she had been left all alone.

Laney pushed the memories away. "Do you really believe the Colby Agency can find the truth in time?"

"To save Rafe Barker in the event he's innocent?"

Laney nodded. That man was her biological father. Was he a monster or a victim? Had he sacrificed his life to save his daughters?

"If anyone can," Hayden promised her, "the Colby Agency can."

The implications of how this changed her life were only just now setting in. But then again, once Clare was stopped was there any reason for anything to change?

"Let's have a look outside Buddy's window."

Laney followed him outside. Despite the sun, she felt cold. She wrapped her arms around herself.

The window was certainly low enough to the ground for someone to be able to climb in were it open. She prayed her talk with Buddy would prevent him from viewing this woman with curiosity. He needed to be afraid of her.

Hayden examined the window carefully. Then he surveyed the ground nearby. Laney followed as he walked all the way around the house. He made a call to Lucas and told him about the incident. Lucas had no news.

The search for Clare was getting nowhere.

Hayden found nothing in the yard. It hadn't rained recently so there were no footprints. And no forgotten evidence.

Buddy's description had been far too vivid to have been a dream. Of that she felt confident. The woman had been here.

At the back door, he hesitated. "Maybe it would be better if Buddy slept in the room with you until this is done."

Laney had been thinking the same thing. "He won't like it. He's a big boy now, you know."

"Maybe we can convince him of how lumpy that sofa is and that I really need a bed to sleep in. Or that you're afraid to sleep alone."

Hayden and bed in the same thought gave her another little shiver but it had nothing to do with fear. "He'd probably go for that."

He hesitated again before opening the door. There was something in his eyes that held her still. Warmed her through and through.

"I'd rather be in your bed," he said, his voice thick with desire. "But your safety comes first."

As if he'd just told her the sky was blue, he turned and walked into the house.

Laney stayed back a minute. She needed a moment to compose herself. For a guy who had given up the player lifestyle, he sure knew how to reel a woman in.

Careful, Laney, don't get in over your head. A few days or weeks from now and he'll be long gone.

She'd had her heart broken too many times already.

When she wandered through the house in search of the man who had somehow banished her discipline in a short enough period to be measured more accurately in hours than days, he unknowingly delivered another blow to her defenses.

Hayden had sprawled on the floor to play Legos with Buddy. Maybe the sight wouldn't have disarmed her so had Hayden not been having a blast with her son.

She'd made a mistake letting him so close. Now she and Buddy would both pay.

Chapter Thirteen

Thursday, May 30th, 1:40 a.m.

Joel lifted Buddy from the car seat in the backseat of his Jeep. He'd checked the perimeter of the yard, then the house to ensure there were no surprises. With the security system in place he wasn't anticipating any surprises inside.

Laney gathered the kid's toys and bear and followed. She was exhausted. The meeting had gone well at the bank that morning and the crowd had been heavy and happy at the saloon tonight—both good things. But she was beat, emotionally and physically.

Two nights in a row without an appearance by Kingston was another good thing. Unless the jerk was up to something that would open a whole new can of worms for Laney. Joel didn't want any more trouble with the guy but if he showed up intending to give Laney a hard time, trouble was what he would get.

In the house, Laney drew the covers back on her bed and Joel settled Buddy there. Once the covers and his stuffed bear were tucked in, Laney gave her boy a kiss and moved quietly out of the room.

Joel almost hated to go. Her scent permeated the air

of her private space. That sweet lotion she wore and that natural, womanly scent drove him mad with desire. From the old iron headboard to the whitewashed wood nightstand, the whole room was her. She had a distinctive flare and he liked that about her. He honestly could not recall ever having paid attention to a woman's taste in decorating.

He hadn't meant for this to happen. This insatiable need to be close to her, to touch and taste her all over, was a strategic error but he couldn't change that now. She was so deep under his skin he wasn't sure there was any hope of backing up now.

Four days being this close and a few before that watching from a distance and he was hooked on the lady.

She was the first woman he'd bared his soul to when it came to his brother's tragedy and his own mistakes. Oddly, he didn't regret going there. He felt good about sharing that with her. It was his job to know everything about her, and somehow giving her something in return felt right.

On all other levels, however, they barely knew each other. The prospects of a relationship were fifty-fifty at best. But he couldn't not want her. She made him wish for those simple things he'd overlooked before.

He joined her in the kitchen. "Would you like a beer?" She stood next to the fridge, that old butcher's table between them.

Laney was nervous. He suspected she had a similar war going on inside. She was attracted to him, too. Occasionally he caught her watching him. He heard the way her breath hitched when he got too close. The idea that she wanted him made him want her all the more.

But he also recognized that she was terrified of getting hurt again. The last thing he wanted to do was hurt her.

She'd suffered too much of that already.

He held up a hand and declined her offer of a beer. "I'm good."

"Coffee?"

If she hadn't looked so hopeful he would have passed. "Your coffee? Anytime."

The smile that lit her face turned him inside out. He loved her smile. Tonight, behind that bar, she had been relaxed and in her element. The folks loved her. She made the High Noon a fun and welcoming place to be.

With the loan worries lifted a little and her ex staying away, she didn't just serve her patrons, she performed a well-choreographed production of smooth moves and snappy dialogue. It was no wonder the High Noon was such a success.

The lady had a gift.

And his full attention.

Once she had the coffeemaker set, he moved up behind her and whispered in her ear, "I couldn't take my eyes off you tonight."

She turned to face him, trapped between his body and the counter. "I hope your boss didn't notice."

Lucas had stopped by for a few minutes. Then he'd gone back on the prowl for his prey. Clare Barker and Tony Weeden had seemingly fallen off the planet. Lucas was having no luck finding the first sign of the two in Beaumont.

"I think every male in the house tonight was watching you, my boss included."

She smiled, her lips trembling. "Is that one of your old player lines or is that a true compliment?"

So the lady needed some convincing, did she? Well, he was way past restraint. No matter that she was his principal and this was business, there was no going back. He was in this for the long haul.

He leaned down and nuzzled her neck, loving the feel of her silky hair against his jaw. He lavished her ear with his tongue then whispered, "You are so beautiful."

"It's been a long time," she murmured. "I'm not so sure this will be as easy to fall back into as kissing."

"We'll take it slow."

She searched his eyes. He showed her with his that she had nothing to fear from him. That he wanted her so, so much. He recognized the moment she made her decision. The worry that had furrowed her brow eased away. Her gaze drifted down to his mouth. He kissed her, softly, slowly. His body reacted instantly, hardening with the need to show her just how beautiful it could be between a man and a woman. He wanted her to know that beauty. To feel all those other emotions and sensations beyond simple lust and desire.

She sidled out of his reach and hurried into the hall. He trailed after her. She made a stop at the linen closet and retrieved a big colorful quilt. She glanced back at him in invitation and he followed her to the living room. He liked following Laney. The view never got boring.

She spread the quilt on the floor. Its once-vibrant hues of red and blue were faded with time. She toed off her boots, rolled off her socks and clicked off the table lamp, leaving nothing but the moonlight filtering in through the windows to guide their way. There was the slightest tremor in her movements. As much as she wanted this, she was still nervous.

He removed his boots and socks, then reached for the clip from her hair and threaded his fingers through that luxurious mane. After tossing the clip aside, he tugged her T-shirt from the waistband of her jeans and peeled it off her slim torso. He had to look at her a moment before continuing. Her body was perfect. Tall, lean but with a nice slender hourglass shape.

She reached behind her and unfastened her bra, allowing it to fall away as he watched. His breath stalled in his lungs as he took in her creamy, high breasts. He reached out, closed his hands over those lush mounds. She gasped. He massaged her breasts, paying special attention to her taut nipples. Then he let his hands glide up her shoulders and gave the same treatment there. Her shoulders and arms were likely tired from making and serving drinks all night. He wanted her completely relaxed. He wanted her to enjoy every moment of this special time between them.

With prompting she turned her back to him and he lavished her neck and upper back with just the right rubbing and squeezing and soft pressure with his fingers. By the time he finished she was moaning with his every touch. He moved his body up against hers, loving the feel of her bottom nestled against his pelvis. With his arms around her, he released the fly of her jeans, but instead of pushing them down, he reached inside and found that hot, damp spot that made her whimper with need. He stroked and teased until she quivered in his arms, her screams of pleasure barely restrained.

He turned her around to face him and he dropped to

his knees. First he kissed each breast, nipped at her nipples, then he slid those tight-fitting jeans down and off.

Slowly, he kissed every part of her. He traced her ribs with his tongue and explored her bellybutton while he kneaded her bottom with his hands. Her fingers fisted in his hair and she quivered with the pleasure building inside her. He restrained his own, refused to give in to the urgency until he made sure this was worth the wait for her. Three years was a long time to wait.

When her breathing became more and more frantic, he slid a hand between her trembling thighs and stroked her some more. Her hips undulated with his movements and then her body tensed. He felt the waves of completion crashing down on her, her inner muscles flexing and contracting around his fingers.

He had to have her soon.

He stood and began to unbutton his shirt.

She opened her eyes and stared for a long moment, watching his methodical movements. Then she came at him.

EMBOLDENED FROM A powerful orgasm, Laney ripped his shirt from his body. She would buy him a new one. Right now she just needed him naked so she could feel his hot skin. She clawed at his belt and fly until they were open. As still as stone and every bit as hard, he watched her every frantic move with an intensity that made her shiver. She wanted him to watch. But more importantly, she wanted to do to him what he had just done to her. She dragged off his jeans. She sat back on her heels and stared at his naked body. He looked amazing. Strong, lean lines. Sculpted muscles. Perfect. She leaned in, inhaled deeply of his masculine scent, then she started to lick. She teased him with her mouth and tongue until he trembled. He tangled his fingers in her hair, begged her to slow down. When she felt him start to throb she drew away. He was heavy with need and she wanted that weight inside her.

Laney fell back onto the quilt she had inherited from her grandmother and opened herself to him. He came down on top of her and filled her in one forceful thrust. She climaxed instantly. His body shook with restraint as he brought her once more to that place. He urged her on until, their bodies shuddering, they found release together.

He rolled onto his side and held her, their bodies still entwined. She snuggled against his chest and listened to the frantic sound of his heart beating. She felt sated and safe.

Eventually she would need to shower and pull on a gown so that she could go to her room and snuggle up to her son. But for now she wanted to be held just like this.

He stroked her hair, kissed her forehead and cheek. She couldn't be sure but she sensed that their lovemaking had affected him as deeply as it had her. She hoped so.

He tipped her chin up to look in her eyes. "You okay?"

She smiled. "I'm better than okay." The truth was no one had ever made love to her like that.

"Yes, you are."

Tears burned in her eyes and she wanted to kick herself for getting all weepy but there was no stopping it. He had made her feel special and she'd needed that so much.

He caressed her cheek. "I don't know about you but I think an early breakfast is in order."

"As long as I get to make the biscuits."

He laughed. "I figure that's a good idea."

They helped each other dress, kissing over and over again. Her lips would be bruised tomorrow, he had kissed her so many times. She decided to forego her jeans, and rushed off to the kitchen in her T-shirt and panties. That she didn't feel the need to cover herself completely in his presence with the lights on was new for her. She'd had a baby and had the marks to prove it. The proof of motherhood hadn't bothered him.

In the kitchen, he was in charge of the eggs and she made the biscuits the way her grandmother had taught her. It felt real, it felt right. Every move was accompanied by a smile or a kiss.

When the biscuits were in the oven, he sat her on the counter and kissed her some more. Each time was somehow different from the last. The way he cradled her face or touched his tongue to hers. Then he lifted her T-shirt to admire her breasts.

He leaned her back against the cabinets. She arched her back, forcing her breasts to jut upward. He explored each one with his fingers and then his mouth.

She tried to hold back from losing herself to his touch, but she couldn't. He had her on the brink of release all over again. He lifted her into his arms and she wrapped her legs around his waist. He fumbled with his zipper until he was free, then, pushing her panties aside, he guided her down onto his erection.

He lifted her over and over, each time letting her slide down that rigid length until they both moaned with release.

Moments later, without even setting her down, he turned off the oven and carried her to the bathroom. They made love again in the shower. Afterwards, he washed her body and she washed his. She learned every part of him. They toweled each other off, went their separate ways to dress and rendezvoused in the kitchen for soggy eggs and hard biscuits.

"Your coffee is amazing," he said after finishing off his cup.

She kissed him and smiled. "One of these days I plan to serve breakfast at the saloon." She loved to cook and she had imagined making beautiful pastries and gourmet omelets to go with the unique blends of coffee she would offer.

"I think that's a brilliant idea." He pulled her against him and settled onto a stool with her in his lap. "You'd need a much bigger staff. Your location is perfect for those morning commuters on the long drive to Houston."

It pleased her immensely that he thought her plan was a good one. "I want to keep the western theme but give it a slight sophisticated quality for morning hours."

"With those biscuits and that coffee, it's a sure success."

"Then maybe I can find the right person to manage the place at night so I can spend more time at home with Buddy."

They talked for a long time about her plans and how she could make those dreams come true. At some point she fell asleep, but was roused as he tucked her into her bed next to Buddy. He smiled down at her and her lips immediately responded.

"Good night." He brushed a kiss across her cheek.

"Night."

When he would have turned away she caught his hand. He stared down at her and her breath left her at how handsome he was. A fact she had noticed over and over since he'd first swaggered into the High Noon.

She peered up into his eyes. "Thank you for protecting us and for making me feel alive again."

He squeezed her hand and smiled before walking away.

Her last thought before she drifted off was of him and how much she wanted this to be real...not just a dream.

Chapter Fourteen

2:00 a.m.

Clare watched longingly as the last of the lights went out in Lisa's home. The man from the Colby Agency had seduced her. Even from the road Clare had been able to see them come together before the lights went out in the living room. Two vague forms falling into each other's arms. She had known that kind of desperation once.

But it had been a mistake.... Except for the three beautiful daughters that had come of that tainted marriage. Fury and misery stormed inside her. She wanted him and all who had helped him to pay for stealing her life.... For taking her babies.

For ruining everything.

Soon they would all know the truth.

No one could stop her now.

"We should take the boy."

Clare turned to her son. "He's beautiful, isn't he?"

Though she couldn't see Tony's fury in the darkness, she could feel the creeping thickness of it. He was angry for her. No one else save him understood what she had been through.... What she had lost.

For years she had sacrificed so much to keep *him*

happy. And he had turned on her, used his silence to make her appear the guiltiest one.

Now he was only three weeks from being a dead man.

Joy shimmered through her. She closed her eyes and prayed that the devil would take him straight to hell.

"We should take him," Tony repeated.

Clare shook off the wonderful thoughts of her husband burning for all of eternity and turned to her son. "He is very smart, too." Perhaps if she ignored Tony's comments he would let the idea go.

"She's a whore."

Clare surveyed the dark house, the turmoil inside her taking on a sharper edge. "She's a good mother." Clare had been a good mother to her daughters...but not to her son.

She had expected him to want to punish her for what she had done so long ago. Instead, he had offered to help. He had prepared for her release and had welcomed her with open arms. She did not deserve his forgiveness.

"Is she a good mother?"

Tension coiled through Clare's body. "She is." Perhaps her son had decided she needed to be punished after all. "She was stronger than me. She kept her son and raised him despite having no one to help."

"She was not raped," Tony rebutted.

Clare wished she could see his eyes. This was the first time they had discussed that part of the past. Had he truly forgiven her? "I was young. Terrified and alone. I didn't know what to do." Though most of her life was a lie, that was the God's truth.

"You had *her*."

Rage rose to an instant boil. Her sister. Janet had

done nothing but hurt her since the day Clare was born. She had learned the truth about her sister. But by then it had been too late. The damage was done.

Tony had paid a heavy price.

Clare had, as well. But now they would have their revenge on them all.

Rafe thought he had won by hiring this illustrious agency to help him. But he had not. Far from it. She was here. She had touched their grandson. She had seen all three of their beautiful daughters.

He would not win. Clare hoped he was afraid. That he lay in that tiny cell at night and wept at the idea that she was free and could do whatever she pleased. There was nothing he could do to stop her the way he had last time.

He was helpless, just as she had been twenty-two years ago. She had trusted him just as she had trusted her sister.

If only dear Janet had realized the error of her ways and run, she might still be alive. But she had remained, steadfast in her certainty that no one would see her lies.

She had gotten what was coming to her, though Clare doubted she had suffered nearly enough. She, too, would burn in hell.

"Yes," Clare said finally in response to her son's comment. "I had my sister." Again Clare wished she could see his face more clearly. "And look what she did to us." She touched his right shoulder. Agony twisted inside her.

"It was my fault."

How could he say that? He'd been a mere child when the accident happened. "She should have been watching you more closely." How could he blame himself?

"She was working and I got in the way."

Tony had told her that Janet had been chopping wood and he'd wanted to help. But Clare sensed that there was more he wasn't telling her. If he told her she would only feel more guilt. He suspected as much and wanted to shield her from it.

What a sweet man he had grown into despite what Clare had done to him. She should have kept him. What good had it done her to return to college and finish her degree?

None.

She had left Tony with Janet with the intention of coming back for him when she could support him. But then she had met Rafe and everything had changed.

Rafe had seemed such a deeply religious man she hadn't dared to tell him about the rape and her illegitimate son. Then she'd fallen so madly in love that she could see nothing but Rafe and the life he offered.

Janet hadn't spoken to her again for years. She had taken Tony away and Clare had been relieved.

Now she had the opportunity to make all of it right. All her past sins would be assuaged.

She sent one last longing look toward her daughter's home. Lisa had done all this on her own. She had been far smarter than her mother. Far stronger. Sarah was the same. Strong, hardworking. Clare had not located Olivia yet, but she was not giving up.

Soon they would all be together for the finale.

"We should go now," she said to Tony.

Ever obedient, he started the car and drove away. He waited a safe distance before turning on the headlights.

Clare sighed. Her plan was coming together, bit by bit. She would not fail.

"We're being followed."

Clare jerked around to stare at the headlights far behind them. "Are you sure?"

"Yes," Tony insisted. "It's that man who has been looking for us all over town. The one from Copperas Cove."

Another from the Colby Agency. Lucas Camp. Clare knew they were trying to stop her.

Fury tightened her lips. She would stop their meddling. Didn't they realize they were working for the devil himself?

"Make sure you lose him."

Tony floored the accelerator, and the car leaped forward. "We need to be rid of him for good."

Clare said nothing. Just a few more days…and it would be done.

Chapter Fifteen

Lucas accelerated. Clare Barker would not elude him this time. He had her in his crosshairs.

The road wound through the countryside that separated Laney's home from the city of Beaumont for some fifteen miles. At this hour he should have no trouble staying on their tail even once they hit the city limits. Traffic would be negligible.

He had known Clare wouldn't be able to resist returning to watch Laney. The new security system had prevented her from getting too close to the house. Instead she and her accomplice had parked on the side of the road and watched from a distance.

And Lucas had been waiting.

The white sedan took a hard right, the vehicle nearly spinning a hundred and eighty degrees before barreling down this new side road.

Lucas made the same turn, his rented sedan fishtailing with the change in momentum, tires screaming in protest.

He wrestled the steering wheel and forced the accelerator to the floor. The car lunged forward, gaining on his mark.

Victoria would be furious at his hazardous driving.

But he could not lose Clare again. She'd gotten far too close to Laney and her son and that was on Lucas.

Another sharp turn, this one to the left. Lucas rode out the precarious maneuver, the smell of burning rubber accompanying the squealing tires.

Weeden appeared to be leading him deeper into the less populated countryside. Lucas wasn't worried. He was armed and ready. Let the bastard make a move.

The red warning of brake lights beamed in his face.

Lucas slammed on his brakes.

Weeden's car slid sideways on the road.

Lucas was going to collide with Weeden's car.

Heart pumping, Lucas cut to the right to avoid T-boning the vehicle.

The deep shoulder of the road threw Lucas's car into a tailspin. He struggled to regain control, but couldn't.

His car plunged off the road…down…down…

A tree stopped his forward momentum.

The air bag exploded, slamming into Lucas's body and forcing him against the seat.

An eerie silence was broken only by the ticking of the cooling engine.

One headlight shone on the trees in front of him.

Lucas gasped. The air bag had knocked the breath out of him. He tried to clear his head and take a mental inventory of any injuries he might have sustained.

His chest ached and…his left leg felt twisted or jammed somehow.

Phone. He reached for the console and fire shot through his right arm. He gritted his teeth against the pain and reached again. It wasn't there. Probably fell to the floorboard, he reasoned.

The sound of someone moving down the embankment on foot snapped Lucas to full attention.

It wouldn't be help... There was no one out here but Weeden and Clare Barker.

The pain making him growl with agony, he tried to get to the weapon in the shoulder holster he wore beneath his jacket. Sweat beaded on his forehead.

He couldn't do it. Damned right shoulder had to be dislocated.

He reached for the door handle with his left hand. Incredibly, the door flew open. Lucas hit the seat belt release and tried to scramble out of the car. Pain roared through him.

A shadow blocked the moonlight.

He looked up into the face of Tony Weeden. His arm was raised high above his head.

Before Lucas could react, something crashed down on his head.

The pain went away.

Chapter Sixteen

Joel was worried. Lucas had not checked in with him all day. The last time they talked was when the High Noon closed up last night. When Joel and Laney arrived to set up for opening around five-thirty this evening there had been no sign of Lucas. No indication that he had slept in the office. His cell phone went straight to voice mail.

Lucas wouldn't just disappear and he certainly wouldn't fail to check in.

Simon and Victoria had been attempting to locate him, as well. Simon had put in a call to Lucas's cell carrier in hopes of learning at least his last known location, by finding out the last cell tower his phone had reached out to. It would take time to muddle through the necessary approvals and Joel sensed that time was short.

Lucas was in trouble.

With the end of the work week approaching, the crowd at the High Noon was thick and rowdy. Good for Laney's bottom line but not so good when Joel was distracted. A guy had to be thankful for small favors, however, and one really good thing was that Kingston hadn't returned.

Maybe he'd ended up in jail or his father had shipped him back off to rehab. The guy needed rehabilitating. For Buddy's sake if not his own.

Lucas had spent the entire day yesterday searching for Clare Barker and Tony Weeden. He'd hit all the motels and hotels his first day in town. Then he'd moved on to restaurants and delis. At the top of his priority list were the cheaper and more out-of-the-way places. He'd found nothing. Like Joel, the man was feeling a little desperate about the situation. But even desperation wouldn't throw a man like Lucas so far off his game.

Joel scrubbed his chin. The only way Lucas would stay out of touch this long was if he had found serious trouble. Simon and Victoria had known him far longer than Joel and the consensus was the same. At this point they had to assume that Lucas needed backup. The problem was no one knew where to look. By late afternoon Simon and Victoria had arrived in Beaumont and were laying out a search grid, with every member of the Colby Agency's Houston office contributing to the search. Backup from the Chicago office had arrived by nightfall. Among those who had arrived was Jim Colby, Victoria's son.

The police had been notified but there was little they could do with no place to start and no evidence of wrongdoing by Clare or her son.

Part of Joel wanted to be out there looking for the older man but he couldn't risk diverting his attention from Laney and Buddy. Damn, this case was growing more complicated and murky with each passing day.

His gaze settled on Laney behind the bar. Like last night, she was on her A game. The crowd was jovial and the money was pouring into the cash register.

No matter how hard he tried to fight it, every time he looked at her, he couldn't stop the images and sensations and sounds from the hours they had spent making love from echoing through his mind...from tensing his muscles with the need to cross the room and touch her.

She had opened completely to him and he had fallen in deep. As crazy as it sounded, considering the short period they had known each other, he now understood the stories his brothers had told him about finding their true loves.

Something grabs you and won't let go.

Joel had no idea what tomorrow held but he sure didn't want to spend it without Laney and Buddy in his life. Even the notion of never seeing them again made his gut twist. Laney had been hurt so badly he wasn't sure how she would see them moving forward. He hoped she would at least consider the idea of exploring this bond between them. For the first time in his life, Joel desperately wanted to have a real relationship. Laney and Buddy made him long for a family of his own.

Not to mention the way Joel had fallen for the kid. God, he loved his nieces and nephews and he'd do anything in the world for any or all of them. This tyke had stolen his heart from the get-go. Maybe that midlife crisis Jeep hadn't done the trick. Maybe there was no outmaneuvering the need to bond with the opposite sex and procreate. Oddly, the idea of having children of his own didn't scare him in the least.

Laney caught him looking and grinned. They'd had breakfast a second time this morning. Buddy had set the menu and helped with rolling out and cutting the fresh biscuits.

Joel's throat tightened. As if all these years of bach-
elorhood had suddenly grown too heavy and had to be
shrugged off, he wondered what it would feel like to
hold a child of his own. To feel the weight of his baby
in his hands and know that for the rest of his life that
tiny human would mean the world to him.

He gave himself a mental shake. *Stay focused, man.*
Maybe he should check on Buddy. See how Tatum was
holding up in the kitchen. The man had been prepping
and cooking all afternoon and things hadn't slowed
down since the last time Joel checked. It may be good
for business, but Tatum was obviously going to need
help in the kitchen if this pace continued.

Weaving through the crowd slowed Joel down. The
bank certainly couldn't complain about this level of
business. Somehow that situation had to work out for
Laney. She had worked too hard to have it all yanked
from under her. If the bank gave her any more trouble,
maybe he'd just have to see what he could do to help.
If she allowed it. Laney Seagers was one independent
lady. And she damned sure knew how to bring him to
his knees. The idea of being so vulnerable to a woman
should feel intimidating but somehow it didn't. It felt
right.

Buddy sat atop a stainless-steel table in the middle
of the kitchen. An array of big pots hung on the rack
above his head. The last time Joel popped in, Buddy
had two big wooden spoons and was using the pots for
drums. Now, a Lego village was taking shape under
his careful attention.

"Hey, Buddy!" Joel gave the boy a gentle punch to
the shoulder. "Looks like you've about got your village finished."

"I think we need a fire truck."

Joel grinned. "Oh, yeah? I'll have to see what I can do about that." He'd decided that he would be worse than all three of his brothers put together when it came to spoiling kids. All these years he'd shaken his head at the way they spoiled their own. Joel would be eating crow on that when the time came.

Slow down. He was already mapping out fatherhood and marriage wasn't even on the table.

Somehow Laney and Buddy made him seriously consider all those things. No, they made him *want* those things.

Buddy stuck his thumb to his chest. "I don't need a fire truck." He crossed his legs, his little cowboy boots scrubbing against the tabletop. "Uncle Tater does. He's trying to burn the place down."

The kitchen was thick with humidity and a heck of a lot warmer than the saloon, even with that crowd out there. "Maybe I'd better check on him."

Buddy nodded. "He's over'helmed."

From the looks of things, Buddy was right. Tatum had three deep fryers going and the grill was loaded down with hamburger patties, chicken breasts and piles of thinly shaved beef. The massive toaster oven was loaded down with buns and sandwich rolls. He had to hand it to the guy, he was organized.

"You got this under control?" Joel dared to ask even after the old sailor shot him a narrowed look.

"Does a cat have climbing gear?" He glanced at the wheel hanging in the window that separated the kitchen from the saloon. The wheel was full with tickets from the waiter and waitresses. "In five minutes that wheel will be empty. Five minutes after that it'll be full again.

It's a good kind of cycle and I've got my system." He waved his hand at the grill.

Joel gave him a nod. "You're a better man than me."

Tatum grinned. "A better cook, for sure."

Joel checked the back door before heading back out to the saloon. Tatum paid no attention. He was too focused on the grill and the fryers. The oven took care of itself, it seemed. Put the bread in at one end, and it rolled out the other onto what looked like a baking sheet.

The saloon was packed now. So far no one was looking for trouble. Joel hoped it stayed that way.

Because he couldn't help himself, he propped at the end of the bar to watch Laney in action. Tonight there were two other bartenders, both female, dressed in the staff garb of a High Noon T-shirt, blue jeans and boots. One hustled between tending bar and waiting tables, depending upon which side of the bar was the furthest behind.

Laney had been going full speed for the past two hours. But Joel had watched her for more than a week now. The woman didn't take breaks until the last customer was happily served.

One of the other bartenders strolled up to him. "You need a drink, Hayden?" Her eyes glittered with a big smile stretched across her shiny lips. The lady was a flirt. But then, flirts and amateur psychologists made the best bartenders.

"No, thanks." He gave the lady a smile. She sashayed away, hoping to impress him with her practiced walk. Didn't work. He only had eyes for one woman.

He watched Laney a minute longer. Long enough for her to toss him one of those smiles that tugged on his heartstrings and then he wandered out into the crowd.

Near the swinging doors two men and a woman appeared to be having a strained discussion. Joel changed directions and headed that way. The lady stormed outside and one of the men followed. The other filtered back into the crowd.

Maybe not a good sign. Joel lingered at the door watching the couple. The woman slapped the man; he crushed her against his car.

Well, hell.

Joel strode toward the two, reached his destination just in time to snag the fool's arm before he slapped the blonde. "I don't think so, pal." He whipped the guy around and shoved him back. "Time for you to go home or to jail. Take your pick."

Behind him the woman took off. Good for her.

"That bitch started it," the guy bellowed. "She offered me her services for twenty bucks and then she tried to drag another guy into it to double her money."

"Whatever she offered you," Joel warned, "you don't hit a woman. You walk away."

"Whatever. I'm out of here."

Joel watched until the hothead had climbed into his truck. Across the lot a snazzy sports car peeled out onto the highway. Some folks just didn't have the sense to enjoy leisure time safely. That kind of behavior got innocent people killed.

A frown tugged at his brow when the blonde started ranting. What the hell was she doing now? She stood at the edge of the lot, evidently shouting at someone who had already driven away. Joel headed in that direction. The sports car was the only one to leave in the last couple of minutes. The truck driven by the guy who'd argued with the blonde peeled out next but the blonde appeared to pay no mind to him.

"What's the problem now, ma'am?"

She whipped around, her eyes wide and wild with something like fear. This was the first good look he'd gotten of her face. She looked familiar....

Damn. "You're the one who showed up with Kingston," he accused. The sports car that had hauled ass out of the lot flashed in his mind again. Not the vehicle Laney had taken the Louisville Slugger to, but a car along those lines.

She started to back away. "I had nothing to do with it. I just did what he told me." She glared at the highway. "Then the bastard drives away without me." A cold, hard reality rammed Joel right between the eyes.

Kingston had been here.

LANEY DEPOSITED THE two cold longneck bottles of beer onto the counter. "Enjoy, gentlemen."

The night's take was on the way to exceeding even the best of her Friday or Saturday nights. Hot damn. She wiped the bar where the two patrons had moved on to a table. With Mr. Teague offering to help and business booming, things were looking up.

Her hands slowed in their cleanup work and she smiled to herself. Things were looking up at home, too. As terrified as she was of getting her heart broken again, she had decided that Hayden was worth the risk.

Joel, she reminded herself. She'd promised to call him Joel from last night on. Seemed only right. When a woman knew a man that intimately, first names were a given.

Her body quivered with remembered desire as snippets of all the times and ways they had made love flashed through her head. No one had ever made love to her like that. As incredible as it had been, it had felt natural and right, as well. No regrets come dawn. Just the relentless desire for more.

Maybe tonight. She trembled at the idea.

Okay, Laney. Don't go falling head over heels after one night.

Giving herself a swift mental kick in the seat of the pants, she turned to go to the kitchen and check on Buddy. It hadn't been ten minutes but—

Smoke rolled from the serving window.

Smoke detectors started to wail.

Laney rushed toward the kitchen door. Tatum burst through the door, almost colliding head-on with her.

"That son of a bitch!" Tatum coughed, his face red as a beet. "He took Buddy. I couldn't stop him. He had a gun."

Laney pushed past him. The kitchen was thick with smoke. "Buddy!"

The back door was open, allowing the smoke to drift out of the room.

Laney's heart sank.

Buddy's Lego village was scattered on the table and floor.

She ran out the back door.

He was gone.

The narrow alley behind the building was vacant save for Tatum's old truck and the Dumpster.

Inside, panicked voices shouted… The music died… But Laney couldn't move.

Her baby was gone.

11:55 p.m.

JOEL WANTED TO KILL Terry Kingston. Not once had he ever really wanted to take another man's life until now. The bastard didn't deserve to live.

The saloon had been cleared, thankfully without injury. The fire department and police had arrived. Two uniforms and an evidence tech had scoured the parking area and the kitchen. For all the good it would do.

The blonde, whose name was Margo Rucker, was being interrogated by the police. Margo couldn't give the license-plate number of the rental Terry had been driving, but she had helped complete the description Joel had gotten when the car spun out of the parking lot. An Amber Alert had been issued for Buddy.

The ache that accompanied that last thought made breathing impossible. He had to find that child. If Kingston got him hurt, Joel would kill the son of a bitch.

Laney was a mess. She paced back and forth in front of the office, furious the police wouldn't let her at the woman and terrified for her baby.

She wouldn't let Joel comfort her or even touch her for that matter.

Tatum had fallen completely apart. He might be a big bad ex-sailor but he was also a father and a grandfather. The guy sat on a bar stool, his head down. The rest of the staff had been interviewed by Joel and the police and then sent home.

Joel's cell vibrated. He dragged it from his pocket. Simon Ruhl. He hoped this was good news for a change. In the last update he'd gotten Lucas was still missing.

"Hayden," Joel said by way of greeting.

"Anything new on Buddy?" Simon asked.

Joel forked a hand through his hair. He wished he had better news to report. "The woman, Margo, said Kingston had spent the past two days coming up with this plan. She has no idea, she claims, where he was going from here. Houston PD has sent a couple of detectives to interview his father."

Luck had, unfortunately, been on Kingston's side tonight. Though he'd arranged for Margo to distract Joel, he hadn't anticipated the rear entrance being locked. But then the toaster oven had jammed and a fire had started. Tatum had put it out easily and quickly, but then he'd opened the back door to let out some of the smoke. Kingston had seized the opportunity. Margo had gotten the text message to "go" the instant Kingston had a way in.

Low-down dirtbag. If he got that boy hurt...

Margo had further stated that Kingston had been drinking but she'd seen him far drunker. Hopefully that was good news. Joel hadn't mentioned to Laney that the guy had roared away from the parking lot like a bat out of hell.

"I put in a call to Houston PD and asked that they put their finest on it," Simon assured him. "How is Laney holding up?"

"About as well as can be expected." Damn Terry Kingston. How could he use his son this way? Was the guy totally heartless?

"Keep her close, Hayden," Simon warned. "Her emotional state could prove a danger to herself and her son. We don't know what Clare Barker and Weeden have planned. It's doubtful Kingston's actions are related to their intentions but there are no certainties here."

"Got it covered." Christ. Joel hadn't even asked about Lucas. "What about Lucas? Any luck with the search?"

"His cell carrier has narrowed down his last registered location as being in the vicinity of Laney's home. Service is sketchy on some of the back roads between her house and the city. They can't pinpoint the area as well as we'd like but at least we have some place to search."

"His intent had been to stay at the High Noon," Joel said, mentally replaying his last conversation with Lucas. "If he changed his mind and decided to stake out the house, he never mentioned it."

"If Lucas had reason to suspect Clare and her accomplice would show up at Laney's home, he would follow that hunch."

"It would help if he'd given me a heads-up." The idea that he and Laney had spent hours making love while Lucas ran into trouble pained him deeply. Joel should have been providing backup instead of indulging in his own selfish needs.

"Lucas has spent a lifetime in covert operations. He's accustomed to following his instincts with or without backup. This was his decision. Bear that in mind."

That fact didn't relieve the regret Joel felt for not anticipating that kind of move out of a man like Lucas. As true as that was, he couldn't regret the bond he and Laney had formed.

Simon ended the call with the assurance he would keep Joel posted and Joel was to do the same.

The office door opened and the two detectives exited. Laney stalled in her pacing and waited expectantly for any answers they may have secured.

"Ma'am," the detective in charge said, "we believe Miss Rucker has given us all she knows and it isn't much. We'll be covering as much ground as quickly as possible in hopes of finding your son and his father without delay. My advice is that you stay home where you can be reached at all times and in the event Kingston decides to drop the child off."

"They do that sometimes," the other detective offered. "They make a rash decision like this out of emotion then reality sets in. You'll need to be home if your boy shows up there."

The two detectives looked as grim and exhausted as Joel felt. But they couldn't possibly have any idea how bad this could get.

Laney thanked the two men and stood like a statue as they moved toward Joel. He braced for whatever bad news they might be about to relay to him that they hadn't wanted to pass on to Laney. He was thankful when she joined Tatum at the bar.

"We have a few calls to make. Outside," the one in charge said. "Ms. Rucker is trying to reach her attorney. We're giving her a few minutes of privacy to do that before we take her in. Make sure she stays put."

The detective's message was loud and clear. Joel had asked for more time with the woman. They were giving it to him. "Count on it."

When they were out the door, he strode to the office.

Margo was fiddling with her cell and swiping at her tears. Joel closed the door and she looked up. "What do you want?" she demanded.

He pulled a chair over to sit knee-to-knee with her. "The police will be taking you to booking in a few minutes."

She blinked back more tears.

"Accessory to felony kidnapping is a serious charge. You'll do time." He leaned forward. "And if the kid dies, you'll end up on death row." Even suggesting that travesty out loud ripped him apart inside.

"I told them everything I know." Her voice trembled.

"He's the kid's father. I didn't know it was kidnapping. He's just trying to get time with his kid."

"Ignorance of the law won't change the charges, Ms. Rucker. You're in deep trouble here but if you help us find him, maybe I can put in a word."

She dragged in a shaky breath. "How can I help you? I don't know anything else! Don't you think I want to get out of this mess? Terry screwed me over on this."

"Think," Joel pressed. "He won't be stupid enough to go home to his father's or to whatever apartment or hotel he uses for sleeping off his drinking binges. But he will go somewhere. Most likely someplace familiar."

Realization dawned on her face. "That mechanic who works on his cars. Makes 'em go faster or something. He hangs out with him a lot. Even slept in his fancy garage a time or two. He got that car he's driving there."

"Who is this mechanic?"

She shook her head. "I've never been to his place and I only met him once but I've heard 'em talk on the phone before." She frowned in concentration. "Studdard or Stuttart. Something like that. He's a big deal around here. Pimps out the motors instead of the bodies. He's kinda famous. He shouldn't be hard for a guy like you to find."

"Anything else?" Joel pushed. "Any friends? Any place at all that he frequents? A restaurant? A department store?"

She laughed. "Terry doesn't have any real friends. Just the ones like the mechanic who make money off him."

"Do you think he'd go back to Houston?" With the Amber Alert he was far more likely to be caught on any main roads and in the larger cities where there was more of a media and police presence. Joel figured he would lay low someplace out of the way until he figured out his next step, which was probably to bring Buddy back just like the detective said. The guy wasn't ambitious enough to have a real plan.

Kingston might be a drunk but he wasn't stupid enough to purposely hurt the kid.

"No way he'd go near his father. They had a big fight this morning. Terry says he's done with his daddy."

Right. His daddy was his money supply. That would be a short-lived position.

Joel took her phone and entered his cell number into her contact list. "You remember anything or you hear anything, you call me first."

Margo nodded. "I'm really going to jail?"

"I'm afraid so."

Her sobs followed him out the door.

Laney waited for him, her expression hopeful, her eyes still filled with terror.

He hugged her and whispered in her ear. "Have Tatum close up. Get your things. We have a lead."

Her breath caught and she trembled in his arms. Then she nodded and rushed to do as he'd asked.

Whatever he had to do to make this right, Joel intended to make it happen. And when he got his hands on Kingston, he was beating the hell out of him. Then Joel would call the cops and give them the lead he was keeping to himself for now…for entirely selfish reasons. Joel wanted to get his hands on Kingston first.

Chapter Seventeen

Studdard Power Engines, Port Arthur, Texas
Friday, May 31st, 6:15 a.m.

Laney felt numb. She thought of all the times Terry had shown up at her house or the saloon too drunk to walk much less drive. He was careless and selfish. He never thought of anyone but himself.

He'd taken Buddy.

She clutched Mr. Bear tighter to her chest. Buddy wouldn't have wanted to go without his bear or without saying goodbye to her. She kept imagining him crying for her.

Laney closed her eyes and prayed again for God to keep her baby safe. The one thing that gave her any relief at all was that she knew Terry wouldn't intentionally hurt Buddy. But the problem with Terry was that he simply was not capable of taking care of himself, much less a child.

"That looks like him."

At the sound of Joel's voice Laney opened her eyes and searched the street. A blue sports car roared into the parking lot. She and Joel had been sitting here for half an hour waiting for the owner, Rudy Studdard, to show up. Her pulse rate started to climb. Was he finally here? The better question was, would he be able to help them?

Simon Ruhl and one of the nice detectives—she couldn't remember his name—had promised to contact her or Joel immediately if they found anything... if there was an accident or a report from a hospital or any word at all about Buddy.

On the half-hour drive from Beaumont to Port Arthur she had seen one of the massive electronic billboards that displayed the face and contact information of any missing child. Seeing Buddy's face on there had been like a bullet to her heart.

Please let my baby be okay. She was terrified by her personal knowledge of Terry's carelessness. He didn't even have a damned car seat for Buddy. Even though Buddy was five, he was still below the weight requirements to use a seat belt only.

He was just a baby.

Despite the police having already checked the low-rent apartment in Beaumont that Margo had said Terry had leased, she and Joel had checked it out, as well. They'd gone to all the haunts the woman had mentioned Terry frequented. Simon Ruhl's contact in Houston had gotten a firm "haven't seen or heard from him" when they visited old man Kingston in the middle of the night. Simon was also pushing the police to move faster on getting a warrant for Terry's cell-phone carrier.

Each hour that passed tore another hole in Laney's heart.

They had to find him.

A tall, lanky man climbed out of the sports car and strolled to the entrance of his garage, which looked more like a showroom for new automobiles. But there were mechanic's bays in the rear. The lot was full of fancy sports cars, not unlike the one Studdard drove, that were protected by an electrified high fence. Concertina wire was rolled across the top. The car Laney had taken the bat to was there. Had her actions propelled this nightmare?

Focus, Laney. She had to keep a clear head if she was going to be of any use to Buddy. He would be counting on her to find him. This was a good start.

Terry had definitely been here recently.

They had gone to Studdard's home first and gotten his wife out of bed. She claimed her husband was out of town and wouldn't be back until morning. And when he got back, she further stated, he would go straight to his shop. She gave Joel the husband's cell number but told him not to waste his time, Studdard never answered it anyway unless it was a client's number that he recognized.

And she had been right.

The wife insisted Studdard would be at the shop between six and seven, no exceptions. His work was his life. She gave the impression of not caring one way or the other as long as the bank account stayed healthy.

"Stay in the Jeep," Joel ordered.

Before she could argue, he got out and called the man's name.

For a moment Laney sat there obediently, too emotionally drained to do any differently.

The man turned, his posture reflecting his apprehension as Joel approached him. Laney was thankful he didn't run. Though Studdard was tall, he was thin. He didn't look like the type to fend off a mugger with his own two hands. His hair was dark and he wore glasses and preppy clothes. Probably expensive. Probably never wore the same getup twice. He and Terry had that in common. Along with the expensive car fetish.

They spoke for a minute and Studdard began to shake his head. Laney's heart sank. Where would they go from here? He had to know something. They had learned that the damned car Terry was driving right now came from this man.

Fury driving her, Laney got out of the Jeep and marched up to the door. Both men looked at her in surprise.

"Mr. Studdard?"

"Laney," Joel said gently. "You should wait in the car."

Studdard looked from her to Joel and back. "I haven't seen Kingston since the day before yesterday when he dropped his damaged car off here and borrowed a loaner."

"But you've talked before," Laney accused, desperate. "Maybe gone out for a meal together. Surely he's mentioned places he likes to hang out or places he might have been or be planning to go." She needed something from this man!

Studdard sighed. "Why don't you come inside and I'll see what I can do." He shrugged. "I know a few others he's done *business* with." He looked at Joel. "If you know what I mean."

"Are you referring to drugs, Mr. Studdard?" she asked.

Laney steeled for worse news. If Terry had gotten into drugs… Oh, God. Her body started to quake. As strong as she wanted to be for Buddy, she couldn't keep the fear at bay.

"Yes. Very recently. That's why I limit my dealings with him to strictly business. I won't take the risk. My clients are the rich and powerful. Whatever they do behind closed doors, they have no desire to do business with anyone with a less-than-stellar reputation."

Laney thought of all the horror stories she had seen on the news where people sold their children for money to buy drugs. Bile burned her throat. But Terry had money… Or had his father really cut him off completely?

Inside, Studdard locked the front entrance behind them and flipped on the lights. "No one else will be here before eight-thirty. I like coming in early to get paperwork done."

"We appreciate your help, Studdard," Joel said. "A missing child requires the attention of everyone who knows the person responsible."

Studdard pushed his glasses up his nose. "Certainly."

He led the way through the showroom of expensive-looking cars. In his office, he flipped on the lights and gestured to the chairs in front of his desk.

"I never gave Terry my personal numbers." He glanced at Laney. "I only do that with close, trustworthy associates. He has this number." He indicated the phone on his desk. "If he called me, the number will be on the caller ID and if he wanted something he will have left a voice mail."

Laney prayed he was right. She sat on the edge of her seat. Joel stood behind her.

"Several calls," Studdard muttered as he scrolled through the numbers. He paused, studied the screen on his desk phone. "And there he is. He called at two thirty-eight this morning." He hit the button to play his voice mails.

Laney held her breath.

He skipped through four calls before Terry's voice floated from the machine. "Studdard, I have a situation."

Thank God he didn't sound wasted. Hope dared to swell in her chest.

"I need another car. ASAP. I can't come to your shop so bring it to the coffeehouse on 365. I'll be waiting. I've got cash. If anyone comes looking for me, you didn't get this call. Screw me over and I'll tell your wife about your extracurricular activities. Hey, and bring me one of your car seats."

Laney gasped, the sound ragged.

Red climbed Studdard's face. "I hope—" He cleared his throat "I hope...this helps in some way."

"Let's go," Joel said. "You're going to help a lot more."

Studdard reared back in his chair. "I've already—"

"He knows my Jeep," Joel argued. "He's expecting you and a new ride. That's what he's going to get." Studdard started to argue again but Joel shut him up with a raised hand. "If this guy gets spooked he could run. A high-speed chase could have a bad ending."

Studdard blinked twice.

"You help us," Joel offered, "and the police don't have to be involved. No one has to know you help friends out this way. Clearly Kingston felt comfortable relaying he had a situation. And considering he's not one of your *trustworthy* clients, I can only guess what you will and have done for those folks."

Laney was holding her breath again, tears brimming

on her lashes. She should have gone to the house for her gun. Then, by God, this guy wouldn't hesitate. Joel had a handgun in his Jeep. He had showed it to her. But Joel insisted he never used it unless there was no other recourse.

Studdard finally acquiesced. "All right."

He selected a modified, as he called it, two-door he felt confident Terry would like. Laney rode in the front with him since she was small enough to hunker down in the floorboard when they approached Terry's car. Joel was slouched down across the tiny backseat since there was no way he could get enough of his big body below the level of the dashboard up front.

Laney consoled herself with memories of her baby. From the first time he had smiled up at her at two months old, she had known they were going to be fine. They had each other and the rest would fall into place in time.

She had let him down.

The drive took less than ten minutes but each one felt like a lifetime to Laney. Daylight had chased away the darkness but the rising sun did nothing to rid her of the chill that had settled deep in her bones.

Her baby had been missing for over eight hours now. Her soul cried out in anguish.

There was a fair-size crowd at the coffeehouse but Terry's car wasn't in the lot. He'd parked across the street in the parking lot of a defunct gas station. He had backed up to the building, so that his vehicle pointed toward the street.

For a fast getaway, Laney supposed. Or maybe to hide his license plate in case the police were looking for him.

"Nose up to him," Joel told Studdard. "We don't want him trying to take off."

Laney hunkered down in the seat. Studdard did as Joel ordered.

"Shut off the engine and get out," Joel told him.

"Okay." The man's voice shook a little now. His fingers fumbled on the keys.

"Stay calm, Studdard," Joel urged. "We have reason to believe he's armed."

"What?" Studdard turned around in his seat. "You didn't say anything about that before."

"Get out of the car," Joel growled. "He's not going to shoot you. He thinks you're here to help. You want him thinking you're not?"

Studdard adjusted his glasses. "But he's just sitting there. Why doesn't he get out?"

Enough of the debating and second-guessing. Laney grabbed the door handle and wrenched the door open. To hell with Studdard. She bailed out with Joel trying his best to grab her and drag her back into the car.

She stormed up to the driver's side of Terry's car. "I want my boy, you son of—"

Laney's knees buckled. Joel caught her before she hit the ground.

There was a hole in Terry's chest... Blood had soaked his shirt and... run down onto the seat between his legs. Where was Buddy? She couldn't see him...not in the front seat or the back.

A surge of adrenaline hit Laney. She jerked from Joel's hold and reached for the door. "I have to find Buddy!"

Joel grabbed her back. "Don't touch anything, Laney."

"I have to find my baby." How had this happened?

Who had taken her baby if he wasn't with his father? Was he cowering in the back floorboard? "Buddy! It's mommy! Where are you, baby?"

Joel gave her a gentle shake. "Let me look, okay? This is a crime scene now and we have to be careful. If whoever did this took Buddy, we can't risk contaminating evidence."

Blackness threatened. Laney barely hung on. Terry was dead. Buddy was gone. Whoever had taken Buddy was willing to kill....

Joel braced her against the wall away from Terry's car. Her body felt cold and hot at once. She couldn't draw a deep enough breath. Where was her baby? What had Terry done? Who had done this to him? Was there even enough room in the rear floorboard for Buddy to hide? Why wouldn't he have cried out to her when he heard her voice?

Because he wasn't here.... Her heart lurched.

Joel moved around to the other side of the car and opened the passenger side door. Laney dared to move away from the wall. Her legs felt rubbery but she managed to stay vertical.

Joel fumbled in the glove box then withdrew from the passenger side as the trunk popped open.

Laney's heart hit the concrete. She hadn't thought of that. Her knees went weak again. *No. Please don't let him be in there....*

After a quick survey of the truck's interior, Joel closed the lid and shook his head.

A crazy mixture of relief and renewed fear flooded her veins. What did this mean? Who would take her little boy?

A drug dealer? A person who wanted to sell her baby to human traffickers or some sick pedophile?

Her heart rose and started to thunder. How would they ever be able to find Buddy now?

Joel's words drifted to her through the haze of panic. He was on the phone. He stated the address and then said that he wanted to report a homicide. He'd called the police.

Dear God. Why would anyone do this? What kind of people had Terry gotten himself involved with?

Images filled her head. Stick figures all lined up in a row...dozens and dozens of them on that motel wall.

She'd watched Buddy through his bedroom window.

The grandma lady...the murderer.

Port Arthur Police Station, 8:30 a.m.

JOEL HAD BEEN INTERROGATED BEFORE. The Port Arthur detective along with the two from Beaumont had questioned him repeatedly about the incident in the High Noon parking lot when Kingston and Joel had exchanged heated words.

Anger came and went as Joel wrestled with his emotions. These guys had a job to do and Joel understood that. But there was a child missing and these guys should be helping look for him, not rehashing irrelevant information.

They'd run Joel's prints just to be sure he was who he said he was. Simon Ruhl had called and offered to come to the station but Joel knew he needed to be on the search for Lucas. The sooner Lucas was found, the sooner Simon and the others could help with this situation.

God almighty, the situation had gone to hell fast.

He'd come here to protect Laney and Buddy and he'd failed.

A female detective was questioning Laney. He wished she didn't have to go through this. Until they released them there wasn't a whole hell of a lot Joel could do.

"Well, all right," the detective from Beaumont in charge of Buddy's case finally announced. "We're going to request support from the FBI. For now, I believe it would be in the best interest of all if you took Ms. Seagers home. We're doing everything that can be done at this time."

Joel stood. "I can appreciate that, but you need to appreciate what she's going through. Sitting around waiting isn't the answer for her peace of mind."

The detective nodded. "We do understand. We'll contact you if we learn anything new."

Joel turned for the door but the detective spoke again. "And for the love of Mike, call us if you get a lead and let us follow up. There's a far less likelihood of the evidence being contaminated."

Joel tossed back the man's own words. "We understand."

Joel walked out. He wasn't making any promises he wouldn't keep. He followed the corridor back to the lobby area. Laney sat in a chair looking devastated and lost. She didn't even look up as he approached.

He sat down beside her. She blinked but didn't look at him.

From the moment he confirmed that Kingston was dead, Joel knew with complete certainty that his murder and Buddy's disappearance had nothing to do with drugs or human trafficking or some sick pedophile.

Clare Barker and Weeden had been watching. Kingston's desperate move had provided an opportunity. Clare had been taken with Buddy—that was obvious. She wanted him. Maybe to reel in Laney.

All Joel had to do was find those two and he would find Buddy. He felt certain of that. For now the boy was likely safe. If the goal was to lure in Laney, they would need Buddy alive.

With the Amber Alert, Lucas missing and Terry's murder, Clare Barker was now wanted for questioning by the police as well as the Colby Agency. She couldn't afford to be out in the open. She and Weeden would need to find someplace to lay low where no one would look for them. Someplace one or both considered safe and way off the radar.

"If you were Clare Barker," Joel said quietly, "where would you go to hide with the grandson you had been dying to spend time with?"

Laney looked over at him. "You think she took him?" Her voice wobbled. Joel nodded.

"She must've taken him. We have to find her, Joel. We have to. I read those articles that were in the photo album," she said. "Their farm was off the beaten path. No one lives there."

Joel managed a weak smile. That was his thinking, too.

Some of the victims' families had bought the place in a tax auction years ago. They'd boarded it up and swore that no one would ever live there again.

"No one would look there," Joel offered. "It's too obvious." He tugged at a strand of her hair. "You know, like in the movies, when you just know the bad guy can't be a certain cliché character because it would be too much of a no-brainer."

Her lips trembled into a faint smile of her own and she nodded.

"I say we take off and head there right now. We could be in Granger by one, maybe sooner since we've missed most of the morning commuters."

"There's nothing else we can do here." Anticipation tinged her voice.

He shook his head. "Nothing. Except wait."

Laney pushed to her feet. "I don't want to wait."

Joel stood. He took her hand in his. "We will find him." She turned to him, her usually glittering brown eyes clouded with fear and misery. "That's a promise," he guaranteed.

As they exited the police station Joel prayed he would be able to keep that promise.

Chapter Eighteen

Granger, 1:15 p.m.

Clare had rocked the boy to sleep. It had taken a while. He'd slept most of the way here but when he'd awakened he had cried for his mother.

She had used this old rocker to sway her girls to sleep when they were little. She was glad it was still here. Much of the old furniture was still here. The house had fallen into grave disrepair, but that could all be fixed in time. She and her family could make something of the place. Turn it back into a real home.

"Sweet boy." She gently brushed the hair out of his face. He was an angel. Beautiful and perfect in every way. Just like his mother was. She had been almost this age when Clare last held her. She had been crying for her bear just as Buddy had cried for his.

Clare wasn't sure how Tony had managed to get the boy away from that rotten father of his but she was glad he had. She hadn't asked any questions and, as usual, her son had offered no explanations. To Clare's way of thinking, Tony was a hero for rescuing Buddy. No man like that drunkard Terry Kingston deserved to have this precious angel.

Now Lisa would want to come to Clare. Tony's plan was a good one. She had worried about how she would convince her daughters to come to her. Especially with the Colby Agency working against her.

The floor creaked and Clare looked up. Tony hovered in the doorway. He looked away when her gaze met his.

"He's precious, isn't he?"

Tony nodded.

She had never gotten to hold him this way. Clare wondered if Janet or the Weedens, the people who had ultimately adopted Tony, had ever once been kind to him. The thought of what they may have done to him besides what was obvious made her sick to her stomach. Clare hadn't known the Weedens but Janet had. Since her release, Clare had learned that the Weedens had been a bad bunch. They were all gone now. The old man and woman had died years ago. Not soon enough for Clare's liking. They had been immensely cruel to Tony if half of what she had learned about them was true. No matter what Tony said about the accident that had caused the loss of his arm, Clare feared the injury had been the result of something far more sinister. She knew her sister too well. Janet had benefited financially from the adoptions of Clare's girls and she suspected the loathsome witch had done the same when she turned Tony over to the Weedens.

"Lunch is ready," Tony announced. "Ham and cheese sandwiches with all the fixings."

Clare caressed the child's soft cheek. "I'll be there in a minute."

"I cut the tomatoes fresh," he snapped. "If you wait, the bread will be soggy."

Clare looked up at him and wondered if watching her

with Buddy made him envious. She wished she could change that. Take away the hurt from the past.

But what was done was done and she had made many mistakes. The most she could hope for was forgiveness or perhaps not even that. If they could all just start over from here, that would be enough.

She looked around at the room that had once been her girls' bedroom. The place was old and run-down for sure. The yard looked like a mess. The clinic that had once been a barn was falling in.

At least the dead who had been buried here had been moved. That was something. The past was behind her now and she wanted to forget those ugly years.

Tony shuffled away. The sound drew her attention to the door. She had disappointed him enough. The least she could do was eat the meal he had prepared.

Anything to make him happy. He had done so very much for her and was prepared to do more.

She placed Buddy carefully on the throw she'd spread on the floor. There was no pillow or proper covers but it would do for now. Children his age could sleep through a war.

Truth was, they were caught up in a war. The battle had scarcely begun.

Tony had told her this morning about his savings. He had plenty of money, he'd said, to fix the old place up if he could buy it back.

That would be nice.

When she had accomplished her goal the world would know the truth and perhaps her home would be returned to her. Wouldn't it be nice if Rafe lived to hear of her good fortune? He would tear out his hair.

She prayed he would suffer every minute of every hour until they shoved those needles into his loathsome veins.

Clare left the room and went in search of her dear son. She owed him so much.

She had seen the spots of blood on his shirt when he brought Buddy to her. But that was irrelevant in this war they were waging. Whatever he had done to bring her grandson to her, she needed to properly show her appreciation.

It was the least she could do with him so willing to sacrifice so much for her.

Tony waited in the kitchen. He had stocked a cooler with fresh sandwich meats and drinks. He thought of everything. Clare wasn't sure what she would have done without him. He seemed prepared for every situation. He had flashlights and changes of clothes. Maps and money. He said that they would find new transportation soon. His idea to come here, the last place anyone would look, was genius.

He was her hero.

A good son.

Clare smiled as she picked up the sandwich he had made. "This is so much better than anything I was ever served in that awful place."

He ducked his head in acknowledgment of her praise. Her son didn't say much but he provided more than she deserved. He had overcome much in his life. Like her, he was a survivor.

They ate in silence for a few moments. Clare didn't like the silence. She had endured far too much of it in prison. She'd had no one to talk to. No one who cared if she lived or died. "Did you find a place to hide the car?"

"Down the road in the turnoff that leads into the woods to an old burned-out house."

"Where the old Martin house once stood." She remembered when the house burned. She and Rafe had just moved here in what the weathermen had called the worst winter in Texas history. Like their old house, the Martins' had nothing but a fireplace to keep warm. It was a terrible tragedy. The whole family was lost in the fire.

Tony shrugged. "Guess so. It's easy to find through the woods beyond the barn."

Barn... He meant the clinic. Where she and Rafe had done their work...when they were happy so, so long ago.

"We can get there quickly if need be," her son noted.

He was worried that they would be found here. But with their photos all over the news now, their options were limited. In truth, taking Buddy hadn't likely been a good idea but she would not spoil her son's glory. His intentions had been good. And she had so desperately wanted to get to know her grandson.

More silence followed. Clare hoped Tony wasn't regretting having helped her. He seemed to have less and less to say to her with each passing day, even if he accomplished more.

The sound of crying broke the silence. Buddy had awakened. Poor child, he was probably terrified.

"I'll get him," Tony grumbled.

"You finish your lunch." Clare set her sandwich aside and started across the room. "I'll get him."

Tony turned sharply. "Wait."

The feral look on his face scared her. Her fingers balled into fists to contain her fear. "What's wrong?"

He rushed past her. She followed, her movements

stiff with uncertainty. He moved to the front window in the entry hall next to the door and peeked out the grimy glass.

Her heart started to pound with the fear swooshing through her veins. "Is something wrong?"

Tony wheeled around. "Go to the car now. I'll get the boy."

Fear snaked around her heart. "The police?"

"Go!" he commanded. "I'll bring the boy."

Clare rushed out the back door and across the yard, the blood pounding in her ears. She fled deep into the woods before she dared to stop.

She gasped for air and tried to hear above the sound of her own heartbeat. How many were here? Her journey could not end this way. There was still much to do. She hadn't found Olivia yet. She wanted to—

A scream filled the air.

Her heart stopped.

Buddy.

Chapter Nineteen

Victoria waited in the lobby, her body numb with fear. The relief she had felt at finding Lucas had been short-lived once the E.R. physicians had examined him.

His right shoulder had been dislocated and his left leg was fractured. But the worst was the head injury. A serious concussion. Once the CT scan was completed they would know the extent of the damage.

Victoria closed her eyes. For nearly twenty-four hours they had searched for him. The last six very near the area where he had been found by a passing motorist.

The thick canopy of trees had hidden his rented sedan from view as the helicopter they'd hired had made pass after pass over the area. Lucas had suffered hours of agony because Victoria could not find him.

Clare Barker and Weeden were responsible for this. Fury unleashed inside Victoria. Lucas had told his rescuers how Weeden had forced him to take the ditch to prevent a horrendous collision that might have killed them all.

He had lain unconscious for hours. When he'd awakened he had endured the pain of scrambling into the

passenger floorboard for his cell. But there had been
no service. He'd had no choice but to start the slow,
agonizing effort of trying to pull his damaged body up
that embankment to the road.

Victoria prayed Lucas had suffered no permanent
damage.

She opened her eyes and took stock of the deserted
lobby. Even the reception desk had a bell one could ring
if service was required. Victoria was alone. Simon and
Jim had been here with her until half an hour ago. She
had dismissed them. There was nothing either of them
could do. They were needed in the search for Buddy
Seagers. Victoria would take care of her husband.

Please let him be okay.

All those months ago they had made the decision
that they would retire, and look at them now. Lucas was
chasing the bad guys as if he were closer to thirty than
sixty. And she was no better. Ferreting out the secrets
of heinous killers.

What had she been thinking?

She would see that this never happened again. Never.
She and her husband were going to make that lifestyle
change they had promised to make. Jim was handling
the agency in Chicago beautifully and Simon had the
Houston office well on its way to fully staffed.

There was no need for her and her husband to be
involved in the day-to-day operations. A nice cottage
on the beach and long walks in the sand were far more
suitable for the years that lay ahead of them.

Victoria would attend to that just as soon as she ensured the woman and her accomplice who had done
this to Lucas were captured and paid sufficiently for
their crimes. And if Rafe Barker was innocent, which

she sincerely doubted, she would set the record straight on that, as well.

"Mrs. Camp?"

Victoria rose, her heart thundering madly as she met the doctor's gaze. "Yes?"

"You may see your husband now."

Thank God.

As Victoria moved toward the door that separated the lobby from the E.R., the doctor explained, "Mr. Camp does have a concussion so we're going to keep him here for a couple of days given his other injuries." The doctor smiled. "But he's going to be fine. In fact, I may need your help in convincing him to stay put. He's rather stubborn."

The good doctor didn't know the half of it. Victoria gave him a reassuring smile. "He'll stay as long as you feel is necessary, Doctor."

He paused at a door in the long corridor. "I'll give the two of you some privacy."

Victoria thanked him and entered the room. She suspected the doctor wanted no part in the debate that would follow. No worries. There would be no debate. She had made her decision and Lucas was not going to sway her.

Her heart melted and her lips spread into a smile when she caught sight of her husband on the examining table, a print cotton gown his only attire. His forehead was bandaged, covering the nasty gash. His right arm was in a sling and his left leg sported a walking cast. But he looked like heaven on earth to Victoria. He was alive, with no injury from which he couldn't recover.

"I suppose it could be worse," she announced as she crossed to his bedside.

He smiled through the pain. She wondered if they had given him any pain medication. The nurse had said it was necessary to wait until after the CT scan for any pain meds.

"I told you I'd be fine."

Victoria had cried copious tears when they'd found him. She wouldn't cry now. She was far too irritated, mostly at herself, and she intended to reveal no weakness. "You knew better than to follow a mark without backup or at least informing someone of your whereabouts. You've done this work far too long to be so careless."

"Correct on all counts, my dear."

The irritation gave way to those softer emotions she had attempted to conceal. "You scared me to death, Lucas."

He took her hand in his and held it tenderly. "I am more sorry about that than you can know." He winked to hide the emotion shining in his own eyes, but she saw it. "Quite frankly, I scared myself."

"Never again." She shook her head firmly.

He started to nod then winced. "Whatever you say, darling."

Victoria couldn't restrain herself any longer. She leaned down and kissed him squarely on the mouth. He caressed her cheek and smiled beneath her onslaught.

"I love you, Victoria."

She blinked back those confounding tears. "I was so afraid I'd lost you."

He squeezed her hand. "You gave me the strength to climb out of that ravine. I knew you would be worried. I wasn't about to let you down."

She managed a wobbling smile. "Very well. I suppose all is forgiven, under the circumstances."

"Good. Let's get out of here. We need to help Laney and Hayden find Buddy."

"All our resources are focused on the search." She tucked the sheet around him. "You and I are staying here for a day or two."

When he started to argue, she reminded him, "'Whatever you say, darling.'"

Lucas surrendered.

She had known he would.

Lucas Camp was a man of his word.

Chapter Twenty

Granger, 1:18 p.m.

Laney froze.

The scream echoed over and over in her head.

"Buddy." His name whispered from her lips.

"Call the police and then Simon," Joel called back at her as he rushed toward the house. "He's not that far behind us."

But they were all too late. Her son was screaming. The screams from her dreams echoed in her brain. Swelled and twisted with the sound of her son's scream.

Laney stared at the house.

This was the place...the screaming place...where the darkness waited. The place of nightmares and the smell of blood and terror.

Laney couldn't breathe. Tears crowded her eyes, her throat.

"Mommy!"

"Buddy," she murmured.

He was here.... And he needed her.

Laney snapped into action. She ran toward the sound of Buddy's scream, her trembling fingers fumbling with the phone.

A gunshot blasted the air. She jerked to a halt. "Buddy! Where are you, baby?"

Nothing. She started running again. She cleared the back of the house, stalled in the yard and turned all the way around. Where was he? Where was Joel? "Mommy's here! Buddy!"

The police! Call the police! Laney hit the necessary buttons.

The dispatcher's voice sounded scratchy, as if the reception was bad. "Nine-one-one, what is the nature of your emergency?"

"Someone took my son." Laney's body shook. Her throat tried to close. "I heard him scream! Gunshots. I need help!"

Another gun blast pierced the air.

"Please! Help us!" she cried.

"Give me your address, ma'am."

The address! What was the address? Laney shook herself, took a breath, then gave the address.

"Stay on the line, ma'am, we—"

Laney couldn't wait. She shoved the phone into her pocket and rushed into the woods calling her son's name.

JOEL CUT THROUGH THE TREES. Another shot whizzed past his head. He ducked.

Up ahead, a male figure with dark hair and wearing a white T-shirt zigzagged through the trees. Weeden.

Joel couldn't get a clear visual on Weeden. Was he carrying Buddy?

Joel lunged forward, keeping low. He cut through the brush and trees making way too much noise. There was no help for it; he couldn't slow down.

If he could get a clear shot…

He stalled.

Nothing moved.

No sound.

Joel forced his heart rate to slow. He listened beyond the sound of his own pounding heart.

"Buddy!"

Laney.

A blast echoed in the air.

Was the son of a bitch shooting at her?

Joel rushed from his hiding place, making all the noise he could, to draw Weeden's attention.

A blast thundered and a bullet hit the tree to his right.

Joel hit the ground. As he lay there, he listened.

Where was that bastard?

Where was Laney?

"Buddy! It's Mommy!"

The voice came from his left.

Joel scrambled up and moved forward and to the right, once again making all the noise he could.

Another shot…hit the ground beside him. Way too close.

Weeden was close.

A flurry of movement drew Joel's attention to his right. He eased between the trees, careful of every step.

He caught a glimpse of dark hair.

Weeden.

Joel moved closer.

"Mommy!"

Buddy.

Joel turned just as the blast echoed. He jerked with the impact, felt the burn of the bullet low on his left side…

He pivoted, used the nearest tree for cover. He touched his side with his free hand. Warm blood oozed between his fingers. *Damn it.*

He had to protect Buddy and Laney. He couldn't let this guy get close to them.

Adrenaline fired through him, and he ignored the pain and rushed forward. Something white flashed between the trees to his left. The T-shirt. The bastard was headed toward the sound of Laney's voice.... Toward Buddy.

Joel charged in that direction.

He spotted Weeden, running...ten yards ahead.

Joel aimed. The bastard darted left. Joel couldn't get the shot without firing into the brush. But Buddy could be in there.

He moved in a dead run parallel with Weeden's path, but suddenly Weeden turned and Joel ducked for cover.

A shot echoed. Bark flew off the tree just above his head. Weeden was shooting to kill.

Fury lashed through Joel. He couldn't throw out any cover shots without looking first. Laney or Buddy could be out there anywhere.

Joel eased from behind the tree, scanned the area around him and moved forward.

"Buddy!" Laney cried.

Joel turned toward the sound of her voice. She was too close.

Another gun blast echoed.

Hot metal tore through his left shoulder and Joel snapped back with the impact.

Weeden darted through the trees.

Fighting through the burn, Joel leveled a bead on him and fired.

Weeden went down.

Relief rushed through Joel, helping him to ignore the pain.

His left arm hanging limply at his side, Joel ran toward the position where Weeden had fallen.

He stopped, studied the ground.

There was blood…but no Weeden.

Joel took stock of the woods around him as he followed the blood trail. The bastard couldn't have gotten far.

A wave of weakness washed over Joel.

He grunted with the pain of lifting his left hand high enough to press his palm over the hole in his side. Sweat poured down his face.

He listened for movement. No sound. No screams… No Laney calling for her son.

He couldn't risk calling out to her or to Buddy.

The ground moved under his feet.

Hold it together.

He had to find this crazy SOB.

Wood snapped behind him.

Joel froze, swayed, then steadied himself to turn—

Something solid slammed into the back of his skull.

He went down.

The sky and trees spun wildly.

Weeden stared down at him, the barrel of his weapon aimed at Joel's face.

"Stop!"

The scream sucked Joel into the darkness.

"BUDDY!" LANEY RUSHED through the woods. She stumbled. She had to find her baby!

Where was Joel?

The gunshots had stopped.... But where was her baby?

She called his name again.

Dear God, please let me find my baby!

Run! Find him! She stumbled again, caught herself and kept going.

"Buddy!"

Where were the monsters who had her baby?

"Joel?"

She cleared the tree line and found herself staring at the back of the old house. A rusty creaking noise floated across the air as the wind shifted one of the old swings.

Wait... She should be going the other way—into the woods. She wasn't supposed to come back to the house. Was she? She hadn't heard Buddy's voice anymore. Where was he?

In the woods. She had to go back in there.

Her baby was in the woods with those awful people. She'd heard someone scream "stop." Not Buddy or Joel.

She turned back to the woods and cried out her son's name. They were in there somewhere.

Why didn't Buddy or Joel answer her?

"Mommy!"

Buddy burst from the woods.

A sound escaped Laney's throat as she hurried to meet him.

She scooped him up and hugged him close, tears blurring her vision. He sobbed against her shoulder, his little body trembling.

"It's okay, baby. Mommy's got you now."

Her breath was trapped in her lungs. Those people were still out there. She had to get Buddy to safety. She needed to find Joel.

Laney's gaze cleared. She turned to run and something in the trees—right where Buddy had come from the woods—caught her attention.

The woman... Gray hair cropped to her chin. A pink dress.

She stared at Laney. Laney stared back. She couldn't move.

Was she coming after Buddy again? Laney told herself to run, but she felt paralyzed.

They just kept staring at each other.

Laney had no idea how many seconds passed but the woman suddenly turned away and disappeared into the woods.

Clare Barker...*her mother.*

More seconds elapsed before Laney could move.

Where was Joel?

Was Weeden still out there? There had been no more gunshots, but could she risk Buddy's safety by running into the woods to look for Joel?

She had to do something. Buddy started to shift around in her arms but his sobbing had eased.

Joel could be injured. She had to find him.

With a big breath, Laney held on tight to her son and rushed back into the woods. "Joel!"

The wail of sirens stalled her. Thank God. She turned and ran as fast as she could toward the front yard.

The third police car skidded to a halt in front of the house as she rounded the corner. Her knees went weak with relief but she kept going.

"We have to find Joel," she shouted to the first officer out of his car. "He's out there...."

"Calm down, ma'am, and tell us what happened."

Laney's mind abruptly cleared. There was no time to waste. "A man and woman kidnapped my son. We found them here. The man is armed. My…friend rushed into the woods after him. There were gunshots. He may be hurt." She broke down then. "You have to find him."

Buddy started to wail. She tried to comfort him but her tears only made him cry harder.

The other officers had already fanned out across the yard but they weren't moving fast enough.

"They have to hurry," she urged. "He could be hurt. The other man had a gun. There were a lot of gunshots." Joel should have come out of the woods by now. He was hurt. Laney knew it. She just knew it. "You have to do something!" she shouted at the officer.

"Ma'am," the officer said calmly, "are you or the child injured?"

She shook her head. What was he waiting for? He needed to find Joel.

"You and your son get in the car where you'll be safe and we'll find your friend."

He didn't get it. "Joel is out there and he needs help. He would be back here by now if not." She was repeating herself but no one was listening. The renewed burn of tears glazed her eyes.

A dark SUV roared to a stop on the road.

Three men emerged. The officer rested his hand on his weapon as if unsure of what would happen next.

"Laney, are you and Buddy all right?"

It was Simon Ruhl.

She rushed to him. "Joel is still out there. There were a lot of gunshots." Her knees went weak again.

Simon turned to one of the other men. "Take care of Ms. Seagers and her son." To the other, he said, "Let's go."

Feeling helpless, Laney watched as Simon and the

other man, along with the officer who'd been trying to calm her, rushed across the yard.

Please, please, let Joel be okay.

Buddy drew back to look at her. His face was drawn in a frown and his eyes were red from crying. "That bad man tried to take me away."

"Did he hurt you, baby?" A new fear trembled through Laney. She prayed they hadn't hurt him in any way. Dear God, she had only just thought of that. What kind of monsters were these people?

Buddy shook his head resolutely. "They didn't hurt me. But I wanted to go home so I got away."

She managed a shaky smile. "What a strong boy you are. You found your way back to Mommy."

This time when he shook his head, his eyes were big. "No, no, Mommy. I couldn't find you. I was lost in the trees. The grandma lady brought me to you."

Laney stilled. She moistened her lips. The memory of the woman staring at her from the edge of the woods flashed in Laney's brain. "Are you sure, baby? Weren't she and the bad man trying to take you away from Mommy?"

"Nope. It was the bad man with the stubby thing." He patted his upper arm. "He took me from Terry. When I woke up I was with the grandma lady."

So Weeden kidnapped Buddy and took him to Clare. He had killed Terry to get to Buddy. The impact of that realization abruptly penetrated the layers of fear that had been swaddling her brain. Terry was dead. No matter how miserable he had made Laney he hadn't deserved to be murdered. Agony swelled in her chest.

"The grandma lady helped me find you." Buddy laid his head on Laney's shoulder. "She's nice."

Laney hugged him so tight he squirmed. Thank God he was safe. Her baby just didn't understand that the woman was not nice. He had no idea.

The man from the Colby Agency standing beside Laney was saying something. She turned to him but he was on his cell phone. She didn't even know his name.

Why hadn't they found Joel yet?

She opened her mouth to demand that this man watch Buddy while she went to search for Joel. After all, there was no need for both of them to be standing here. But he spoke first.

"They've found Hayden. EMS will be here any second. They were notified as soon as the Granger police were on the scene."

What did that mean? "How badly is he hurt?"

"I'm sorry, ma'am, I can't answer that."

Laney tilted Buddy's chin up. "Mommy needs to go help Mr. Joel so I need you to stay with this gentleman until I get back."

"Ma'am, it would be best for you to stay here."

Buddy clung to her. She couldn't leave him like that and she couldn't risk taking him back into those woods. There was no way to know where Clare and Weeden were at this point. Laney's heart twisted in agony. She prayed Joel wasn't hurt too badly.

Just when she thought her heart would be crushed with worry, four men, two of them uniformed officers, rounded the corner of the house carrying Joel between them.

Laney rushed to meet them, her heart thundering. "How is he?"

"He's unconscious," Simon answered. "We can't assess the full extent of his injuries but he's breathing and his pulse is strong."

As they reached the front yard, the ambulance arrived.

Laney stayed back while the paramedics did their work. Joel's face was ashen. His shirt was bloody around one shoulder and along his side. He didn't move. Didn't open his eyes. She struggled not to cry. She didn't want to upset Buddy any further but she was scared to death. There was so much blood.

Finally, they loaded Joel onto a gurney and headed for the ambulance.

She hurried along beside them. "Is he going to be okay?"

"We hope so," one of the paramedics said without looking at her.

Fear lanced her heart. Why couldn't anyone tell her what she wanted to hear?

"Laney."

She turned to Simon, who gestured to his SUV. "Come with us. We're following the ambulance."

He helped her and Buddy into the SUV. Laney couldn't take her eyes off the ambulance.

The ambulance spun away. Simon maneuvered the SUV onto the road behind it. The police stayed at the farm to look for Weeden and Clare Barker.

But they were gone.

Simon introduced her to the other two men. The only name that stuck was Colby. One was named Jim Colby. She remembered Lucas mentioning him…. He was Victoria's son.

The men spoke quietly but Laney wasn't really listening. She kept thinking about the way the woman,

Clare, had looked at her. What did she want? Was she giving the orders? Had she told Weeden to kill whoever got in their way?

Laney closed her eyes. She had Buddy back safe and sound. If Joel was okay, those two things were all that mattered at the moment.

Clare Barker could disappear and never come back for all Laney cared. She wished she had never heard that name.

Chapter Twenty-One

Beaumont Hospital, 6:05 p.m.

Laney paced the small E.R. waiting room. Buddy was asleep in a chair. Bless his heart. When he woke up he would be wild with a sudden burst of energy. She wished she could take a power nap right now and wake up refreshed.

But that was impossible. She didn't dare close her eyes.

She'd taken Buddy to the hospital cafeteria and he'd eaten like he was totally starved. But he had assured her that the grandma lady had fed him.

Simon had called and briefed her on what they and the police had found. Weeden had taken at least one bullet. They had followed the blood trail to an old, burned-out house down the road from the former Barker residence. And that was where the trail ended. It was believed that Clare and Weeden had left their getaway car there.

The police had an APB out for both Clare and Weeden along with the description of their car. Hospitals and clinics had been alerted to be on the watch for a wounded one-armed man.

Simon felt certain they would not seek medical assistance unless the injury was life-threatening. Weeden was a nurse so as long as he was conscious he could instruct his mother in how to attend to his wound.

Laney stopped midway across the lobby. She kept thinking about how the woman had stared at her. About the house and how it had felt to be there. The screams from her lifelong nightmares had come from that house. Laney knew that now.

Whatever had happened in that house, as a four-year-old child she had blocked the memories. She wondered if the older one, Olivia, remembered anything more clearly.

Laney stared beyond the glass wall that separated the E.R. waiting room from the emergency parking area outside. News crews had gathered.

The world now knew that Clare Barker had left prison with an agenda to find her daughters who were, in fact, alive.

Laney had two sisters.

"Laney."

She turned at the sound of her name, her heart rushing into her throat. But it was not a nurse or a doctor. The woman's dark hair was sprinkled with gray but rather than looking old, she looked sophisticated. Her face was very attractive and she wore an elegant suit. Was she someone from the hospital staff? Was she about to deliver news that Laney did not want to hear?

"Yes?" Laney held her breath.

"My name is Victoria Colby-Camp. Do you have any news on Joel's condition?"

Laney was so exhausted she wasn't sure whether to be relieved or disappointed. "Nothing yet. He's been in surgery for two hours. But he was stable and had re-gained consciousness before they took him to surgery." Laney was still furious they hadn't let her see him.

But, if they made him well again, she could live with that.

Victoria smiled. "Joel is strong and determined. Like my Lucas."

"Oh, gosh. Your husband is here. How is he?" Joel had gotten the call en route to Granger that Lucas had been found. That was how Simon and his entourage were able to arrive so quickly after her and Joel. Joel had explained their suspicions to Simon. And since Lucas had been located, Simon and his team headed that way, as well.

"He's fine," Victoria said. "We expect to be able to go home in a day or two."

"That's great." Laney had so much she wanted to say to this woman but she was absolutely drained and nothing in her head was straight. "I want to thank you for all your agency has done to protect my boy and me."

Victoria peeked past her and smiled. "Your son is an amazing young man. Simon told me how well he handled this ordeal."

Pride welled in Laney's chest. "He is something." She just hoped she could get over the idea of never let-ting him out of her sight again. Laney turned back to Victoria. "Things might have turned out way different if it hadn't been for you and your agency." She shook her head. "I don't know what we would have done with-out Joel."

Victoria took Laney's hand in hers and gave it a squeeze. "We will continue to ensure your safety until this is done. You have my word."

A fresh wave of tears filled Laney's eyes. "Thank you." With Buddy safe, if Joel was okay Laney could live with whatever came next. What difference did anything else make as long as those she loved were safe?

That was the thing… She loved Joel. No question.

"I'll check in with you when I return." Victoria waved to someone beyond the glass. "Simon and I have an errand to run."

Laney watched her go.

Thank God for people like Victoria Colby.

Polunsky Prison, 8:00 p.m.

VICTORIA HAD BEEN ESCORTED to the same cold, sterile room as the first time she had met with notorious serial killer Rafe Barker. Warden Prentice had been less than happy with her demand to see his infamous prisoner at this hour, but Victoria had refused to take no for an answer.

In less than three weeks Rafe Barker would be executed for more than a dozen murders. That first time she had come here it had been at his behest. A letter begging her to help him protect his daughters—the daughters he had been accused of murdering twenty-two years ago—had swayed Victoria and brought her here when the warden had insisted she was wasting her time.

Now, almost ten days later, her husband and one of her investigators lay in Beaumont Hospital barely having escaped death. Another man was dead. Janet Tolliver was dead. Fury stoked to a blaze inside Victoria. This had to stop.

Whatever Rafe knew, and she suspected there was a great deal that he wasn't telling her, she would learn now. Or else the agency was washing its hands of this case beyond protecting Sadie, Laney and Olivia.

Each time she thought of how Lucas could have so easily died, she wanted to tear something apart. And that sweet child. Anything could have happened to him today. The child's father, no matter his sins, had been murdered today.

This was enough. No more games.

The door of the interview room opened. Victoria jerked from her troubling thoughts and braced for war. Two prison guards escorted Barker into the room. The leg irons around his ankles and the belly chain coiled about his waist rattled as he was ushered to the chair directly across the table from her just like before. The nylon glides whispered across the tile floor as the chair was drawn back.

"Sit," one of the guards ordered.

Barker followed the instruction given, his gaze already heavy on Victoria. He settled into the molded plastic chair. The second guard secured the leg irons to the floor and the chains on Barker's hands to the underside of the sturdy table that was all that stood between him and Victoria.

"We'll be right outside, ma'am," the first guard said to her, "if you need anything."

"Thank you. We'll be fine."

When the door had closed behind the guards, Barker continued to stare at her, his faded brown eyes dull and listless. "Something happen?"

He had refused to speak to her since her second visit here when she had informed him of how his confidant and nurse, Tony Weeden, had double-crossed him. That he uttered even those two words now surprised her and at the same time infuriated her.

"My husband and one of my investigators were almost killed today. Another man was murdered by your former friend, Tony Weeden. We now have reason to believe he also killed Janet Tolliver."

Barker said nothing. Yet his gaze never deviated from her.

"Your grandson," Victoria said, making this personal, "was abducted by Clare and Tony."

He flinched.

So he wasn't made of stone. "Tony murdered the child's father and then snatched the little boy with the stench of clotting blood still on his clothes."

Silence.

Victoria braced her hands on the table and leaned forward. Fury had whipped to a frenzy inside her. "What does she want?"

"To finish what I stopped her from doing twenty-two years ago," he uttered in a monotone that made Victoria want to grab him and shake him.

"Weeden took her back to the home the two of you shared. From the looks of things, the intent was to take up residence there again."

The bastard said nothing.

Rage tightened Victoria's lips. "If you know something that will help us stop her, for the love of God, tell me."

Barker leaned forward. Victoria refused to back off.

He stared deep into her eyes. "You can't simply contain her," he whispered. "She's pure evil. I had her contained and they set her free. She won't make the same mistake twice." He leaned away. "Now my daughters will pay the price for the mistake of this so-called justice system."

There was a cryptic message there. "What are you saying?"

He leaned forward again. He waited until she did, as well. Victoria hated the idea of being this close to him.

"The only way to stop her is to kill her." He leaned back far enough to look into her eyes once more. "And I don't think you've got it in you to do that, Victoria." He laughed, a dry rusty sound. "She knows it's you trying to stop her now. And she will do everything in her power to make you pay, too. Trust me, I know."

"She will not stop me," Victoria guaranteed.

Rafe stared at her a moment. "We'll see."

Beaumont Hospital, 9:30 p.m.

WHEN SHE FELT HIS HAND MOVE beneath hers, Laney opened her eyes and sat up straighter. She'd almost dozed off in this uncomfortable old chair.

Joel was watching her.

She smiled. "You're awake." Thank God, thank God. He'd come through the surgery just fine but she wasn't satisfied until he opened those beautiful brown eyes to her.

He managed a lopsided smile. "I dreamed about you."

Her lips trembled at the sound of his voice. His words were so sweet but just hearing him speak made her more happy than any one thing in her entire life except for the birth of her son.

"I hope it was a good dream." She moved to his bedside, took his hand fully in hers.

Uncertainty cluttered his face. "Buddy?"

She glanced at her son curled up on the blanket by her chair. "Sleeping like a rock. He's fine." There was so much she wanted to tell him about how Clare had sent Buddy to her. But that would all have to wait.

Joel released a breath. "Thank God." He looked troubled again. "What about Weeden and Clare?"

She hated to tell him this part. "They got away. But Weeden was injured. So far he hasn't shown up at any clinics or hospitals. As far as we know, anyway."

"I hit him at least once." Joel grimaced. "For a one-armed guy he packs a hell of a blow."

"Are you okay? Do you need more pain medication?" She didn't want him to suffer any more than necessary.

"I'm good." He searched her eyes a moment. "As long as you and Buddy are here, I'm perfect."

More of those sweet words that gave her hope. Laney had done a lot of thinking during the past few hours and she had made some decisions. Maybe they were the wrong ones but there was only one way to find out. "I've been thinking."

He squeezed her hand. "I'm pretty sure you do a lot of that. You're a smart lady."

If he didn't stop she was never going to get all this said. "Anyway, I've decided to sell the house and the saloon and go as far away from here as you're willing to take us."

His gaze held hers but he said nothing. Doubt usurped her confidence, terrified her. Had she read his feelings for her and Buddy wrong?

"You've worked hard on that house and on that saloon, what with all the renovations and building the business. Why would you give that up?"

Well, he'd certainly skirted the real issue. But she couldn't have been that wrong. "If getting out of here ensures that we're all safe, I absolutely will."

For a stretch that felt like a lifetime he searched her eyes some more. "I may be flat on my back right now but I guarantee you I will do a better job of protecting you and Buddy as soon as I'm out of here."

Oh, no. She hadn't meant to make him feel as if any part of what had happened was his failure. Good grief! "But I don't want you to have to protect us like that. I want to be someplace safe."

He tried to rise up on his elbows, grimaced at the effort.

"Wait. Let me raise the bed." Nervous now, she fiddled with the buttons until she was able to raise the head of the bed, putting him in a slightly more upright position. "There."

He wrapped long, strong fingers around hers. "The problem with your plan is that until Weeden and Clare are stopped, they'll keep coming after you. Whether she wants a simple reunion or has some evil agenda, we can't be sure. But her actions indicate the latter. If she only wanted a simple family reunion, mailing out invitations would have done the trick."

Laney thought of how Clare had helped Buddy find her. "If she just wants to see us, why doesn't she say so?"

"That's the part that troubles me. Whatever her reason for approaching the situation like this…it's wrong. We can't take the risk that she'll just give up and go away. We have to square this thing away."

She understood all that. But that wasn't what she meant. Or maybe it was. She was too damned confused. Too exhausted and too scared and worried to beat around the bush. She wanted to get to the point that had nothing to do with the Barkers.

"I love you, okay?" Oh, God, she'd said it. "I don't want you risking your life to protect us. If that means we have to pull up stakes and move away, that's fine. I'm ready to go."

She'd put her cards on the table.

The longer he stared at her without saying a word, the more she quaked inside.

"Come here." He tugged at her to get her to sit down on the edge of his bed. "I've had a few chicks toss the whole I-love-you thing at me."

Laney's heart sank.

"It was a game and I knew it at the time. Frankly, I always wondered how my brothers had found their soul mates. I thought maybe fate had played a big trick on me."

She wanted to say something but her heart had surged into her throat and she couldn't. She simply couldn't.

"What I do know is that no one has ever offered to give up everything they've worked for just for me." He traced her cheek. "I don't know what I did right to find you or to deserve you and Buddy in my life but I'm sure as hell glad I did."

She tried to hold them back, she really did, but it didn't work. The tears slid down her cheeks.

"I love you, Laney, and I love Buddy. If you let me, I'll spend the rest of my life protecting you."

What was he saying? She'd been so worried about right now she hadn't even thought about the future. "Does that mean you want to take us with you when you go?" That was the closest to a reasonable question she could come up with.

"It means I want to stay here with the two of you."

All the other worries crowded in on her. "If I can't swing that loan we may be on the street." It was the ugly truth.

"You won't need that loan. Not only will we be paying that off but we'll be doing some upgrading."

"You don't have to do all that." She wanted him, not his money.

"I want to do all that, Laney. I want to give you the life you deserve." He swiped at her tears with the backs of his fingers. "And as soon as I'm out of this damned hospital, we're going to find a ring and a minister and we're getting married. Buddy can be my best man."

Laney's breath caught.

"That is, if you'll have me as your husband."

She nodded. "I was hoping you would mention that otherwise I was going to have to do the proposing myself." She felt giddy, wanted to jump for joy.

"We'll have a celebration at the High Noon. We'll have Tatum burn the mortgage in that toaster oven of his."

Laney laughed. "That little incident almost gave the poor guy a nervous breakdown." She'd checked in with him and he had the High Noon under control. "I'm thinking of giving him a raise."

"Make him manager."

Not a bad idea, she thought. "But then what will I do?"

He tugged on a lock of her hair until she leaned down close enough for him to brush a kiss across her lips. "You'll stay home and raise all those babies we're going to have. And watch me teach Buddy how to be the best ballplayer in Texas."

She smiled. "Are you suggesting I stay barefoot and pregnant?"

He grinned. "Only for the first few years."

She raised a skeptical eyebrow. "How about I co-manage with Tatum and we'll negotiate the barefoot and pregnant thing? Deal?"

"You drive a hard bargain, ma'am, but you have a deal."

This time he deepened the kiss and Laney knew for an absolute certainty she had won that negotiation.

Whatever happened from this moment forward, she, Buddy and Joel were a family.

Nothing could stop them.

* * * * *

"I got a call from the stalker today."

A sharp intake of breath as Mac leaned forward was his only reaction. Pretending his nearness didn't affect her, she relayed the conversation.

"Are you sure that was wise? What if this person has grown more unstable? What if she's dangerous? You know she said you would pay."

"I've always known this person is unstable."

Agitated, as much by how badly she wanted to touch him as she was by the situation, she jumped from her chair and began to pace.

"Why do you think she'd be breaking in to my house and calling me?"

A muscle worked in Mac's jaw. "You do realize you are putting yourself in danger?"

Swallowing hard, she boldly met his gaze. "It's time to end this, once and for all. I'm counting on you to keep me safe."

First published in Great Britain 2012
by Mills & Boon, an imprint of Harlequin (UK) Limited,
Eton House, 18-24 Paradise Road, Richmond, Surrey TW9 1SR

© Karen Whiddon 2012

ISBN: 978 0 263 89573 5
ebook ISBN: 978 1 408 97255 7

46-1112

Harlequin (UK) policy is to use papers that are natural, renewable and recyclable products and made from wood grown in sustainable forests. The logging and manufacturing processes conform to the legal environmental regulations of the country of origin.

Printed and bound in Spain
by Blackprint CPI, Barcelona

THE COP'S MISSING CHILD

BY
KAREN WHIDDON

MILLS & BOON

Karen Whiddon started weaving fanciful tales for her younger brothers at the age of eleven. Amidst the Catskill Mountains of New York, then the Rocky Mountains of Colorado, she fueled her imagination with the natural beauty that surrounded her. Karen now lives in north Texas, where she shares her life with her very own hero of a husband and three doting dogs. Also an entrepreneur, she divides her time between the business she started and writing. You can e-mail Karen at KWhiddon1@aol.com or write to her at PO Box 820807, Fort Worth, TX 76182. Fans of her writing can also check out her website, www.karenwhiddon.com.

To my family, because they are above all the most important part of my life.

Chapter 1

The bright sun felt warm on his skin. If he'd been here for no reason other than a desire to enjoy the weather, Mac Riordan would have stopped and turned his face up to let the bright rays try to heat blood that these days always seemed chilled. Instead, he glanced around while keeping his quarry in sight, taking in the lush greenness of the park crowded with citizens enjoying the early spring air.

He couldn't believe the hunter's rush he felt at this planned-for encounter. Finally, after all this time, he'd meet the woman who had, inadvertently or not, stolen everything he had left to live for.

He'd planned this carefully, just happened to take a stroll along the tree-lined, paved walking path when the very woman he'd come to town to find strode past him on her daily walk—Emily Gilley. He'd been watching her for a week, after all, and figured an accidental meeting in the park would be a great way to meet her.

True, if he wanted this to appear unintentional, keeping up with her confident pace without looking as though he was stalking her might prove difficult, though not impossible.

He doubted she'd find him suspicious. From what he'd heard about the east Texas town of Anniversary, everyone was friendly and trusting and looked out for each other. If this was true, then Emily Gilley would have no reason to worry about a friendly stranger.

He allowed himself the slightest of grim smiles. If only she knew.

So far, he'd been careful. After all, he'd only been in town for three weeks. It was just long enough to establish his brand-new trucking business and to put out a few feelers about her, the woman he'd spent several years trying to locate: Emily Gilley, twenty-nine-year-old widow of one of the most notorious drug dealers on the Eastern Seaboard. She'd changed her name, taking back her mother's maiden name Gilley, and altered both the cut and the color of her hair, all to help her disappear. But for someone with the far-flung resources to which he had access, finding her had been a matter of time and a tenacious effort. He was fortunate to still have a lot of the tools from his law enforcement days at his disposal.

Her long, blond locks were now dark, short and spiky. Instead of designer fashions, she wore clothing that looked off the rack at a big bin department store. She'd gone from a glamorous life in Manhattan to this: a tiny lakefront community ninety miles east of Dallas.

As he hurried around a bend at the end of the trail, trying not to appear in too much of a rush, he nearly ran into her. She'd stopped at the weathered wooden bench that marked the entrance to the paved parking lot of Sue's Catfish Hut, which was crowded with lunchtime patrons.

She was stopped and turned to face him, apparently willing to wait for him to catch up.

This was going even better than he'd hoped, he thought with some satisfaction. And then he got a look at her annoyed expression.

Hands on her hips, she glared at him, her brown eyes full of anger mixed with only the barest hint of fear. "What do you want? Stop following me! If you're trying to creep me out, you're succeeding admirably."

He dipped his chin, sending her an abashed smile he hoped she'd find reassuring. "My apologies. I had no idea this was a private trail."

Instead of growing flustered, she shook her head, sending her shaggy spiked hair rippling. "It's not. But I walk here every day on my lunch break, and I know almost everyone in town. Every time I look up, you're right behind me. You never pass me or fall back. And while this is the first time I've seen you here, you have to understand how such behavior can make a woman feel threatened."

"Threatened? Interesting choice of words." He crossed his arms. "I'm new here, and I mean you no harm. I wasn't aware being a newcomer and taking a walk were crimes."

Narrowing her eyes, she studied him, apparently not buying his too-easy, confident patter. In his experience, overly suspicious or outright paranoid people usually had something to hide. But then again, she had a point. He was a stranger who was following her, and her former husband had been a drug dealer. No doubt, looking over her shoulder had been deeply ingrained in her psyche. She'd be foolish not to worry. And one thing he'd learned about Emily Gilley, formerly Cavell, was that she was anything but stupid.

Finally, she took a deep breath, exhaling it slowly.

"Look," she said, her tone reasonable this time rather than furious, "you've been following me way too closely. What matters is that you've made me very uncomfortable." Swallowing hard, she studied him, her caramel gaze unflinching. "And even though this is a small town, one can't be too careful."

It was especially true for a woman like her, with so many secrets to hide.

He nodded, feigning chagrin. "Again, I apologize. If I'd known I was frightening you, I would have dropped back or—" he grimaced ruefully "—I would have tried to pass you."

Rather than accept his apology, she straightened her shoulders and lifted her chin. "You said you're new in town, right?"

"Yes." Relieved and slightly surprised that getting to know her was going to be this simple, he gave her a practiced, easy smile, holding out his hand. "Mac Riordan."

Instead of a handshake, she simply continued to stare him down. Only when he'd dropped his hand and frowned did she speak again in a cool, measured tone. "Welcome to Anniversary, Mac Riordan. I don't know who you are or what you want, but in the future, please leave me alone.

Tamping down shock, he feigned confusion instead. "Ma'am, I—"

Backing up slightly, she tilted her head and peered up at him. "Let me ask you something. Are you the one who mailed me the note? It was postmarked Dallas. Is that where you're from?"

"Note?" He eyed her warily. Had someone tipped her off about his arrival? "What note? I have no idea what you're talking about."

"You didn't send me an anonymous note? Cut out letters on white paper?"

Was this a joke? Then, as he realized what she'd said, his former cop instincts made him ask, "Is someone sending you threatening notes?"

Again he got the sharp, brown-glass stare, as if she thought if she tried hard enough she could read his mind. Since he'd been looked at all kinds of ways by all sorts of people in his previous life in law enforcement, he let her. Silence was often the best interrogation method of all.

"You didn't answer my question. Are you from Dallas?"

"No," he fired back. "Albany, New York. Now tell me about this note."

"That's none of your business," she said calmly, her spine so rigid he thought it might snap. Then, apparently considering he might in fact be harmless, she swallowed, still eyeing him warily.

"I'm sorry. I didn't mean to be so rude. I've got to go." She mouthed the words, sounding anything but. Without another word, she marched off, her spiky dark hair ruffling in the breeze.

Watching her slender, lithe body as she went, he couldn't help but respect that she knew enough to be wary. Because if their situations had been reversed, he'd have done exactly the same. People on the run from former lives couldn't afford to befriend curious strangers.

This was exactly the reason he had to make sure he gained her trust—no matter what it took.

Even as she hurried away, Emily Gilley felt the tall, dark-haired stranger's gaze boring into her back. She felt flushed and hot, though not entirely from her brisk walk. Instead, she worried about the man with the striking cobalt eyes. At first glance, the tinge of gray in his hair had made him look older by at least a decade. But up close, his rugged face appeared to be only a few years older than she. Mid-thirties, perhaps, a handsome, muscular man who moved with easy grace. Any other woman would have been intrigued by his blatant masculinity, his self-confident virility.

Not she…she knew better. Sex on the hoof didn't last past the morning, and men like him were nothing but trouble. After all, she'd been married to one once.

This man singled her out. Why? She couldn't help but wonder if this attempt to appear older was deliberate, an effort to camouflage who he really was—or *what* he was.

He was a threat. She couldn't believe his sudden appearance the same day after getting her first threat since moving here was a mere coincidence. How could it be?

The unsigned note that had appeared in her mailbox that morning had been similar to the ones she used to get back in New York. Letters cut and pasted from a magazine, the three sentences read exactly like the ones she'd received before. Her stalker—and Ryan's, for the note always mentioned her five-year-old son by name—had somehow found her here, in an innocuous small Texas town.

This meant it was time to move on.

She considered, suddenly exhausted by it all, she could run again. Or she could stay—and fight.

Because quite frankly, she liked living here in Anniversary, Texas. She'd made friends, and while her receptionist job at Tearmann's Animal Clinic wasn't glamorous, she loved the sheer ordinariness of it. All in all, she'd made a cozy home for herself and her son here.

Damned if she would give that up without a battle. She'd paid enough for crimes she hadn't even committed. Never mind that she'd been completely clueless about her husband's nefarious activities. A lot of people thought she should still be held equally responsible, especially now that Carlos was dead.

Without any idea why, she'd always assumed the threatening notes had come from one of Carlos's mistresses. She knew of two, and there'd probably been more. Any one of them could have viewed his death as a breach of promise and his wife as the rival who got everything—especially since Emily had always suspected one of those women had been the one to birth her son and give him up for adoption, no doubt at Carlos's urging. She could only hope he hadn't forced the issue, which would mean there was another woman out there mourning the loss of her son.

Even though Emily could definitely sympathize if that was the case, she was Ryan's mother now, and she'd made a good home for him here. The only thing she wanted to do was pretend her former life had never happened. All she'd brought with her from that life was her son. He was all that mattered.

Hurrying from the walking trail and across the parking lot to Sue's Catfish Hut, she refused to look over her shoulder at the man. She sensed him still standing where she'd left him, watching her. She could feel his gaze burning into her back.

"Afternoon, Letty." Lifting her hand in a friendly wave to the elderly cashier, Emily slid inside the empty booth. She spent quite a few of her sixty-minute lunches exactly the same way—a brisk walk around the park and then a bite to eat at Sue's with her friend Jayne Cooper.

"Hey, lady." Jayne plopped into the seat opposite her. Jayne's normally frizzy blond hair had been tied back in a ponytail. She worked in the police station down the street, one of three dispatchers. "Who was that man you were talking to in the park? He looks like that new guy who moved here from up north somewhere. I can't remember his name."

Surprised, Emily tensed and then forced herself to relax. Good grief, she was tired of being suspicious of everything and everyone. She'd honestly believed she'd gotten over that, until the stalker's note timed with the appearance of the strange man had brought all her old fears back to life.

"He said his name is Mac Riordan. He said he's new in town."

"That's right, he is." Snapping her fingers, Jayne nodded. "Everyone in the sheriff's office has been talking about him. Apparently, he and Renee Beauchamp go way back. He moved here a couple of weeks ago and opened a trucking company. He bought the Stamflin place out on FM 3356."

Emily simply nodded. "So he's legit then?"

Now Jayne studied her closely. "As opposed to what? Some crazed serial killer? You are the biggest worry-wart I know."

Somehow, Emily managed to effect a careless shrug.

"That comes from living in Manhattan. You can't be too careful there."

As Jayne was about to speak—no doubt to launch into her favorite topic, the bliss of bucolic existence in Anniversary—their friend Tina appeared with two tall glasses of iced tea. "Here you go, ladies. Are you both having the usual today?"

"Yes," Emily and Jayne answered in unison.

"Good." Grinning widely, Tina winked. "I already put in the order ticket. Lord, help me if you ever decide to walk on the wild side and try something else."

Just then, the front door opened, and the noisy dining room went abruptly quiet for a moment before the noise level resumed. Emily's heart sank. Mac Riordan's large frame filled the doorway and he scanned the room.

When his gaze connected with hers, Emily tensed, resisting the urge to duck under the table. Just because the man decided to have his lunch at the same place didn't make him her stalker. Right?

"Oooh, my," Jayne breathed. "Emily, honey, why didn't you mention that he is absolutely gorgeous?"

"You saw him in the park."

"From a distance, Em. Only from a distance."

"Emily? You know him?" Tina asked sharply.

When Emily shook her head, Tina narrowed her heavily made-up eyes. "You're blushing," she pointed out. "Why is that?"

Blushing? It was true that her face felt warm, but Emily never blushed. "I just met him a few minutes ago in the park, that's all," she said, aware she sounded as if she was trying too hard to be casual.

"Uh-huh." Clearly believing there was more to the story, Tina nodded. "I'm calling an immediate lady's night this Friday. Mexican food and margaritas. I can't wait to hear all about this."

"There's nothing to tell," Emily began. "I…" The words caught in her throat as Mac began slowly making his way toward her booth, drawing the gaze of every busybody in the restaurant—in other words, just about everyone.

Jayne and Tina grew wide-eyed as he approached them. Idly, Emily wondered why it seemed every woman in the restaurant appeared to be drooling, then pushed the thought away.

Her skin prickled as he dipped his chin at Tina, then Jayne, before facing Emily. "I'd like to have a word with you, if you don't mind," he said in a quiet yet authorative voice.

"I'm about to eat lunch," Emily told him firmly, refusing to look at either of her friends, though she could feel them staring in astonishment.

"Fair enough. How about after?"

Most of the other patrons in the restaurant made no attempt to hide their avid eavesdropping. Slightly desperate, Emily hesitated. She hated to think that this one chance encounter could undermine all of her attempts to fit in this town.

"Fine," she finally said, just to make him go away. "Now please, let me eat my lunch in peace."

For an answer, he dipped his chin again, then moved away to take a seat at the bar. She couldn't help but notice he'd chosen his stool with care, claiming the one closest to the front door so he could stop her if she tried to make an escape.

"Well, well, well," Tina said. "I think there's a lot more to tell us about than a chance meeting in the park."

The kitchen chose that moment to ring the bell, signaling Tina that she had an order up. Relieved, Emily watched her go, aware she'd been temporarily spared from answering. Not that there was anything to tell, though she knew her friends would never believe that.

As Tina left to fetch their lunch, Jayne regarded Emily curiously. "Are you all right?" she asked. "You look a bit pale."

Keeping her hands under the table so her friend wouldn't see her wringing them, Emily frowned. "I don't understand why he wants to talk to me. I've already said everything I need to say when I ran into him in the park."

"Which was?" Jayne prompted.

"Basically, to leave me alone."

"Wow. Way to win friends and make enemies."

"Oh, come on." Irritated, Emily eyed Tina making her way toward them with their lunch. "You would have done the same if you'd been walking alone and some man started following you."

Jayne shook her head, dislodging pieces of her ponytail. "Sweetie, he's drop-dead, to-die-for hot. What's wrong with you?"

"And he followed me relentlessly. Even in here. Tell me you don't think that's weird."

This prompted Jayne to snort inelegantly. "That kind of weird is like a gift from heaven. I mean, look at him!"

Tina reached their table and set down their catfish in front of them. "Here you go, girls. Have you noticed every single woman in here is eyeing your Mr. Tall, Dark and Handsome?"

"He's not mine." Picking up her fork, Emily stabbed a corn bread hush puppy with her fork, popping it into her mouth to discourage further questions. As she chewed, she studiously avoided looking in the direction of the lunch bar.

Jayne and Tina had no such compunction.

"Well, if you don't want him, mind if I have a try?" Tina finally drawled, her east Texas twang as thick as syrup.

"Go right ahead," Emily answered once she'd finished chewing. "Just be careful he doesn't murder you in your sleep."

"Emily!" both women chided.

"You've got to get over that paranoia." Shaking her head, then her hips, Tina sashayed away. Emily picked at her food, her appetite gone.

"You really are upset about this, aren't you?" Jayne asked, taking another bite of the crisp golden fish.

"I'll be fine." Her automatic answer, made even now to a woman she counted among her friends, meant she wasn't. But her self-protective instincts, awakened after the craziness that had followed her husband's death, refused to stay dormant for long. Experience had taught her nothing was ever as it seemed.

"Are you going to talk to him after we eat?"

Emily took a long drink of her iced tea. "I guess so. Hopefully, I can convince him to leave me alone."

"Maybe he just wants to ask you out on a date."

Emily's forced laugh told her friend what she thought of that idea. "No. He doesn't. Believe me."

From her expression, Jayne clearly didn't. "Do you want me to come with you when you talk to him?"

Surprised and grateful, Emily touched the back of Jayne's hand. "No, but thank you for offering."

The sympathy in Jayne's eyes made Emily's throat close up. Trying to regain her equilibrium, she stabbed a piece of fish and forced herself to chew it.

"Sometimes you remind me of Rocco," Jayne said. "When we got him from the Boxer rescue, he was terrified of every move we made."

At her friend's analogy, Emily had to smile. "You're comparing me to your dog?"

"Believe me when I say that's the highest compliment I could pay you. It took Rocco six months to begin to trust me. I've known you four and a half years, and I still wonder if you'll ever stop being shocked at the kindness of others," Jayne mused. "I know you don't like to talk about your past, but you seem to be wound a bit too tight. If you ever need someone to lend an ear…"

This line of conversation, while hardly new, had the potential to go on for hours. Over time, she'd told both her best friends about her past, at least the part before Carlos. Unlike Ryan, she hadn't been fortunate enough to be adopted. Due to poor health and a variety of childhood diseases, she hadn't even been shuttled from foster home to foster home. Instead, she'd spent her childhood in an orphanage, venturing out into the world alone as soon as she turned eighteen. She'd met Carlos shortly after that, and the whirlwind courtship and marriage had seemed exactly what she'd needed.

Ah, the naivete of youth. Emily checked her watch. She had ten minutes left before she had to return to work.

Tapping her watch face and shaking her head at her friend, she ate a couple more bites of her fish before blotting her mouth with her napkin.

"I've got to go, or I'll be late," she said, tossing her payment on the table.

"What about him?" Still eating, Jayne jerked her head in Mac Riordan's direction. "You told him you'd talk to him. And since you can't get out the door without going past him…"

Though she already knew the time, Emily made a big show of checking her watch once more. "I hope he can make this quick and painless."

Still, despite her misgivings, her mouth went dry the closer she got to him. Mac stood as she approached, placing his money on the counter and falling into step with her as they headed out the door. Though her heartbeat immediately started racing, she kept her face expressionless and waited until they'd emerged into the bright spring sunshine before speaking.

"All right," she told him. "I work down the street, and I have five minutes left on my lunch break. What do you want?"

Instead of answering, he took her arm. Immediately, she tensed, causing him to drop his hand. He shot her a look but didn't comment on her defensive body language.

"Let's walk and talk," he said.

Without responding, she set off at a brisk pace for the vet clinic. She hated the way she felt hyperaware of him, hated the way a single glance at him made her insides go all weak and warm.

When they'd covered half the distance without him telling her what he wanted, she finally stopped and turned to face him. "Why do you need to talk to me?" Though she spoke in a soft voice, she made sure a thread of steel ran through it. "I don't know you, and I'd like to keep it that way."

"You mentioned a threatening letter," he began.

"I never said it was *threatening.*" Despite the alarm bells clanging inside her head, she still felt an insistent tug of attraction.

"Cut out letters? Come on. Why else would you ask if I mailed it to you?" he said in a reasonable tone. "I'm new in town, and we've never met before today, so that's the only way your question makes sense."

Put that way, he sort of had a point. But his supposed concern didn't excuse his odd behavior. At one time, she would have allowed herself to feel flattered. Now she could only feel threatened. "Look, you've been following me. First on the walking path, then you came into the restaurant and made a public scene."

Now he tilted his head. "That was not a scene. I have nothing to hide. Do you?"

She shuddered, unable to conceal her reaction. "If that's not creepy, stalkerish behavior, I don't know what it is. So I'll ask you one more time, what do you want?"

"To help you."

"Of course you do." Unable to rein in her sarcastic response, she crossed her arms. "Out of the goodness of your heart, right? You don't even know me. And I sure as hell don't know you."

"Cop instincts, I guess. I used to be a detective in the Albany Police Department. Your sheriff's department can vouch for me."

Wearily, she nodded. Jayne had said something of the sort. "You still haven't told me what you want."

"I'd like to offer my services," he said, his gaze steady.

"No, thanks." She shook her head.

"For a fee, if that will make you feel better. If you need protection, I can help."

Dumbfounded despite herself, Emily looked away. Whatever she'd expected him to say, it hadn't been this. The idea of having help of some kind—any kind—felt so seductive that she nearly swayed with relief.

But she didn't…because she knew better. Despite his movie-star good looks and the tug of sexual attraction she felt when she looked at him, she couldn't afford to trust him. She couldn't allow herself the luxury of letting her guard down. The sins of her husband's past were too numerous.

"Look, I appreciate your offer." Softening her voice, she tried to appear as if she meant it. "In reality, I had a couple of blind dates with a guy who liked me way more than I liked him. I'm pretty sure that's all this is."

Devilishly handsome, he studied her. With his hawk-like features and his too-sharp blue eyes, everything about him spoke of inherent strength. Ah, but she knew better than most how appearances could be deceiving.

"Give me his name, and I'll talk to him," he said. "If it is him, I'll make sure he doesn't bother you again."

She recoiled, unable to help herself. Her late husband had been such a man, promising to take care of her, keeping her shielded from the rest of the world. At first, she'd found this charming. It wasn't until later that she'd realized she'd been slowly suffocating.

And when she'd found out her entire marriage, her entire life had all been nothing but a pack of lies, she'd known she shouldn't have been surprised. But she was. And hurt and betrayed. She'd vowed she'd never be so blind again.

This was why, even though this man's rugged profile made her want to melt inside, she wanted to play it safe and send him away—with a smile, if possible.

Because the last thing she needed was to make another enemy. God knows she had made enough of those already, thanks to Carlos.

Chapter 2

Careful not to flash a confident smile, Mac waited for Emily to accept his offer. Though he'd never been anyone's bodyguard, he felt he'd do a superb job. Being a former cop had its advantages.

"No, thank you," she said instead and then turned and hurried inside Tearmann's Animal Clinic, leaving him standing alone on the sidewalk. Scratching his head, he grimaced, wondering why he'd even thought this would be easy. Years of experience should have taught him that nothing ever was.

Turning, he headed back toward the parking lot where he'd left his pickup truck. The other day he'd been talking to his friend and former partner Joe, who still worked for the Albany P.D. Joe had speculated that someone like Emily Gilley was a chameleon. She could change everything about herself to suit the place and

the occasion. Now that he'd met her, Mac thought Joe
might be dead-on accurate about this.

He'd have to regroup and replan. His quarry was nervous and wary—and rightfully so. He'd been watching
her from a distance ever since he'd arrived in Anniversary. Despite the time he'd put in learning about her and
her routine, he'd yet to catch a glimpse of Ryan, the boy
she passed off as her son.

This, he vowed silently, would become his number
one priority.

Heart pounding and hands shaking, Emily walked
over to the front desk, summoning a smile for Sally,
the gum-chewing redhead who covered the reception
area every day while Emily had lunch.

"You look like you've seen a ghost. Are you all
right?" Sally asked, tilting her head and peering at
Emily with concern.

"I'm fine," Emily lied, managing a limp smile. "It's
kind of hot outside, and I think I got kind of dehy-
drated, that's all."

Immediately, the older woman's frown cleared. "I'll
bring you a bottle of water from the back." She hurried off, leaving a trail of strong perfume in her wake.

As soon as she was gone, Emily sank down in her
chair. She fought against instinct—the urge to run
away, to quit her job, drive home immediately, pack
her and Ryan's things and get the hell out of Texas. She
wanted to run…again…away from anything she per-
ceived as a threat…away from him.

She took a few deep breaths. Sally returned, bearing the promised water. As Emily opened her mouth
to speak, the phone rang. Waving her thanks to Sally,

Emily answered, keeping her voice steady and professionally polite.

After she completed that booking—a morning spay—some clients came in: the Jones family with their three pugs. After that, a steady stream of phone calls and customers kept her busy. Somehow the afternoon flew by without her once thinking about Mac Riordan and the danger of his beautiful, casual smile.

Finally, the last appointment left and Emily locked the front door. She rushed through her normal closing duties, straightening the waiting room magazines and making sure the front door glass was smudge free. If she hurried, she'd make it to Mim's Day Care where her son attended the after school program half an hour before closing time, and she and Ryan could swing by the grocery store and pick up the boxes of macaroni and cheese she'd been promising to make him, along with his beloved hot dogs, for supper.

The next morning, Emily woke with a renewed sense of purpose. She refused to allow herself to be run out of town. She just had to figure out the best way to fight. Sure, Mac Riordan was handsome and a charmer, but Carlos had been the same. She knew how to deal with men like him, even if it meant pushing away the simmering attraction she felt for him.

Feeling strong, she went to wake Ryan.

She sat down on the edge of his rumpled bed and watched him sleep, her heart bursting with love. As usual, seconds after she touched his shoulder, her son opened his eyes wide and held out his arms from a hug. Her throat clogged and her eyes filled as she wrapped her arms around him, breathing in the shampoo scent in his clean hair.

"I love you, mama," he murmured, his voice full of sleep and sounding younger than his five years.

She cleared her throat, smiling mistily. "I love you too, Ryan."

As she poured him cereal, a good compromise between the sugary one he'd wanted and the totally healthy one she had chosen, she found herself taking comfort in the familiar routine. No matter what kind of day she had at work, sharing her mornings with Ryan and looking forward to the evening ahead kept her motivated to have a positive day.

After breakfast, she followed him to his room to check out his clothing choices. Once she'd approved those, which happened more and more often these days, she grabbed the car key, buckled her son in his car seat and left.

"Have a good day." Leaning down to kiss her squirming son's cheek, she breathed in the apple juice and soap scent of him and wished the knot in her chest would ease.

"I will." Ryan shifted from one foot to the other, clearly eager to hurry inside his kindergarten classroom but equally loathe to abandon his mother.

"Go on, then." She gave him a tiny push, smiling as he tore off without another glance at her.

Looking at her watch as she left the elementary school, she waved at Mrs. Parsons, the assistant principal who always took morning duty at the front door, before hurrying to her car. The small gray Honda had been old when she'd purchased it, but it was clean, dent-free and it ran well, which was all she cared about. Every day she had to get Ryan to school and then pick him up from day care after. That, combined with her job and weekly trips to the grocery store, didn't seem to be more than the little car could handle.

Now though, she had one more errand she wanted to run before she had to be at work. Emily planned to pay a visit to the sheriff's office. One thing she'd learned being married to Carlos had been that the squeaky wheel got the grease. If she didn't push, she knew they'd ignore her worries over the anonymous letter. They had no idea of her life story and the reason she took such things seriously, and if she had her way, they never would. That said, she had no intention of ending up one of those horrific stories you see on the evening news.

She'd make sure the Anniversary Police Department viewed her threatening letter as...well, as threatening as she did.

Already in her office, Renee Beauchamp looked up as Emily approached. Though her brown eyes appeared bright, the faint dark circles under told a different story.

"Good morning," Emily said firmly, stepping into the sheriff's office uninvited and taking a seat in one of the two chrome-and-cloth chairs facing the desk. "I'd like a moment of your time."

Renee nodded, her expression showing nothing but professional interest. "What can I do for you, Ms. Gilley?"

"I'm here to find out what you've learned about the letter." Another trick Emily had learned was to state things as though they were fact, rather than ask questions. This conveyed both a sense of confidence and of purpose.

"Nothing, actually." Renee steepled her fingers on the desk in front of her. "We've had very little to go on, and since there was no specific threat—"

"Oh, but there was," Emily interrupted firmly. Pulling her copy from her purse, she read the relevant line. *"I know what you've done. You've stolen what is mine and you'll pay for what you did. Tell the truth, or risk everything."*

Nodding, Renee leaned forward. "While I appreciate and understand your concern, the letter is too vague. If, for example, it read 'I'm going to plant a bomb in your garage' or something, we'd have cause to act. But the wording 'you'll pay' conveys nothing."

Biting back an instinctive response, Emily swallowed back her anger. Just because the sheriff spoke factually didn't mean she didn't have a private, visceral reaction. As a woman, she must. Emily knew she had to appeal to this if she wanted help.

"Do you have children, Renee?" Emily asked softly.

A quick shadow appeared in Renee's eyes, then vanished. "No, I don't."

She held up her hand as Emily opened her mouth to speak. "But that doesn't mean I don't get where you're coming from."

"Then how can you tell me it's not a threat?"

"Because the letter did not directly threaten you or your son," Renee said gently. "And if you read it again, you'll see there is absolutely no specific threat in there—at all."

Incredulous, Emily had to force herself to close her mouth. "You honestly don't believe 'you'll pay for taking him' puts me—or him—in any danger?"

"Ms. Gilley—"

Bulldozing through whatever platitude the other woman was about to offer, Emily stood. "Ryan is adopted, Renee. I know you had no way of knowing that, but I can't help feel this letter is somehow related to that."

A tiny frown appeared between the sheriff's perfectly arched eyebrows. She sat up straighter, giving Emily a piercing look. "All right. I'll check it out. I'll need to ask you a few questions."

"Of course." Emily watched while Renee grabbed a pen and pad.

"Did you go through a service, or was the adoption privately arranged?"

"It was private." Emily managed to sound confident. "My former husband—I'm a widow—handled everything. But I located all the records he gave me back then and would be glad to provide you with copies."

"I'd like that." The sheriff stood, holding out her hand. "Just bring them by at your earliest convenience."

Standing also, Emily shook hands. It was almost time for her to head to work. "Thank you. I will."

"Have a good day."

"Oh, I have one last question." Turning in the doorway, Emily tried for both a casual expression and carefree voice. "What do you know about Mac Riordan?"

To her surprise, Renee laughed. "He's an okay sort of guy. He's new in town, and I don't know him that well, though my friend Joe speaks highly of him. Mac used to be a cop, up in Albany, which is where Joe works. I heard Mac kind of spooked you a bit."

"He did, a little." With a cheery wave and a manufactured smile, Emily let herself out, sighing. The damn letter had succeeded in erasing nearly four and a half years of security, all at once. Mac Riordan's appearance had made things even worse. After all, Albany was only several hours north of Manhattan.

She didn't just have her own security to worry about.

She had to keep her son safe. Clearly she had a decision to make—and quickly.

Once at work, Emily pushed the letter from her mind…and Mac Riordan, as well. Though as her lunch hour approached and she prepared to head out for her daily walk, she couldn't help but think of him. Surely he'd taken the hint and wouldn't show up in the park today.

If he did, she'd have to accept that he was stalking her. And then she'd have to quit her job, pick up Ryan and go home and pack, running away in the middle of the night without a single goodbye to anyone.

Heart pounding and feeling queasy at the thought, she shook her head. Maybe if she tried to think logically, it was possible the man simply liked her. She'd felt a sort of electrical connection, despite having all her barriers up. From the way he'd looked at her, blue eyes dark and full of promise, he'd felt it, too. Exhaling, she laced up her sneakers and nevertheless prayed he wouldn't be there.

He wasn't. The pressure in her chest and the sick feeling in her stomach eased a little as she enjoyed a quiet, uninterrupted walk. The sun shone brightly; a few white, fluffy clouds dotted the sky like sheep; and birds sang, dogs barked, and people all around her enjoyed the bright spring day.

After, perspiring slightly and feeling pretty good, she stepped into Sue's Catfish Hut and greeted her friends. As she took her usual seat, she couldn't help but do a quick scan of the restaurant for a sight of those broad shoulders and dark gray hair.

Again, Mac Riordan was conspicuously absent. For the first time all day, she allowed herself to relax, even though a tiny part of her felt disappointed at his absence. She enjoyed her meal, chatting with Jayne and Tina and sipping iced tea.

She went back to work with a light step, allowing herself to believe everything just might turn out to be all right. By the end of the workday, she felt almost normal.

After helping close up the veterinary clinic, she hopped in her car and headed over to the day care.

As soon as she arrived, Ryan flung himself at her, holding on to her legs with a fierce grip.

"Finally," he groused. "It took you forever to pick me up. I'm all played out."

She couldn't help but laugh at his choice of words. The after school programs at Mims's Day Care tended to lean toward organized games, most of them physical. The tall trees made the heavily shaded playground the perfect place for youngsters to run off pent-up aggressions or simply play.

"Well, now you get to rest," she said. "Grab your stuff and we'll go."

He did as she asked, snatching up his camo backpack and waving goodbye to his friends.

Once she'd buckled him into his booster seat, she climbed in the front and started the engine.

"How's a tuna casserole sound for dinner?" This should be a sure hit since he always loved the one she made, using the leftover mac and cheese from last night and adding a can of peas and a can of tuna.

"No. I want a Good Times meal." Looking mutinous, little Ryan crossed his arms and lifted his chin. "With fries. No tuna."

Tired as she might be, still Emily managed to summon a smile for her son. "Rough day at school?" she asked, leaning over the backseat and ruffling his hair.

"Yep. And at Mim's, too. I'm tired of playing."

This was a new one. "Tired of playing? You? Why?"

"Because they always make me be the bad guy."

Emily blinked. "Really? Why?"

He looked away, his lower lip quivering. "I dunno. Mommy, can we please get a Good Times meal?"

Though she'd planned on making the casserole and eating it for a couple of days, she relented. "Sure, I guess I'll just get a salad or something."

Apparently everyone's children wanted Good Times meals. The drive-thru line had six cars already waiting. Emily debated going inside, but judging from the crowded interior, she'd be better off waiting in her car—especially since Ryan kept fidgeting, whining and protesting he was too big for a booster seat, even though the law stated he had to weigh a hundred pounds before graduated to just being buckled into the seat belt.

"You've still got some growing to do," she informed him.

"I haven't been weighed lately," he said huffily. "Now I'm a big boy. I bet I weigh a hundred and five now."

Considering him solemnly, she somehow kept from smiling. "Okay," she finally said. "When we get home, we'll check."

He pumped his little fist up in the air. "And next time I go in the car, I can buckle up like a big person?"

"If you weigh over one hundred." Which she knew he didn't.

"And I can ride in the front with you?"

"We'll see." Finally, they reached the window. Placing her order, she glanced back at her son, who'd finally fallen quiet. He was staring at something in the parking lot. As she followed his gaze, she recoiled. Mac Riordan stood next to a large white pickup truck, talking to another man. As far as she could tell, he hadn't seen her.

Struggling to hide her fear, she handed the money to the window cashier, accepted her order and put the car in Drive. Heart pounding, she pulled away, using only her rearview mirror to make sure she hadn't been spotted.

All the way home, jumpy and unsettled, she kept checking to make sure they weren't being followed. Nothing out of the ordinary occurred, and they pulled into the driveway slowly.

Not for the first time, Emily wished she could afford an automatic garage door opener. How much simpler and safer it would be to just hit a button, pull into the concealed garage and close the door behind you, all before even getting out of the car.

If she stayed in Anniversary, she'd have to put money aside to buy one.

Parking, she gave the rearview mirror one final check before unlocking the doors. The smell of fast-food made her stomach growl, and she was glad she'd opted for a grilled chicken sandwich instead of a salad. She needed something a bit more substantial today, especially since she knew she wouldn't be getting much sleep.

Making decisions had never been her strong suit. She literally had to force herself to act at times—especially if she didn't have a clear picture of potential repercussions.

She wished she could be one of those kinds of people who could go with their gut, trusting their instinct. Not her...she always required the facts.

Helping Ryan out of the car, she took his hand. Together, they walked up the sidewalk to the front of their circa 1960 rental house. Then she realized something was wrong.

"Hold on." Grasping Ryan's hand firmly, she stopped. "Don't move."

Though she'd locked it securely that morning, the front door was slightly ajar and obviously unlocked. Someone had been—or was still—inside her house.

Chapter 3

Since Emily wouldn't hire him as her bodyguard, Mac knew it was time to go to plan B. He sauntered into the Anniversary Police Department, intent on asking Renee for a job. To his surprise, she sat at the front desk in the receptionist's chair, typing up something on a decrepit manual typewriter.

"You got a minute?" he asked.

"Sure." Pinning him with her direct gaze, she dragged a hand through her short hair. "Perfect timing, Riordan. I've been meaning to call you and ask you to come in. Follow me," she ordered, jumping to her feet and giving Mac a hard look as though she thought he might run off.

When they reached her office, she took a seat behind her desk and indicated he should sit in what he thought of as the suspect's chair...interesting.

Taking a seat, he leaned back, crossing his arms.

He'd let her go first, since obviously she had something on her mind.

In typical cop fashion, Renee got right to the point. "How well do you know Emily Gilley?"

"I've only met her one time, in the park." It was a truthful answer—especially since Renee didn't need to know about all the research Mac had done to find her, and more importantly, to find Ryan.

"You seemed very interested in her."

He spread his hands. "What can I say? She's a pretty lady." Again, he only spoke the truth.

Renee seemed to sense this—or at least, he hoped she did. "You know, Riordan, I'm just doing my job. I actually believe you."

"Good to know." He allowed a slight smile. "I did offer to be her bodyguard. She turned me down flat."

Staring, Renee narrowed her eyes. Then, apparently deciding he was serious, she dipped her head, grinning. "I should tell you that I ran a check on you and talked to your former partner back in Albany. Joe and I go way back. He had nothing bad to say about you."

It was unsurprising. Joe was his best friend, and Mac had been a very good police officer. He would still be, if he hadn't left his job. But Joe had understood that finding Ryan had become more important to him than anything else.

"And on top of that," Renee continued, "Joe put me through to your lieutenant. Just like our mutual friend Joe, your former boss speaks very highly of you."

"Good to know." Aware of his precarious position, he debated whether or not now would be a good time to broach his proposal. On the one hand, if Emily and Ryan were in serious danger, then he couldn't afford to wait. On the other, he didn't want to do anything that would make Renee even more suspicious of him.

To his surprise, Renee broached the subject for him. Dragging her hand through her cropped blond hair, she tapped her pen several times on her pad of paper. "Emily's scared. I'm beginning to think she might have a good reason to be. Unfortunately, we're really short-handed here."

Though her words kick-started his heart into over-drive, he held himself perfectly still and merely nodded.

Appropriately encouraged, she continued. "I know you have a trucking business to run and all, but would you consider coming to work for me part-time? Like a few hours a week?"

While he pretended to consider her offer, she tossed out what for him clenched the deal. "I'd really like you to handle the Emily Gilley case exclusively."

A thousand thoughts raced through Emily's mind. First and foremost, she had to keep her son safe.

"Don't move," she repeated.

"But I'm hungry," Ryan started to whine, raising his face to hers. Something he saw in her expression must have gotten through to him, because he instantly went silent.

"What's wrong, Mama?" he whispered, his blue eyes huge in his small face. "Is everything okay?"

No, everything was not okay—though she didn't say that out loud to her five-year-old. "I don't know yet," she said instead, moving them backward. "I think we need to get back in the car and call the sheriff."

She wouldn't panic. She couldn't, even though she knew if her front door was open that someone had been in her house.

Backing out of her driveway, she drove to the corner gas station and mini-mart and parked.

"Go ahead and start on your Good Times meal, honey," she told Ryan, handing the brightly decorated box back to him. "Remember, no toy until you finish your meal."

She waited until he was happily munching away before taking a deep breath and pulling her phone from her purse.

Keeping the doors locked and the engine running, she made the call. When she asked to be put through directly to Renee, the dispatcher immediately did so—yet another difference between living in a large city and a small town.

Speaking quietly and calmly so she wouldn't alarm Ryan, she told Renee what had happened. "I didn't go inside," she said. "I have no idea if anyone is still in there."

"That's a wise move," Renee said. "Where are you now?"

Emily relayed her location.

"Stay put. We'll meet you there in less than five minutes," the sheriff promised. "The car will be an unmarked cruiser. No lights or sirens."

"All right." Disconnecting the call, Emily shoved her phone back into her purse and eyed her sandwich. It now looked wilted and completely unappetizing, though probably due more to the circumstances than the actual appearance. Even the thought of trying to eat made her stomach roil.

Law enforcement pulled up just over four minutes later, the unmarked Chevrolet still looking official and police-like. It was not Renee, Emily realized, but another officer, which was unusual since the Anniversary Police Department was so small.

Squinting, Emily tried to make him out. The passenger door opened, and a familiar dark-haired, broad-shouldered man emerged. She squinted, certain she wasn't seeing correctly. But as he approached, she realized that Mac Riordan, while not decked out in a crisply pressed navy police uniform, wore a police badge pinned to his button-down shirt.

As he walked toward her car, she was struck once again by the way he exuded masculinity. He was one of those men who, with one glance at their steely gaze, could make a woman feel safe and protected.

Foolishness, she chided herself. Nevertheless, her mouth went dry as he approached. Mac Riordan looked…different. She waited in silence until he reached her.

As if he sensed her confusion, he gave her a reassuring smile. "I'm working for the sheriff's office part-time. Renee asked me to handle your case."

Stunned, at first Emily didn't know how to respond. "But—"

Interrupting, his rich voice washed over her like waves in a storm. "I can assure you I'm completely qualified. I spent ten years at the Albany Police Department, working my way up from patrol to homicide detective."

"I'm sure you are," she said faintly.

Relief warring with trepidation, she opened her door.

But as she started to get out of her car, Mac waved her back.

"I want you to follow me, all right? I'm going to ask you to remain in your car while I make sure your home is safe."

Swallowing hard, Emily nodded. She had to be careful to hide any evidence of fear from her son, who watched the exchange with wide, curious eyes.

"Why are the police here, Mommy?"

Putting the car in Drive, she again checked her mirrors before pulling away. "Because I think someone might have been inside our house, honey."

He cocked his head, apparently unable to decide how to take this news. "A bad person?" he finally asked

"Maybe." She shrugged, as if this was not important. "We have no way of knowing. That's why we're letting the police check this out first."

"Maybe it was a bear!" Giggling, Ryan made a roaring sound. "Or maybe a deer got inside like that video we watched on the computer one time."

Thank goodness for his vivid imagination and his innocence. "Maybe," she allowed, even though there were no bears anywhere near their part of the country, unless one counted the bears living in the Dallas Zoo. "I guess we'll just have to wait and see."

"Can we take a video of our own, Mommy? Pleeeease?"

"We'll see." She gave him a reassuring smile, just in case he sensed her jangled nerves. "Let's wait until we find out what exactly got inside, okay?"

Nodding, he resumed playing with the little plastic airplane that had come with his meal.

An eternity passed, but finally they reached her street. The police car pulled into her driveway, and Mac motioned to Emily to park in the street one house down. She did as he asked, unwilling to take any chances with her son's safety.

Heart in her throat, she watched as Mac got out and headed toward her house. As he went around to the backyard, Emily turned around to distract Ryan, not wanting him to notice that Mac had drawn his gun.

"Let's go ahead and eat, honey," she urged watching as he tore into his Good Times meal.

While he ate, she alternated between keeping an eye on him and watching her house. Trying to will her heartbeat to slow down, she took a tiny bite of her grilled chicken sandwich. Chewing what tasted like ashes, she managed to choke it down and swallowed hard, setting her food aside.

Ryan had finished his burger and half his fries and was already restless. "Mommy? What is the policeman doing inside our house?" he asked, squirming in his seat. "Can we go inside yet?"

About to answer, she spotted Mac heading toward her car, his large form making her feel ridiculously safe. "Just a minute, sweetheart."

Rolling down the window, Emily peered up at the handsome man, trying not to hold her breath. "Well?"

"You've been burglarized," he said grimly. "Though I can't tell for sure what they were after. Your TV, stereo and computer were all untouched."

"Jewelry, maybe?" A lot of the more valuable pieces in Emily's collection had been given to her by Carlos, so she wouldn't mind too badly if they'd been stolen. After all, she had renter's insurance.

"I don't think so," he answered, his professional expression warring with the heat in his blue eyes. He glanced once at Ryan, then quickly back to her, keeping his gaze fixed on her face.

"Is it safe to go inside?" she asked, hating the note of breathlessness that had crept into her voice and hoping he put it down to her being upset about the break-in.

For an answer, he opened her door. "Come on. The

house is clear. I'll have you take a look, but glancing quickly through your things, it doesn't appear the intruder touched anything."

"Then why—" Emily started to ask, then looked down, reeling in shock. Suddenly, she *knew* exactly why the intruder had been in her home.

When she raised her head again to meet Mac's gaze, she hoped her expression was calm. "In my office—" she began, ignoring his proffered hand and climbing out of the car.

"What about me?" Ryan asked, fumbling with his seat belt. "I wanna go, too."

Emily glanced at Mac, receiving a nod of confirmation that it was safe. He seemed to be making a studious effort to avoid looking at her son, which, since it made no sense, was probably a figment of her imagination. "Of course you can come. We're home, after all. We're safe here." She emphasized the word *safe,* so Mac would not say anything unduly alarming within Ryan's hearing.

"Good." Her five-year-old sounded unfazed, cheerful rather than frightened. He jumped out of the car, landing on both feet with a solid *splunk.*

"Hey, there," Mac said from behind her, making her start slightly, which Ryan noticed. When he looked up, he saw the unfamiliar man for the first time. Pulling on her leg, her son tried to disappear behind her.

"Honey, it's all right," she soothed. "This is Deputy Riordan. He's here to help us find out who broke into our house."

Ryan peeked out from around her leg. Glancing from her boy to the man who now crouched down to put himself at Ryan's level, she was surprised to see a look of naked, awful pain on Mac's craggy face.

She was about to ask him what was wrong but forced herself to hold her tongue.

"Go ahead and say hello to the nice policeman," she urged softly.

Holding himself rigidly, her brave little boy eased out and around her and then held out his hand. "I'm Ryan Gilley," he said politely, exactly as she'd taught him.

Gently taking the small hand, Mac swallowed hard as he shook it. Again, she realized he appeared to be in the throes of some deep, strong emotion, which made her wonder if she'd been right, and he'd actually lost a child.

"Pleased to meet you, Ryan," Mac finally said, his voice husky. "I like your backpack."

This was exactly the right comment to make. Ryan had spent hours searching for the perfect backpack. He'd ignored the popular cartoon characters and chosen a green-and-tan camouflage material pack. When she'd asked him why, he'd told her he wanted to be a hunter when he got older. Since he wouldn't even harm a spider, insisting she carry it outside rather than squishing it, she couldn't imagine that ever happening, but let it go.

"Thanks." Glancing up at Emily, Ryan edged closer. "Come on, Mommy. I want to make sure nobody stole any of my toys."

Exchanging a quick glance with Mac, Emily nodded and held out her hand for Ryan to take. He did so and then began tugging on her, clearly in a hurry to get inside the house.

Stepping into her living room, Emily stifled a gasp. The place hadn't been merely burglarized—it had been trashed. It was torn up, tossed around and destroyed on purpose. Though Ryan continued to pull her in the general direction of his bedroom, she couldn't help but slow and try to take in the sheer scope of the damage.

"Hang on a minute, Ryan," she said sharply. "Stay here with Mommy while I look around."

About to protest, Ryan glanced from her to the sheriff's deputy and nodded instead.

While she stood, trying to take in the scope of the destruction, all she could think of was to be thankful she and Ryan hadn't been home. She could clean up the mess, replace whatever had been stolen, but if anyone had harmed her son… The very thought made her shudder.

Wordlessly, Mac came up beside her, placing a hand reassuringly on her shoulder as if he knew her thoughts.

Instantly, she jerked away. "Where's Renee? I'd really hoped—"

"You do want to find this stalker, right?"

Emily stiffened. "Of course. It's just—"

"I'm assigned to your case. And I'm good. I promise you that I will find this guy."

The brief urge that had her wanting to lean against Mac appalled her. She nodded, wondering why she had such a strong, adverse reaction to him. It wasn't as if the man had actually done anything to warrant her mistrust and suspicion—well, aside from following her into Sue's Catfish Hut the first time they'd met. Maybe it was her persistent, instantaneous attraction to him.

Could she trust him? Did she even have a choice?

Aware both he and Ryan were watching her expectantly, she forced a pleasant, if humorless, smile. "All right. Why don't you tell me what you're going to do about this?"

Spreading her hands to encompass the total trashing of her home, she realized she was perilously close to tears. That knowledge alone was enough to cause her to shore up her shoulders, take a deep breath and lift her chin.

"We'll find the guy," he said simply. "I promise you that."

"Thank you." She hoped he didn't notice the catch in her voice. Glancing down at her son, who now seemed engrossed in playing with the toy that had come with his Good Times meal, she sighed. "What now?"

"Take a look around and see if anything is missing," Mac said, his deep voice rolling over her in a wave of calmness.

The sick dread in the pit of her stomach refused to leave, but Emily forced herself to head toward the room she used as an office. Luckily, this was right next to her son's bedroom.

"Mommy!" Ryan crowed, tugging his hand free and catapulting onto his bed. "They didn't touch my toys!"

After a quick inspection of his room, including under the bed and in the closet, Emily left him happily playing with his trucks and went to check out her desk.

"They were looking for something among your files," Mac said quietly behind her. File folders and paper were strewn all over the desk, chair, foldout couch and floor.

A manila folder sat open and empty on top of her desk. Before she even picked it up to read the label, Emily knew what it was.

"Ryan's adoption records," she said out loud. "They stole Ryan's adoption records."

Spinning, she grabbed Mac's arm. "You've got to help me. Whoever broke in here is after my son. You've got to help me protect him."

Mac's sharp blue gaze searched her face. "Do you have other copies?"

"Of course." Punching the on button, she powered up her computer. "I scanned them and saved them, both here and on CD."

"I'd like copies."

"Of course." As soon as the computer booted up, Emily clicked on the folder and printed them off, handing them to him.

"Was anything else taken, besides your son's adoption paperwork?" he asked.

"Not that I can tell." Twisting her hands together, she tried to sound unaffected.

"Let's check the rest of the house," he said. Without waiting for an answer, he turned and went down the hall to the next bedroom—Ryan's room.

It, she reflected thankfully, appeared untouched. Oblivious to his mother's chaotic thoughts, Ryan cheerfully played with a couple of his trucks, ignoring the adults.

Mac paused at the doorway, watching silently, as though the cheerfully untidy mess was more than he'd expected.

"Do you have children?" she asked softly.

He started, as if her question had brought him out of deep contemplation. "Currently, no." His abrupt tone made it sound like the topic was both painful and closed.

"I'm sorry." She shrugged, suddenly feeling uncomfortable again. "Please excuse the mess. Ryan's only five, which is why—"

"No need to explain." His back to her, he stepped into the room the way one might enter a church. Again, she cursed her overactive imagination. There was no logical reason why a man—a sheriff's deputy and experienced police officer—would act in such a way.

Unless...

She blinked. Though she didn't know him well enough to ask, again she wondered if he'd lost a child.

"Was anything taken from here?" he asked, directing the question to her rather than Ryan.

"No," Ryan answered, without looking up from his trucks. "All my stuff is okay."

"Thanks." Flashing her son a reassuring smile, he moved close to Emily and spoke in a low voice. "Would you mind taking a quick look around and letting me know if you see anything missing? Just in case?"

"Of course." Horrified at the thought, she took a step forward, trying to mentally catalog Ryan's toys. After a preliminary sweep of the room, heart in her throat, she looked at Mac helplessly. "Honestly, he has so much. Do you really think someone would—"

"Probably not." He touched her shoulder, the gentle grip meaning to reassure her. "After all, your stalker seems more concerned with you and the adoption than with your son himself. I'm sure there's nothing to worry about."

They were good words, but the idea of someone taking one of Ryan's toys like some kind of trophy opened up an entirely new world of terrifying possibilities. Again, she felt the strong urge to gather her meager belongings, pick up her son and run as fast and as far as she could.

"Emily?"

Realizing Mac had been talking to her, asking her something, she forced herself to concentrate on him. "I'm sorry," she said. To her surprise, she sounded relatively normal. "What did you say?"

"I asked you if you could walk with me to the other rooms."

With her heart skipping a beat, she couldn't help but glance back at Ryan. Loath to leave her son, conversely she didn't want to alarm him.

"He'll be fine," Mac said. "Let him play."

"Just a couple of bathrooms and the laundry room." He stepped into the hall and gestured. "Lead the way."

Heartbeat far too rapid, she headed for the hallway and her bedroom, with Mac following. While she'd begun to think Mac Riordan might be an okay kind of guy, something about him still felt a bit off, though she'd be hard-pressed to specify exactly how.

He searched her room first. She noted how he moved with a brisk efficiency, treating her home and her belongings with respect. Appreciating that, she felt the tightness in her chest begin to ease somewhat.

When they'd finished, they wound up back at the front door. "Is that it?" she asked. "Is there anything else you need?"

Considering, Mac cocked his head. "Now that we've finished checking out your house, I have a few questions. I'll need a minute or two of your time."

"You've got it." Though she knew he wanted to ask her about her past, which normally would have caused her to shut down completely, she also realized she'd need to answer honestly. Otherwise, there was no possible way on earth that this small-town sheriff's department could even remotely understand what they might be up against.

Making an instant decision to tell the truth, though not all of it, Emily led the way to the kitchen. "Have a seat. I'm guessing this might take a while."

"That depends on how much you have to tell me." When Mac's humorous tone failed to produce an answering smile, he grew serious. "Why don't you start with what you know was actually taken? Why Ryan's adoption records?"

She considered her words carefully, an actual ingrained habit since she'd chosen this way of life.

"I was married to a…criminal." Wincing as an expression of understanding filled Mac's sky-blue eyes, she held up her hand. "No, it's not what you think. I didn't know about him until after he died. My husband is dead."

"I'm sorry to hear that. Did he die of natural causes?"

No one but a cop would have thought to ask such a thing. "No." She debated whether or not to elaborate, then realized with a bit of internet research he would learn the truth regardless. "He was murdered."

Silently, Mac waited.

She took a deep breath, forcing herself to continue. "My name wasn't always Emily Gilley."

"I see that." Tapping the copies of the adoption papers he'd been handed, he eyed her with a law enforcement officer's intent stare. She'd become very familiar with that look in the months immediately following her husband's death.

Steeling herself, she continued trying to relive a past she'd hated. "After the investigation, I learned some things—a lot of things—that I hadn't known about my husband."

"Go on."

"My husband was Carlos Cavell. I had my name legally changed to Gilley after his death." She did this right before she and Ryan had vanished from their old life.

Immediate comprehension dawned in Mac's face. After all, everyone knew of Carlos Cavell. The name had been blazed everywhere in the news after his particularly gruesome murder. Though she'd tried to stay out of the spotlight, inevitably photos of her and Ryan had appeared. Since then, she'd changed her appearance quite a bit. So far, that had been enough.

"Not a bad disguise," Mac commented wryly. "But you still haven't told me why you felt the need to disappear."

"Whoever killed Carlos—and the police were unable to determine even a reasonable suspect—came after me and my son."

Agitated, unable to sit still, she began pacing. "I think it might have been one of his mistresses. I told the police that and they investigated, but they couldn't find anything. So I did the only thing I could. I sold everything, took whatever cash was left after paying the debts and ran."

"Here, to Anniversary."

"Yes. Until now, we were settling in nicely. I really liked it here."

Mac immediately picked up on her use of past tense. "Liked? Are you planning on leaving?"

Chewing on her thumbnail, she forced herself to stop. "I'm not sure. If this keeps up, I have no choice."

"You don't even know if this incident is related."

"How can it not be?" Emily protested. "This intruder took Ryan's adoption records. That was the crux of the threats to begin with. Something about the way Carlos got our son."

"Did he use an adoption service?"

"No. It was a private adoption. Apparently lots of money changed hands. I'm guessing, though I don't know for sure, that whatever channels Carlos went through weren't exactly on the up-and-up."

"As long as both parties signed the necessary paperwork and the documents were filed in a court of law..."

With her throat closing up from the panicked feeling in her chest, she debated whether to go on. In the end, she couldn't risk Mac not understanding the awful truth she suspected—that Ryan was her husband's natural son with one of his mistresses. No way was she letting anyone take her son away from her. She'd die first.

In a quiet voice, she relayed her suspicions.

"I've tried to trace the adoption," she admitted. "Any records beyond what I had were completely destroyed. It's possible—though not certain—that my husband may have obtained Ryan's birth certificate illegally."

To his credit, Mac showed no reaction—as if he heard stories like this every day. Then again, maybe he did.

"So what you're telling me is that you aren't one hundred percent sure you have a legal right to your boy."

Just hearing the words made Emily feel as though she'd been punched in the stomach. She wanted to double over, and only a supreme act of willpower kept her standing upright.

"I—" briefly she closed her eyes "—I don't know."

Now Mac pushed back his chair and stood. As he moved closer, she figured he meant to shake hands and held hers out accordingly.

Instead, to her complete and utter shock, he wrapped his muscular arms around her and gave her a quick hug.

"I'll keep this information between us for the time being. Right now, our focus is on finding whoever wrote you that letter and broke into your house."

Blinking back tears, she stepped out of his embrace and nodded. "Thank you."

Expression enigmatic, he simply watched her, as though waiting for her to say something else.

Chapter 4

Not reacting as Emily bared her soul to him was one of the most difficult things Mac had ever done. Only years of training and working on the streets enabled him to keep his face expressionless. When he'd impulsively hugged her, he half expected her to shove him away and order him to leave.

Instead, she finally nodded and thanked him. He felt thankful that she had no idea of the emotions swirling inside him. He couldn't stop marveling, amazed and humbled by the way he felt now that he'd finally gotten to see his son—after five years, three months and twenty days of missing him and wondering what had happened to him.

One look and he'd known. Even though he hadn't yet taken the DNA test, he knew Ryan was his. Gazing at the dark-headed boy, he saw his wife, Sarah, in the boy's chin, the tilt of his head. And Ryan had Mac's eyes and nose and the full head of dark hair, exactly as Mac had when he'd been a child.

Maybe soon he could reclaim what he'd lost, and they could be a family together.

Then he glanced at Emily, painfully aware of the way she and Ryan interacted. She clearly loved the child she considered her son, and the feeling was mutual. For the first time, Mac wondered what kind of damage he would cause if he tried to take Ryan away from the woman he called Mommy.

Emily cleared her throat, bringing him out of his tangled thoughts. "Well, then. What's your plan?" One brow raised, she waited, a study in contrasts. Her delicately carved facial structure seemed at odds with her lush, passionate mouth. Her short, spiky haircut didn't go with her faded jeans and high-collared blouse.

Eyeing her with as much professional dispassion as he could muster, he cleared his throat. "I have a few more questions about your life before you moved here."

"I see." Appearing resolute, she indicated the kitchen table. Graceful and willowy, her exquisite beauty made her appear both fragile and wild. "Go ahead."

"I need to know…" He paused, searching for the right words. The question he wanted to ask her was one he'd wondered ever since he'd learned she'd adopted the infant he believed was his son. "I need to know if you knew there was something unusual about where your son came from."

Was that guilt that flashed across her mobile face or sorrow?

"No," she said.

He decided to continue to press her. "You never questioned your husband?"

"I never had a reason to, before all this started." Her

careful, measured movements spoke of the depths of her agitation. "You have to understand that being married to a man like Carlos Cavell came with some benefits. One of these seemed to be the ability to cut through a lot of red tape. When we originally applied to adopt an infant, we were told it could take up to three years."

Keeping his expression neutral, he nodded. "And how long in actuality before you were told about Ryan?"

"Six months." She looked down, as though her answer was somehow shameful. And maybe it was, he thought, because any sensible, rational woman should have suspected something was wrong. Or would they?

"Did you go through the same agency that you initially applied to?"

Lifting one shoulder in a shrug, she still wouldn't meet his gaze. "Honestly, at the time, I didn't even question anything. I was just so overjoyed to be getting a baby of my own."

Waiting, he eyed her while she took a deep breath, then looked down. "Actually, I've been unable to make any of the records he had in Ryan's file match up with anything even remotely concrete."

Squinting at her, watching for even the slightest sign that she was hiding something, he waited. He'd long ago learned in situations like this that silence seemed to generate more answers than questions.

Finally, after appearing to be lost in thought, she raised her head and again met his gaze, her big brown eyes soft and defenseless and absolutely beautiful. He felt an unwilling jolt of attraction, which he quickly suppressed.

"You must have your own thoughts about that," he said, his even tone belying the importance of the question. "Where do you think Carlos got Ryan?" His heart pounded as he waited to hear what she would say.

"As I mentioned, my, er, husband had a mistress. Actually, more than one." She gave him a stiff smile, unable to disguise her worry and her hurt. "I'm thinking that Ryan is actually Carlos's son with one of them. He must have forced her into signing the adoption papers. Now she wants her son back. Honestly, if that was the case, I can't help but feel sorry for her."

Startled, he managed to keep his expression noncommittal. "That's one possibility," he said, though in truth he knew it wasn't. "We'll definitely check into that."

She nodded. "Look, Mac—I mean, Deputy Riordan. I don't understand any of this." Though she squared her shoulders and lifted her chin, the quiver in her voice, whether genuine or artificial, made him want to comfort her. No doubt, he thought cynically, that was what she'd hoped for.

Chiding himself silently, he tried to remember he wanted to keep an open mind. There was a chance, no matter how small, that she might not have known that her baby had been stolen right out of the hospital nursery. Emily Gilley could be, as unlikely as it might seem, entirely blameless.

Plus, there was one other thing he needed to consider. When Renee Beauchamp had sworn him in as a deputy, he'd taken an oath to protect and serve. No matter what crimes he suspected Emily Gilley of committing, he now had a sworn duty to help her with her current situation, which, he admitted to himself fiercely, he would have regardless. Because anyone threatening her also threatened Ryan.

He needed to get to know her, try to figure out what

kind of person she was and if she could have knowingly taken someone else's child and claimed him as her own.

Someone else's child. He gave himself a mental shake. It was time to stop hiding from the painful truth.

If what he suspected was factual and Emily Gilley had stolen his son from the hospital nursery, then Ryan Gilley was actually *his* son, the only family he had left in the world.

Mac could only hope this was true. Otherwise, he had no lead to go on, no chance in hell of finding his boy.

While he'd searched for his missing child for five years now without success, he'd begun to despair of ever actually finding him—especially as time went on.

This, too, was his fault. He couldn't help but blame himself. If he'd been more vigilant, he would have managed to keep his son safe. But everything had happened so damn fast. The car crash that had killed his wife, Sarah, had consumed him, and he'd barely acknowledged the baby they'd been able to save. Occupied with an awful grief, he'd buried Sarah, meanwhile trying to figure out how on earth he was going to manage a tiny infant. The day after the funeral, the hospital had called him with the news.

His baby had gone missing right out of the nursery. His department, his own coworkers—people he'd worked with side by side, day in and day out—had handled the case for him since he'd been banned from working on it.

As if that had stopped him. But when lead after lead hadn't panned out and years had gone by, he'd gradually begun to lose hope until his partner, Joe, had uncovered information leading to Emily Gilley and her adopted son, Ryan. Everything—from the adoption shrouded in secrecy, to the time frame and age of her child—pointed to her.

All he needed was proof. And truthfully, he also wanted to know why. He couldn't imagine what kind of twisted, desperate need would drive someone to steal another's child.

Looking at Emily Gilley with an instinct he'd honed after years of police work, he wouldn't have thought she'd be capable of such a heinous act—her husband, maybe, but not her.

The need for answers had been gnawing inside him for months now. If he could prove without a doubt that her son, Ryan, was actually his boy, the infant he and Sarah had decided to call Taylor, Mac intended to get him back in his life—no matter what.

The longer she sat across from Mac Riordan in her brightly painted kitchen, the more uncomfortable Emily became. This room, with its deep red walls and clean white cabinets, had been the only one she'd bothered to change in the rental house. She'd made the kitchen into her sanctuary, envisioning casual meals and noisy children's birthday parties and early morning cups of coffee while the sun rose.

Now, with the big man wearing the deputy sheriff's badge pinned on his impossibly broad chest sitting across from her, the kitchen suddenly seemed too small, closed in, almost alien. She felt as if she were actually seated in a police interrogation room, being questioned about some crime that she hadn't committed.

Ridiculous. Her imagination, always exaggerated, wasn't doing her any favors here. After all, *she had done nothing wrong.*

But a certain cynical look in Mac's bright blue eyes

made her feel culpable somehow, which again, was absurd. She was the victim here, not the perpetrator.

She didn't know the man, so how could she even think she could decipher any expression in his vivid gaze?

While he appeared lost in thought, she studied him. His prematurely gray hair, rather than aging him, gave his craggy face character. Just one look from his sapphire eyes brought a visceral shock that she felt deep within her belly.

He unsettled her. It was strange and disconcerting, too, to say the least. These feelings were entirely unwelcome. She had no business being attracted to a man— any man—when her life was entirely in turmoil.

"All right," he finally said, appearing to reach some sort of decision. "Let's talk about suspects. We've got potential mistresses. Earlier, you mentioned some guy you went on a blind date with. Tell me about him."

She sighed, thinking of her failed attempt to be normal. "I'm pretty sure Tim is harmless."

"Let me be the judge of that."

Instead of fixating on the way his mouth quirked appealingly at the corner, she swallowed. "Would you like something to drink?" she asked, because she needed a distraction. "I've got iced tea, lemonade and water."

"Water would be great."

Glad she was able to occupy herself by filling two glasses with ice, then the cold water she kept in a pitcher in the fridge, she turned and placed their drinks on the kitchen table.

He reached for the glass. "Thank you," he said, drinking deeply. She found herself watching the strong lines of his throat as he drank. "About this Tim. What's his last name?"

"Keeslar. Tim Keeslar. My friend Tina set this up. You've met her. She's a waitress at Sue's Catfish Hut."

He nodded, writing down the last name. "Tell me everything you know about him."

"I really don't think—"

"Please." He touched the back of her hand, his fingers both protective and soothing. "Humor me."

"He's tall and slender, longish dark hair. Not bad looking." She shrugged, slightly embarrassed. "He owns his own home and drives a big Ford pickup."

"What does he do for a living?"

"He owns the auto-parts store on Fifth Street."

After noting all this, Mac looked up, brow raised. "And he's single? Has he ever been married?"

"I don't think so, but I can't say for sure. We only went out twice." She rubbed her suddenly aching temples, trying to remember. "I don't know."

"That's okay. I can easily find that out. Tell me why you thought he might be your stalker. You said he liked you way more than you liked him."

Feeling foolish, she relayed how, after declining a third date, Tim suddenly started popping up everywhere she went. "If I went to a movie with Jayne or Tina, Tim was there. I couldn't go anywhere—the grocery store, the dry cleaners, downtown—without running into him."

"Did you confront him?"

She gave him a wry smile. "I'm pretty sure you know the answer to that."

He asked a few more questions. He was very thorough, and she liked the way he carefully noted her responses.

"*Now* do you take me seriously?" Emily asked him

quietly, amazed at her sense of relief now that she'd gotten everything off her shoulders.

He gave her a sharp look and a frown. "Emily, I've always taken you seriously. I'd be a fool to do anything else."

Then, while she was puzzling over his cryptic statement, he drained the last of his water, stood and dipped his chin. "I'll be in touch," he said, and let himself out.

Driving back to his fledgling trucking company, Mac mulled over the dramatic change that had occurred in his life—almost overnight. Originally, he'd come to Anniversary with no plans to ever work again in law enforcement.

Using his savings, he'd started up a trucking company, specializing in flatbed freight hauling. To his surprise, business had been good—so good, in fact, that earlier that week he'd decided he needed to hire his first nondriver employee. He needed someone to book loads both through trucking brokers and directly through shippers using not only the phone but personal contacts and the internet. This meant he had to find someone with trucking experience who didn't want to be a truck driver.

This was not a small order in a town the size of Anniversary.

He had an interview scheduled that afternoon with the first person to respond to his ad, a young man named Chris Pitts. According to the résumé he'd emailed, his father and two brothers were all truckers, which of course made Mac wonder why Chris wasn't.

He had an immediate answer to that question when Chris rolled into his shop in a wheelchair.

"Old football injury," he said in response to Mac's

questioning look. "Can't climb in and out of a truck. Also, my body can't take the pounding of the road. But I can still work, just not as a truck driver."

"As long as you keep my trucks loaded, you can do laps around the yard in your wheelchair if you want," Mac responded. When Chris grinned, Mac knew that, barring any real oddities in the interview, he'd found his dispatcher.

Even better, Chris wanted to start work immediately. "Tomorrow morning?"

"I'll be here." The two men shook hands, and Chris wheeled himself out. Following, Mac watched as the younger man used a specially equipped van. He stepped forward, but Chris waved off his offer of assistance.

"I've got it. I've been doing this on my own for a few years now." Chris flashed another big grin, and after stowing his wheelchair via an electronic lift, waved and drove away.

Watching him go, for the first time in far too long, Mac thought his life might finally be on the right track. He was once again doing the kind of work he'd been born to do and—even better—his job gave him up close and personal access to not only Emily Gilley but Ryan. He couldn't have planned things better if he'd tried.

After Mac left, Emily tried to put her house back in some semblance of order. At odd intervals, tears threatened, which infuriated her as she angrily wiped them away. How long would she and Ryan have to pay for a greedy, unethical man's misdeeds? She'd been naive and foolish when she'd married Carlos Cavell, looking past the gaping inconsistencies between what he told her and the reality of his actual life.

In fact, she'd been so willingly blinded that it wasn't

until after Carlos's death that she'd learned not only had he kept more than one longtime mistress but he'd been involved in some shady if not outright illegal deals and left her in debt up to her eyeballs.

The chain of restaurants that she'd believed provided their income were barely functional, losing money and, if the NYPD were to be believed, operated as a front for Carlos's money-laundering operations. There'd been debts and deals and a stack of unpaid bills.

She'd been in the process of selling everything, including her lavish home, when the first threat had arrived. To her horror and shock, the double-paged rambling missive had hinted that she'd somehow stolen her son. This had so terrified her that she'd rushed to check the adoption records even before contacting the authorities.

All the paperwork on Ryan's adoption appeared to be in order, but appearances were deceiving. After making a few phone calls and doing some online research, she learned the adoption broker listed had never existed.

In other words, the adoption papers were entirely fake—forged by Carlos or his associates. For what reason, she had no idea.

Truth be told, she really didn't want to know. Ryan had come to her an infant and, at the time of Carlos's death, was still a tiny human being who was her son— body, heart and spirit. They were linked in deeper ways than mere flesh and blood.

She couldn't take a chance losing him.

So she'd kept silent about the threats, continued liquidating her assets, paying off the debts and making plans.

Then when she had nothing left to tie her to Man-

hattan, she and Ryan had gotten up one morning and
quietly disappeared.

Now that four and a half uneventful years had passed
since she'd left, she'd begun to relax, to allow herself
to feel safe.

Not anymore, though. It appeared her stalker had
finally found her.

By the time the sun began to rise, Emily had nearly
finished downing her second cup of strong coffee. She
sat alone in the kitchen, one scented candle her only
source of light. Ryan still slept, blissfully unaware of
the storm clouds of chaos threatening his world.

What to do, what to do… Every instinct screamed
run, but truth be told, she was tired of running. She'd
settled in here in Anniversary, loving the feeling of actually living an ordinary life.

Still, she had to face facts. If she didn't run, then
what were her options? If she stayed and fought, she'd
have to learn who the stalker was and what exactly he
or she wanted.

Most importantly, was Ryan at risk? Restless, she
got up and poured herself another cup.

First there was the cryptic note, then the break-in.
What next?

Picking up the note, she reread the words. *I know
what you've done. You've stolen what is mine, and you'll
pay for what you did. Tell the truth or risk everything.*

Hand shaking, she read it again. It was cryptic, to
be sure. But she had nothing of value except her child.

While she knew she didn't know what really had
happened with her son's adoption, she'd done nothing
more than welcome an infant into her life five years
ago. Believing her husband was on the up-and-up, she'd

been full of happiness to finally have the child she was unable to conceive—Ryan...her boy...her son.

Since then, she'd given him everything a child could want, not the least of all which was her heart. As to telling the truth, how could she do that when she didn't even know what it was?

Forcing herself to be analytical, she read the note a third time. All of the messages had been variations of this same threat. She'd stolen something from the stalker. Tell the truth or risk everything. Renee was right. As far as threats went, that was awfully vague. She supposed she ought to be grateful the stalker hadn't written something like "you and the boy will die."

But despite the lack of specification, the notes still terrified her. She supposed she really didn't want to know the truth, didn't want to learn what her husband had done to bring her this child.

Because, in the end, none of it mattered. Ryan was hers. She'd give her life protecting him if it came to that.

Pacing, steaming cup of coffee in hand, Emily eyed the clock, willing her heartbeat to slow. She couldn't think rationally if she allowed panic to take over.

First things first, she had to decide what course of action, if any, to take immediately. As the first light of sunrise began to dapple the trees, she took a deep breath. She decided to call in to work and ask for the day off. Once she let them know what had happened, she felt certain they'd be sympathetic, which was just one of the reasons she loved working there.

Aware the clinic opened at seven for surgery drop-offs, she made the call and, exactly as she'd suspected, she was told in no uncertain terms to take a personal day.

Hanging up the phone, she poured another cup of

coffee. As she did, the tightness in her chest eased somewhat. Funny how accomplishing even one small thing made her feel a tiny bit better, more in control of her life.

Next, she debated whether or not to take Ryan to school. In the end, she decided normalcy would be the best for him, so she woke him and helped him choose his clothes for the day.

Driving him to kindergarten, the sheer ordinariness of the act made her regret taking the entire day off from work. But after seeing her son safely ensconced in his classroom under the watchful eye of Ms. Penney, she headed home to try and make order of her ransacked home.

As soon as she got there, though, she decided to go in to work for the afternoon, once she'd finished straightening out her house.

An hour or so later, having tidied the living room and gotten her office back into some semblance of order, she wandered into the kitchen to see if she could squeeze one final cup of coffee from the nearly empty pot. As she sipped the lukewarm beverage, she eyed the clock. If she made herself a quick lunch and changed clothes, she could arrive at the office shortly after noon.

Later, after arriving at the bustling veterinary clinic, she was glad she'd decided to go in. The busy ordinary workday would help take her mind off her problems. She needed to be calm and rational in order to think.

Luckily, the day flew by. A steady stream of clients kept her busy. Before she knew it, the wall clock showed five minutes until closing time.

Just as she was about to lock up and head out, her cell phone rang. It was Mrs. Mims, the day care director and owner.

"Emily, you'd better get over here quick," she said, her normally calm voice quivering.

Instantly, Emily's heart leapt into her throat. She asked about Ryan. "Is he all right?"

"He's fine," Mrs. Mims assured her, clearly trying for calm, although she sounded out of breath and agitated. "But earlier—" she hesitated, then continued in a rush "—a man tried to grab him off the playground. His teacher and one of the parents were able to stop him. The sheriff's department is on the way."

Chapter 5

Heart pounding, Emily murmured something in reply and hung up the phone. After she grabbed her purse, she rushed to the front door, dizzy and nauseated. Someone had tried to snatch Ryan. The words played over and over again, a terrifying litany echoing inside her head.

Had this been completely random, the act of some sick pervert wanting a child, any child? Or was this tied into the threats and her past life? Did they even matter? Either way, her son had nearly been harmed.

Taking deep breaths and fighting off the dizziness and the panic, she broke every speed limit on the way to the day care. When she pulled up, two police cars blocked the entrance, lights flashing blue, white and red.

Once she'd parked behind them, she cut the engine and ran to the entrance. Renee Beauchamp and Mac

Riordan waited just inside the doorway, with a clearly rattled Mrs. Mims.

Emily hurried forward, and Mac moved to intercept her.

"Easy now," he said, correctly interpreting Emily's frantic fears. "Everything's going to be all right." He spoke in a soothing voice, taking Emily's arm and steering her into Mrs. Mims's office. "Ryan's fine."

A single chair rested in front of Mrs. Mims's desk. Emily had sat there once before, when she'd enrolled her son in the day care, and later the after-school program. As she let Mac guide her to that seat now, she realized her entire body had begun to tremble.

"I want to see my son." She forced out the words through lifeless lips. "Please."

Before she'd even finished speaking, Renee shepherded Ryan into the office. Emily shot up out of the chair, dropping to her knees and enveloping her boy into a tight hug.

"Mommy?" Squirming, Ryan pushed her away. "What's wrong?"

It dawned on her that her son had no idea of the danger he'd just faced. Emily took a deep breath. When she looked up and met Mac's gaze, she realized he looked nearly as rattled as she felt.

"Nothing's the matter," she managed, swallowing hard. "I just missed you."

Nodding, Ryan appeared to accept this at face value. Then, with a five-year-old's aplomb, he eyed Renee and Mac, his expression grave. "Was there an accident?"

Exchanging a quick look with Emily, Mac squatted down to put himself at Ryan's level. "No, not exactly. We wanted to talk to you about the man you met earlier, when you were in the playground."

Ryan's troubled expression cleared. "Oh, him. He wasn't a bad man."

Emily's heart skipped a beat, but she managed to keep her expression neutral. "How do you know he wasn't bad, honey?"

"Because even though he was just like that man in that movie—you know—*Stranger Danger,* he really didn't want to hurt me."

Mac crouched down, putting himself at Ryan's level. "Why don't you tell us exactly what happened?"

"Okay." Moving in closer to Emily, as though he needed reassurance, Ryan appeared to carefully consider his words, adopting a serious manner far older than his five years. "First, he said he had candy, and if I wanted to have some I had to go with him."

Emily winced. Feeling the sudden tension in his mother's body, Ryan stopped, peering up at her. "Mommy? Are you all right?"

Only when she'd nodded and tried to smile reassuringly did he continue. "When I told him no, he said he had puppies in his van. Just like the cartoon we watched in preschool," Ryan said scornfully. "I'm only five, and I know better than that."

"Van?" Mac asked, his deliberately casual voice at odds with his intense gaze. "What color was the van?"

Ryan shrugged. "I don't know. I never saw it. He said it was parked around the corner." Then, again looking up at his mother, he scrunched up his little freckled face into a concerned frown. "You told me never to go with strangers, right Mommy?"

Chest so tight she wasn't certain she could speak, Emily nodded. "Yes, I did, Ryan." Praying her hand wouldn't shake too badly, she reached out and ruffled his hair. "You did good, son. I'm proud of you."

Ruffling Ryan's hair, Mac stood. "Let me take you home," Mac murmured to Emily.

"I don't want to go home," she said, surprising even herself. Then, noting the way Ryan gazed up at her in concern, she forced another smile. "I was thinking about taking Ryan out for pizza since he did so well today."

Ryan beamed. Looking from his mother to Mac, he smiled. "You can come, too, Mac," he offered. "Mommy might feel better if we have a policeman with us."

Raising a brow, Mac and her son shared a conspiratorial grin. "Pizza it is," he said, as though he knew there was no way Emily would refuse him.

And he was right, she thought ruefully as she walked, still weak-kneed, toward the door with her son and the man who'd promised to protect them.

When Mac held out his hand for Emily's keys, he half expected her to ignore him. It was a testament to her state of mind when she simply handed them over without a word.

Driving with Emily in the passenger seat and Ryan buckled into his booster seat in the back, he couldn't help but imagine if this is what it would be like to be a family—something he'd always wanted and knew he'd never have.

From the pinched look on Emily's face and Ryan's uncharacteristic silence, he doubted either of them was thinking along the same lines.

"Are you all right, little buddy?" he asked, watching the boy who might be his son in the rearview mirror.

Ryan nodded without speaking. Mac glanced at Emily, half expecting her to crumple at any moment and dissolve in tears, which wouldn't be good—at all. He needed her to be able to stay strong to protect her son.

Instead, she sat ramrod straight, staring ahead and lost in thought. Judging from the set of her jaw, she was furious.

Good. That meant she wouldn't give up without a fight. He reluctantly admired that.

They arrived at Paul's Pizza Palace, which he was pleased to note wasn't overly crowded. He parked the car and hurried to open Emily's door, then stood guard while she helped Ryan out of his booster seat.

Once inside, they went through the buffet line and, plates stacked high, they followed while Emily chose a booth. Mac approved of her choice. Away from the windows and tucked into a back corner with a good view of the door, they had both privacy and a clear escape route if needed.

Chiding himself for being paranoid, he ate his pizza and tried to relax. This should be a moment he savored. It wasn't every day he got to share a meal with the boy who might be his son.

He'd nearly succeeded when Emily touched his arm. "I know that man."

At the urgency in her voice, Mac turned to see who she meant. Across the room crowded with lunchtime diners, his new dispatcher Chris sat with his chair wheeled up to a table.

Eyes wide and stricken, Emily had gone pale as a sheet. "What's he doing here?" she whispered.

"That's my dispatcher, Chris," Mac said. He tried to sound normal despite the fact that she looked like she'd seen a demon emerge from the bowels of hell. "Do you know him?"

"Yes." Mouth grim, she nodded. "His name isn't really Chris."

Silently, Mac cursed. He should have run a comprehensive background check. "Are you sure?"

"Yes." Studiously avoiding glancing across the room, Emily pretended to study the menu. "That's Franco DiSorinne. He was one of my husband's most trusted men."

Mac clenched his jaw, resisting the urge to reach across the table and take her hand in his. "Okay, say it is him. Do you have any idea why he would be here, pretending to be someone else? It's been what, five years since Carlos died?"

When she raised her head to meet his gaze, he saw panic in her eyes. "I don't know. I've received various threats over the years, but until recently, they'd died out." Shaking, she leaned close so Ryan wouldn't hear. "We need to find out if he's the man who tried to grab Ryan."

Glancing at Ryan, who had finished his pizza and was busy playing a game on Emily's phone, Mac shook his head. "He didn't say anything about a wheelchair," he said, sotto voce.

"Wheelchairs can be fake," she shot back in a whisper. "You should know that better than anyone. I'll bet he can walk just fine. Franco wasn't in a wheelchair the last time I saw him."

Debating whether to confront his dispatcher here or wait until Chris—er, Franco—showed up for work in the morning, Mac decided there was no better time than the present.

He pushed up from the booth and stood. But when he glanced across the room, Chris was gone.

"I'll talk to him in the morning," he said, meeting

Emily's troubled gaze and holding it. Unable to help himself, he reached across the table and covered her hand with his own. "Don't worry. If he's behind this, we'll take care of it."

Though she nodded, the worry and fear never left her eyes. "You know what?" she announced, pushing her barely touched meal away. "I'd prefer if you could clear this up tonight. Right now, I'd like to go home and let you get out there and do your job."

Since he couldn't fault her logic, he nodded. Ryan had finished eating and bounced in his seat, asking to go to the video arcade every few minutes. Undeterred by his mother's constant *no*'s, he continued to push, sending Emily perilously close to the edge.

When Mac stood, a clearly relieved Emily helped Ryan to his feet. "We're going home," she said firmly, steering him away from the brightly lit arcade.

"I'll need you to drop me off at the day care so I can pick up my car," Mac said quietly. Emily nodded, and again he felt the urge to comfort her, to reach across the seat and pull her into his side. Of course, he did nothing.

They drove away in silence, both lost in their own thoughts, managing to ignore Ryan's persistent, low-key whining.

When they pulled up in front of the day care, Renee's department vehicle was still parked in the lot. Mac got out, taking one final long look at Ryan, so he could sear the image on his heart. He told a clearly distracted Emily goodbye, advising her to make sure she locked all her doors, and watched as she drove off.

Then he climbed into his police cruiser and went looking for Chris Pitts, aka Franco DiSorinne.

An hour and a half later, he admitted defeat. Nothing checked out—not the information Chris had put on his employment application or a search of the state database. Neither Chris Pitts or Franco DiSorinne were listed as residents of Texas.

Weary, he decided to call it a night. On his way home, he ran through a drive-thru and picked up a burger and fries for dinner. It was not the healthiest solution, he knew, but with the kind of day he'd had, the last thing he felt like doing was cooking anything.

Once home, he walked out to the small wooden building he used as his trucking company office. Even though Chris or Franco had only worked as his dispatcher for a short time, he'd done a wonderful job. Not only would he be sorely missed but next to impossible to replace. Every truck had remained loaded and busy, and Chris had even set up some bookings for the rest of the week.

Mac grimaced. It was too bad he'd somehow found the perfect employee who'd turned out to be bogus.

Returning to his kitchen, he sighed and opened the takeout bag and began to chow down, standing up. As he finished eating, washing down his food with a cold beer, his cell phone rang. Caller ID showed it was his friend and former partner, Joe Stalling.

"Hey, Joe." Grinning, Mac took a swig of his beer and leaned back in his chair. Since Joe still worked as a detective for the Albany P.D., his calls always filled Mac in on all the happenings there.

"Hey, yourself." Joe's grin came across in his voice. That was one of the things Mac had liked best about the other man—his tendency to find amusement in the worst situations. Considering his job, working in the Crimes Against Persons—Family Unit, and the types of gut-wrenching cases he'd had, Joe was lucky to have managed to avoid burnout after five years at the same job.

Others sometimes found his ever-present smile off-putting. But Mac knew each officer had his own way of dealing with all the horrific and senseless acts of violence. Joe's dogged sense of humor was his.

Mac trusted him more than he had anyone since his wife Sarah. They'd all been good friends, back in the days before the car accident had taken Sarah's life. In fact, Joe was the only person who knew the true reason Mac had resigned from the force and moved to Texas. He filled Joe in on taking the part-time job with the local police department but made no mention of Emily or her break-in.

"Have you seen the kid yet?" Joe asked.

Mac hesitated. He didn't know why, but he didn't want to admit that he'd met Ryan. For now, he wanted to keep it private, between him and Emily and the boy.

"No," he lied. "I've only just met Emily, the mother. I'm trying to take things slow."

The other man snorted. "Hell, you've been there over three weeks. How much slower can you go?"

Taking another swig of beer, Mac decided not to respond. Instead, he cut directly to the chase. "Do you have any new info for me about Cavell or his wife?" Joe had promised to use the vast law enforcement network to keep Mac informed if anything else surfaced about Emily's former husband.

"There's a ton of information, but I had to jump through hoops to get it." Joe sighed. "Since I'm in Albany, upstate, it hasn't been easy. NYPD is pretty tight about releasing anything to an outside agency."

Startled, Mac blinked. "NYPD? This was a federal investigation. Since you worked with them once, I thought you were going through them."

"I'm trying, but you know as well as I do that getting anything from the Feds is like pulling teeth. I'm also relying on an old friend at the NYPD. He's worked there for years."

Mac frowned. This didn't make a lot of sense. While agencies frequently shared information, the Feds were notoriously tight-lipped with cases of this caliber, which was no doubt still going on since Carlos Cavell's death was the only part of the huge investigation that had actually been solved. They'd have been more likely to talk directly to Joe since he'd done work with them in the past on this case. Mac didn't think they would share with NYPD unless they had a damn good reason.

However, Joe had no reason to lie. If he said NYPD had info, then Mac believed him.

"So did you get something?" Mac asked.

"Yep, though I don't know if there's anything useful. My contact emailed me everything he had. There's a lot of paper. I'm sorting through it bit by bit. I'm hoping to finish up by the end of this week."

"Thanks." Curious, Mac scratched his head. "What reason did you give NYPD for wanting copies of the files?"

Joe laughed. "First off, I didn't go through official channels. Second, I used the good old standard— ongoing investigation. My buddy didn't ask a lot of questions. He owed me a favor, so I called it in."

"I really appreciate that," Mac said and meant it.

"No problem. Hey, Mac?" Joe's voice rang with fierce determination. "When you get to see the kid, take a cell phone picture or something and send it to me. I'd really like to see it, okay?"

Mac found himself grinning, his inner turmoil easing somewhat. Sometimes he really missed his friend. "Sure will, buddy. Talk to you later."

Placing the phone on the table, Mac picked at the last of his fries. Joe was so hopeful for him and really enthusiastic over the prospect of Mac finally being reunited with his son. Mac appreciated that. It felt good to actually have a good friend on his side—especially since Joe's tireless efforts on Mac's behalf had led to him being the one to actually find Ryan.

Scratching his head, he drained his beer. He couldn't help but wonder why he felt so reluctant to share his good fortune with Joe. Maybe it was because he didn't yet know the truth. That had to be it.

Satisfied, he wandered into the living room and turned on the TV. For the first time in years, he found himself looking forward to tomorrow and the new day. Maybe in Anniversary he'd finally found a place he could call home.

When the doorbell chimed a little after 5:00 p.m., Emily's first inclination was to ignore it. After all, she and Ryan were going to spend the next couple of hours lounging in front of the TV, trying to regain a sense of normalcy.

Still, just in case Mac had decided to come back for some reason, she looked through the peephole.

An unfamiliar blonde woman stood on her front step. She was young, pretty, and wearing a low-cut, formfitting red dress and four-inch platform heels that wouldn't have been out of place on a stripper. Curious, Emily opened the door. "Yes?"

Long-lashed and heavily made-up brown eyes stared her down. "Are you Emily Cavell?"

Instantly, silent alarms went off. "My last name is Gilley," Emily answered. "What do you want?"

Undeterred by Emily's icy tone, the blonde continued to study her. "I'm Desiree. Maybe Carlos mentioned me?"

Carlos. With dawning horror, Emily realized who this woman was. She was one of Carlos's former mistresses. Her heart began to pound. It took every ounce of willpower not to slam the door in the woman's face.

"What do you want?" Emily asked again.

"I need to talk to you." Desiree looked pointedly past Emily toward the living room. "Can I come in?"

"No." No way was she letting this woman inside the house where her son lay sleeping. Instead, she stepped outside, closing the door firmly behind her. "If you want to talk, then talk," she ordered. "Otherwise, I'm going to have to ask you to leave."

"Oh, not yet," Desiree said grimly. "Not until I've gotten what I came for."

At that moment, Emily realized the vulnerable position she'd just put herself in. Unarmed, without even her cell phone, she stood outside in plain view. If anyone wanted to ambush her, she'd be easy pickings.

Instead of responding to what sounded like an overt threat, Emily simply crossed her arms and waited. She kept her back to the door, the handle within reach in case she needed to beat a hasty retreat.

"Carlos gave me some jewelry," Desiree said when it became apparent that Emily wasn't going to question her. "A beautiful diamond necklace and tennis bracelet. He took them to get them professionally cleaned."

"And?"

Desiree coughed delicately. "Well, he died before returning them. I'd like to get them back."

Though her relief was so great that Emily nearly laughed out loud, she managed to keep her face expressionless. She'd thought this woman had come looking for her son. Instead, she wanted some baubles?

"Was that what this was all about? The threats, the break-in?"

"Threats? Break-in?" Desiree sounded genuinely puzzled. "I have no idea what you're talking about. A friend in the NYPD told me I would get my jewelry back when the investigation into Carlos's death was complete. But I didn't."

"The investigation wound down several years ago," Emily pointed out.

"I know." Desiree pouted prettily. "And believe me, I was bummed when you disappeared. But my friend found you and told me to go see you. So here I am. I'm ready to collect what belongs to me."

Emily froze. The last sentence was lifted right out of the threatening notes. Suddenly afraid, she forced herself to lift her chin and hide her fear. "I'm sorry. I don't have your jewelry."

Desiree frowned, a small crease forming between her perfectly shaped brows. "I don't believe you."

"Everything Carlos had was liquidated to pay debts. I never saw any diamond necklace or bracelet."

"These were very valuable—" Desiree began.

Emily had had enough. "I understand, and I'm sorry," she said, turning to go back inside.

Desiree grabbed her arm. "I've come a long way. I'll report you for theft."

Emily jerked away, heart beating a furious tattoo in her chest. "Go right ahead. Now I'm asking you to leave my property."

The other woman didn't move. "Or what?"

"Or I'm calling the police."

Inside, the phone rang. Praying Desiree wouldn't try to force her way inside, Emily turned, yanked open the door, stepped around it and slammed it closed in the other woman's face. Still stunned and shaken, she slid the dead bolt into place before running to grab the still-ringing phone.

"Emily?"

Mac. She closed her eyes. Thank God. "Please come," she croaked. "Come quick."

Five minutes later, she heard his car screech down her street and pull up in her driveway. By the time he reached her front door, she thought she'd managed to pull herself together, gathering her shredded composure into some semblance of rational normalcy.

Yanking open the door, she stepped aside so he could enter. Instead, he pulled her close for a quick hug. Dazedly, she wondered if he hugged all his victims.

Once he'd released her, she swallowed hard and raised her head. "One of Carlos's mistresses was here."

Mac nodded. Jaw clenched and steely eyed, he looked both concerned and furious. "Tell me what happened."

When she relayed what Desiree had said, his expression grew thunderous. "Did she admit to breaking into your house?"

"No." She pushed away the urge to step closer to him in the hopes he'd hold her again. For some foolish reason, being close to him gave her strength.

"What about the threatening note?"

Again she shook her head. "I'm guessing it was her, don't you think?"

"I never guess when it comes to this kind of thing. Remember, we have more than one suspect. There's that guy you dated, Tim Keeslar. I haven't been able to locate him yet. And there's my dispatcher, Chris, or Franco or whatever his name really is. Now we've got this woman."

She watched as he pulled a pad and pen from his pocket. "Tell me everything you remember. What was her name?"

"I almost hate to say it," she admitted. "It's pretty cliché. She said her name was Desiree."

One corner of his mouth twitched, but to his credit, he didn't laugh. He asked several more questions, jotting down all her answers. When he'd finished, he put away the pad and pen and stood staring at her for a moment.

Suddenly tongue-tied, she colored as she realized she'd been staring at his mouth.

Full of longing, she met his gaze, aware he'd most likely been able to see her completely inappropriate desire.

Instead of commenting, he took a step toward her. She moved toward him and somehow wound up exactly where she wanted to be—in his arms.

Chapter 6

He tasted like spearmint and safety, and as Emily relaxed into his embrace, she could feel the tight leash he kept on his passion. Despite that, explosive currents washed over her, making her body throb.

Unconsciously, she leaned into him and deepened the kiss. The sheer maleness of him sent shivers to her core. Briefly, she wondered if he felt the same, then decided she didn't care.

He held her snugly, making no effort to break away, and when she raised her head to take a breath, he reclaimed her lips almost instantly. The kiss was heady, despite its odd gentleness, and left her mouth burning.

She wanted none of this; she wanted more. She wanted…giving up the struggle for rational thought, she returned his kiss with a recklessness that wasn't at all like her.

When they finally broke apart—this time for good—

both of them were breathing heavily. His eyes had gone dark, but his expression had turned to stone.

"That shouldn't have happened," she began. "I—"

"I agree." His harsh voice sounded raw. "Let's pretend it didn't and stick to business."

Though his swift dismissal stung, she knew he was right. While she struggled to organize her thoughts, he moved toward the door. "I'll see what I can find out about this Desiree. If I locate her or find any information about her I'll be in touch."

"Thank you," she answered. "Though I may not be here after today."

He froze. Apparently, that had been the wrong thing to say. "Where will you be?"

With a casual shrug, she hoped her tone sounded as expressionless as his. "I'm thinking about simply packing up and leaving town."

"Running? Again?"

"Don't talk as though you know me," she said, her sharp voice masking her hurt. "I'll do what I think best. I won't leave unless I have to. I want Ryan to have this." She spread her arms, turning to encompass her ordinary house with the lush suburban yard. "A place he can put down roots. Friends he'll have through all his school years. A sense of permanence. I don't want to yank him from town to town, always on the run, always looking over our shoulders."

"That's commendable," he said. "Fighting is always preferable, at least as far as I'm concerned."

There was something in his voice. "Is that what you've done?" she asked softly. "Fought for what you want?"

Her question startled him. Dark emotion flashed in

his eyes a second before he slammed the lid down on it. "It's better than running," he repeated.

She noticed he didn't answer her question. Fine. She didn't really care anyway. She only had enough energy to worry about her son. "If things get bad enough where I have no choice, then both Ryan and I are out of here. We'll go in the night, without notice to you or anyone else. Do you understand?"

"Of course," he said, "but I doubt it's going to come to that. Believe me, I want to catch this guy as bad as you do."

Nodding, she swallowed hard and then took a big leap of faith. "Then I need you to do one more favor for me. I need you to help me find out the truth about Ryan's adoption. I think if I can do that then we can figure out who this crazy person is and why he or she is stalking me."

Despite the earth-shattering honesty of the kiss they'd shared, Mac could barely contain his shock at her trusting words. If Emily truly meant what she'd just said—and the raw sincerity in her voice told him she did—he had to believe she really didn't know what the truth about Ryan.

In all the scenarios he'd imagined, he hadn't thought of this possibility. He'd been prepared for so long to do battle with the woman who'd stolen his son and now... now the best thing he could do was reserve all judgment and guide her to the truth about where her son had come from. But could he do so and remain objective? That was the question. He didn't know the answer, but he'd certainly have to try.

With a start, he realized she watched him with trust and hope shining naked from her beautiful brown eyes.

For half a second he felt like a heel then realized he'd done nothing wrong.

"I know we've been over this, but we need to go over it again. Let's start at the beginning." Hand at the small of her back, he gently guided her toward the house. He liked touching her. Something about her delicate, willowy physique brought out the protector in him. He hadn't felt at all like that in the time since his wife had died and his son disappeared. Since he'd been unable to protect either one of them, he supposed that was natural.

But feeling like that about Emily was all kinds of wrong—at least until they learned the truth about whether or not she and her former husband had been the ones who'd stolen his son.

When she took a seat on her sofa and motioned him to the chair, her caramel eyes blazed with determination and suppressed anger. While he reluctantly admired her spunk, he didn't want her doing anything brave and crazy.

"I've already told you everything I know," she began, her words trailing off as he shook his head.

"I know, but even if we've already gone over this, I want you to tell me everything you remember about adopting Ryan. There might be some kernel of information there that you might have overlooked."

"All right." Sitting back, she briefly closed her eyes, as though she needed to gather her strength to relive the past. Watching her in this unguarded moment, the way the light reflected on her creamy skin and the sexy way the shagginess of her dark hair set off her delicately carved facial structure, he fought the urge to touch her, to pull her close and lend her strength. Ridiculous, yet even as he mentally scoffed at his own foolishness, his body stirred at her unconscious loveliness. She was everything he was not—beauty and grace and compassion, a perfect mother for Ryan. Though her marriage had failed, she'd make some man a wonderful wife.

Damn. Throat aching, he looked away, cursing the fact that he had to struggle to regain his composure. He swallowed hard, and forced himself to concentrate. "Start at the beginning," he urged, his voice remarkably steady. "I assume you and your husband had been trying to conceive."

Her amazing eyes flew open, briefly reflecting her anguish when she thought of that long ago time. For a moment, she bowed her head, and when she lifted it again, he knew how hard it was for her to bare her soul to him.

"Yes," she said. "I wanted children. Carlos said he did, but I think he only agreed because if I was busy with babies he would be free to do whatever he wanted."

Something stirred in him at her unguarded words—something foolish and dangerous and completely misplaced. Clearing his throat, he kept asking the questions that he knew he must. "Yours wasn't a happy marriage?"

"No." The admission seemed to startle her. "I truly didn't know my husband when I married him. I thought I did, really. But like a lot of other young women, I overlooked a lot of things. Many of those I believed I could change once we were married."

"Change how?"

She ducked her head, her face coloring as though embarrassed. "With the power of my love." She sighed, then continued. "I did love him once."

He didn't comment. How could he? Once, he'd been exactly the same with his wife, Sarah. Luckily

for them, she'd settled down, tamed her wildness and
began working on their marriage. Otherwise, he had
no doubt they wouldn't have lasted past the first year.

"I know what you mean. I've forgiven much," he
said. "In the name of love."

"Thank you." Her relieved smile told him she appreciated the small kindness. "Anyway, Carlos humored
me with what he called the baby obsession. But no matter what, I just couldn't get pregnant."

"So you had tests?"

"No." Her expression clouded. "He refused. I don't
think he could have handled it if he learned the infer-
tility was his fault. He was so—" she waved a hand
vaguely "—macho, you know?"

He didn't know. He'd never met the man. But from
the videos he'd watched of police interrogations, Carlos
Cavell had been a preening peacock of a man. Mac
couldn't even begin to picture him with a woman like
Emily.

"Go on."

Twisting her hands in her lap, she continued. "Anyway, after a while of trying, he said he was done. He
told me if I wanted a baby so much, then I needed to
go ahead and adopt one. His only stipulation was that
the child be a boy."

"He wanted a son." Odd how even now with the
other man long dead, the thought could infuriate Mac.
Unwilling to wait for the adoption to go through the
proper channels, which took time, when Carlos had
wanted a son, he'd simply hired someone to steal one.

"Yes. He wanted a son. I would have been happy
with either a boy or a girl, so that didn't matter to me."

Briskly, Mac forced himself to continue the questioning. "So you decided to adopt. Who began the process?"

"I did. Carlos was far too busy to have time to do something like that. But when he heard me complaining about how slow everything seemed to be going, he took over."

They covered a few more things, like the fact that every single place she'd contacted had pointed out the long waiting list. Whether church group or private agency, if she wanted an infant, she'd better be prepared to wait.

"And one of the things Carlos didn't have was patience," she said. "He told me he was going to pull some strings. I don't know what he did, but he called me one day and told me to get the nursery ready. Very soon we were going to have our very own baby."

"And you didn't question how he'd accomplished such a miracle in six months' time?"

"We've already covered this." Stretching, she met his gaze, though her own was hooded, looking inward. "I was so overjoyed that I was finally having my dream of a baby come true that I didn't question him. He was my husband."

Mac nodded, wondering why of all the women in the world this one got to him. They should be sworn enemies, and instead, he found himself wanting to hold her. "And then?" he prompted.

"Then, exactly as Carlos had promised, I had my baby. Ryan." Her smile was genuine, full of love. "He was only a few days old when they brought him to me. I've often wondered about the mother who gave him up—even if she was one of Carlos's mistresses, which I've suspected she was."

Carlos's mistresses? Really? It took every ounce of self-control not to react to her comment.

He didn't understand how the hell she could say such a thing. Could she truly believe that Ryan's mother was one of Carlos's many lovers? He truly didn't think Emily was that clueless, but her words left only one possibility—the same one he'd already reached.

She didn't know. He felt it like a physical blow to his chest. She honestly did not know.

Looking down, he briefly closed his eyes. Of all he'd expected when he met this woman and of all the scenarios he'd imagined, he'd never pictured this likelihood.

Emily Gilley might truly be innocent. If she really had no idea at all that the baby she'd adopted had been stolen, then she was blameless, as much of a victim as he was—judging from her statement about Carlos's mistress, She wasn't the slightest bit aware that her son legally belonged to someone else.

Or…he forced himself to hang on to his cynical nature. The other possibility was that Emily was a damn fine actress.

Until he knew for sure, he couldn't allow the lure of her compelling beauty and warm personality to sway him.

"After you adopted Ryan, did your marriage get better?" he heard himself asking, waiting for her answer even as he inwardly winced.

"No, not really. I actually was on the verge of asking for a divorce when he was killed."

Now *this* was news. Evidently she'd been successful at keeping this information out of the media, which meant, he reflected, that she most likely hadn't confided in anyone.

"Why?" he asked.

Expression troubled, Emily raised her caramel-colored gaze to his. "I don't know. Sometimes I think I wasn't meant to be married. The man I'd loved, the man I'd believed my husband to be, that person was entirely fabricated. Carlos kept his true self separate from me, from our marriage. Gradually, over time, bits and pieces came out. To be honest, I was secretly relieved when I learned he had mistresses."

Blindsided, Mac didn't understand. "Relieved? Why?"

"Because then I had something concrete on which to blame my marriage's failure. I had a rational excuse to leave."

Still he didn't get it. "If you were unhappy, then why'd you need an excuse? Why didn't you just go?"

Now she stared at him, looking incredulous. "We had a child. We were a family."

"And you wanted out. Are you saying you had to justify your own unhappiness?"

A brief quiver, the slightest hitch in her breathing, told him that his comment had hit home.

"Yes," she admitted. "I needed to justify wanting to leave him. Despite the lies and the illegal activities it turned out he was involved in, on the surface Carlos was a model husband. He didn't beat me—in fact, he treated me more like precious china. He provided well for us. We never wanted for anything."

"But you weren't happy."

She sighed. "That's not the issue. When there's a child involved, you don't just walk away and split up a family that easily."

God, he wanted to kiss her. Instead, he forced himself to think—really think—about her words. After all, he knew about the various trouble spots that could strike a marriage. He'd lived them. In fact, his wife Sarah had admitted she'd decided to get pregnant in a last-ditch hope of saving their marriage. The fact that she hadn't consulted with him first had actually made things worse—until the baby inside her became real.

Then, he had begun to believe that maybe she was right. Once they had a child together, everything would be all right. They'd work things out.

"That makes sense. I get that. But Emily," he continued, gentling his tone, "how could you not know what Carlos did? He was constantly in the news for one thing or another. How'd you rationalize his multiple arrests, the fact that the Feds had him on their radar?"

"Put like that," she said wryly, "I sound pretty stupid. But the short answer is I didn't know. Ryan kept me busy. I did a lot of charitable work for the animal shelter and a couple of other local charities. Whenever I happened to see the occasional news story, he always had a good explanation."

"How do you explain away being indicted for wire fraud? Or being the head of a large drug cartel?"

"*Suspected* head," she pointed out, even as she shook her head. "And he claimed the indictment was a business rivalry gone bad."

When he opened his mouth to speak again, she held up her hand, letting him see how her fingers trembled. "Look, Mac, I knew Carlos wasn't a good person. I guess I didn't want to let myself see exactly how bad he actually was. But once he was murdered, I had no choice."

They stared at each other for a moment in silence. Her agitation and frustration were nearly palpable, and again he struggled, hands fisted at his sides, to keep from touching her.

Seeing her like that, her glossy dark hair sticking up as if she'd just gotten out of bed, so sexy and slender and fragile-looking, he ached to gather her in his arms and hold her close. Though she tried so hard to be strong, he knew from personal experience that everyone had a breaking point.

The question he faced was this: Did he want to be the one who broke her or the one who helped her hold things together?

Things were coming full circle.

It all came down to this. Did he still believe Emily Gilley had knowingly stolen a baby—his child— named him Ryan and made him her son? Or because she wanted a baby so badly, had she turned a blind eye to her husband's worst crime? Was she as innocent as she appeared to be?

When he'd made the decision to come to Anniversary, his plans had been clear-cut and sharp: find out if Emily Gilley's Ryan was truly his son and go from there.

Now…he didn't know what to think. He'd spent many years in law enforcement and had always believed he had a good eye when it came to people. Every instinct he had kept telling him that Emily Gilley was exactly as she appeared—good, kind and loving. She didn't even appear to realize how her stunning beauty affected men.

Disgusted with himself, he swallowed. If he kept on letting his emotions—and frankly, his libido—control him, he'd eventually mess things up. And since Ryan was all he had left in this world to call his own, he couldn't let anything interfere with their reunion.

Of course, he still had to determine if Ryan was actually his son. This, he reminded himself sharply, must always be his focus—no matter how sweet and charming and sexy Emily might appear.

Emily had run out of words when her cell phone rang. Grateful for any distraction that would keep her from oversharing any more with Mac, she answered.

"Hello, Em!" Jayne Cooper's excited voice boomed into her ear. "I just wanted to remind you about tonight."

"Tonight?" Emily drew a blank. "What's tonight?"

Jayne laughed. "Surely you didn't forget. Tonight we're meeting at The Cheesy Pepper for girls' night. We've been planning this all week, remember?"

With all the craziness that had been going on, Emily had completely blanked on the fact that they'd made plans earlier in the week. "I can't," she said unequivocally, filling her friend in on what had happened.

"I heard some of that from Ed," Jayne told her. "And if anyone needs a break, it's you."

Emily couldn't even imagine trying to have fun after something like this—and said so.

"You need to unwind," Jayne insisted. "There's nothing better for that than a night out with your best friends."

"I could do dinner but nothing more. But—" and she meant this, sort of "—unfortunately, I haven't even booked a babysitter. And you know how hard it is to find a good one this late on a Friday." Since Jayne had two children herself, she'd know it was nearly impossible.

"You forgot to get a sitter?" Jayne asked, sounding a bit shocked. Then she clucked. "I'm sorry. Of course you forgot. You've certainly had a lot to deal with this week."

Relieved, Emily swallowed, trying to get words out past the sudden lump in her throat. "I'm so glad you understand," she began.

"Oh, I do. Completely. And that's why you need a girls' night out more than ever." Determination rang in Jayne's voice. "My husband is watching our two, and I'm sure he wouldn't mind one more. They're planning on ordering pizza. Bring Ryan over. He likes to play with Charlie. He'll have a blast."

Emily blinked. "I don't know…"

"Yes. You. Do. I'm not taking no for an answer."

Finally, Emily had no choice but to tell her friend the truth. "I'm afraid to leave Ryan. This nutcase seems to be targeting him."

"Sweetheart, you know Ed is a sheriff's deputy, right? He's fully aware of your situation. He won't let anything happen to your baby."

"I'd rather—"

Jayne bulldozed on as though Emily hadn't spoken. "Now bring Ryan over to my house around six. You don't have much time. And wear something cute. We are going out on the town."

"Dinner only," Emily protested weakly and too late. Listening to the click that meant Jayne had disconnected the call, Emily shook her head, trying to smile and failing miserably.

How could she do this? Go out with her friends and pretend everything was normal? Instead of what— sitting home alone jumping at every outside sound?

She sighed. Maybe Jayne was right. Perhaps a night with Tina and Jayne would help Emily quit worrying. After all, it couldn't hurt. And, as Jayne had pointed out, her husband Ed worked for the sheriff's department as a deputy.

While she was there, Emily resolved to ask him what he thought of Mac Riordan. She still wasn't sure she entirely trusted him.

"Earth to Emily," Mac said, startling her. Somehow, she'd managed to forget he was there. "Is there a problem?"

"No," she answered, debating whether or not to tell him her plans. Then, because he'd no doubt find out from Ed anyway, she filled him in on Jayne's call.

"I think that's a good idea," he said, surprising her. "You need to take a break from this craziness. Dinner and a drink with your friends might go a long way to helping you feel better. I don't know about you, but I always think more clearly when I'm relaxed."

Since he'd just voiced her own thoughts exactly, she considered him. "You don't think Ryan will be in any danger? Because if there's the slightest chance—"

"Ed can handle things. He's been a deputy for a long time."

Still she hesitated. "I don't know…"

He touched the back of her hand. Though his touch was light, she still felt a shiver of electricity. "If it'll make you feel better, I can go over there and hang out with him while you're gone. Two deputies are better than one."

Astonished, she looked up. His posture seemed casual and friendly, but he seemed to be keeping himself perfectly still, as though holding his breath waiting for her answer, which made absolutely no sense whatsoever.

"You'd do that?" she asked slowly. "Give up your Friday night to help Ed keep my son safe?" She couldn't believe it. While she could tell Mac was dedicated to his job, this went above and beyond.

"Of course." He grinned. "Actually, it would be a win-win situation. I don't have any plans, and I like the heck out of Ed. We could play cards or something."

With two deputies, her son would be safer at home than with her. And she really could use a break. Deciding, Emily slowly nodded. "I'll take you up on that. I have to pick up Ryan from school. Jayne wants us there around six."

Mac stood. "I'll be there around the same time."

Hyperaware of him, her skin prickled when he walked by. Even Emily's halfhearted attempt to rationalize that this was because of her lingering suspicion fell flat. She knew—and she'd be lying to herself if she pretended otherwise—that something about him attracted her in a way no man had done for years.

Studying him from under her lashes, she tried to analyze her reaction. He radiated confident masculinity, though in an entirely unselfconscious manner. Her husband had once been such a man—or so she'd thought. Only a lot of Carlos's confidence masked a bone deep, vicious insecurity. Somehow she doubted Mac Riordan had a single self-doubting bone in his broad-shouldered body.

Then she wondered why she even cared. All that mattered was finding the creep who'd been stalking her and Ryan. Once he'd helped her do that, she'd doubted she'd ever see Mac again, no matter how strong the attraction.

Showing him out, she watched as he walked to his car, unable to resist admiring his broad shoulders and the way his jeans fit his backside. She even liked the way he walked—a sort of take-the-bull-by-the-horns, no-nonsense stride.

Then, as he started the car and drove away with a

friendly wave, she chastised herself. The last thing she needed in the middle of all this craziness was to develop a crush on anyone, especially on the handsome sheriff's deputy assigned to help her.

Chapter 7

Once he'd put away his notebook and left her house, Mac drove home, unable to resist singing along to the music on the radio. With his heart light for the first time in months—hell, *years*—he felt as if he'd been given an amazing, stupendous gift. In fact, he couldn't believe his luck. Emily had essentially given him a free pass to spend time getting to know his son.

He shook his head, grinning like a fool. His son. Even though he didn't have proof—only a DNA test would be able to prove that—he knew in his heart the truth. Ryan was his. And whether Emily had knowingly stolen him or not, nothing could change that.

Calling Ed, he gave his coworker a heads-up. The poor guy sounded, while a bit bewildered, really happy to have company while he babysat. When Mac mentioned a game of Texas Hold 'em, Ed grew even more enthusiastic. He volunteered to go to the store and get chips and dip in preparation for guys' night in.

Briefly, both men discussed the chance of the stalker putting in an appearance. Neither felt this was even a remote possibility, though they would be on their guard just in case.

Hanging up, Mac drove home. Now all he had to do was grab something to eat and then mentally prepare himself for the night. Nervous, anxious and excited all at once, his stomach doing flip-flops, he wondered if he'd even be able to choke down some dinner.

This news was so momentous that he could scarcely keep it to himself. Inside his living room, he paced, trying out a dozen different scenarios and rejecting each one. He'd simply have to play this by ear.

Taking out his cell phone, he toyed with the idea of calling Joe but decided at the last minute against it. He wasn't ready to talk about this—not now, not yet, while everything was still so fragile and new. He'd give the relationship with Ryan time to develop before he'd feel safe to share details with anyone else. Since Joe was his best friend, Mac knew his former partner would understand.

He felt a smudge of remorse for hiding the truth from his best friend. Soon, he'd remedy that. He knew Joe would be overjoyed when he learned Mac had not only met his son but was getting to know him, too.

Humming softly under his breath, Mac fixed himself a sandwich and washed it down with a diet soda. He wished he'd asked Emily what kind of toys Ryan liked but then remembered his brief foray inside the boy's room and smiled. He'd run by the store on his way to Ed's later and pick up some small gift for his son.

* * *

Friends, Emily thought happily, were one of life's greatest blessings. In New York, she hadn't made too many friends—at least not genuine ones. Most of the people who attached themselves to Carlos Cavell and his wife only hung around for the status or because they wanted something for themselves.

After Carlos's death, the truth of this had been hammered home when all of the women she'd hung out with suddenly didn't answer their cell phones or return her calls. Her friends here in Anniversary were one of the many reasons Emily valued her life in the small town.

Guilt stabbed her as she wondered if it was wrong to be so happy about having some time with Jayne and Tina, sans child. Though intellectually she knew this respite from worry was a good idea, she couldn't shake the guilt. Any other time she would have acknowledged that she deserved this—she put in her time both as a full-time worker and a mommy.

But any other time, she didn't have some wacko after her for an imaginary crime. She could have withstood this, she thought, if only the stalker hadn't involved her son.

Then she thought of Mac Riordan with his quiet sense of purpose, and her doubts silenced. Ed and Mac wouldn't let anything happen to Ryan, and she needed to let go of her guilt and enjoy her time with her friends.

This resolved, she mentally reviewed the meager contents of her closet. It had been so long since they'd had a girls' night out that she could hardly think about what to wear. One aspect to this was the way she'd need to go about preparing.

A night out on the town in tiny Anniversary, Texas, was quite a bit different than a night out in Manhattan, New York. Here in Anniversary, cowboy boots and jeans were the perfect going-out attire. She really liked the fact that she didn't have to wear stilettos and a short dress. She also loved that she didn't have to be "on," worrying about a stray photographer or a flash going off in her face. Being married to one of New York's most notorious men had made her a minor celebrity there. Here, she was just plain old Emily Gilley, a single mom who worked in the vet's office.

And, she thought to herself with a smile, she had two of the best friends a woman could ever want.

With the simple acceptance of childhood, Ryan was unsurprised to see her early for the second day in a row.

"Everything all right, Mommy?" he asked, climbing into the car.

"Yep," she answered, chucking him under the chin. "How'd you like to go play with Eva and Charlie tonight while Mommy and Jayne go out?"

"For dinner?" He frowned, apparently not sold on the idea.

When she nodded, his frown deepened. "Will I get to eat first?"

"I think Ed is ordering pizza."

Just like that, his little face cleared. "Oh, okay. As long as Ed makes Eva share with me and Charlie."

That settled, she waited until Ryan had finished buckling himself in and drove home to plot what to wear. Despite Jayne's and Mac's reassurances, she vacillated between wanting to call off the entire night and being excited at the idea of taking a few hours to catch up with friends.

In the end, she decided to go through with her plans. Both she and Ryan could use a diversion.

A couple hours later, she pulled up to Jayne's small

ranch house with a hyperactive Ryan bouncing in the car seat. He'd gotten more and more excited the longer he considered the prospect of a night playing with his friend Charlie. She almost pitied Ed and Mac having to deal with him.

With Mac's patrol car parked in front of the brick house and Ed's in the driveway, the place looked well guarded. Her heart lightened a few more degrees, and she began to think she might be able to enjoy herself after all.

As soon as she turned the engine off, Ryan unbuckled himself, yanked the door open and took off running for the front door. Following behind at a more sedate pace, Emily couldn't help but grin. So much for worrying that her son would miss her.

Jayne met her at the door, giving her a big hug as Ryan tore past. "You didn't tell me Mr. Tall and Delicious was coming over," Jayne whispered.

Concerned that maybe she should have asked her friend's permission, Emily grimaced. "Sorry. I'm pretty sure he said he was going to clear it with Ed."

"He did." Jayne hugged her. "I was just teasing."

Aware of her red face, Emily shrugged. At Jayne's knowing look, she shook her head. "He's helping protect Ryan. Nothing more, nothing less."

"Oh, yeah? Then why are you blushing?"

To her consternation, Emily felt her face grow hotter. It was for no good reason, either—that is, if she didn't count the persistent smoldering attraction that always seemed to be simmering between them. "Are you ready?" she asked, pretending to ignore Jayne's expectant expression. "I'm starving."

"Sure." Jayne shrugged. "Let's go say goodbye to

the rug rats, and then we'll go pick up Tina. I'm glad she didn't have to work tonight."

As they walked into the living room, Emily saw Mac and Ed sitting side by side on the sofa, while Ryan had joined Charlie in front of the big-screen TV, already engrossed in a video game. Eva, a few years older, sprawled on the armchair, reading a book.

Mac's gaze swept over her, and he grinned. Giving her a thumbs-up, he winked.

Emily felt her blush deepen. Next to her, Jayne laughed. "If you two can quit making googly eyes at each other, we wanted to say bye. We've got to go pick up Tina, and then we're heading out."

Pushing himself up off the sofa, Ed crossed the room and gave his wife a quick kiss on the lips. Glancing at Emily, he smiled. "Don't you worry any, hon. Ryan's in good hands."

Face still flaming, she smiled back. "Thanks."

"Are you ready?" Practically bouncing on her feet, Jayne was clearly eager to go.

"Just a second. Bye, Ryan," Emily said. Her son didn't even turn and look at her. Instead, he lifted his hand in a backward wave without taking his eyes off the video game.

As she and Jayne left the room, Emily sighed. "I suppose it's good that he's not going to miss me at all, right?"

Her friend gave her a curious look. Then apparently realizing Emily was serious, she smiled and gave her a shoulder bump. "Why should he? Ryan and Charlie are friends. They'll have a blast tonight. Poor Eva. It's going to be guys' night at my house—video games, pizza and cards. Though as long as they leave her alone and let her read in peace, she'll be fine."

Emily nodded, saying nothing.

Apparently, her nervousness showed. After they got in the car, Jayne reached over and gave Emily a quick hug. "And you'll be all right, too. I promise. Now relax and let yourself have fun."

"I'll try," Emily said, meaning it.

Taking his cue from Ed, Mac kept his demeanor relaxed and easygoing, though his insides were churning with emotion. He tried not to focus too much on Ryan, though he couldn't help but be hyperconscious of the boy who was his son. He'd trashed the idea of buying a gift, realizing such a gesture might be viewed with suspicion.

While Charlie and Ryan battled it out in their video game and Eva read, Ed got out a deck of cards and a couple of beers. The house had an open layout, and the kitchen table had a clear view of the living area. The two men played a few games of poker, using chips instead of money. They talked shop, though since Ryan was present, they didn't touch on the Emily Gilley stalker case. Mac found the complexity of the other cases interesting, amazed such crimes occurred in a small town like Anniversary.

When the pizza arrived, Ed made the boys turn off the TV and Eva put her book down and join them at the table. They had three large pizzas, probably too much, but Ed said he'd rather have extra food than not enough.

To Mac's surprise, Ryan climbed into the seat next to him.

"Hi," Ryan said, reaching for a slice of cheese pizza.

"Hi, yourself." Mimicking the boy's motions, Mac chose a piece of the same pie.

Taking a big bite, Ryan chewed, studying Mac all the

while with a string of cheese hanging from his mouth. "Are you my mommy's boyfriend?" he asked.

Mac nearly choked. He glanced at Ed, saw from the other man's grin that he'd get no help there and managed to swallow. "No," he said, hoping he sounded more nonchalant than he felt. "I'm trying to help your mom catch the bad guys who broke into your house."

Snagging another huge bite, the boy nodded. "I think it's the same people who were after my dad."

Hearing another man referred to as Ryan's dad didn't hurt as much as he'd expected. Again, Mac exchanged a glance with Ed. "You remember people being after your father?"

With a shrug, Ryan helped himself to another slice. At the same time, Charlie went for the exact same one. Even though there were several other identical pieces to choose from, a minor scuffle ensued, mostly consisting of shoving and elbowing and Charlie yelling.

"Enough." Ed didn't shout, but he didn't have to. The authority in his voice was sufficient to instantly quiet the boys. Mac viewed his coworker with admiration as Ed admonished the children to be nice and share.

Then, with both boys quietly munching on their pizza and Eva still ignoring them all, immersed in her food, they happily continued the meal. Ed glanced at Mac, then at Ryan and did a double take.

"That's so weird," he said, chuckling. "You and Ryan look enough alike that you two could be related."

Mac froze. With an effort, he pasted what he hoped was a surprised look on his face and turned, pretending to study the boy. Ryan gazed back at him, a surprisingly serious look in his nearly identical blue eyes.

"I don't know. Maybe." Mac shrugged, as if the issue was of no importance, as if his heart wasn't pounding.

"We have the same color eyes," Ryan said. "Blue." Sounding proud, he looked from Mac to Ed and back again. "My mom's eyes are brown."

"So you know your colors," Charlie scoffed. "Big deal. I learned those in preschool."

"So did I." Ryan punched his arm, no doubt meaning to emphasize his point.

"No more of that." Ed's stern voice stopped Charlie from sure retaliation. "If you want to play some more of that video game, you two need to eat your pizza peacefully."

"Fine," Charlie huffed, again reaching for another slice at the same time as Ryan. But as it looked like another mini-battle would break out, a sharp look from Ed had each boy taking separate pieces and eating them in silence.

"I have to admire your parenting skills," Mac said after the children had finished eating. The boys had resumed playing their game, and Eva had retreated to her room with her book.

"Thanks." Ed grinned. "It comes with the territory."

"I don't know." For the first time since he'd seen a resolution to his obsessive quest to regain his son, he questioned whether or not he'd be able to be a good father.

"You just do what your dad did with you, that's all." Stretching, Ed gathered up the empty pizza boxes. "As long as it worked, that is."

"I didn't have a dad." Though Mac didn't usually talk about his past, he needed answers or reassurance and thought Ed would be the man to help him. "My mom raised me alone. She died of ovarian cancer right after I got married when I was twenty-five."

"Wow. I'm sorry to hear that."

Mac shrugged. "It was a long time ago."

"You never even had a stepdad?"

"Nope." He smiled to show Ed it really wasn't a big deal.

"Okay." Jamming the pizza boxes in the large trash can, Ed wiped the table off with a paper towel. "I guess it doesn't matter since you and your wife never had kids, right?"

Rather than commenting, Mac began to shuffle the cards. "Let's play."

"So…" Tina took a sip of her mango margarita before leaning forward to peer at Emily. "What's going on with you and Mac Riordan?"

Emily blinked, ignoring how her heart leapt into her throat at the mention of his name. "Going on? Nothing. He's working for the sheriff's office and trying to find out who's stalking me."

Tina and Jayne exchanged a meaningful look while Emily felt her face grow hot—again. What the heck was wrong with her?

"I think it might be a bit more than that," Jayne pointed out gently. "After all, he's at my house right now with Ed, helping watch Ryan."

"He is?" Clearly intrigued, Tina's eyes widened. "Do tell."

Both women eyed Emily expectantly.

"There's nothing to tell. Seriously." Grabbing a chip from the basket in the middle of the table, she plunged it into the bowl of warm *queso* and ate it slowly before reaching for another.

"Emily." Placing her hand on Emily's arm, Tina leaned close. "He's hot, he's single and obviously he has eyes for you. Why not give him a chance?"

Looking down, Emily tried not to react. She'd have to be a fool to get involved with another man after what Carlos had done to her. But they didn't know that. After all, Jayne and Tina meant well. These women were her friends.

"I'm not in the market," she said lightly. "Look what happened when I agreed to go out with Tim Keeslar."

Tina groaned. "Okay, so that was a mistake. I'm sorry for setting you up with him."

"I know Mac was trying to locate him," Jayne put in. "He wanted to ask him some questions and make sure he doesn't turn out to be your stalker."

"He's not my stalker." Emily knew she sounded weary, but she couldn't help it.

"How do you know?"

"I don't, but I think he just really liked me and I wasn't ready to be in any sort of a relationship. And I'm still not," she said pointedly.

"Ah, but this is totally different." Tina grinned. "Tim Keeslar is no Mac Riordan. I can't believe you don't find him attractive."

Ignoring the way her face heated, Emily grabbed another chip. "I didn't say that. He's a very handsome man. I'm just not in the market. I already told you to go for it, Tina, if you think he's so hot."

Laughing, Tina had the grace to look abashed. "He's not interested in me. I already tried flirting with him, and he had about as much interest in me as I have in Wendell Wayne Barnes."

Since everyone in Anniversary knew Wendell Wayne believed himself madly in love with Tina, despite the fact that he was thirty years older and looked like he never bathed, this cracked Jayne up. Emily even had to laugh, glad she'd rerouted the conversation away from her love life—or lack thereof.

The waiter chose this moment to bring their sizzling fajitas: chicken for Emily, beef for Jayne and shrimp for Tina.

"Corn and flour tortillas," he announced. "Do you need anything else, ladies?"

In unison, they shook their heads. Both Jayne and Tina had to wipe their eyes; they'd been laughing so hard.

Silence fell for a moment while the women dug in.

But Tina wasn't done. She'd barely loaded her tortilla with meat, cheese, guacamole and sour cream and taken a bite when she looked at Emily. "Now you are aware that Mac Riordan is about the hottest man in town, right?"

"She's right," Jayne chimed in. "Except for my husband, that is. What she's trying to say, honey, is if you're holding out for something better, you're wasting your time. Mac's it."

"Can we change the subject, please?" Emily kept her voice friendly but firm. "I need this night out to forget about my problems, not rehash them."

Jayne raised one perfectly arched brow. "Are you saying Mac is a problem?"

"No. Yes. Oh, stop." Swatting her friend, Emily grabbed a second corn tortilla and began loading it up with chicken, refried beans, rice and shredded cheese. She bit in, rolling her eyes. "This is heaven."

They finished their meal and a second margarita each, except for Jayne since she was driving.

"One order of sopaipillas, please," Tina told the waiter. "And three forks."

With a nod, he hurried off to get their dessert. As

they watched him go, Jayne looked beyond him and frowned.

"Check out that woman over there, near the tortilla-making machine," she said, lowering her voice. "Do you think she's a hooker?"

Both Emily and Tina turned to look. The instant Emily saw the heavily made-up bleach-blonde in the skin-tight dress, her heart sank. Desiree was sitting in a corner booth with Franco, enjoying giant margaritas and laughing, heads close together.

Closing her eyes, Emily drew on every ounce of inner strength she possessed to keep herself from reacting—at least physically.

Though her heart raced, she managed to chuckle while Tina and Jayne thoroughly trashed Desiree. But when they switched to speculating about the hunky man with her, Emily felt sick.

Still, she had no choice but to remain in place, pretending to have a good time. At least with her back to the other woman, there was still a chance Desiree wouldn't notice her—not so if Emily got up to leave, though.

Cursing under her breath, Emily tried to steer the conversation to something else, bringing up Mac out of sheer desperation. To her relief, her friends eagerly latched on to that topic, until Desiree and Franco got up to leave.

"Look at those shoes," Tina breathed. "How can she even walk in them?"

Counting to three so the other couple would be well on their way to the door, Emily finally turned to look. She caught the back of them, noting that Franco had gotten rid of his fake wheelchair.

Once they'd left the restaurant, despite her roiling

stomach, Emily struggled to at least pretend to enjoy the rest of the night. Neither Jayne nor Tina appeared to notice anything was wrong, which meant her acting abilities must have improved.

Still waiting on the sopaipillas, Jayne's cell phone rang. She answered and listened before muttering something unintelligible and ending the call.

"Is there a problem?" Emily asked, immediately concerned about Ryan.

"I'm not sure," Jayne said slowly. "That was Ed. He got a phone call from someone who claims to be Ryan's parent. He said he couldn't tell if the caller was a man or a woman. Do you know who the people are who gave him up for adoption?"

Dumbfounded, Emily stared. "No. But this is exactly what's been going on…the letters, the break-in. And I got several hang-ups at work, the day I was out after the break-in."

"Are you all right?" Both women viewed her, concern written all over their faces.

"No." With her throat closed up, Emily found it difficult to speak.

"Oh." Obviously troubled, Jayne looked down at her plate before raising her eyes to meet Emily's. "I think we'd better skip dessert and head home."

"Right." Emily jumped to her feet, feeling as though her heart would pound right out of her chest. Had Desiree made the call after leaving the restaurant? "What did this person say? Did he or she threaten Ryan?"

"No. Oddly enough, the only threat was made toward Mac."

"What?" Emily couldn't believe it. This was a new twist. "I don't understand."

"Well, despite your protests that you and Mac aren't

involved, I'm guessing Ryan's biological parent thinks you are. And this doesn't appear to make him or her very happy."

"That makes no sense. Even if we were—and we're not—what does that have to do with Ryan?"

Until now, Tina had remained silent, but now she moved forward and put her hand on Emily's shoulder. "Maybe it's the idea that you two are going to make a family with Ryan. Stalkers are usually crazy," she said. "Most times their actions don't make much sense."

Jayne signaled for the check. "She's right. This guy—or gal—could be convinced that you, as well as your son, belong to him. Any male seen as threatening this fantasy would be considered a danger."

"Which is why he or she threatened Mac." Emily's dull voice mirrored the ache beginning to thrum inside her skull. She fidgeted while Jayne paid the bill, promising to reimburse her friend later.

"The question I have now," Jayne said as they hurried out to her car, "is what is Mac going to do about it?"

Chapter 8

Staring blankly while Ed relayed in a voice too low for the boys to hear exactly what the caller had said, Mac clenched his jaw. Who was this person claiming to be Ryan's biological parent? This reminded him yet again that while he was ninety-nine percent certain Ryan was his stolen infant, apparently someone else believed differently. Until a DNA test was run, there'd be no way to know for certain. Gut instinct didn't count.

"And you didn't recognize the voice?" Mac asked.

"No. I couldn't even tell if it was a man or a woman. Whoever it was used some kind of voice-distortion software, like the kind you can get over the internet."

Mac cursed.

"Jayne and the girls are on their way home," Ed continued. "I hated to mess up their night, but this is too important to ignore."

"I agree." Mac didn't have to feign his anger. For the

first time, he wondered how accurate Joe's information had been. Was it actually possible someone else was Ryan's birth parent? Like, as Emily had mentioned, one of Carlos's mistresses?

If that turned out to be the case, he thought with a weariness that struck deep inside all the way to his soul, that meant his real son was still out there somewhere. And the likelihood Mac would find him five years later was highly improbable.

"I've contacted the phone company," Ed was saying. "They're running a trace on the call. If we can get an originating number, we'll know where the perp's hiding out."

"Right." But Mac knew what the trace would yield—a disposable cell phone, a "burn" phone, which was untraceable.

He squinted at Ed. "What did Jayne say?"

"They were going to leave right away and head home."

"Do you know how much she told Emily?"

Ed stared back. "Probably everything. Why?"

He glanced at the boys, still engrossed in their game. "Just wondering how much interference to run."

Ed grimaced. "I know what you think, but from what I've seen of Emily Gilley, she'll be cool as ice around her kid. You don't have to worry about that."

"I never did get a hold of Tim Keeslar," Mac groused. "The manager at the parts store he owns said he was on vacation. I checked his house, and no one is there."

"If he went out of town, he went salmon fishing up in Alaska. He goes every year about this time. But he should be back by now."

"Good. I'll try him again tomorrow," Mac said.

A moment later, the front door opened, and the

women rushed into the room. Jayne and Tina immediately crossed to the kitchen to join Ed and Mac. Emily instead walked calmly over to where the boys still sat transfixed in front of the TV.

He watched while she bent over and calmly kissed Ryan's cheek, murmuring something in his ear.

"I don't want to go home yet," Ryan whined.

Straightening up, she crossed her arms. "Now, please."

Amazingly, Ryan put down the controller and jumped up, following his mother without further protest. She came over to the group of adults, hugging Jayne and Ed and kissing Tina's cheek.

When she reached Mac, she stopped and held out her hand. "Thank you for your help tonight," she said, her touch as cool as her polite and distant voice. "Ryan and I are leaving now."

Before he could even frame a response, she turned her back to them, marching toward the front door. Sensing something was up, but not sure what, Ryan trotted along at her side.

After he cast a quick look of apology at Ed and the others, Mac rushed after her. He caught her just as she yanked the front door open and stepped outside.

"I'm going with you," he said, his tone leaving no room for argument.

She didn't even turn around. "Fine," she said, her voice so emotionless that it told him exactly how frightened she was inside.

His chest squeezed. How he wished he could protect her from this, from all of what was coming.

"Are you okay to drive?" he asked, trying to sound as if he only spoke because of his part-time profession as deputy.

"I only had one margarita," she said, her back ram-rod straight, the line of her neck graceful. "And maybe one sip from my second. Plus I ate. I'm fine."

"Good. I'll follow you in my car."

Her only response was to dip her head in a curt nod.

When they got to her place, the motion-detection lights came on. Parking in front of the garage, he made her wait inside her car while he checked out the perimeter. Everything was still locked up tight, exactly as she'd left it.

He soon returned to her and rapped on the driver's side window. "All clear."

She got out slowly, with an instinctive grace he couldn't help but admire. Ryan, now sleepy, appeared to be in no hurry to go anywhere. She had to coax him, finally standing aside and letting Mac pick him up and carry him into the house.

"This way," she said, her voice low, leading the way to Ryan's room. "Just put him on the bed."

Once he'd complied, she began the process of getting the groggy five-year-old out of his clothes and into his pajamas. "We've still got to brush our teeth and wash our face and hands," she said. "Come on, Ryan. Help me out here."

Though Mac ached to assist her, he remained in the doorway, pretty sure she wouldn't appreciate his help. When she finally remembered him standing there, she flashed him a quick and polite smile.

"Why don't you go wait in the living room? Help yourself to a drink. I'll join you in a few minutes."

Eyeing her bending over the boy who might be his son, jaunty wisps of hair framing her heart-shaped face, he felt a peculiar sort of catch in his chest. Careful to reveal nothing in his expression, he simply nodded and moved away to do as she'd asked.

After rummaging through her refrigerator and locating a diet cola, he prowled around the living area, struck again by how completely at home he felt there. He'd lived in a lot of places since Sarah had died and he'd sold their house, unable to bear living with the memories. Most of them had been temporary, and none of them had ever made him feel at home.

Even the small place he'd purchased here in Anniversary felt like an impersonal mockery of everything he'd hoped it would be. At the end of a winding dirt road the frame house had looked to him like something out of a Norman Rockwell painting. He'd felt the impact, the raw wanting in his gut the first time he'd seen the place and known he had to have it. He'd been hopeful that this would finally become his home.

However, since moving in, he'd only unpacked a few boxes and done absolutely nothing to fix it up. Once again, he felt like a stranger in his own home, which told him this came from within him.

Shaking off the uncharacteristic melancholy, he took a seat on the edge of her couch. Then, restless, he got back to his feet and resumed prowling.

"Hey." Her soft smile told him she had no idea how sensuous her husky voice sounded. "Thanks for coming with me. He's asleep now."

"Does he usually go to bed this early?"

Glancing at her watch, she grimaced. "On school nights, yes. Since tomorrow is Saturday, I normally let him stay up later. He must have been really tired."

He studied her heart-shaped face and felt the familiar tug of desire. He wanted to kiss her. The urge to taste her lips again came out of nowhere, buffeting him like a sudden storm, taking him completely by surprise. Staring at her, he saw her pupils darken to chocolate and knew she felt it, too.

Their gazes locked. He could have sworn something intense passed between them. Heart pounding, he took a shaky breath, debating. Then her expression locked down and she moved away, answering his question without him even having to ask it.

With her back to him, she spoke, her voice hard and tight. "I saw Desiree and Franco tonight at The Cheesy Pepper. He was walking, not using a wheelchair."

He froze. "Why didn't you tell me that earlier?"

Arms crossed, she spun around to face him. "There was too much going on. The phone call…" Her voice broke, and he realized how perilously close to breaking she was.

Desperately trying to distract her, he said the first thing that came to mind. "Your house looks great. This is exactly how I wish my place looked."

"Thanks." She gave him a ghost of a smile that wobbled on the edges. "I don't have a lot of money, so I did the best I could. This is sort of how I imagine a basic suburban family home would look."

He focused on one word. "Imagine? You don't know? Where'd you grow up, on a farm?"

Her lush black lashes swept down to cover her eyes. "No, not exactly." Her tone told him to drop the subject. Feeling as if he were a treasure hunter, he didn't want to. As distractions went, this was a doozy.

"No farm, no suburbia. Hmm." Scratching his chin, he pretended to consider other alternatives. "A commune?"

His pitiful attempt at a joke didn't make her crack even the barest of smiles. Instead, she shook her head.

Though her expression was serious, at least she no longer appeared on the verge of collapse.

"If you really want to know, I grew up in an orphanage. I wasn't lucky enough to be adopted like Ryan."

He blinked. This floored him. In all the information he and Joe had put together, neither man had seen anything about that. Her husband Carlos must have used his considerable influence to bury that bit of information about his wife's past, though why, Mac didn't know.

"I'm sorry," he said. "I didn't mean to bring up old wounds."

She shrugged. "Don't be, it was a long time ago, and I'm over it."

Truly curious, he studied her. "What was that like?"

Something changed in her expression—not a total shutdown but close. "I don't…"

"Of course you don't have to tell me if you don't want to," he told her, his voice gentle, aching again to touch her. "I've never even been inside an orphanage. I can't even imagine how it must have been."

Eyeing him, she fingered a silky tendril of hair. "Living there wasn't that bad. I mean, it was all I knew. The hard part was staying there when a lot of the other kids got adopted or went to foster homes."

"And you didn't?"

"No." She didn't bother to hide the hurt in her caramel eyes. "I was a sickly child. Rheumatic fever, various infections—you name it, I had it. For that reason, they always passed me over. I didn't understand. At first, I though it must have been because I was bad, so I was super well behaved. Then, as I grew older, I went the opposite way and rebelled."

She grimaced. "In retrospect, I'm lucky I didn't end up in jail or worse."

"How long did you live there?"

"Until I was eighteen. That's how the system works. Once you age out, you're on your own. Luckily, I had a job at a fast-food place, and I'd been smart enough to save up some money, so I was okay."

The records Joe had dug up had indicated she'd married Carlos at twenty. "And then you met your husband."

"And then I met my husband." She sighed. "We were married four years."

When he only nodded, unsure how to respond, she tilted her head, openly studying him. "How about you? What's your story?"

Though he usually didn't talk about his past, he'd opened up. He really couldn't do any less.

"The usual. I never knew my father. I was raised by my mother in Albany. Became a cop after college. Married fairly young." Swallowing, he knew his light-hearted tone was all wrong, but using it always helped ease the pain. "My wife died in a car crash a little over five years ago."

Moving toward him, she squeezed his arm. "I'm sorry."

He prayed she wouldn't ask about children.

"What about your mom?" she asked instead.

"She passed away when I was twenty-five. Ovarian cancer."

"Ouch." She winced. "I'm sorry."

"Me, too," he said and meant it. "But like you said, that was years ago."

Spreading his hands to keep from touching her, he grimaced. "Enough talking about the past."

"Tell me how the investigation is going," she said, the breathy hitch in her voice the only thing that told him she was just as affected as he. "Have you found out anything at all?"

Looking down, he took a moment to gather his thoughts. "On the adoption, no. I've got a friend working with the NYPD and a private investigator in Manhattan. But since your former husband was under investigation by the FBI, everything is locked up tight. I'm still working on that."

"Thank you." She still wouldn't look at him. "It's so weird that I can't find even the tiniest trail to tell me where my son came from. I know a lot of adoptions are closed and I could understand that, but I can't even find any record that Ryan even existed."

Inwardly wincing, his stomach tightened as he debated whether or not to tell her about the newborn baby who had been stolen from Albany Medical Center right around the time she'd adopted Ryan. How would she react, learning the baby she thought of as her own might have actually belonged to him?

Might was the operative word, he reminded himself. He still didn't know for certain.

His cell phone rang, a welcome distraction. It was Renee. He listened to what she had to say, answered in the affirmative and concluded the call. Emily had turned and watched him silently, her eyes huge.

"That was Renee," he told her. "While we haven't had any luck locating Tim Keeslar, who's apparently out of town on vacation, we have managed to locate the hotel where Desiree and Franco are holed up. I'm on my way to meet Renee there now."

She nodded. "There's no point in worrying about Tim. If he's gone, he couldn't have broken into my house."

"True, but we have no idea when he left or if he is

even gone. And even if he didn't break into your house, he could have sent you the letters and made the phone calls." Her next words made him pause.

"Only if he somehow imagines he's Ryan's biological father," she said, "which I'm sure he does not. So cross him off your list."

He'd been a cop for so long that her words made him suspicious—almost as if she cared about this guy and didn't want him to be a suspect. An unfamiliar emotion twisted inside him. Without giving himself time to think, he reacted, crossing the space between them and, hands on her shoulders, pulling her close. "Why do you say this?"

Though she shivered, she didn't pull away. "Because when I went out with him, he wasn't real happy when he learned I had a son. I got the impression he was only interested in one thing, if you know what I mean."

Unfortunately, he did. Letting her go, he narrowed his eyes at the thought of another man touching her—any man. "I still want to talk to him."

She shrugged. "Keep me posted, please," she said, her tone a clear dismissal.

With a nod, he let himself out.

Driving to the address Renee had given him, glad he had time to calm his unruly body, he tried to push Emily from his thoughts and focus on the task at hand.

When he pulled up in the motel parking lot, the place looked deserted. Parking, he surveyed the area before getting out of his car. Well-lit and clean, this was a far cry from the sleazy place he'd pictured.

Of course, Anniversary was a much smaller town than Albany.

As he walked toward the motel office, a car pulled

up. Long, lean and shiny, the older model Cadillac would have looked at home in a classic car show.

His first thought was whoever drove this car wanted to be noticed. And when the front door opened and Chris Pitts, aka Franco DiSorinne, stepped out, the inference was that he had nothing to hide.

Turning, Mac hurried over. When Chris—or Franco—glanced up and saw him, he hesitated just long enough to allow Mac to reach him and draw his gun.

"I'd like to talk to you," Mac said, weapon up and ready. "Keep your hands in the air."

Franco didn't move. "Unless you're arresting me, I have nothing to say to you."

"Hands up," Mac barked. "Where's Desiree?"

Surprise flashed across Franco's face. "How do you—never mind. She's safe, and I'm not letting the likes of you bother her."

Renee would be here any minute now to provide backup. Mac just needed to keep the other man calm. "Why'd you do it, Franco? Pretend to be someone else so I'd hire you?"

Franco didn't react. Not even mild surprise showed in his stony expression.

"Come on, man." Mac tilted his head, though he kept his pistol up and ready. "I really liked you. I've done nothing to be treated that way. Why'd you do it?"

"Nothing against you." For the first time, Franco allowed himself a smug smile. "I needed cover, and your job opening provided it."

Now they were getting somewhere. "Cover? For what?"

But Franco wouldn't respond.

Another car pulled into the parking lot, headlights illuminating them. Renee turned on the blue and red lights before parking and getting out. She, too, approached with her weapon drawn.

"Where is she?" Renee barked. "Tell her to come out with her hands up."

Though Franco didn't move, he shifted his eyes toward the closest unit. Number 227. Perfect.

"I know where she is," Mac told Renee. "Cuff him, and I'll get her to come out."

"Hands behind your back."

Waiting until he saw Renee nudge a cuffed and furious Franco toward her squad car, Mac went up to the door of Room 227 and banged on it with an open fist. "Police. Open up."

Nothing. He glanced up at Franco and saw the other man smiling. But why? There were no back entrances to the motel rooms, so Desiree couldn't have escaped. Maybe Franco thought small-town officers wouldn't break into the room.

Taking a deep breath, Mac debated whether or not to try and kick in the door. Despite what television cop shows aired, such a move was never easy.

As he deliberated, a shot rang out.

"Get down," he yelled, dropping by reflex. Renee, however, wasn't so lucky. When he looked back for her, she was already on the ground, bleeding.

Immediately, he got on his radio and called dispatch for an ambulance as well as backup. But before he'd even finished speaking, the door to Room 227 opened and a woman who could only have been Desiree emerged crying, with her hands up.

Chapter 9

Ed Cooper took charge of the prisoners, booking Desiree with a charge of assault to a police officer with a deadly weapon. Franco was charged as her accomplice.

Mac followed the ambulance to the hospital. As far as he could tell, Renee's wound wasn't life-threatening, which was a relief. The bullet had grazed her shoulder, taking out a good-size chunk of flesh with it. Still, he wanted to be there for her and help in any way he could.

A few hours later, with Renee settled, her wound cleaned and bandaged, groggy with the meds she'd been given for the pain, he took his leave and headed down to the station to see what Ed had been able to find out.

"We're still holding them but not for long. They've both already lawyered up," Ed told him, with no small amount of disgust. "The only thing the girl would say was she shot Renee in self-defense."

"Self-defense?" Mac shook his head. "She shot a uniformed police officer."

"I know. It's weak. But that's what she's going with. How's Renee?"

Dragging his hand through his hair, Mac realized exhaustion had him seeing double. "She's okay. They're keeping her overnight, but I expect she'll be discharged tomorrow morning."

"Which is Saturday. At least we've got until Monday before their lawyer can get the judge to set bail." Ed grimaced. They both knew how this worked. Worse, Mac figured Franco and Desiree would vanish once they'd posted bond.

"I need five minutes," he told Ed.

"But—"

"Just go get a cup of coffee." Already walking away, Mac pointed in the direction of the break room. He didn't look back to see if Ed had done as he'd asked.

Franco and Desiree were being kept in separate holding cells until Judge Carrodine opened court on Monday morning and their attorney could petition for bail to be set. Mac chose to visit Desiree first.

She looked up when he entered the cell. Black mascara streaks ran down both cheeks as she regarded him suspiciously. "What do you want?" she asked.

Ignoring her question, he stared at her, unsmiling. "You're in a lot of trouble, you know."

"My lawyer will take care of this," she said without conviction. "He said not to talk to any of you."

Shaking his head, he continued to stare her down. "Why'd you do it, Desiree? Shooting a police officer is a pretty serious thing."

"I didn't mean to shoot her," she protested, apparently already forgetting her attorney's instructions.

"When you knocked on the door, I thought you were one of Franco's enemies."

She said this despite the fact that he'd identified himself as police loudly and clearly. Mac let that one go. "What do you want with Emily?" he asked casually. "She said you came to her house."

Desiree frowned, her worried expression replaced with one of contempt. "Carlos's stupid wife? She stole my jewelry, and I want it back. I need the money."

It was the same story she'd given Emily. If Desiree was after Ryan, she was doing a good job of pretending otherwise. Actually, Mac believed her. Women like her had no interest in children—their own or others. All they cared about was money.

This was exactly what Desiree had said. She was telling the truth, at least about that. Still...

"You came all this way for a necklace and bracelet?"

"And earrings." Sniffing, she swallowed. "These weren't ordinary diamonds, you understand? I saw the receipt. Carlos paid nearly two hundred grand for the necklace alone."

Damn. He knew Emily had sold everything to pay off her debts, but she hadn't mentioned very expensive diamonds. He'd have to ask her about that.

Turning, he exited her cell without another word and went next door.

Franco didn't even look up when Mac entered. One look at his clenched jaw and hunched shoulders told Mac he was barely holding back his rage.

"I might be able to get them to cut you a deal," Mac said casually, "but I'll need some information from you."

When Franco met Mac's gaze, he didn't bother to hide his anger. "Go away."

Staring him down, finally Mac nodded. "Suit yourself. Both you and your girlfriend are gonna do hard time for shooting a cop."

"I didn't shoot anyone," Franco snarled.

"Desiree says differently. She told me she was only doing what you told her to do." Mac felt no compunction about lying. He really didn't expect Franco to believe him. If the other man had been an associate of a mobster like Carlos Cavell, he'd been around the block enough times to know better.

Still, on the off chance that he was wrong, Mac crossed his arms and waited.

Finally, Franco spoke, glaring at him. "Tell me your deal, and I'll think about it."

"I need you to tell me what you want with Carlos Cavell's wife."

For an unguarded moment, Franco's expression mirrored his shock. Apparently, whatever he'd been expecting hadn't been this.

Jaw set, he looked away. "No comment."

Mac shrugged, feigning nonchalance. "All right, then. Let me know if you decide you want to talk about a plea."

Franco didn't respond, though Mac waited, silently counting to ten.

Then he let himself out.

Exhausted beyond reason, Mac knew he should get in the car, drive home and get some much needed sleep. Instead, though it was late and he thought she'd probably be asleep, he found himself pulling up in Emily's driveway.

Parking, he killed the engine and sat in the car. A light shone yellow from her kitchen window, and he used that as enough reason to get out and go tap quietly on her front door.

To his surprise, she opened it instantly, as though she'd been watching out the window and waiting for him.

About to speak, instead he pulled her into his arms and just held her, drawing comfort from the fresh shampoo-and-soap scent of her.

He didn't know how long they stood there, holding on to each other, but finally, as he swayed from exhaustion, she broke away and gently led him into the house, closing and locking the door behind her.

"What happened?" she asked quietly.

"First, I need to ask you about some diamonds. Desiree said the necklace alone was worth over one hundred thousand dollars."

She shook her head. "I didn't find anything like that."

"All right." He searched her face. "Desiree shot Renee."

Emily gasped. "What?"

Dropping into her chair, he relayed the night's events. She listened quietly until he finished, finally dropping to her knees alongside his chair.

"Is Renee going to be all right?"

He nodded, trying not to look at her mouth and unable to keep from remembering the explosiveness of the kiss they'd shared earlier. The rasp of his own breathing and the thump of his heartbeat mingled with hers. Despite his exhaustion and her earlier anger, the electricity between them still hummed in the air, too powerful... seductive...dangerous—especially now when his guard was so completely down.

He didn't move, couldn't move, even though he knew he was on the verge of doing something foolish.

Seeming to sense it, too, she moved restlessly against his leg. His mouth went dry as he watched her, realizing he'd never seen her as wildly beautiful. Desire stabbed deep inside him. Sensing his regard, she dragged her hand through her short, dark hair, biting her lip as she looked away.

He nearly groaned out loud. Hell, he wanted her. He wanted to bury himself inside her—right here, right now.

Again their gazes locked. She stopped moving and something—desire? heat?—flickered in her face. Motionless, her caramel eyes molten, she appeared to be waiting. He tried to throttle the dizzying surge of wanting, of need, but as she raised herself up onto her knees, he knew he fought a losing battle.

Roughly, he pulled her to him. Though she didn't resist, she trembled against his touch, settling on his lap. His body, already aroused, responded with a surge of heat.

"Emily?" he rasped, hoping she'd understand what he asked.

"Please. Hold me."

Though he knew he was in trouble if comfort was all she wanted, he did his best to simply hold her, though he knew she could feel his arousal pressing against her perfectly shaped bottom.

Turning to him, her full breasts flush against his chest, she clung to him, soft curves fitting him perfectly. When he slid his hand down her shoulder to the swell of her breast, he hesitated, heart hammering in his chest, hoping she wanted this as badly as he.

Apparently she did. She pressed her mouth against

his throat, where the pulse threatened to leap out of his skin. His heart lurched.

"Yes," she whispered. Then, pressing against him, she kissed him with a hunger that matched his, her soft, sweet lips more persuasive than any words could have been.

He let his mouth move over hers, devouring her, drinking her in, wanting more—so much more.

But was this...wrong? With his heartbeat pounding in his ears and heat blazing through his veins, he could scarcely think of anything but the feel and scent of her.

Emily, Emily. And though his mind told him to resist, his damn body refused to listen. She kissed him again with an unmistakable sense of urgency, and she took his hands, encouraging him to touch her.

Was he actually shaking? Pushing away the thought along with his doubts and his questions, he traced the hollow of her throat, the slope of her shoulders, her sides to reach the curve of her hips. He pulled her toward him, wanting her closer than was humanly possible. He knew she could feel just how much he wanted her. Despite his mammoth arousal, he tried like hell to maintain control. He wanted to let her be the one to choose how far this went.

As if he had the right to take this any further.

And then, she lifted her small, delicate hand and traced the outline of his erection, hard and rigid and ready, and he was lost. He tried to speak but only succeeded in a groan, and when she kissed him again, she continued to stroke him to madness with the certainty of her touch.

Though she already straddled him, when she began to move her softness against him, what little restraint he'd managed to hang on to completely and utterly vanished. Breathing harshly, he grabbed her wrist, holding her away.

"Stop," he bit out the word. "It's been way too long since I—"

"Shh." Brushing her lips against his, she got up and took his hand and led him into the bedroom. He went, dazed and tormented and too damn aroused to care.

Closing the door behind her, she kissed him again, this time warm and lingering and full of promise. Slowly she began unbuttoning her soft cotton nightgown, her seductive smile inviting him to help.

So he did—or at least, he tried. His fingers felt too big and ungainly. Fumbling with the buttons, he hoped he wouldn't tear the cloth, especially when she undid his belt.

A tangle of clothes and bodies, they undressed each other, each touch erotic, every kiss a sexy tease. She helped him pull his T-shirt over his head, trailing kisses along his chest, biting at his nipple. He sucked in his breath, self-control already shredded, while great shuddering waves of desire rocked him to the core.

Naked, bodies slick with perspiration and need, they came together as though they'd both been starving. And if he thought about it, he had.

Though he tried to be gentle, he could no more control his raging desire than he could a tornado. And she, she urged him on, apparently craving him as much as he did her.

When he would have gently eased them onto the bed, she grinned and pulled him instead, sending them sprawling, limbs intertwined in a sensual tangle.

They kissed again, his aroused flesh pressing into her soft belly then, as she moved, the warm apex of her womanhood. Bending his head, he caressed her breasts with his tongue, trying like hell to slow things down. He wanted to try to make this last.

But she had other ideas. Arching her back, she moaned, blindly reaching and capturing his hard-on with her hand, squeezing and moving her hands up and down seductively.

"Emily," he warned. "Easy."

Again she laughed, a husky sound of joyous sensuality. "I'm ready for you."

Knowing if he entered her now that he'd lose control, he used his finger instead, finding her wet and ready and hot—so hot. His body surged against her leg as she convulsed around his finger.

Damn. He wasn't going to be able to wait too much longer.

"I need you inside me," she breathed. Wiggling her body against his hand, she rose up against him and pushed herself down over the length of him, sheathing him deep inside her.

He bit back a moan. The pleasure was purely explosive. Slowly, he started to move, savoring the feeling. Thrashing, she bucked her hips, taking him in faster until he couldn't think, until there was only him and her—their bodies joined together.

"Mac!" Shuddering, she found her release, bringing him to his at nearly the same instant. The waves of pleasure seemed to go on and on, taking him by storm.

Finally, both spent, their naked skin moist and warm, they lay silent, holding each other, not speaking.

Sometime after that, she slept.

Eventually, after forcing himself not to think too hard about what had just happened, he did, too.

When he woke, the clock on the nightstand read 5:03 a.m. Quietly, he eased himself out of the sheets;

found his jeans, socks, shirt, shoes; and got dressed in the darkness.

Sneaking out before dawn was something he'd only seen in movies. This was another first in this bizarre chapter of his life.

Great. He'd done a lot of things in his past that he wasn't proud of, but this took the cake. He'd obviously been thinking with what was in his pants rather than his brain. How could he make love with a woman when he planned to be the one to completely ruin her life?

Emily was already wounded, shattered, and he'd begun to suspect she'd been wronged almost as much as he had. He had no business even becoming friends with her, never mind becoming her lover.

Worse, he already wanted to make love to her again.

Since he always tried to be honest with himself, he knew that despite his misgivings, he couldn't stay away from her. Even if he didn't have concern for Ryan's safety as an excuse, he genuinely *liked* Emily. He wasn't going to let anything happen to her—not on his watch.

And if it turned out Ryan was the infant who had been stolen from him five years ago, he'd try to work out some sort of visitation schedule rather than cutting her completely out of Ryan's life. He suspected both of them would need such an arrangement to stay sane.

Briefly, he tried to imagine the future. He couldn't. He knew what he'd like, knew too that such a thing would not be possible if he continued to pursue his planned course of action.

He needed answers, needed to know the truth.

Since right now he couldn't have them, he did the cowardly thing. He left Emily asleep in her bed without saying goodbye.

* * *

After Mac left, Emily lay still between the sheets with her eyes closed, doing some serious thinking. She'd always been a light sleeper, and she'd come awake the instant he slipped from the bed.

Though part of her longed to call him back to her, to wrap him in her arms and entice him to make love yet again, the rational side of her was glad he was going without her having to ask him to. She'd never let Ryan wake up to find a man in her bed, even Mac, whom Ryan liked and trusted. Maybe it would happen eventually, depending on how things played out, but not now—not while everything was still new and shiny and full of potential.

She wasn't even certain she wanted this. At this stage in her life—and in Ryan's life—she didn't need a relationship…especially with all the craziness going on with the stalker. Diamonds? It would be so ironic if all along her stalker had been after missing jewelry rather than Ryan.

It would be ironic and a blessing. While she knew nothing about diamonds, if she could believe with certainty that no one was after her boy, she'd finally be able to breathe again.

Until she knew for sure, she needed to focus on her son, make sure she gave him an ordinary, perfect life—the kind she'd always dreamed of for herself. Mac would only complicate things, but she'd be lying if she tried to pretend he wouldn't make a fantastic father.

And what little boy didn't need a father?

Turning around various possibilities, she punched her pillow and tried to will herself back to sleep. She didn't need this now. But what she needed and what she wanted, however, were two different things.

Mac Riordan had shown her how to desire again. Being with him had made her appreciate her femininity and reminded her of all the ways a male companion and lover could enrich her life.

But she knew better than anyone how this sort of sweet, sharp happiness could turn and plunge a knife into one's chest. Did she want to risk such pain, letting herself care about this man she barely knew?

After leaving Emily's, Mac headed home, showered and got ready to face the day. He stopped in a Patty's Coffee Shop and snagged breakfast and several cups of piping hot coffee. The food helped with the unsettled feeling roiling inside him.

Then as he'd done for years, he shoved his personal problems on the back burner and focused on his jobs.

After checking on his trucking business and wishing his former dispatcher, Chris Pitts, had been a real employee, he headed downtown to the hospital. He wanted to talk to Renee. This case, at least to him, had suddenly grown incredibly complicated.

With this latest wrinkle, was the stalker after diamonds, and if so, why the phone call from someone who, mistakenly or otherwise, believed he or she was Ryan's biological parent? With Carlos's former mistress and goon arriving in town together, Mac knew he needed to enlist help. He needed to talk to Renee first, and then he wanted to phone his buddy Joe back in Albany. He really hoped Renee could call in some outside law enforcement agency, maybe even the Feds.

Arriving at the hospital early that Saturday morning, he headed up to Renee's room, hoping she'd be awake and able to talk.

She sat up in her hospital bed, evidently having just finished breakfast.

"You got a minute?" he asked, stopping just inside her doorway.

"Sure." She dropped her fork and motioned to one of the visitor's chairs. Flashing him an amused smile, she shook her head. "Ed called and filled me in on everything. I'm glad we've got the shooter and her accomplice in custody. Nothing much is going to happen with that until Monday when Judge Carrodine goes back to work."

He nodded. "I know. I wanted a minute of your time."

"Sure." Leaning forward, she focused her direct gaze on him. "What's up?" With her short hair and larger-than-life bravado, she could have looked masculine but didn't. Instead, her shorn locks framed her heart-shaped face, emphasizing her femininity rather than detracting from it.

Mac had begun to consider her a friend. "About the Gilley case. Things are escalating. Not only does the stalker seem to think he or she is Ryan's birth parent but we've got two individuals in town who are part of Emily's past. They claim to be looking for some valuable jewelry. On top of that, we still don't know if any of these people tried to grab Ryan. I'm worried this person will try again." He took a deep breath. "I think Emily and Ryan are in danger."

Renee leaned forward. "Even with those two in custody?"

"Even so. Because I'm not a hundred percent convinced they are behind all this."

"Seriously? Crossing her arms and ignoring her bulky shoulder bandages, Renee frowned at him. "Who else could it be? If they really think Emily has their diamonds, maybe they wanted to grab the kid for insurance. You know as well as I do that holding him for ransom would be a viable way to get what they clearly think his mother has stolen."

"Too obvious. Neither one of them has even mentioned Ryan. But the caller did. This person—whoever he or she is—seems to think Emily stole his or her baby. They aren't happy with my involvement with her."

Expression thoughtful, Renee considered his words. "I don't know. Who are you thinking?"

"I'm not sure. Even though Tim Keeslar is supposedly out of town, I'd really like to talk to him. Because the stalker appears to be upping the intensity. I'm afraid he or she is going to make a move soon."

She'd gone utterly still. "How can I assist?"

Carefully, he spoke. "If you have any contacts inside the FBI that could help, that would be great. I'm gonna call Joe and get him working on this, as well. I still need information on the adoption."

"I agree. Because, unless Carlos Cavell stole this baby directly out of a hospital, there have to be records somewhere."

He held his breath, watching her to see if she knew she'd just stated what he believed to be the truth behind Ryan's appearance in Emily's life.

Continuing, she appeared oblivious. "I'll see what I can find out," Renee promised. "I should be out of here by lunchtime today, according to the doctor. I'll go directly to the office and get to work."

"While I appreciate that, I think you'd better rest." Mac patted her hand. "You just got shot, remember?"

"I wouldn't even call it that," she said, her mouth twisting wryly. "The bullet just grazed me. I'm fine.

As soon as they discharge me, I can go back to my normal life."

Mac managed a smile and a nod. Grabbing his car keys, he turned to go. Next up, he'd call Joe and get him to start working on the case. Joe had contacts inside the FBI who could really come in handy.

Letting himself out, he got in his car and pulled out his cell.

Joe picked up on the first ring, as though he'd been expecting the call. "Hey, buddy."

"Hey, yourself." Quickly he outlined the situation.

When he'd finished, Joe whistled. "I had no idea things were heating up so much down there."

"Will you see what you can find out about Franco DiSorinne and a woman named Desiree Smith?"

"Is that her real last name?"

"It's what's on her ID."

"Okay. Will do. I'll be back in touch as soon as I find out something."

Hanging up, Mac allowed himself a slight smile. Joe always had his back, even though he now was two thousand miles away.

Satisfied he'd done everything he could for now, he shifted the cruiser into Drive and headed home. He'd spend a few minutes working on the trucking business before driving out to Emily's that afternoon to check on her.

Finally going back to sleep, Emily didn't get up for a few more hours, glad it was Saturday. When she woke, she wasn't too surprised to find herself missing Mac. Her body felt pleasantly sore from their lovemaking the night before.

Still, she was glad he'd left—especially since she

had an inquisitive son who would be sure to ask a lot of questions that she wasn't ready to answer.

Stretching lazily, she showered and then headed into the kitchen. She brewed herself a pot of coffee, heavily doctored it with cream and artificial sweetener and drank a cup while gazing out the back window.

Fear no longer ruled her life, she realized. For the first time she could remember, she actually felt anticipation and hope for the future. She felt strong and capable and ready to deal with anything. It'd been nice to know so many people in her new hometown had her back.

Especially Mac. Smiling, she shook her head. Baby steps, baby steps... She'd deal with her burgeoning feelings for him as they came.

When Ryan finally woke up around nine, she made blueberry pancakes, letting him eat them in front of the TV while he watched his cartoons, something he only got to do on Saturday mornings.

Pouring herself her second cup of coffee, she wandered out onto the patio. The bright blue, cloudless skies promised a hot day, but at this time of the morning, the outside temperature hovered in the low 80s.

Watching a squirrel raid one of the bird feeders, she took a seat in her favorite rocking chair, the one she'd bought from a display outside of a restaurant. She'd purchased the chair because it represented the kind of home she'd never had. It was one of the few possessions she'd brought with her to Texas. When she'd married Carlos, she'd hoped they could build that kind of home, but it hadn't worked out. So now, she and Ryan were working on making it on their own.

And now she was thinking of Mac. Again, images of him intruded into her world.

Last night had been...fabulous. She stretched her

body, aching in an unfamiliar yet recognizable way. Though the last thing she'd intended was to get involved with anyone, she couldn't deny their connection.

Thinking about more coffee, she wandered back inside. Still watching cartoons, Ryan glanced up at her and smiled. The sight of his freckled face filled her with joy. She collected his plate and took it into the kitchen to wash up.

She filled that morning with mundane tasks, trying not to think about the stalker, the two people currently being held by the sheriff's office or about Mac. She sorted laundry, started the wash, dusted and vacuumed, taking comfort in the ordinary domestic chores.

Outside, she heard the distinctive sound of the postal truck delivering the mail.

Walking out to get it, when she opened her mailbox, Emily frowned. Stuffed inside, along with the usual catalogs and bills, was a special delivery envelope addressed to her.

Seeing it, she froze. Since she hadn't ordered anything, she could only think it had been placed there by her stalker rather than the mail carrier.

Immediately, she called Mac.

"I'll be there in ten minutes," he told her, his deep voice sending warmth through her suddenly cold body. "I'm on the other side of town. Don't touch anything, okay? As a matter of fact, wait for me inside your house."

Agreeing, she hurried back inside, locking the dead bolt behind her.

Mac arrived in less than seven minutes, which meant he must have driven as fast as he could without using lights and sirens. He jumped out of the car, looking reassuringly big, his muscular shoulders straining the fabric of his shirt. As he strode up her sidewalk, his massive, purposeful presence quickened her pulse against all reason. Again, she flashed back to the night before, and her body flushed all over.

Chiding herself, she opened her door and met him halfway. It took every ounce of self-possession she had to keep from throwing herself into his arms.

Damn. She had it worse than she'd thought.

As he gazed at her, standing so close she could feel his body heat, she knew he was thinking about it, too. Her instinctive response to this realization was so powerful that she shivered and moved away.

She cleared her throat and tried to focus her scattered thoughts. "It's in the mailbox," she told him, her voice husky.

He nodded, his nearness still overwhelming. "Wait here," he ordered, his voice as rusty as hers had been.

Of course she couldn't. Hurrying along after him, she stood back a respectful distance while he opened the metal box and peered inside.

First he extracted her regular mail, handing the letters and catalogs and flyers to her. Then, working carefully, he removed the padded envelope marked Priority.

"So far, there's nothing to worry about. This came through the postal service," he told her, showing her the stamps. "The postmark shows it originated in Dallas. The postmark is smudged, but it looks like it was mailed yesterday or the day before. There's no return address."

She nodded. Raising her eyes, she found him watching her, the heat of his gaze making her sway toward him.

"What do you want to do?" he asked softly, the intensity in his voice palpable. "I can take it with me and open it in the sheriff's office, or we can cut it open right here, right now."

She forced a smile, aware she fooled neither of them. "I have to see what's inside."

Nodding, he pulled the precut tab. As he scanned the contents, his face shut down. Jaw clenched, eyes narrowed, he passed her the papers.

Instead of a note, there were photographs. Printed on an inkjet printer, the poor quality attested to inferior paper. Each and every one of them was of an infant, clearly in a hospital bassinet.

Gazing at them, at first she didn't comprehend. Then, when she did, she didn't understand. "These are...Ryan. At birth. Before I adopted him, I'm guessing."

"Yes." His voice, choked and raw, mirrored her emotions.

Disoriented, she looked up, trying to process not only this but Mac's reaction. Expression shuttered, he looked like a man in pain.

The photos proved that this stalker was truly her worst fear come to life. "Ryan's actual birth parent, someone who might not have willingly given him up." Just thinking of what that meant shattered her.

"Emily..." Mac reached for her, hand on her shoulder, his gentle touch oddly comforting.

"They mean to try and get him back, to take him away from me." Her fear and misery felt like a heavy weight pressing on her chest. "I can't let them do that. He's my son, my baby. He'll be lost without me. And I..."

Unable to finish the sentence, she bowed her head, the hot ache in her throat threatening to overwhelm her.

With a muffled curse, he pulled her close, wrapping her in his strong arms. Grateful, she let him hold her.

The suffocating sensation that had begun to tighten her throat eased somewhat.

"I don't think you need to worry about that," he said placing a light kiss on her forehead before holding her at arm's length. "We need to talk. There's something I have to tell you."

Folding her arms around herself as if the gesture could bring some warmth, she waited.

A muscle worked in his jaw. His eyes were tortured. She didn't understand why, but he seemed to be struggling with some sort of awful pain. "Though I don't recognize those pictures, I'm guessing they were taken right after Ryan was born, in the NICU."

Helpless, she nodded, willing him to continue.

"First off, you don't have to worry about Ryan's mother coming to try and reclaim him." The harshness of his voice spoke of great emotion, though she could read nothing in his shuttered gaze.

"How do you know this?"

Swallowing hard, he appeared to struggle to speak. "Because I believe Ryan's mother—" his voice cracked, despair darkening his features "—was my wife, Sarah. She died in a car accident on the same day he was born."

At first, she didn't comprehend. Then, ice spreading through her veins as she stared at him with dawning horror, she gasped. "That means you're—"

"Ryan's biological father."

Chapter 10

Emily felt sick. Raw emotion overwhelmed her. Backing away, she stumbled, nearly going to her knees. Terror shot through her, fear laced with fury. "Get away from me."

"Wait." He moved toward her, regret and longing warring in his eyes. Expression grim, he reached out as though to grab her. Somehow, she evaded him, rushing away from him, from the man she'd believed was her friend but who'd turned out instead to be her darkest enemy. She couldn't bear the sight of him.

"Get the hell away from me. You'd better leave, right now—before I call the police."

Since he was, in essence, the police, he didn't comment. Instead, he kept coming, his broad shoulders heaving as he tried to breath. "Listen to me. Please. I'm not your stalker. I swear to you I'm not. I don't know who that is."

"Then who are you?" she cried, despair and anguish twisting her insides.

"A man who's spent the past five years searching for his son." He let out a long, audible breath. "You have no idea what that's like."

She stared at him and she struggled with her confusion. Feeling as if the sky had turned to ice, then shattered and began crushing her, she shook her head. "I don't understand."

Regret flickered in his gaze. "I believe Ryan is my son. Five years ago, my wife was in a car wreck, and he was born prematurely." He cleared his throat, apparently trying to find the right words. "She died delivering him, and while I was burying her, my baby was stolen from the hospital."

Perplexed, she made a choked, desperate sound. "I'm sorry that happened to you, but what are your reasons for thinking Ryan is that child? If I remember right, your baby was born in an Albany hospital. I lived in Manhattan when I adopted Ryan."

"I haven't figured out all the details," he admitted, lifting his chin.

She no longer cared. "This is ridiculous. How dare you come here with this pile of—"

"It's true," he insisted.

Straightening her spin, she looked him in the eye. "I'm sorry you had such an awful thing happen to you, but you're mistaken about Ryan. He's not your missing child."

He took a step toward her, stopping only when she gave him a withering stare and yanked open the door.

"I think you need to leave," she said, crossing her arms.

"Ryan is my son." He lifted his chin.

"You have no proof."

"No, I don't." His mouth twisted. "Therefore, I'd like a DNA test. If you won't consent to one, I'll get an attorney."

Stunned and horrified, she could only stare. For a moment, she couldn't even breathe. "And then what?"

"And then we'll have to see." Posture rigid, he moved away. He didn't turn and look back at her before climbing into his car and leaving.

"I'll die before I let him take Ryan." Pushing her uneaten salad around in her plate, Emily let her dejected resolve show. She'd only thought things had been bad with the stalker and Desiree and Franco. This claim by Mac felt like the proverbial last straw.

Jayne eyed her, sympathy darkening her gray eyes. "Do you think he's your stalker, too?"

"No." Emily passed her hand over her eyes, wishing she could somehow make this all go away. "That's the weird part. This other person—I don't know if it's a man or a woman—also believes they are one of Ryan's birth parents."

"What about the mistress?"

"It could be her," Emily admitted. "And I still haven't figured out Franco's part in all this."

"Maybe he thinks he's the father, too."

Emily shook her head. "Anything is possible, I guess."

Leaning over, Jayne patted her hand. "Then a DNA test is the only way to go. It makes sense."

Finally, Emily gave up her futile attempt to get some nourishment. Her queasy stomach wouldn't allow her to eat anyway. "I can't risk it." Leaning forward, she decided to confide in her best friend. "I'm seriously thinking about packing everything up and leaving town in the middle of the night."

Jayne's mouth fell open. "No, you can't."

"It may be the only way I can keep my life from falling apart. I've got to protect Ryan."

Before she'd even finished speaking, Jayne had begun shaking her head. "Don't you want to know the truth? If Ryan really was stolen from Mac, then he is his son. There's nothing you can do to change that, and furthermore, Mac deserves to be in Ryan's life. It'll be best for both of them. Surely you two can work out some sort of arrangement."

She was right. Emily closed her eyes, still feeling sick. "So what do I do?" she whispered. "I'm so afraid."

"You have to believe Mac just wants a relationship with Ryan, not to take him away from you. He's not a monster."

"I don't know," Emily said bleakly. "He slept with me to get closer to my son."

Jayne gasped. "He...what? Seriously?"

"Yes." Emily closed her eyes. She dropped her lashes to hide the hurt. "I actually thought we might be beginning a relationship. I can't believe I was that stupid."

Jayne squeezed her hand. "Let's be proactive rather than reactive. Even though it's the weekend, let's get Ed involved and go talk to Renee. Don't forget that they still have Desiree and Franco in custody. I have a feeling she'll be in her office."

"Why?" Emily shrugged in resignation. "What good is that going to do?"

"First, I think you need to talk to Franco and Desiree yourself, in person. Second, we're going to make Mac tell Renee about his personal involvement in this. I'm betting she doesn't know." Jayne gave her a de-

termined look. "We've got to get to the bottom of this
once and for all."

She nudged Emily, half hug, half push. "Sweetheart,
it's time to pull out all the stops and find out who is your
stalker and what, exactly, they want before something
worse happens and someone gets hurt."

She despised him—and rightly so. Mac called himself seven kinds of fool all the way home. He hadn't
meant to spill his guts the way he had. It went to show
how sex could mess with a guy's brain. That had to
be it. He'd been feeling all warm and cuddly and even
thought he and Emily might have started something
worth preserving—and not just for the sake of his relationship with his son.

Stupid, stupid, stupid.

He wouldn't be surprised if she didn't try to run.
Hell, he wouldn't blame her if she did.

Hating like hell the way he was shaking, he put in
a call to Renee. "I need to talk to you. I haven't been
entirely honest...."

"Yes, I know," she said, her voice steely and decid-
edly unfriendly. "I've got Emily Gilley and Ed and
Jayne Cooper here in my office."

His stomach clenched. "They're already there?" That
had been fast. He could scarcely wrap his mind around
the events of the past few days. Everything had begun
to run together. Once, everything had seemed so clear-
cut. Now, he no longer knew what he wanted.

"Yes," Renee answered, "and you'd better come in
right now. Emily is very upset. Understandably so. We
have quite a bit to talk about, don't you think?"

Inhaling deeply, he knew she was right. After all,

he wasn't the only one with secrets that needed to be revealed.

"I'm on my way," he said, concluding the call. He'd put his truth out in the open, and now the time had come for Emily Gilley to do the same.

Inside Renee's office, Emily felt torn. While Renee spoke to him on the phone, she paced. "I'm not sure I'm up to seeing Mac. Not right now," she protested, wishing she didn't feel as if her heart had splintered in half. "Not yet. Not after what he did."

"You have to, sweetheart," Jayne murmured, grabbing her and putting her arm around Emily's shoulders. "This is a neutral place. It's all for the better."

Pretending she didn't see the long look that passed between Ed and Jayne and Renee, Emily took a deep, shuddering breath. "Let me go check on Ryan."

"He's fine," Renee put in. "Eva and Charlie are watching TV in the break room with him. I've got one of my assistants in there keeping an eye on all of them."

Emily nodded, aware of both anticipation and dread. When Mac had told her who he was and what he believed to be the truth, again she'd had to fight not to react on impulse. Trying to stand still, to deal with this latest crisis was a new form of torture, especially when every protective mothering instinct she had screamed at her to grab her son and run—fast and far. She knew she could disappear in another state, another small town. After all, she'd done it once before.

But eventually, as it always did, her past would catch up with her. In this instance, she knew Mac would not rest until he found her again. And she couldn't blame him.

Because, whether she agreed with him or not, he truly believed Ryan was his son.

"Do you think he is?" Renee asked bluntly, almost as if she'd read Emily's mind. "Ryan's father, that is."

"I have no way of knowing." Emily paused to catch her breath, her misgivings threatening to turn into full-blown panic. "I know nothing of my son's history or parentage. I've always understood that the adoption was arranged through a private broker my former husband contacted."

Renee waited, apparently aware Emily hadn't finished speaking.

"There's also Desiree and Franco." Emily inhaled. "For the longest time, I've believed that my husband fathered Ryan with one of his mistresses. I've suspected she is my stalker—Ryan's biological mother."

"Desiree?" Renee watched her with a keenly observant gaze. "In other words, you think your former husband is Ryan's true father."

"Yes."

"That all makes sense, too," Jayne breathed. "And the mistress could have resented giving up her son, so she's the one threatening you."

Emily nodded. "Even though this all happened in New York, I think she might have followed me here to Texas to try and get Ryan back. Though why she won't admit it is beyond me. She keeps talking about some jewelry."

"Maybe she plans to blackmail you," Jayne put in. "Have you considered that?"

"That's another possibility," Renee agreed.

"I hadn't thought of that." Emily closed her eyes. "And here I was actually feeling sorry for her, thinking she might have been forced to give up her baby. If she's planning to try blackmail, she'll soon figure out that I have nothing. You can't get blood from a stone, so if that's the case, she's way off base."

"Then Mac comes along and says he's the father." Renee's lips thinned. "What a nightmare."

Relieved that someone actually understood, Emily spoke with quiet, worried firmness. "Yes. Mac's story came out of nowhere."

Jayne rubbed the top of her back, no doubt trying to console her. Knowing if this continued, she might choke up—or worse, dissolve in tears—Emily moved away. She gave her friend an apologetic look as she went to stand as far away from the door as possible. There wasn't room to pace or she would have done that instead.

Clearly not understanding, Jayne moved also, taking a place at Emily's side. At the move, Emily felt a rush of gratitude. She'd never had a friend like Jayne, someone willing to have your back no matter what.

Just as Emily was attempting to compose a way to tell Jayne how much that meant to her, Renee stood. "Why don't you and I go have a chat with Desiree? Just the two of us."

Once again feeling a discomforting sense of finality, Emily found herself nodding. She stepped away from Jayne, her head held high. "Lead the way."

Following Renee down the long hallway to the back part of the sheriff's department, Emily mentally rehearsed what she wanted to say to the woman who might or might not be the mother of her son.

"I think you might have a private word with Franco, too," Renee said, her tone conversational. Something about the too-casual sound of it made Emily stop and look at her.

"Just me?"

With a shrug, Renee flashed a rueful grin. "Both Desiree and Franco have hired lawyers. They won't even say boo to me. But maybe they'll be different with you."

Though her heart had started pounding and her mouth had gone dry, Emily nodded. "If one of them is responsible for making my life a living hell, then I'd like to know."

"Good girl." Renee's grin widened as she patted Emily's shoulder. "Here we are."

As they paused at the metal door, Emily caught herself wishing that Mac was by her side, which surprised her. She supposed she'd need time to get used to the idea that he had become her enemy.

"This is where we're holding Desiree," Renee said as she unlocked the door.

"I'm not sure I want to be alone with her," Emily admitted.

"Oh, you won't be. I'll be standing right by the door watching, though I won't participate in any discussion you two might have. All right?"

Since she didn't appear to have a choice, Emily nodded.

Desiree looked up as they stepped inside, her hostile expression not boding well for the chance of any meaningful conversation.

"Emily wants to have a word with you," Renee announced.

"I have nothing to say to either of you." Desiree sneered, her gaze sweeping over Emily disparagingly before returning to Renee. "Leave me alone."

Though Renee's jaw tightened, she didn't respond.

Taking a deep breath, Emily stepped into the room. A small holding cell, the room had the basic necessities—a cot, a chair, a sink and in the corner a toilet with a plastic shower curtain that could be pulled around for privacy.

Perched on the edge of the cot, with her extensive makeup still intact, Desiree wore the petulant and wounded look of a martyr. "My lawyer says I'll be out of here as soon as court opens up Monday morning. So go away, and quit bothering me."

Ignoring her, Emily took another step closer. "I want to talk to you about my son."

Desiree's perfectly shaped brows rose. "You have a kid? Carlos never mentioned that to me."

Stunned, Emily stared. "How long were you two together?"

Waving a languid hand, her scarlet nails flashing, Desiree smiled. "Two years," she said proudly. "He'd just left my apartment the day he was murdered."

Though this statement probably should have bothered Emily, she'd long ago come to terms with Carlos's multiple infidelities. Briefly she wondered if Desiree knew she'd been one in a long parade of others, then decided nothing would be gained by mentioning that.

"You don't know about my son?" Emily asked softly, not sure whether to believe her.

Emphatically, Desiree shook her head. "I don't like kids. Why do you care what I think about your son anyway?"

"No reason." Glancing back at Renee, who stood with arms folded near the exit, Emily dipped her chin to indicate that she'd finished.

"You're really stupid," Desiree said as Emily prepared to leave the room. "And I know you have my jewelry. I'm not leaving until I get it back."

Turning, Emily met the other woman's gaze straight

on. "I don't have any jewelry. Everything was sold to pay off Carlos's debts."

Desiree narrowed her eyes. "You sold my necklace? That was my price for giving Carlos the ultimate gift."

"Ultimate gift?" Emily froze. "What exactly did you give him?"

But Desiree's expression had shut down. "None of your business. Leave me alone."

Once out in the hallway, Emily exchanged a look with Renee. "I don't know what to think about her."

"I think she's telling the truth." Renee frowned. "She doesn't know anything about Ryan."

"Maybe not, but what ultimate gift did she give Carlos? Do you think she could have given up her baby?"

Renee eyed her for a moment before slowly nodding her head. "I suppose it's possible, but what matters to us right now is if she did she doesn't want him back, I don't think she's your stalker."

Emily wanted to protest but didn't. Renee wouldn't understand why she still wanted to know if Desiree was Ryan's birth mother. Then again, maybe she would. After all, if that was the case, Mac's claim to fatherhood was completely misguided.

Oddly, this thought didn't make her feel any better.

"Are you okay?" Renee asked, concern plain in her eyes.

Emily nodded. "Let's go talk to Franco."

This time, when she stepped into the small room, after a quick, rage-filled glance, Franco refused to even look at her. Every attempt at conversation was met with "talk to my lawyer."

After the fifth response, Emily shrugged and motioned to Renee that she was ready to go.

As they were walking back to Renee's office, Mac arrived. He strode through the front door, his powerful, well-muscled body moving with easy grace. His closed-off expression gave nothing away. Emily glanced at him, trying like hell to study him dispassionately and wishing her heart still didn't skip a beat when she looked at him.

The same hopeless attraction flared—even now that she knew he was her enemy.

Seeing them, he stopped, indicating with a sweep of his hand that they should precede him. As they filed into Renee's small office, everyone in the room stared at him, including Emily.

Devilishly handsome, the air of isolation around his tall figure might have been only her imagination—or not, considering the hostility with which everyone in the room regarded him.

Those piercing sapphire eyes locked on her. "Emily." She noted he kept his hands at his sides, clenched into fists. Who was he angry with—her or himself? Why did she even care?

For the space of a heartbeat, she stared back at him, struggling to find the right words. It turned out there were none.

He measured her, his look cool and appraising. She studied him back, unable to keep from drinking up his powerful male beauty with her eyes. As if he knew, for an instant his impossibly blue gaze sharpened. Her traitorous pulse quickened in an involuntary response.

She should have hated him for what he'd done to her, the way he'd made her have hope and desire again when she thought she never would. But as a mother, she could understand the depth of the love that drove him—love for a child he'd never known. If Ryan really was his, how could she even think to take his son away from him now?

Yet how could she bear to give up her baby?

"I'm sorry," he said, his words meant only for her, his expression grim. She shriveled inside at his words, aware she could not accept his apology. How could she, when she didn't even understand why he bothered to make it?

"I trusted you." Her voice broke. Even worse, she knew he could read the hurt and accusation in her eyes. More than anything, she wished she could turn her heart cold, change it to stone, so this raw, primitive grief wouldn't overwhelm her.

Once again, as though she sensed Emily's inner agony, Jayne put her arm around her shoulders, pulling her close and giving Mac her best back-off-from-my-best-friend glare. Emily loved her for that.

Clearing his throat, Ed shuffled his feet awkwardly, clearly wishing he was somewhere else, anywhere else.

"Emily? Are you all right?" Renee stood like a weary Amazon, her desk her shield, looking from Emily's little group to the man standing alone near the doorway, his handsome face a dark mask.

With her throat closed up, Emily could only nod, which apparently was enough.

"All right, then. Why don't we start with you?" Renee said to Mac, before including the others in her sweeping gaze. "I think we all have a right to know the truth. Are you the one who's been terrorizing Emily here?"

Mac blinked, his mask slipping for a moment to reveal shock. "I… No. I have no idea who that is."

"Obviously, this person believes he or she's the boy's natural parent," Renee continued. "I've talked to Joe, and he admits that neither of you have found any conclusive evidence proving that you're the father, either."

At that, Emily felt the weight on her chest lighten somewhat.

"Why don't you tell me—us—what exactly are your reasons for believing Ryan is your son?" Renee asked.

Mac shifted his weight, hesitating as he measured her for a moment before inclining his head. He watched Emily, clearing speaking directly to her. "As you know now, your husband was under investigation. The Feds were watching him. NYPD was helping. They asked my partner, Joe, to be a part of that investigation. He's a whiz at anything electronics related, one of the best in the country. He was on loan from the Albany P.D."

"So?" Crossing her arms, Renee regarded him the way she might regard a hostile witness. "What has all that to do with any of this? Get to the point."

Mac met her gaze, unblinking. "I will. Joe was there when my wife died. Hell, he helped pull her out of the wrecked car. He was at the hospital when my son was born."

One corner of his mouth twisting upward in a grimace, he continued, his voice bleak with sorrow. "Joe also was there in Manhattan, watching via hidden cameras, the day your adopted son appeared—exactly one day after my own baby was stolen."

Emily's heart dropped into her stomach. She could only imagine how he must have felt. Somehow, from somewhere, she found her voice. "While I'm sorry for your loss, you still haven't given me a valid reason to believe that my son was—is—your missing baby."

Pinning her with his gaze, a swift shadow crossed his face. "Joe recognized him. When he saw Ryan, he called me immediately, though doing so was against protocol. He swore the kid was a dead ringer for my missing son."

Emily felt as if ice had crept into her every pore. Swaying, she closed her eyes for a moment, trying to gather her composure. Her sorrow and worry and fear had become a huge, painful knot in her heart.

"Why didn't you simply ask me back then?" Emily whispered. "I'm sure Carlos and I could have cleared things up immediately."

One muscle worked in his jaw, as if he held his emotions in check. "Because I couldn't. Due to the nature of his investigation and how close they were to an arrest, I had to wait until the Feds made their move. The night before the sting was supposed to go down, Carlos was murdered."

Closing her eyes, Emily struggled to swallow past the ache in her throat. She knew the rest. "And I disappeared," she whispered.

"Exactly."

They all went silent for a moment, digesting this.

"What about the pictures of Ryan in the hospital nursery that Emily got from the stalker?" Renee eyed him like a hawk. "Have you ever seen them before?"

"No," he admitted. "Though they could have been any infant in any hospital. The little knitted cap on the baby's head looked familiar."

"A lot of hospitals use those for preemies," Jayne retorted. "That doesn't mean anything."

"You're right. It doesn't. That's why I'd like a DNA test to solve this once and for all."

"Once you were able to seek out Emily, did you contact the authorities to help you look for her?" Renee asked, her voice still brusque.

Now Mac looked down. "No, we did not."

"Why not?" Her glance clearly said she thought he'd been foolish. "You were a cop. You know we help our own. I'm sure the Albany P.D., hell, the NYPD would have pulled out all the stops to help you."

Jaw clenched, he shook his head. "First off, we had no proof. Second, Joe went out on a limb for me. Telling me could have jeopardized the investigation. I couldn't risk it."

"So Emily vanished with the baby you believed was yours. And you had no idea where she'd gone?" Renee asked, her tone sympathetic.

"Right. No idea whatsoever." He shrugged his shoulders. "It took me four and a half years to track her down."

Shocked, Emily met Renee's eyes before slanting a look at him. "You were stalking me."

"Not like that," he said, his dark gaze full of pain and regret. "I swear to you that wasn't me."

Before Emily could respond, Renee held up a hand. "You moved here because she lived here?" she asked, narrowing her eyes at him.

He didn't look at Emily when he answered. "Yes."

"And befriended her and got her to trust you," Jayne put in, the accusation in her voice mimicking the way Emily felt.

Mac didn't answer. He didn't have to—his actions spoke for themselves.

"Was your coming to work for the sheriff's department part of this plan, too?" Renee asked, her vexation evident in the lines that creased her brow.

"No, that simply happened. Circumstances. Maybe. What does any of this matter now? Look." Including them all in his gaze, he gestured. "Despite what you all think of me, I didn't intend for anyone to get hurt. I have been searching for my son for five years. I don't expect any of you to understand that, but finding him was—is—the only thing that made life worth living."

Watching him, Emily empathized. She should hate this man, not sympathize with him. Yet who was she to say she would have done things any differently had their situations been reversed?

She might not be Ryan's birth mother but he was the son of her heart—and would always be, no matter what the outcome of all this…no matter who had biological rights.

Blinking, she realized someone must have asked her a question.

"Emily," Jayne prodded. "Do you want to press charges?"

"For what?" Dragging her hand across her eyes, Emily pushed away her exhaustion, focusing on the fear. Fear would keep her sharp, help her make sure she didn't make any mistakes that could potentially endanger her son. "Though he's been dishonest, Mac hasn't committed a crime."

Jayne looked at Renee, who slowly nodded. "She's right. As a matter of fact, I'm going to recommend that we shelve this topic for now and focus on catching this wacko who's been tormenting our Emily."

"I'd like to continue to help," Mac put in, startling Emily, and from the look on Renee's, Jayne's and Ed's faces, them all.

Then, as Emily opened her mouth to protest, he held up a hand. "Hear me out. Who better to protect Ryan than someone who cares about him? I can promise you I'd give my life for him. You can't ask for much more than that."

This time, rather than keeping his emotions locked

inside, he let her hear the anguish in his deep voice, see the torment in his eyes. Guilt and anger and fear and…all the same emotions she had tumbling inside her. They shared this, if nothing else.

Actually trembling, a tear slipped silently down her cheek as she watched him, aching.

Renee glanced from one to the other. "I'll leave that up to Emily. Honey, what do you want to do?"

Emily slowly nodded. "I'd like him to help."

"All right." Renee turned to face Mac. "I'm going to let you stay on the payroll but only because we need to catch this stalker. That is your only duty, understand?"

"I understand," he said. "I want that stalker caught as badly as anyone here."

"I doubt that," Emily said, before she thought better of it. "Thank you," she told Renee, turning away from Mac, unable to keep looking at him. "I'll be going now."

Then, giving Jayne's arm a squeeze in gratitude and nodding at Ed, she went to collect her son and head on home before she shattered into a thousand pieces.

Chapter 11

Mac watched her go. The instant she'd disappeared from view, everyone turned to stare at him: Jayne, as if he was something distasteful she'd found under a rock; Ed with curiosity; and Renee with a drained sort of compassion.

"What the hell were you thinking, Riordan?" Renee asked. "Do you have any clue?"

He gave her a rueful smile. "Not really," he admitted. "I'm sure that must be really apparent to the rest of you."

"It's okay, man." Ed came forward, earning a death glare from his wife. "I would have done the same thing if someone had stolen Eva or Charlie."

Despite her obvious desire to side with her friend, even Jayne had to nod in agreement. Regardless of that, she stepped forward, poking him in the chest, her gaze shooting daggers at him.

"Don't you hurt Emily," she said, drawing out the words so he'd understand they were important. "I don't care what you feel you have to do. I even understand some of it. But Emily loves her boy, and he loves her. She'd do anything for him. Get that? Don't you do anything to mess that up."

"I won't," he promised, realizing he meant it. "I'm going to catch this stalker. You wait and see. Once I do, then we'll find out the truth about Ryan's parentage."

"But—" Jayne began, until Ed squeezed her shoulder in warning.

"A man has a right to know the truth about his son," Ed growled. "Don't begrudge him that."

Ridiculously grateful, Mac tried to summon up a smile. When he couldn't even manage that, he nodded, knowing the other man would understand.

As he turned to go, his cell phone rang. Joe's number showed on the caller ID. Immensely grateful that his friend—rather through some sort of cosmic connection or mere coincidence—had chosen to call just when Mac needed him most, he answered.

"What's up?" Joe asked, his cheerful voice somehow easing a bit of the knot in Mac's chest.

As he hurried outside, Mac filled his best friend in.

"You need me?" Joe asked, the seriousness in his tone telling Mac he only needed to say the word.

"I'm okay." Even though he wasn't.

"Listen, I have some vacation time coming. I'll book a plane ticket and head on down there," Joe said, as though he knew everything Mac hadn't put into words.

"I don't know…." The protest was only a token, and both of them knew it.

"I'll call you with my flight information," Joe said firmly. "You can pick me up at the airport."

Capitulating, Mac ended the call. He should have talked to Joe sooner. Now that he had, he felt better than he had in days. Having someone on his side—not just anyone but a savvy criminal investigator—would definitely go a long way toward helping him learn the identity of Emily's stalker.

Driving home, listening as Ryan chatted happily in the backseat, Emily felt utterly and completely depleted. As though by his actions, Mac had stripped all the vitality out of her, laying her inner soul bare and exposed to the unfriendly elements. She'd come to think of him as a friend. No, she'd come to think of him as more than that....

Ruthlessly, she cut off the thought. It was too dangerous and completely and utterly foolish. But Mac was right about one thing. If she was going to protect Ryan, she had to find out the truth about his parentage.

Was he Mac's son? Or, as she'd long suspected, Carlos's with one of his mistresses? After all, Carlos had always claimed that Emily had been the reason they couldn't have a child of their own, even though neither of them had ever been tested. His refusal to allow not only tests but also in vitro fertilization told her she would never have the child she craved. She'd labeled herself barren, in her darkest moments, when she'd despaired of ever having the children she craved. Adoption had been the only option Carlos would consider.

And then Ryan had come along, like the brightest, shiniest gift, the greatest blessing Carlos could have given her. Her son was her world, the family she'd never had, her heart. She could no more lose him than she could live without breathing.

Could she risk this? How could she not?

Reluctantly, she faced the fact that the time had come for her to know the truth. First up was to find the stalker, which, since no one appeared to be having any luck, she'd have to do on her own.

She had a plan. Despite Desiree's denial, Emily was willing to bet Carlos's old mistress was the stalker, which meant if she'd been the one to birth Ryan, Mac had the wrong baby. And since Desiree must have signed away her rights—no doubt in exchange for cash—she wouldn't have as much of a chance of gaining full custody. That was assuming the documents could be found. No doubt they were among the boxes of paperwork the FBI had seized after Carlos's death.

That was it. Emily actually smiled to herself the first time all day. If she could get Desiree to admit to being the stalker, she could take the first step to end this craziness once and for all. The DNA test would just be icing on the cake. Her life would go back to normal, and her future with Ryan would be safe and secure.

Her plan had only one flaw: Desiree's repeated denial. What did the other woman hope to gain? And where did Franco come in on all of this? His arrival— with Desiree—was too much of a coincidence. That meant the two of them were concocting some sort of plan.

What a mess. Briefly, she closed her eyes, wondering what had happened to her cherished dreams of a life in a clapboard house with a white-picket fence, playing in the sprinklers on a warm summer day.

Now she was embroiled up to her elbows with two people—one known and the other not—who believed themselves to be Ryan's rightful parent.

The truth of it was—no matter the biology or

genes—she was Ryan's mother. And if she had any say in things, no one could ever take that away from them.

Glancing at her watch, aware her rather shaky plan hinged on the hope that the stalker would call her personally this time, she began to mentally rehearse exactly what she would say. And she still had to decide if she should let Mac in on her plan.

Sunday passed in a blur of indecision. Mac must have picked up the phone to call Emily at least half a dozen times, always reconsidering. Joe's flight would be in around nine that evening, so until then, he was just killing time.

He puttered around the house, restless as a caged lion but unwilling to go into town and risk running into Emily or any of her friends.

Finally, Mac made the two-hour drive to the airport. He parked outside in the arrival area of Terminal C and waited.

When Joe finally emerged, striding across the pavement, several women did double takes, making Mac grin. "New haircut?" he asked, as Joe pulled open the passenger door and, after tossing his carry-on in the backseat, climbed inside.

"Yep." Joe grinned back, shaking Mac's hand. "Ladies seem to like it." Shrugging, he settled back. "Tell me everything."

So Mac did, starting at the beginning. Joe listened without interruption. With every word, Mac felt more and more at ease, as if unburdening himself to his best friend had removed a huge pile of rocks from his chest.

When Mac wound down, finishing with his declaration to Emily and the meeting at the sheriff's department, Joe winced. "Ouch," he said. "Maybe not the best move."

Concentrating on driving, Mac glanced at Joe and grimaced. "I know, but I couldn't keep lying to her."

"You have *feelings* for her?" Joe sounded incredulous. "We're talking about Carlos Cavell's widow? The woman who stole your son?"

"We don't know that," Mac protested, aware that by doing so he was answering in the affirmative.

"We don't?"

"We're not a hundred percent certain."

"Mac!" Joe leaned forward, peering up at Mac like he was afraid his best friend had lost his mind.

"Well, it's true," Mac continued. "I've asked for a DNA test. Until we do that and I get the results back, there's no way we can be—"

"Take me to meet him," Joe interrupted. "I'll bet I'd know after one look at him."

Mac glanced sideways. "Just like that, huh? You're serious?"

"Yes."

Mulling this over, Mac finally shook his head. "Things are too volatile right now. You'll eventually meet him, I promise."

"It's your call," Joe said. "You know who else I want to hang out with? Renee. I haven't seen her in ages."

Mac nodded. "We're nearly there. If it's okay with you, we'll grab a beer and then make tonight an early one. It's been a long day."

"Sure, no problem," Joe said easily. "I'm going to be here a week. There's plenty of time to get everything done."

The next morning, Mac got up and, after he and Joe killed a pot of coffee and demolished six fried eggs, drove his friend over to Emily's house. They stopped at a doughnut shop along the way and picked up a dozen assorted as a sort of peace offering.

"Are you sure she won't mind?" Joe asked, for what had to be the third or fourth time.

"Reasonably," Mac answered. "Though she has to be at work by nine, if we time this right, it'll work out. Even if she won't spend much time with us, at least you'll get to see Ryan."

"Fantastic." Joe stretched and yawned. "I called Renee while you were in the shower. She and I are having lunch later."

Mac nodded, already thinking about Emily. As they pulled up in her driveway and his heart began to pound, he told himself it didn't matter if she rejected him. If she didn't want to let him in, he'd hand her the doughnuts and go on about his business.

Joe got out with him, one hand on Mac's shoulder in a show of support as Mac rang the bell.

A moment later, Emily answered the door, looking both frazzled and beautiful. Her short, spiky hair was messier than usual, reminding him of the way she'd looked after they'd made love. His body stirred, though he immediately clamped down on that chain of thought.

Next to him, Joe made a sound of approval low in his throat.

"What do you want?" Her gaze locked on his before she deliberately let it slide away to inspect Joe.

"Truce?" He held out the box of doughnuts.

Staring at him, unsmiling, she shook her head. "No, thanks. I'm not interested."

Joe stepped forward, his brilliant smile in place. "Hi. I'm Joe Stalling, Mac's friend from Albany." He held out his hand.

Taking it, Emily briskly and efficiently dispatched with pleasantries. "Nice to meet you," she said, before turning back to Mac. "After all this, you think you can show up on my doorstep with a box of doughnuts and expect me to forgive you?"

He winced, aware of Joe watching silently. "I'd really like to talk."

"It's Monday, and I have to get Ryan to school." Pointedly, she glanced at her watch. "We're already running late."

"How about after?" Though he hated begging, he supposed he deserved this for what he'd done to her.

Stepping back, she attempted to close the door on him. "I have to go to work."

"Remember I'm still working your case," he reminded her, grateful when she paused. "Joe has years of experience working in New York. He's kindly offered his assistance."

This, more than anything else, got her attention.

Finally, she nodded. Leaving the door open, she stepped back, motioning for them to come inside.

"Wait here," she ordered, turning her back on him and disappearing into the hallway.

Standing in the small tile square that marked her foyer, he gazed out at the colorful living room of the house that had once felt like home. The aroma of fresh coffee filled the air, and he could hear the sounds of Emily helping Ryan get ready for school.

Mac felt a longing so sharp it was painful, well aware that he might have once stood a chance of being part of this…if only he'd kept his mouth shut…if he'd been willing to build a life based on a lie.

"Pretty nice," Joe commented, looking around. When Mac didn't respond, he slugged his arm. "And now that I've seen her, I can understand how you two got involved."

Throat aching, Mac could only nod.

A moment later, Emily returned, a freshly scrubbed and grumbling Ryan at her side. Next to him, Mac felt Joe instantly go on full alert.

"Hey, Mac!" Ryan grinned, sauntering over toward Mac and holding up his hand for a fist bump. Smiling, Mac bumped him back.

"I brought doughnuts," he said, holding up the box and drawing Ryan's gaze back to him from Joe.

"Ryan already ate breakfast," Emily put in, her pinched voice matching the flatness in her eyes.

"Please, Mom? Can I have just one?" Ryan pleaded, alternating jumping up and down and shooting covetous looks at the doughnut box.

Mac wanted to side with Ryan but, afraid if he did so he'd have the opposite effect, said nothing.

"Please, please, please?" Ryan kept on. "Just one teeny chocolate glazed doughnut? Pleeeeeease?"

Finally, with a small smile at her son, Emily gave in. "Just one," she said, ruffling his head. "And you'll have to eat it on the way to school."

Crouching down, Mac lowered the box to Ryan's level, letting him open it. "Choose whichever one you like."

The boy didn't even hesitate. "That one," he said, snagging a chocolate-topped doughnut. Mac handed him a napkin, unable to tear his eyes away as Ryan bit in with obvious delight.

"Hi, there," Joe ventured when no one made a move to introduce him to the child. Like Mac, he crouched down, putting himself at the same height as Ryan. "I'm Joe, Mac's friend."

"Hi." Barely glancing at him, Ryan focused all his attention on his sugary treat.

"I've got to take Ryan to school," Emily said, eyeing Mac and then Joe from under her long lashes. "Do you want to wait outside in your car? I should be back in five minutes or so."

Careful not to show how hurt he was that she rightly no longer trusted him enough to let him wait in her living room while she was gone, he nodded. "Sure."

As he trudged to his patrol car with Joe and the rest of the doughnuts, he couldn't help but wonder if she meant to return. He couldn't blame her if she went on to other things and left him sitting alone in her driveway.

"Ryan doesn't look at all like I expected," Joe said thoughtfully once they were safely inside the patrol car. He flashed Mac a halfhearted smile. "Though I swear I can see Sarah in him."

Mac felt too queasy to smile back. He opened his glove box and removed the DNA test kit he'd brought. "I was going to give her this, but now I don't know if it's a good idea."

Frowning, Joe looked from the book to him. "You gotta do what you gotta do."

And that, for Mac, pretty much summed everything up in one neat sentence. Still, that didn't mean he had to like it.

He and Joe waited silently, each lost in their own thoughts.

Seven minutes later, Emily pulled in alongside them. He started to get out of his car, but she motioned him back.

"We can talk right here," she said, lifting her chin.

"In the car?" he asked, stung yet again. "I'd really like a little privacy."

Wearing the pained expression of a martyr, she made a show of checking her watch before reaching for the back car door handle. "You're the one who brought a friend."

Point taken.

Getting in, she dipped her chin in a nod at Joe, then returned her attention to Mac, eyeing him like a fly trapped in a web watching a spider.

Mac eyed Joe, considered asking him to leave, then thought better of it. He noticed his friend watching Emily in the rearview mirror rather than turning around to face her.

"What do you want?" she finally asked.

Taking a deep breath, he leaned over the console and placed the doughnut box next to her on the backseat. "As I've said, I'd like a DNA test." He crossed his arms. Despite the pain and contempt he saw flash in her eyes, he held his ground. "That's the only way we'll know for certain."

"And then what?" Despite the slight tremor in her voice, she held her head high. "If he is your son, are you planning to sue for custody? You have to know I'll fight you with everything I have."

He dipped his head, not sure how to answer. He owed her the unvarnished truth, but he was no longer one hundred percent confident he knew what the truth was.

"I don't know," he finally told her. "Let's deal with that bridge when we cross it."

"I see." The bitterness in her tone told him she didn't really. "I'll go by the drugstore and pick up a DNA test kit."

"No need. I already have one." Heart hammering in his chest, he held it out. He'd ordered it first thing after arriving in Anniversary. "I'm going to use the same lab the sheriff's department uses. Renee said we can get faster results that way."

Instead of taking it, she crossed her arms. "I don't have to do this, you know. I can make you get a lawyer, and we can go to court. I can delay this for months, maybe even years."

At her words, Joe tensed but said nothing. Mac could tell from his friend's profile that Joe wanted to jump into the conversation in Mac's defense. While he appreciated that, Mac was glad he didn't.

Aching, Mac regarded Emily. "Yes, you could do that. But I have to think you'd want to know the truth, too. For yourself and for Ryan."

She opened her mouth and then closed it.

"Not to mention getting rid of the stalker. If it turns out Ryan is my son, this other person will have no claim on him."

As his words registered, she swallowed hard. Finally, mouth twisting, she took the proffered box. He couldn't help but notice how her hands trembled as his did. "You might not be his father, you know."

"I know," he said, though he didn't believe that for an instant. "Your stalker and your former husband could be the birth parents."

At his ready agreement, she stiffened. "Yes. Or there's a third possibility. Neither of you could be a genetic match. Ryan could be exactly as he was presented to me—a baby whose mother gave him up for adoption—someone completely unknown."

Joe quietly snorted. They both ignored him.

"Anything's possible," Mac finally said.

Emily stared at him. The hope she couldn't hide, along with the stark pain in her beautiful eyes, nearly undid him. "I never meant for this to happen," he muttered, trying to pretend Joe wasn't eavesdropping on the entire conversation. "You, me, none of that."

"Really?" Again she crossed her arms, shooting several glances at Joe, as though wishing he'd give them some privacy and leave. "What did you mean to happen exactly? You came into our lives, ostensibly to help find my stalker, comforted me, pretended to care about me…"

Her voice broke, and she turned away to stare out the window. The way she hunched her shoulders told him how hard she tried to hold on to what had to be the shattered remnants of her self-control.

More than anything, he wanted to take her arms. It was part of his penance that he couldn't.

Half of him wanted to ask for the DNA test kit back, to tell her never mind and ask if they could simply go back to the way they'd been before. He'd seen a glimpse of the possible future, a future so full of hope and love and happiness that he'd scarcely dared to believe it. But he'd known then as he did now that if they were going to try and forge such a potential life they could have no lies in between them. Ah, but that didn't make him want it any less.

Still, he knew that no matter the outcome he had a right to know the truth. *They* had a right to know. *Ryan* had a right to know, too. Even Emily had to see that.

He hadn't meant to hurt her. Clearly, he had hurt them both. Hell, if she felt one tenth as bad as he did, it's a wonder she could even look at him.

The future he'd begun to envision had also vanished, like wisps of smoke in a gale force wind.

"I'm not going to leave Anniversary, you know," he finally said. "No matter what happens."

At these words, she turned to face him, every angle

of her body speaking defiance. "I don't care what you do."

They both knew this was a lie.

When he didn't immediately respond, she nodded. Then, clutching the DNA test kit, she climbed out of his car and went back to her house, her back ramrod straight and her gait stiff. Unlocking her front door, she slipped inside, never once looking back.

Mac shot Joe a warning look, letting him know he'd better not say a word. Then he started the car and drove off.

Once inside, Emily crumbled. Tossing the stupid DNA test kit as far as she could, she stomped into her kitchen, pouring herself a big mug of her own coffee, dumping his down the drain. She'd be damned if she'd drink his.

Before she'd realized it, half an hour had passed. Almost out the door, her house phone rang.

Caller ID read *Unknown Caller*. Maybe…heart suddenly pounding, she answered.

"I'm glad I caught you before you left for your job," the metallic voice said. Due to the amount of distortion, she couldn't make out whether the caller was male or female. It sounded like a sexless computer android.

"I'm not playing your game." Emily kept her voice even. "I'm sick and tired of you hounding me."

"Tough," the computer-generated voice sneered.

Ignoring this, Emily continued. "If you really feel that Ryan is your child, why the secrecy? Don't worry, I know Carlos had a mistress. He had more than one, so if this is Desiree, you'll still have some proving to do. Come forward. Let's meet and see if we can hash this out."

The silence on the other end of the phone line told her she'd succeeded in startling her caller.

"You lie," the person said.

"No, I don't." Keeping her tone light, Emily sighed. "It seems Ryan is a popular child. I've already got one person claiming to be his father who has asked for a DNA test. What's one more? Why not add your name to the mix?"

Again the caller went quiet. When he or she spoke again, the androidlike tone sounded thick and even more unsteady. "Are you serious?"

"Dead serious," Emily answered, then winced at her unfortunate choice of words. "Either put up or shut up."

"Stupid woman. I'll meet you. At your place. Look for me, because I won't be calling to let you know when to expect me." There was a click, and Emily knew her stalker had hung up. Whether it was Desiree, Franco or a complete stranger, Emily knew she'd finally set things in motion toward a conclusion.

Placing the phone back in the cradle, she realized she was shaking. Suddenly, she didn't want to be alone in her house any longer. She snatched her purse off the counter, hurried to her car and went in to work.

Luckily, the vet clinic was busy all day and time flew by. She skipped her daily run, vaguely afraid to go near the park, and grabbed a quick sandwich from the deli down the street. She ate at her desk, explaining she had a lot of paperwork to catch up on due to her absences.

Whenever the image of Mac came to mind, she ruthlessly pushed the thoughts away. But as the day wore on, she found herself wondering if she should tell him that she'd spoken with her stalker. Someone needed to know what she'd done. Since Mac had a vested interest in catching this person, too, filling him in would be a smart idea.

So what if the idea of seeing him again had her stomach tied in knots?

She waited until thirty minutes before closing time to call his cell phone. He answered on the second ring, the deep timbre of his voice sending a jolt into her heart.

Though she knew she could simply tell him what she'd done over the phone, she suddenly wanted to see him in person.

"We need to talk," she said.

"Name the time and the place and I'll be there." The hopeful huskiness in the statement made her regret her impulsive decision.

She couldn't back out gracefully—not now. "Come over around seven. That'll give me time to fix Ryan dinner."

"I can come earlier and bring something. Chicken, pizza, burgers you name it."

Wearily, she closed her eyes. "No, thank you. I need to talk to you while Ryan is occupied. His favorite television show comes on at seven. He won't be listening in if we talk in the kitchen."

After the vet clinic closed, Emily picked Ryan up at the day care and went home. She cooked Ryan's favorite hamburger-and-macaroni dish, and they ate together. Despite the ball of worries lodged in her stomach like lead, she choked some down and managed to smile and nod as Ryan recounted his day at both kindergarten and day care.

Dinner finished, Ryan went to take his bath before his show came on, and she washed the dishes. Every sound, from a particularly insistent blue jay outside to Ryan turning off the faucet, had her jumping. If real life were like the campy horror movies she used to watch when she was younger, the stalker would be jumping out of her closet at any moment.

Luckily, that didn't happen.

Trying to laugh at her fears, as it grew closer to seven, she couldn't keep herself from checking out her reflection in the mirror. After brushing and then spiking up her hair, she smoothed a little lip balm over her lips and waited for the doorbell to chime. She refused to pace or give in to the temptation to keep taking peeks out the window.

Despite her halfhearted attempts to act normal, she didn't fool her son.

"Mom?" Ryan asked, emerging from the bathroom already in his pajamas, his dark hair still damp. She breathed in the clean scent of Ivory soap and hugged him tight, only releasing him when he protested.

"What's up, kiddo?" she asked.

"Is someone coming over?"

Since he didn't know anything about what had happened, she nodded. "Mac is, sweetheart. How did you know?"

He grinned. "You're still wearing your work clothes and makeup, Mom." Lifting his small hand for a fist bump, he crowed in triumph, making her smile. "Normally, you change."

"You're right. I guess I can't put anything past you, huh? Your show's about to come on, so you'd better turn the TV on."

The words had barely left her mouth when the doorbell chimed, instantly sending her heart into overdrive.

"That's him! That's him!" Ryan yelled, running toward the door.

"Wait!" she shouted, going after him, reminding him

she needed to look through the peephole, but she was a few seconds too late.

Not knowing who was on the other side, he yanked the door open just as she reached him.

Chapter 12

Luckily, Mac stood on her doorstep rather than the stalker. After shooting Mac a stay-put glare, Emily turned the same look on Ryan. Upset and furious, she grabbed her son and moved him back. "How many times have I told you we don't open the door without checking to see who's out there?"

His blue eyes widened at both her tone and her actions. "But you said Mac was coming over. I knew it was him ringing the doorbell."

"That doesn't matter," she chided, still shaking from the burst of adrenaline. "That could have been anyone. We have to be careful. You know that."

For a second, Ryan looked like he wanted to argue. Then, apparently thinking better of that, he hung his head, his lower lip wobbling. "I'm sorry, Mommy."

She hugged him close and breathed a kiss on his forehead. "Okay. But promise me you'll remember next time, okay?"

"Okay." Sniffling, he raised his head. Then he grinned, eyeing the paper bag Mac held. "Whatcha got?"

"Ryan!" About to apologize, she closed her mouth as Mac crouched down, holding the bag out toward Ryan.

"Why don't you look and see?" Mac said.

Reaching for the bag, her son had the presence of mind to glance at her for permission. She yanked her gaze away from Mac's and slowly nodded, giving her permission.

With that, Ryan snatched it and yanked it open. "Cookies!" he breathed. "Oh, Mom. Can I?"

"May I," she corrected automatically. Though she limited sweets, occasionally she let Ryan indulge. "Yes, you may."

"Can—may I have a glass of milk to go with them?"

Though she kept a pleasant expression on her face, she felt awkward, dealing with her son in front of the man who might be his biological father. Still, she kept her voice neutral and consoled herself with the knowledge that her son didn't suspect anything was amiss. "Of course, if you promise to use the coaster on the coffee table. I'll bring it to you in a minute."

"Thank you so much!" Impulsively, Ryan gave Mac a quick hug, then tore off to the living room to plunk down in front of the television just as the opening credits started for his show.

Still feeling self-conscious, she avoided meeting Mac's gaze. "He'll be busy for the next half hour. Come on into the kitchen."

As she led the way, she could feel his eyes burning into her back. She had to fight an overwhelming—and completely stupid—need to turn and walk into his arms and let him hold her. Instead, she busied herself pouring Ryan's milk, feeling the heat of Mac's gaze as she carried it out to her son.

When she returned, she flashed him a halfhearted smile and pulled out her chair at the kitchen table, motioning for him to do the same. She tried not to watch as he settled his large body, dwarfing the ordinary chair.

To give him credit, he didn't try to rush her. Instead, he simply placed his tanned hands on top of the table and waited.

"Where's your buddy?" she asked, stalling despite her resolve.

"He and Renee went out," he said, unsmiling. "They're old friends who go way back."

Swallowing, she nodded. For her part, she took an inordinate amount of time getting settled, unable to keep from fidgeting. This felt more uncomfortable than she'd thought it would.

Finally, once she was seated, she squared her shoulders and looked directly at him, surprised at how painful that was. "I asked you to come over because I got a call from the stalker today."

A sharp intake of breath as he leaned forward was his only reaction. Pretending his nearness didn't affect her, she relayed the conversation, tumbling her words over each other in an effort to get them all out.

When she'd finished, Mac sat back, jaw clenched. "Are you sure that was wise?" Emotion deepened his sapphire eyes, changing them to midnight. "What if this person—let's say you're right and she actually is one of your former husband's mistresses—has grown more unstable? What if she's dangerous? You know she said you would pay."

"I've always known she's unstable." Agitated, as much by how badly she wanted to touch him as she was by the situation, she jumped from her chair and began to pace. "Why the hell else do you think she'd be breaking into my house and calling me?"

A muscle worked in his jaw. "You do realize you are putting yourself in danger?"

Swallowing hard, she boldly met his gaze. "It's time to end this, once and for all. I'm counting on you to keep me safe."

Though he didn't react verbally to her words, something smoldered in the depths of his eyes.

"Do you think you can do that?" she pressed.

"I can," he promised, his voice husky. "You can count on that."

"Thank you." Now that the hard part was over, she exhaled and pulled a chair out to take a seat before reconsidering. "Would you like something to drink? I have cola, iced tea, lemonade or water."

"Water is fine, thanks."

After she'd placed their glasses on the table, she again took her seat, gripping her glass with both her hands.

His bare arm, tanned and muscular and silky with hair, rested on top of the table. She fought the urge to touch him, to stroke his skin and see the desire blaze into life in his eyes. Even now, when she knew he'd used her, she still ached for him. How foolish was that?

"All right, let's get what details we can. Are you reasonably certain the caller was female?" He sounded exactly like the cop he was—professional and detached... too detached. Though no doubt his calm, reassuring tone was meant to soothe, conversely she wanted to shake him up, ruffle his feathers, make him show emotion—any emotion.

In the other room, Ryan laughed out loud at his television show, a reassuringly normal sound that was so out of place with this discussion that she jumped.

What the hell was wrong with her? She took a deep breath. "No. I'm not certain at all. There was no way to tell. As you know, whoever it was uses some kind of computer-generated voice software."

"But they agreed to meet you. Did they say where?"

Aware he wasn't going to like this, she took another deep breath, wincing. "Here. Whoever it is plans to come here. And he or she said they'd show up unannounced."

He reached across the table and captured one of her hands in his big one, startling her. "I don't like this," he said.

"Of course you don't." Though she didn't pull away, she couldn't resist a verbal jab. "After all, someone else actually might have a valid claim to what you think is yours."

This time, when pain flashed across his rugged face, she steeled herself and didn't break their locked gaze.

He leaned forward, toward her rather than recoiling away as she would have expected, keeping her hand trapped in his. He looked big and powerful, and she knew a second's fleeting longing that he would always be there to protect her and keep her safe and warm.

This proved that fools never, ever changed.

About to open her mouth and ask him to leave now that their business had been concluded, a slight hesitation in his expression made her wait.

"Listen, I've been thinking about this. About him." Speaking quietly, he glanced back toward the living room, where Ryan sat still engrossed in his program, eating his cookies and drinking his milk. "I wanted you to know that I'm not going to try and take him away from you."

"What?" She blinked, blank, amazed and disoriented. "Say that again?"

"If the DNA test proves I'm—" he lowered his voice again "—if it proves I'm his father, I'm not planning to try and sue for custody."

All she could do was stare and then stupidly ask him why not.

"You're his mother now." He gave her a long look, full of rueful warmth. "I wouldn't take that away from him, away from either of you. But I would like to work out some sort of visitation agreement with you. So I can be in his life, help him grow up. And assist you if you need me."

Shock siphoned the blood from her face. Dizzy, for a moment she thought she might actually faint. Shaken and momentarily speechless, she found herself gripping his hand so hard the tanned skin turned white.

She stared at him, her heart pounding. "Are you..." The words caught in her throat. Swallowing hard, she tried again. "Do you really mean that?"

"Of course I do. If Ryan is my son, I have a right to share in his life but not to ruin it. He loves you, and I can see how much you love him."

Almost afraid to believe it, she focused on her breathing—in and out, trying to center herself, attempting to accept his words as truth. This felt like a miracle, as if her prayers had not only been heard but answered.

Eyeing him across the table, his generous mouth quirked in the beginning of a smile, she couldn't catch her breath. With her throat aching and tears pricking the back of her eyes, she wasn't sure she could speak.

What a wonderful, amazing man.

Again, she longed to go to him and wrap her arms around him. Instead, she pushed past the emotion clogging her voice. "Thank you," she said, the warmth in her voice warring with the huskiness of raw emotion. "I can't tell you how much that means to me."

Now he did smile, dazzling her. "I'm not your enemy, Emily. I never was."

In the other room, the familiar jangle of a popular commercial came on. Ryan appeared, carrying the wadded up cookie bag and his empty milk glass. He froze when he saw his mother's tear-filled eyes and devastated expression.

"Mommy? Are you all right?"

"Of course I am!" Pushing herself up, she took his glass from him, carrying it to the sink and rinsing it out. The very ordinariness of the action helped calm her. "Throw your empty bag in the trash," she told him, glad she sounded relatively normal again.

Once he'd done that, she crouched down and opened her arms wide. "Come here, you."

He ran over, gave her a quick hug and then began squirming when she tried to keep him close. "Mommmmy! My show's coming back on."

As soon as she let him go, he rushed back into the other room.

"See what I mean?" Mac's eyes were suspiciously bright. Seeing that, she gave in to impulse and went to him, hugging him from behind. The instant her arms wrapped around his shoulders, he froze, as if her touch was too much for him to handle just then.

She felt foolish, immediately backing off, though she refused to apologize. If anyone deserved a hug, Mac did.

A moment later, he uncoiled himself from his chair.

"I'd better be going. Before I do, I'll call Renee and make sure she's arranged for twenty-four-hour surveillance."

Biting her lip, she hesitated. After all that he'd given her that night, she knew she owed him this much. She decided she'd go for it and say exactly what was in her heart. "I thought this was your case."

In the middle of paging through the contact list on his phone, he paused. "This is," he said slowly, a question in his eyes.

"Then wouldn't you be the one doing surveillance?"

"We take shifts. I'm not sure who's on tonight."

"I asked you to come over." She took a deep breath, then plunged on before she thought better of it. "Why don't you just stay here? I have a foldout couch in my office. You can sleep there."

Staring at her, when he finally offered her a slow, arresting smile, she knew he'd accept her offer.

"Let me run to my house and throw a few things into a bag. I'll be back in less than an hour," he said, his deep voice vibrating with emotion.

Throat tight, she followed him to the door, watching as he got into his car and drove off. Then she secured the dead bolt and the other lock, hoping her stalker didn't decide to make an appearance in Mac's absence.

As he drove away, Mac finally admitted to himself the truth. He loved her—with every beat of his heart and more. He loved her. And he could never let her know. He wondered if fate would ever stop laughing at him.

He'd found his son, true. But he'd also found the woman with whom he wanted to spend the rest of his life.

Allowing himself a moment to dream, he pictured them: he and Emily and Ryan together. A family.

But now she'd never believe he wanted her for herself. She'd always believe he only said he loved her because of the child they shared. Sadly, he couldn't blame her. So he'd best learn how to be grateful for what he could have.

At least he'd once had a family—unlike Joe, who'd never married. That's why Mac had been glad to see the spark of interest between Joe and Renee.

The knowledge that his friend might finally have something going on in the romance department made Mac happy. Joe had always been the perpetual bachelor, dating a large variety of girls but never getting serious. He'd even refused to bring a date when he'd gone out with Mac and Sarah, claiming being a single third wheel was better than introducing his best friends to women he didn't love.

Though Mac had found this slightly odd, Sarah always seemed to find it amusing. Good-naturedly, Mac had humored them both.

As he thought of this, he was struck by something else. Remembering those days no longer felt as painful. He hummed under his breath and realized this was because not only had he finally located his son but he'd found a woman with whom he wanted to spend the rest of his life.

He merely had to stop an overzealous stalker and then spend all his time showing her that they were meant to be together.

Throwing a couple of clothing changes into a gym bag, he grabbed the essential toiletries. He tossed the bag in his car, checked his mailbox and his answering machine, then climbed into the car and headed back toward Emily's.

As he pulled out of his driveway, his cell phone rang. It was Joe.

"What's up?" Mac asked good-naturedly.

"I need a favor." Joe sounded distracted, almost upset. "I ran out of gas in my rental car and need you to bring me five gallons. I'm stuck in the middle of nowhere." He rattled off a location clear on the opposite end of town.

Glancing at his watch, Mac knew he didn't have time. "I'm going to call one of the other deputies to meet you. I have somewhere I really have to be."

"Come on, Mac," Joe groaned. "I have a huge flower arrangement in my car, along with a giant stuffed toy bear. Since they're for Renee, I really don't want anyone else in the department to see them. Imagine the ribbing she'd get. Please come yourself. It will only take a few minutes. I promise."

Again Mac checked his watch. It had only taken him twenty minutes to get home and pack. Running out to rescue Joe would take at least that long. He didn't want to leave Emily alone in case the stalker chose that night to pay her a visit.

"I'll do what I can," Mac finally told Joe. "Rescue will arrive in a few minutes."

Aware Mac would be back soon, Emily tidied up while letting herself imagine various scenarios, all of them erotic. She couldn't imagine what had possessed her to invite the man to stay overnight in her home, but now she was glad she had. Though she knew it would be difficult to resist temptation. Did she even want to resist? That was the million-dollar question.

She sighed. Despite his enigmatic exterior, she sensed his inner vulnerability, especially concerning her son. Rather than pushing her away, his Achilles' heel pleased her and made her desire him even more.

But she would have to table her wants and needs right now. They had more important issues to worry about.

Once she'd finished straightening up the house, she sent Ryan to brush his teeth and pulled out the sofa bed. She found sheets in the linen closet and made the bed up for him, imagining Mac's tan skin against the smooth sheets. Smiling at the image, she finished making the area as comfortable as she could.

When the doorbell chimed a scant thirty minutes later, Emily wiped suddenly sweaty hands down the front of her jeans and grinned. That had been really quick. She'd just gotten Ryan tucked into bed.

After unlocking her dead bolt, she opened the door, her welcoming smile fading as she belatedly realized she should have followed her own rule and used the peephole.

It wasn't Mac standing on the doorstep. It was Mac's friend, dressed in a hoodie and jeans. This time, she got a good look at his blond hair, tanned skin and blue eyes—the same color as Mac's.

"Can I help you?" she managed to ask politely, though before she finished speaking she already knew. Heart pounding, she tried to close the door, but he stuck his foot inside and gave it a heave, sending her stumbling back against the wall. He pushed his way in, kicking the door shut behind him.

"I've come to get Ryan," he said, his tone coolly menacing as he pulled out a pistol and pointed it at her. "Bring him to me. Now."

Emily stared, even as panic coiled in the pit of her stomach. She didn't know what to say, how to choose the right words—something that wouldn't set him off. She had to do something to buy her a little time until Mac returned. Because there was no way in hell she was letting this man take her son.

When she didn't respond, the man took a step closer, a shadow of annoyance darkening his face. "I mean it. Get the boy. Now."

Instead of moving, she studied him. His compact medium build spoke of latent strength, and he walked with a fighter's muscular stance.

Either way, his presence here didn't compute. Though he appeared extremely dangerous, he couldn't be her stalker. After all, Albany, New York, was a long way from Texas, and he'd just gotten into town.

So what did he want with her son?

Either way, she'd die before she'd let him take Ryan.

"Did you understand me?" The silken voice he used to ask the question made her even more ill at ease. "I'm not asking again. Get Ryan."

"What do you want with my son?" she demanded, refusing to let him see how much he frightened her.

"*Your* son?" His laugh came rimmed with icicles. "Do you mean the baby you had stolen from the hospital nursery so you could adopt him?"

She felt as if her breath had been cut off as she glanced uneasily over her shoulder. "If this is some misguided attempt to help Mac, you need to stop. He wouldn't want this. He and I are already working something out. I know you're his best friend, but this is completely unnecessary."

At her words, he gave her a black, layered look. "You honestly think—"

Before he could finish, the doorbell rang. Mac? Her heart leapt into her throat as she instinctively turned toward it.

"Don't move," Joe barked. Keeping the gun trained on her, he crossed to the door and checked the peephole. "Perfect," he said, unlocking the dead bolt. "Reinforcements."

Franco and Desiree stepped inside. Desiree's overly made-up eyes widened at the sight of the gun. Franco, on the other hand, appeared unfazed. He faced Joe and cocked his head. "Did you find the diamonds?" he asked.

"Not yet," Joe answered. "I'm sure it's here somewhere. Right, Emily?"

Afraid to move, she slowly shook her head. "I'm sorry, but like I told Desiree earlier, all of the jewelry was sold."

"And that's why we're going to grab the kid," Franco sneered. "Because I'll bet you find the diamonds real quick if you're worried about your son."

Emily froze. "That's why you want Ryan?" she asked softly, watching both Franco and Joe. "Because of some stupid, nonexistent diamonds?"

Joe started to speak, but Franco cut him off. "Half a million of ice isn't stupid. Now go find the jewelry or we're taking your kid."

Terror skittered a path up her spine, giving her an involuntary shiver. "Please," she appealed to Joe. "You're Mac's friend. You have to know he believes Ryan is his son. Don't do this."

Joe laughed, a bitter sound. "I know what he believes. He's always believed that. But I know better. Ryan isn't his son. He's mine."

"Yours?" she repeated. Was that madness glittering

in his eyes or certainty? Either way, she knew she stood on dangerous, unstable ground.

She needed to buy enough time for Mac to return. Mac was her only hope.

"Please." She kept her tone cordial, like that of a hostess speaking to a welcomed guest. "I'm confused. Mac told me the exact same story, except he said Ryan is *his* son. He can't be both."

He stared hard at her, his mouth twisting. She looked back as calmly as she could, hoping he couldn't see the wild tattoo of her rapidly beating heart.

Finally he looked away, appearing to be considering her words. Though judging from the tight grimness of his jaw, she didn't have long before he lashed out again.

Inwardly shuddering, she prayed she could pull this off. Time…she needed time. And she needed Mac. She could only hope he returned soon.

As he considered her words, his handsome face twisted in rage, a caricature of the icily composed man who'd faced her a moment ago.

"Sit down." Motioning with the gun toward her sofa, he waited.

She sat.

"Let me tell you about me and Mac." He sneered the words. "We've been best friends since we were in the third grade. We competed for everything, too. Sometimes I won. Sometimes he won. Neither of us really minded—until Sarah came along."

"Mac's wife?"

"That's right. She and Mac started dating, and then they married. I tried, but I couldn't let her go. All along, I was the proverbial third wheel. Mac used to tease me because I never brought dates around them."

The way he looked at her, as though she was supposed to comment, had her scrambling for something noncommittal to say. "You sound like you all were a close group of friends."

A muscle worked in his jaw, making her think she must have made a mistake. But then he slowly nodded. "We were. Until Sarah realized I loved her and began to love me back."

Mac sighed. Though he'd debated honoring Joe's request, he couldn't risk leaving Emily alone much longer—not with the stalker about to show up at any moment. Luckily, he'd called Ed, and he'd agreed to go help Joe. Now Mac was on his way to Emily's. He'd already been gone longer than he deemed feasible.

Pushing the accelerator to the floor, he sped toward Emily's house, praying he wasn't too late.

He got there in less than ten minutes, noting the unfamiliar car parked in her driveway. The maroon sedan looked vaguely familiar, despite its spectacular ordinariness.

He parked in front of a house two doors over. He approached on foot, with his service pistol drawn.

Instead of going to the front door, he ran to the side. Keeping close to the building, he rushed around to the back. Of course, being prudent and careful, Emily had locked the door. However, he was willing to bet she was like thousands of other people and kept a spare key stashed somewhere nearby.

He found it inside a fake rock she'd evidently purchased for that purpose. Quietly, he unlocked the back door and slipped inside.

From the other room, he could hear voices. A man stood with his back to him, and it appeared Emily was seated on the couch.

Not taking the time to consider, he rushed across the kitchen into the den, weapon raised.

"Sheriff's department. Hands where I can see them," he ordered, adrenaline pumping so hard it took him a second to recognize the man with a gun pointed at Emily.

"Joe?" Despite his shocked disbelief, Mac kept his best friend in his sights. "I thought you'd run out of gas on the other side of town."

Joe's mouth twisted. "I thought you would be on your way to help me."

Mac frowned. "I sent Ed. What the hell is going on?"

Before he'd finished speaking, Franco rushed out of the bedroom, gun drawn. "Drop it, cop."

"Or I shoot Emily," Joe said.

Because he had no choice, Mac dropped his gun.

Moving quickly, Joe kicked it aside.

"I found it!" a familiar feminine voice trilled. Desiree tripped into the living room, grinning. She held a battered cigar box in her hands. "It was in the kid's room, in a toy box, under a bunch of stuffed animals. He never even woke up."

"Open it," Franco commanded, keeping his weapon trained on Mac.

Slowly, she did, licking her brightly painted lips as she displayed the stunning diamond jewelry inside. "There's even more," she breathed. "I'll bet there's a million bucks worth of stuff in here. Maybe more."

"Perfect." Franco smiled back. "Now we'll be leaving. Go, honey. Go."

Desiree headed toward the door, Franco right behind her, gun still drawn. "Are you coming, Joe?"

Joe shook his head. "Hold on," he barked. "We're not done here. I want the kid."

Mouth open, Franco stared. "Why? We've got what we want. Let's go."

"No," Joe snarled, his gaze flicking from Emily to Mac and back to Franco. "We're not leaving until I get what I want. I need you to back me up. I came here for Ryan. I want my son."

"Your son?" Both Mac and Franco spoke at the same time. Mac kept his gaze trained on Joe, who had his pistol pointed at Emily. Franco still stood near the doorway next to Desiree, weapon raised.

Joe's expression of fury warred with the sadness in his blue eyes as he nodded. "I know you thought he was yours. But he's not. He's mine. Sarah was going to tell you—actually, we both were going to tell you that night at dinner. But then she had the accident and…"

Mac could only stare. "Are you insane? Sarah wouldn't have cheated on me. And not with you. You were—are—like a brother to me. To both of us."

Joe laughed. And then Mac knew.

A tumble of confused images ran through his mind. None of them made sense. "How could you? You're my best friend. I trusted you like a brother."

For an instant, regret darkened Joe's chiseled features. "I'm sorry. We never meant for anything to happen. But we grew so close.…"

Keeping his eyes trained on the man he'd believed was his best friend, Mac tried to understand. Inside, something clicked, an answer finally sliding into place.

Instead of anger or grief, he felt only…bitterness. He would have thought learning such an awful truth about his wife and the man he'd called his friend would rip his heart out. But in the past five years, he'd done a lot of questioning. In hindsight, a lot of things about his marriage hadn't added up.

And now Mac had to face the fact that the baby he'd believed to be his might in reality be Joe's.

That hurt more than he would have believed possible. "Mac," Joe said, "you've got to understand. Sarah and I truly loved each other. She was going to ask you for a divorce so we could marry and raise our child together."

Our child... The baby Mac had always believed was his.

Now Joe's beyond-the-pale assistance in the search for Ryan all made sense.

Even so, it took every ounce of willpower Mac possessed to keep from staggering under the impact of Joe's words. Now that they'd been spoken, looking back, he wondered how he hadn't seen something, guessed anything. Had he really been so blind?

"You had no reason to doubt her," Emily said, almost as if she read his mind. "Or him."

Mac kept his gaze trained on Joe. "Now I understand why you were so fanatical about locating the baby. You kept on even when every lead seemed to be a dead end. But not because you were so desperately trying to help a man who'd lost everything. You did it because you had a vested interest."

"I lost everything, too," Joe cried, pain flashing in his blue eyes.

"Maybe you have, but that doesn't explain how we've ended up with this. Both of us armed and against each other."

Franco cleared his throat, drawing their attention.

"Look," he said, reaching for the front door. "This is all very touching and all that, but I got what I came for."

Brandishing the cigar box like a weapon, Desiree grinned. "Me, too. Looks like sending you all those letters finally paid off."

"Letters?" Emily asked. "Those were from you?"

"Yep," Desiree said proudly. "You took what was mine. I wanted it back. Now, I've got it. I hope it works out for you with all this." She gestured at Joe and Mac. "But Franco and me, we gotta run."

"Don't move," Joe ordered. Then, when Franco ignored him, Joe shot him in the back.

Chapter 13

Emily gasped as Franco fell, a bloodstain spreading over his upper shoulder.

"You shot him." Desiree's voice echoed Emily's disbelief. "Oh. My. God."

Blue eyes narrowed, Joe looked from Desiree to Mac to Emily. "So what? Consider this proof that I'll do what I have to do to take back what's mine."

Sobbing, Desiree sank to the floor alongside Franco, still clutching the all-but-forgotten cigar box.

Heart pounding, Emily flinched as Joe took a step toward her. She prayed the loud gunshot hadn't awakened Ryan.

"Go get the boy," Joe ordered again, this time through clenched teeth.

Emily shook her head, breathing in quick, shallow gasps. "No."

"Put the gun down," Mac ordered. "Come on, Joe. There's no way you'll get away with this. It's over."

Joe didn't move, the barrel of his gun never wavering from Emily. "It's not over. Either I get my son or I'll shoot Emily."

"That makes no sense," Mac growled.

Joe glared at him. "It makes just as much sense as what you did. You befriended her, all so you could take what you thought was yours. We're not so different, you and I. I want what's mine."

Shaking his head, Mac took a step closer to Joe. "Without a DNA test, we have no way to know for sure that you're the father."

Afraid to breathe, Emily watched as Joe eyed Mac.

Then, apparently seeing a hint of uncertainty in Joe's expression, Mac kept talking. "Sarah and I were still intimate right up until she died," he said. "I could just as easily be Ryan's biological father as you."

Face mottling with rage, Joe's jaw worked. "You're lying," he sputtered, waving the gun in the air between Emily and Mac. "Sarah told me she wasn't—"

Behind Joe, Desiree slowly got to her feet. Mascara had made black streaks run down her cheeks. Moving slowly, she raised the cigar box and slammed it in the back of Joe's head.

Joe staggered, clearly stunned.

"Get down!" Mac dove for him. Out of reflex, Joe squeezed off a shot. It went into the roof above Emily's head, sending plaster raining down on her.

Elbow to the throat, Mac knocked the pistol away ~~fro~~m Joe. Emily scrambled to retrieve it. Desiree stood ~~nea~~rby, shaking.

Mac grimly cuffed his best friend and began reading him his rights. "You have the right to remain silent—"

"Mom?" Ryan said, sleepy-eyed and standing in the doorway closest to Joe. "What's going on?"

Emily's heart stuttered. "Ryan, go back to your room," she told him, breathless and shaky but stern. "I'll be in there in a minute. I promise."

To her relief, the little boy turned immediately and disappeared around the corner.

"Wait up, Ryan." Handcuffed and subdued, Joe stared in the direction the boy had gone. "Please, let me see him. Just once more."

"No." Emily lifted her chin and glared at him. "If you'd gone about this in a different way, I might have considered it. But you've not only endangered me but him. You have no rights, as far as I'm concerned."

Then she looked at Mac, shaking with the after-effects of shock and a sudden, furious rage. "Do I need to call 911?"

"I can call it in," he said quietly. "Go tend to Ryan."

"What about Franco?" a clearly shaken Desiree asked. "We need an ambulance. He's still alive."

"We'll get him some help," Mac promised. "Please, sit down before you fall and hurt yourself."

Though she nodded, Desiree sank to the ground alongside Franco, who still hadn't moved. Emily noticed the other woman continued to cradle her box of precious jewels as though they were a lifeline. Personally, she was surprised that Desiree hadn't fled when she had the opportunity. She must really have cared for Franco.

Shaking her head, Emily hurried out of the room. The last thing she heard was Mac calling dispatch.

When she reached Ryan's room, her little boy launched himself at her. She held him and attempted to calm him. Though half-asleep, he'd seen the strange man and the guns. She'd explained things simply, by saying Joe had been a bad man and since Mac was a policeman he'd arrested him. Luckily, Ryan didn't appear to have seen Franco lying on the floor.

Downplaying any danger, including the gunshot that had awakened him, she smoothed his dark hair away from his perfect little face and kissed his forehead.

"Do you think you can try and go back to sleep?" she murmured. "It's a school day tomorrow, and I know you don't want to miss kindergarten."

He clung tightly to her and shook his head violently. "That man was going to shoot you, wasn't he?"

"It's all right, sweetheart. Mac saved us."

Her little boy raised his head and met her gaze, looking much older than his five years. "I want to tell him thank you," he said.

"You can, later. I promise." She kissed him again, love making her chest tight. "He has to get that man to jail and then there's paperwork and all kinds of boring stuff. You can thank him in the morning."

Rather than arguing, he nodded, eyes already half closing. She continued to hold him, rocking softly and murmuring in a soothing voice.

When his even breathing revealed he'd fallen back asleep, she eased her arms out from under him. Once his head was on the pillow, she covered him and got up. About to leave, she stopped, unable to keep from standing near the side of his bed and gazing down at him with her heart full of wonder and love.

He was her baby...her son. No matter what the DNA

test proved, nothing would ever change the relationship she had with him.

She closed Ryan's door behind her and prayed the wail of the approaching sirens didn't awaken him again. She went to rejoin Mac and Desiree.

Later that night, after the ambulance had taken Franco to the hospital, Emily answered a barrage of questions. Renee handled the investigation herself, despite her bandages and the obvious pain her shoulder wound caused her. Desiree had to hand over the jewels and was arrested on charges of breaking and entering. She was bundled into the sheriff's car, along with Joe, who faced a barrage of charges.

Mac insisted on escorting Joe downtown himself. He left without even a backward glance at Emily. She supposed he was still stunned over Joe's revelations. She couldn't help but wonder what kind of woman Mac's wife had been to have an affair with her husband's best friend.

Though Mac had clearly not believed her when she said she hadn't known about the diamonds, she'd only told the truth. The one area she'd never thought to search was her son's toy box.

Wandering into the kitchen, she poured a glass of white wine and drifted back into the living room. More than exhausted, she felt drained. As she collapsed on the sofa, she knew her life was about to change. She couldn't put it off, couldn't run and hide. She had to face her future—Ryan's future—straight on, with her head held high.

After all, she'd done nothing wrong and everything right.

Sipping her wine, she reflected on Mac's promise

not to take her son away if he was the father. With those words, he'd managed to erase all the shadows over her heart.

Except what would happen if Joe was Ryan's biological father, rather than Mac? She supposed it wouldn't matter now. It looked like Joe would be going away to prison for a long, long time.

She carried her half-finished glass to the sink, rinsed it out and went to bed. Everything could be dealt with in the morning. What she needed now was sleep.

Once all the necessary paperwork had been completed and with Joe and Desiree safely in custody and Franco recuperating in the hospital, Mac finally headed home as dawn began to lighten the eastern horizon.

Joe's revelations had stunned him. But now, while he hated learning he'd been played for a fool by his wife and his best friend, he'd found a sort of acceptance. All that was ancient history and completely insignificant compared to what really mattered to him now.

All that mattered was Emily and Ryan...Ryan and Emily. When he crawled into bed as the sun came up, their names were the last two things on his mind.

Later that morning, a ringing telephone jarred him out of a deep, dreamless sleep. Instantly alert, he answered.

"Did I wake you?" Emily asked, her husky voice sending a thunderbolt of desire straight through his groin.

"I'm okay," he managed to say, rubbing his eyes and ˌinting at the clock, trying to read the time. "How ˌt you?"

ˌast night was tough, but it's a new day."

"And Ryan?" he asked.

"Ryan was a little upset last night, but this morning he seems fine. I just dropped him off at school." She took a deep breath. "I was wondering if you had a few minutes to talk."

He couldn't squelch the warm glow that spread through him. "Would you like to have breakfast?"

"Thanks, but I've already had it several hours ago." A thread of nervous determination ran through her voice. "Could you meet me at the sheriff's department in, say, thirty minutes?"

He frowned but kept his tone light. "Sure. Would you mind telling me why?"

"I'd rather not. See you there." She disconnected the call.

Now what? Refusing to speculate, he took a quick shower, towel dried his hair and got dressed. Since it was nearly one, he skipped his normal coffee and snagged a stale, leftover doughnut on the way out.

Driving the speed limit, he arrived at the same time as Emily. He turned in just as she pulled up into the parking lot.

Though she had to have noticed his car, she continued on inside without even glancing at him, her back ramrod straight.

A kernel of worry lodged in his stomach. What was going on? He parked and went inside.

Emily waited for him inside Renee's office. He raised a brow at her as he walked in. "What's up?" he asked.

She motioned to a box in the middle of Renee's desk—the DNA kit. "We need your sample. I've already gotten Ryan's, and Renee is going to get Joe's."

Renee handed him a swab. "Go ahead and swab the inside of your cheek and place that inside this bag."

Again he looked at Emily, but she wouldn't meet his gaze. He did as Renee had requested. When he'd finished, he turned the bag around but didn't hand it to Renee—not yet.

"Are you sure you want to go through with this?" He laid a gentle hand on Emily's arm. "You don't have to, you know."

"Yes, I do." Though she met his gaze bravely and spoke in a calm voice, he could see the worry in her caramel eyes. "You were right, what you said before. I have to know the truth. And Ryan should know who his father is."

He nodded, feeling a sense of finality as he accepted her decision. His life—everything leading up to this point—clicked into place as he handed the sealed bag to Renee. Unable to resist, he glanced at Emily, only to find she was intently watching Renee.

"I'll hand carry this to the lab we use for crime scenes," Renee said. "They're in Dallas, and they promised to get the results as quickly as possible. We'll include not only yours and Joe's samples but one from Carlos, as well," Renee told them.

Emily started at that. "How is that possible? Carlos has been dead five years."

"NYPD has some on file. I pulled a few strings, and I'll need you to sign some forms. Since Carlos's widow is the one requesting it, I'm confident they'll [ge]t our request. We should know in three days tops," [sh]e said.

"[W]ill you inform Joe of the results?" Mac asked,

keeping his voice steady. "Even though it's likely he'll be transferred to the county jail?"

"Of course. I can visit him there." A shadow crossed Renee's face. "I have to say that I was surprised. I had no idea he was involved in any of this."

"Me, either," Mac said grimly.

"You lost a friend."

"No, I learned the man I'd thought of as a brother was a backstabbing, wife-stealing liar." Aware of the bleakness of his tone, Mac looked away, lost in thought.

He couldn't help but wonder if he'd really known Sarah at all. She'd been nearly full-term when she'd lost her life in that accident, all the while maintaining that she and Mac were the parents. He wondered how long she would have kept up the farce. Had she truly known which man actually was the baby's father, or had she only suspected? That was one question to which he'd never know the answer.

As Mac turned to go, Emily voiced what they both feared. "What if Ryan really is Joe's son?"

Renee shrugged, looking at Mac.

He squeezed Emily's shoulder, glad of an excuse to touch her. "We'll deal with that when we come to it."

Though she nodded, he could tell from her downcast eyes and closed off expression that the idea troubled her greatly.

It worried him, too. But he refused to let the outcome of the DNA test affect the plans he'd made for the rest of his life—plans that, no matter what, included Emily and Ryan.

The next three days passed in a blur. Emily kept busy. In fact, Jayne and Tina told her she seemed positively driven. She worked hard, kept busy and managed to avoid Mac, though doing so was easy since he appeared to be also avoiding her. She couldn't exactly blame him. Still…

She didn't know what she would do if the DNA test revealed that Joe was Ryan's father. She prayed it would be Mac. Thinking how things had changed almost made her smile. A few days ago, she would never have believed she'd be hoping Mac would have a connection to her son.

Her doorbell chimed, making her jump. As if her thoughts had summoned him, Mac stood on the front porch, wearing his uniform and looking impossibly handsome.

Glad Ryan was still at school, her traitorous heart skipped a beat at the sight of him. Even now, even after knowing he'd played on her attraction to him and used her to get closer to Ryan, she still wanted him.

Schooling her expression into a bland, pleasant look, she opened the door. "Hey."

His gaze raked over her, sending an involuntary shiver down her spine. "Do you have a minute?"

Slowly, she nodded, struck dumb by the power of her own foolish need. Blood humming in her ears, she stepped aside, indicating he could follow.

As he moved past her so she could close the door behind him, she couldn't help flashing back to when she'd been locked in his embrace. She shook her head to dispel the disturbingly carnal images. Even now she ᵃ̶ᵉᵈ things had been different.

e'd actually allowed herself to believe in a future. ʳᵃs progress, was it not? Progress. Right…when she couldn't even perceive of a future without him. It was more of a step back than anything else.

She loved him. The power of that knowledge made her wince. She couldn't let him know. To protect herself, she knew she'd need to call on any shred of latent acting ability she might have in order to talk to him as if what he'd done, what they'd shared, hadn't mattered.

"What's up?" she asked Mac, perching on the edge of the couch as though she didn't have a care in the world. Her voice sounded serene and steady, even though her insides were quaking.

"I came to apologize," he told her, a ghost of a smile flitting across his handsome features. "I know to you it seemed like I tried to get close to you because of Ryan, and maybe in the beginning, that's all it was. But something changed."

Keeping an iron grip on her emotions, she waved his words away. "No worries," she said brightly. "I don't have any hard feelings against you."

His expression darkened. "You might be listening, but you're not hearing what I'm trying to tell you. This is important, Emily. To both of us."

"To both of us?" she echoed, surprised by the flash of anger she felt. Suddenly, she'd had enough of pretending. "Is it? So I'm supposed to sit here and let you say whatever you feel you have to in order to salve your conscience?"

Shaking his head, his brittle smile softened. "That's not why I'm here. Yes, you deserve an apology— actually, you deserve so much more."

Inwardly, she cringed. "I don't—"

"Let me finish." He came closer, stopping within touching distance. "Something started between us…

something with potential. I didn't intend for that to happen, but—"

Horrified, she cut him off. "I don't want your pity."

"This is not about pity," he growled, grabbing her and pulling her into the crush of his embrace. Stunned by the instant desire warring with fury, she stiffened rather than struggled, fighting against her instinctive response.

"Let me go," she said, barely getting the words out before he covered her mouth with his own.

Her resolve shattered with his kiss. Hunger, passion and more blazed to life, and she clung to him, dizzy and trembling and full of need.

When he finally raised his mouth from hers, his impossibly blue eyes blazing, she couldn't make herself pull away. There was an implicit claim in his embrace. daring her to deny what had sparked to life.

"This," he said quietly, nose to nose. "We have the potential of something special between us. You see it. I know you do. No matter what happens with the DNA test."

She couldn't answer, couldn't allow herself to hope, couldn't even begin to find the words. Forcing herself to look away from him so he wouldn't see the truth in her gaze, a movement out the front window caught her eye.

"Look," she gasped, moving away to stare at the sheriff's cruiser pulling into her drive.

"Renee." He sounded as worried as she. "The DNA test results must have come back already."

Heart racing, Emily nodded. As she moved toward loor, he touched her shoulder, stopping her.

romise me you'll think about it," he said, letting the hope that shone fierce from his blue eyes.

Giving the barest of nods, she answered. They went to the door together, standing side by side, arms touching.

Renee glanced from one to the other but didn't speak as she held out the results.

Emily accepted the tan envelope from the other woman, amazed that her fingers didn't shake.

Again, Renee's sharp gaze swept from Mac to Emily and back again. "Is everything okay?"

Numb, Emily nodded. Mac did the same.

"Then, I'll leave you two alone," Renee said, turning and marching down the sidewalk. She got back into her car and drove off.

Once her car had disappeared from view, Mac took Emily's left hand and led her inside. Fingers still locked with hers, he closed the door and locked it. Though she wanted to let herself relax into his touch, she couldn't.

Jittery, jumpy, she fingered the envelope, wondering why she felt so reluctant to finally learn the truth.

As if he sensed this, he squeezed her hand, his fingers gentle and warm. "Do you mind waiting to open it? I'd like to settle things between us first."

Hesitating, fighting the urge to let herself lean into him for comfort, she decided to go ahead and speak the truth. "I'm not sure we have anything to settle."

"But we do." He took a deep breath, studying her intently. "I want you to know this. If Joe is the biological father, I'll help you fight any attempt he might make to gain custody."

At first she couldn't quite process his words. When she finally did, she supposed they made a twisted kind of sense. "Why? Because you want to get him back for sleeping with your wife?"

"No." He dragged his hand through his hair. "For the same reason as before when I told you if I was the father, I wouldn't try to take your son from you. Because I want what's best for Ryan. Staying with you would be the best for him."

Staring at him, she saw the truth of his words in his face. "You honestly mean that, don't you?" she asked with a dawning sense of wonder. "No matter what the outcome of the DNA test, you truly care about my son."

"And about you," he put in quietly. "I know it's early and we're barely getting to know each other, but there's something there. Tell me you feel it, too."

The tenderness in his gaze made her knees weak. Tongue-tied and feeling warm, she couldn't speak so she nodded instead.

"This is your choice," he continued, the intensity in his voice telling her he meant what he said. "If you'd like to try—to give us a try—let me know. If not, tell me that instead and I'll back off. Either way, I'll respect your wishes."

He sounded so formal, so endearingly old-fashioned. His nearness, overwhelming and familiar at once, made her giddy. "I'd like to try."

The warmth of his smile felt like a reward. "I'm glad," he told her. He moved in close as though he meant to kiss her, but she held the envelope up like a flag.

Stopping in his tracks, he eyed her.

"Are you ready?" she asked, only the faintest quiver in her voice.

Despite the muscle clenching in his jaw, he nodded. "I guess so. Go ahead and open it."

Then it all came down to this. This moment, whatever was written on a small piece of paper, had the life-shattering capacity to change her world—their world.

Staring at the sealed envelope, heartbeat drumming in her ears, Emily finally shook her head. "I can't...." She shoved the results at him. "Here, you should be the one to open it."

To her surprise, though he held out his hand and accepted the envelope from her, he appeared reluctant. His blue eyes, full of trepidation, met hers before he nodded.

"Let's go into the kitchen," he said.

Emily followed him, the knot in her throat growing as he tore it open and extracted a piece of paper. As he began to read silently, his eyes narrowed, but otherwise his expression gave nothing away.

"Well?" she asked anxiously, reaching for the solid strength of his arm, unable to help herself. "What does it say?"

A cry of relief broke from his lips. "I'm the father. Ryan is my son."

Then, while Emily stood frozen, excitement and relief and fear all warring inside her, he swept her into his arms.

As he held her, a warm glow of peace and satisfaction came over her. His shoulders shook, and still he clung to her, obviously in the grip of strong emotion. With his hands locked behind her back, she held on, honored that he'd chosen to share this moment with her.

Finally, he raised his head. "Thank you," he said, his voice hoarse. "I meant what I said before. I won't take him away from you. But I'd still like to be part of yours and Ryan's life," he began, his deep voice simmering with emotion.

Inside her, everything stilled. She had to know, she

had to be sure. "Ryan will like that," she said, watching him, aware her heart shone in her eyes.

Taking a step closer, his eyes blazed with emotion. "What about you?" he asked. "Would you like that, too? Because Emily, I want to be with you and Ryan both—not one without the other."

A tentative happiness blossomed to life. "Are you sure?" she asked softly.

Crossing the room in three swift strides, he swept her into his arms and kissed her again. "Very sure."

Neither spoke for a long time after that.

* * * * *

NORWAY

Martin Gostelow

JPM GUIDES

land of the Vikings

CONTENTS

people of the far north

the outdoors life

hardy flora and fauna